Talk to Me

Jules Wake

Published 2014 by Choc Lit Limited
Penrose House, Crawley Drive, Camberley, Surrey GU15 2AB, UK
www.choc-lit.com

A CIP catalogue record for this book is available
from the British Library

ISBN 978-1-78189-063-9

Printed and bound by CPI Group (UK) Ltd, Croydon, CR0 4YY

For Donna, for being there every step of the way and
Tricia & Dad who always believed.

Acknowledgements

Writing a book is a bit like being an athlete, except perhaps with a bigger bottom. It looks as if you do all the work on your own but actually there are lots of people alongside.

Thanks, therefore, go to the Choc Lit team who really put things on track. Hugs to all my fellow Choc Lit authors for their unwavering support and encouragement in the grandstands.

Extra special thanks to Moira Lea who introduced me to Louise Allen and the Romantic Novelists' Association. Louise does sterling work coordinating the RNA's New Writers' Scheme and without her this book would never have seen the light of day. I'm very proud to be a member of the RNA, through which I've made so many friends, received so much advice and been the recipient of such generosity of spirit. It really is an amazing organisation.

Of course nothing very much would have been written without my cheerleaders, the wonderful Jude Roust, my RNA partner in crime and the Tring Writers' Circle, Sue, Indra, Clive, Nick Cook, Janet, Katy, Sandra, Graham and Helen, as well as those dear friends who put up with me forcing early drafts on them, Justine, Sam, Helen D & Mel (even though her suggested title didn't make the grade).

Factually correct thanks to Jen & Shane O'Neil for police procedure and cocktails!

Last to my family who love me enough not to care about a less than spotless house and funnily enough, never once, complained about having frozen pizza again – my lovely children Ellie, Matt & gorgeous husband Nick (who still would like to believe the hero is based on him – sorry darling he's not).

Prologue

If anyone could still look masculine in baby pink, it was Daniel. The fleece dressing gown, several sizes too small, emphasised his broad shoulders and revealed a subtly muscled chest dusted with a tantalising 'V' of dark blond hair.

His sheepish smile revealed a chipped tooth, which never failed to disarm me.

'Morning.' The tentative word had a tinge of huskiness as he stepped out of the bathroom.

All my hormones leapt to attention, the miserable traitors.

'Hi,' I squeaked back, with all the allure of Minnie Mouse, blushing like an over-ripe tomato. Why couldn't I be cool, calm and sophisticated about this morning-after stuff? He'd stayed over. For the first time. Perfectly normal. People got off with each other at parties. Came back. Spent the night. No biggie.

Should I offer him breakfast? Coffee? No, he didn't drink coffee. 'Do you want a cup of tea, I was just ...' I nodded towards the kitchen, keeping my eyes fixed on his, wishing I'd shaved my legs before last night's party instead of being a lazy trollop.

'Thanks, Olivia, that'd be great,' he said with far more enthusiasm than a bog-standard cup of tea warranted. I'd hoped he'd retire to the lounge while I made it, but no, he had to trail down the corridor behind me.

Doing my best not to look his way, I busied myself filling the kettle, getting teabags and mugs out, straightening tea towels and wiping counter tops that didn't need wiping. Even so, I could see that the belt on the dressing gown had loosened and even more of his chest was exposed. The inside of my mouth felt as though every drop of moisture had been sucked out.

Automatically I spooned two sugars into his tea and stirred, then stopped. The intimacy of the moment glowed between us as I handed him the mug. His fingers brushed mine, and at his touch a spark of electricity raced up my arm and a punch of longing hit me. I ducked my head, looking at the ingrained dirt in the lino that hadn't yet been replaced. Friends. We were friends. I could do this. He didn't need to know.

'Thanks Olivia ...' his voice trailed off, as if derailed by a sudden awareness of the situation. 'Maybe I ought to, er ...' He looked over my shoulder back down the corridor toward my flatmate's bedroom '... see if Emily would like one.'

There he'd said it. Said her name. My current lodger, Emily. My stomach doubled over as if a demolition ball had slammed into it. It might as well have done.

Giggles were coming from the room next door, still audible above Steve Wright's bloody Sunday bloody Love Songs. Probably not the best choice that morning, especially not when he had to go and play the world's most weepy ballad, Nilsson's 'Without You'. What the hell had gone wrong last night? My hormones had been doing the lambada in great expectation for the last week. Flirtatious texts had been exchanged between Daniel and me on a daily basis. A slinky, killer top had been bought to go with my favourite black trousers, which clearly begged the question was I wearing any underwear? All to no sodding avail. I really had thought that after all those years of near misses, we were finally going to cross the Rubicon.

Nilsson was building to a pitch. 'I can't liiiiiive, if living is without yoooooou. Can't live, I can't give anymororoor.'

Utter nonsense. Of course you could live, you just got on

with it and you certainly didn't waste time feeling sorry for yourself listening to pappy songs on the radio.

A fresh gale of laughter came through the thin wall and I could hear Daniel's gruffer tones. Then it went quiet. My overactive imagination saw Emily's face alight with laughter and then the laughter cut off by a kiss.

Stomping to the radio, I abruptly turned it to Radio 4 and got long wave by mistake. Great, cricket. I raised my eyes heavenwards. Not helping here.

Couldn't someone be on my side? Couldn't I have a break today? Cricket had its own connotations. All related to Daniel.

Not many people realised it but he was my friend first – but the minute he met my dad and brother, Ben, with that strange instant sports exchange men have, they discovered a mutual adoration of cricket. Before I knew it Daniel had joined the village cricket club, White Waltham, and became an inescapable fixture in my life and almost part of the family as my cousin, Barney, and cousin-in-law to be, Piers, played for the same team too.

I had to get out of the flat. I might as well go and do what I'd been putting off for ages and see if I could find the perfect outfit to wear to my cousin Lucy's forthcoming wedding. A horrible thought suddenly struck me. Please God don't let Daniel invite Emily to be his partner at the wedding. No, they wouldn't last that long. Surely this was just a one-night fling thing. Wasn't it?

Chapter One

What was it with wedding speeches? Whatever happened to, 'I'm nervous as hell? Doesn't my bride look great? Thanks for coming.'

As if he could hear my thoughts, Daniel looked across and gave me one of his zillion-kilowatt smiles, followed by a discreet wink as the groom proceeded to launch into a speech worthy of the Pride of Britain awards.

My heart did its usual Olympic gold-winning, one and a half somersault dive sending a hot flush around my system. Six weeks. He'd been going out with Emily for six, sodding, interminable weeks now and I still had that stupid reaction around him.

I gave a tense, polite smile back. I could do this. Friends, we're friends. Always have been and – I had to accept it once and for all – always will be.

Oh Lord, think brick walls, drowning orphans, paella with big juicy prawns and bits of chorizo ... but it was no good, as usual my pulse was off, tripping the light fandango and making me feel slightly light-headed. Then the come down, the realisation. I felt sick. Again.

As Emily's hand crept around Daniel's shoulders I focused back on Piers the groom and his rambling tale of finding true love in Neasden in three minutes, trying to ensure that my face said completely-enraptured-by-this-story. I'd heard it before from Lucy but if I so much as glanced at the couple across from me, I might spontaneously combust in flagrant jealousy.

And now I felt small-minded and petty. They were happy. I should be happy for them.

The room erupted with laughter. I'd missed the groom's

punchline. He was raising his glass to make the toast and then we were all on our feet.

Indecent or not, I left the table abandoning my half-eaten dessert and headed to the ladies before everyone else. All the mirror told me was that my eyes were over-bright but that I still looked relatively normal. Jealousy did funny things to you on the inside and I was convinced it might start showing any day now on the outside.

Unfortunately I couldn't skulk in the loos for the rest of the reception so, tucking my clutch bag under my arm, I headed in search of much-needed liquid refreshment. Of course I bumped straight into my mother who must have been staking out the bar waiting for me, as she knows there's only so long I can go without a glass of wine. She flicked a triumphant glance at my Auntie Brenda, who was looking vibrant in a fuchsia pink silk suit.

'Well, Olivia, isn't that amazing? Lucy met Piers on a speed-date.'

'Yes, Mum. I did know.' And just because the bride and groom had met at a speed-date didn't mean the rest of the world should try it. Quite frankly, pulling out my own toenails with a pair of rusty pliers had more appeal. Unfortunately Lucy's success had given my other entrepreneurial cousin Barney a bright idea.

'See, it can work.' Her eyes twinkled, encouraging and pleading at the same time.

'Yes and I'm sorry,' I said, not feeling sorry at all. 'It's really not my thing. Anyone want a drink?'

'You do know that Barney's speed-dates are for the discerning single,' Auntie Brenda interrupted, her bright red curls clashing with her outfit as they bobbed with enthusiastic maternal pride. 'He doesn't let just anyone in, you know. Invitation only.'

'I know, Auntie Bren. Sounds wonderful,' I lied.

Wonderfully awful. 'I'm sure Barney's doing brilliantly, but—'

'Olivia! You need to get back out there,' butted in my sister Kate.

No. All I needed was a drink. And where had Kate popped up from? It wasn't as if Mum needed reinforcements. She and Auntie Bren were doing just fine on their own.

'Honestly, Mum. She's turned into a right bore. No sense of adventure.'

And going to live in a plush flat in Sydney's Darling Harbour made her Ranulph Fiennes? A pioneering spirit she was not. Other people went off to Australia with a well-worn rucksack that had earned its Glastonbury stripes, not a set of matching luggage Victoria Beckham would envy.

'That's not kind, Kate,' said Mum, determined as always to treat us fairly, before turning to me with that I'm-concerned-about-you expression on her face. It was becoming a permanent fixture.

So I'd lost a bit of weight I could ill afford to lose. It had absolutely nothing to do with unrequited love – it was just a bit tricky eating sometimes. I'd taken to hiding in my room with a good book whenever Daniel was around, which meant I skipped a few dinners. Thankfully he was staying over a lot less now and I could top up at breakfast time.

'It would be nice, though, if you helped your cousin.' Mum was off again, like a seagull with a chip on the seafront. 'He's just starting his business. We should support him.'

'The royal "we"?' I asked with a flippancy I didn't feel. In fact I felt a bit like that poor soggy chip – about to be gobbled up. I knew exactly where this was heading. 'So you and Dad will be coming too?'

'Don't be silly now, dear.'

'What about you?' I turned to Kate with a limp grin. If I was going down, she could come too.

'Sorry, hon, but I'll be off back to Oz soon. Wouldn't want to get their hopes up and then disappoint ... besides I've got Greg.'

Ah yes, the perfect surf-stud stockbroker she'd met within a week of arriving in Australia. From her description of him you could bet the two of them made a stunning couple on Bondi beach or wherever the beautiful people of Sydney go. Kate is gorgeous and reminds me of one those pedigree Weimaraner dogs, all glossy and sleek. Me? I'm more like a Golden Retriever: long legs, brown eyes and lots of blonde curls – although not quite so dopey.

'Olivia,' chipped in Auntie Brenda. 'Pretty girl like you. Barney's desperately short of attractive women, you know.'

Blatant flattery wasn't going to get her anywhere, especially not where Barney, my least favourite cousin, was concerned.

'It's time you got back in the water,' said Kate, her voice gentling with concern.

'What?' I said, determined that the smile on my face didn't slip. Red herrings were called for and quick. 'I've been in the water plenty, I just don't like to get in too deep.' Short and sweet suited me fine, although recently those had begun to pall.

'Olivia! Don't be like that. You really need to get over him.'

I gave her a startled glance. Oh God! Did Kate know? I thought I'd done a rather fabulous job that day, keeping my feelings hidden; smiling a lot, laughing too loudly, avoiding looking in a certain direction. Look folks, I'm having a fantastic time. I'm not the least bit in love with Daniel. Not the least bit bothered that Emily's all over him. Not the least bit ... imagining what it would be like for him to lean over and nibble that little bit between my neck and ear ... no, no don't go there.

Kate's face was bright with curiosity. Oh bugger, her

sibling antennae were better tuned than I'd suspected. Had she sussed me after all?

'Mike didn't deserve you ...'

Phew. Wrong. Thank you, thank you. Mike was another mistake, a different one. You'd think I was piling them up. He was Jurassic period, definitely ancient history. She was digging in the dark but I wasn't about to set her straight.

And then squinting over her shoulder, I spotted Daniel with Emily.

'Why not try it?' Kate finished.

Her face, drawn in earnest lines, made me want to hug her. She hadn't a clue.

Like a shopaholic with the credit cards cut up, but unable to stay away from the shops, my eyes sneaked another peep beyond Kate. Emily's hand was snaking up Daniel's back, her fingers toying with the blond hair at the nape of his neck.

You'd think seeing them together all the time would have given me some kind of immunity by now, like building resistance against germs, but no, every time I saw the two of them together, I caught the cold all over again.

How wet was I? I needed to do something. Take positive action and stop being so pathetic and spineless.

I turned so that Kate's head obscured the two of them. Alternative therapy. Medicine. That's what I needed. It'd taste bloody awful but it might do the trick.

'OK.' I'm not sure who was more surprised by my calm acquiescence – me, Mum or Kate? Auntie Bren just smiled serenely.

That was it. Traffic light green for go. Kate's face lit up with a gleeful smile. I smiled back, ignoring the spasm of panic that clutched at me. I'd only said I'd go. She was going back to Australia soon. I could always get out of it later. I was brilliant at coming up with ideas, a creative thinker allegedly, according to those silly management profiles they do at work. I could dream up a million excuses. Voluntary root canal work, knitting lessons, appendicitis – any one would do.

Unfortunately, I hadn't taken account of the cunning Machiavellian strand lodged within Kate's DNA.

Daniel felt Emily nestle in next to him. Soft, warm. Her cleavage on display, inviting. He put an arm round her and looked down at the white-blonde hair. No denying, she was gorgeous especially when she smiled sleepily up at him, her eyes hinting at sex. Sweet, uncomplicated and very feminine.

Looking around the room he saw the DJ methodically packing up his kit with the kind of fierce concentration that said, 'I'm off duty and headed home'. It was that time of night. Even the waitresses had been roused from their earlier resigned inertia and were whipping glasses off tables with super-heroic speed.

Across the table, Olivia and her sister had their heads together, tawny blonde and glossy brunette. His eyes narrowed as he watched Olivia lift her half-full wine glass. Her heart wasn't in it. She'd been putting on a brave face all day. He felt for her but it went with the territory. This was what she'd signed up for. As she took another sip she looked up and caught him watching. A tight-lipped smile flashed across her face.

Served her right and then he immediately regretted the thought. Unkind and unfair. No one deserved to be unhappy but God he wanted to shake her. Getting herself into such a mess.

Women, he'd never understand them, although he'd always thought he got Olivia. Straight arrow. Sensible, down to earth. He winced. Made her sound boring and she wasn't. How long was it that they'd known each other now? Since the second term of the first year at university. She was a fixture in so many of his memories. The voice of reason on nights out when student antics threatened to go too far. Calming things down in curry houses when the laddish behaviour overstepped the mark. And yet she always achieved it with humour and authority, without coming across like a Head Girl.

Daniel could see where she got those traits. Her family all had that same natural ability to lead without appearing overbearing.

Shit, what would her parents say if they knew? With a marriage as solid as theirs, he felt sure they would be horrified if they heard their daughter was going out with a married man. He could barely believe it himself. He sighed and felt Emily wriggle as he tightened his arm around her.

He gave himself a mental shake. Nothing to do with him. She was a grown woman and had made her bed. Good job Emily had tipped him off that night at the party otherwise he'd have gone ahead and made a right dick of himself. You thought you knew people. Just went to show you didn't always know them as well as you thought. Emily had sworn him to secrecy, making him promise not to tell Olivia he knew. Something he regretted. Part of him wanted to remind her how awful it had been when his mother had an affair and the other part, the one that wanted to shake the living daylights out of her, couldn't believe she could forget. It felt like a betrayal.

He shook his head trying to shake away the hollow feeling. Olivia had to really love this guy.

Daniel gritted his teeth at the memory of the near miss. Emily's hand fluttered along the length of his tense jaw and then down over his thigh. He had a good idea where it was headed. Simple and uncomplicated, that's what he wanted. He certainly didn't want to be sitting here dwelling on the past and wondering what the hell Olivia was playing at.

Emily's hand moved up, her fingers sliding into the waistband of his trousers. He looked down to see the suggestive tilt of her eyebrow and her rosebud mouth pursed in invitation. He bent his head to kiss her. Yes, Olivia had made her bed, it was nothing to do with him.

Chapter Two

As he and Emily collected their breakfast from the extensive buffet, he caught sight of the two sisters and headed over to the table they'd commandeered in the corner of the dining room. Olivia looked a bit wan this morning. Not that it seemed to have affected her appetite; she seemed absorbed in mopping up the last dregs of fried egg with a piece of bread.

'Do I detect that you've just scoffed a full English?' he teased, feeling guilty that he'd not made more effort to talk to her the previous evening.

She looked up, her eyes darting away briefly before they slid back to make contact. She did that a lot these days. Guilty conscience.

'Golly, Sherlock.' Her smile was feeble but that wasn't unexpected. She'd never worn hangovers particularly well. 'No flies on you.'

'Did you really eat a full cooked breakfast?' asked Emily, her eyes widening as she slipped into a chair and tucked into a solitary croissant. In her dainty hands it looked huge as she nibbled it delicately. 'Gosh, I don't know how you could.'

Startled he glanced at Emily wondering if there was more to her words but there was a dimple in her cheek and her blue eyes were guileless.

'Lucky Olivia has such a fast metabolism,' Kate's voice floated out from the business section of the *Sunday Times*.

He smiled. Kate could be such a bruiser. So different from Olivia. Tact had bypassed Kate. She said what she thought, whereas Olivia always managed to find something positive in people. Obviously where she was going wrong with her married man. He was bound to be a wanker.

'Our Olivia's always been a tall, skinny wench,' Kate

continued in a mock Yorkshire accent. Then she gave a sigh and rustled the paper.

Olivia smiled reluctantly as she caught his eye. It was all show. They both knew Kate only ever read the fashion pages.

'Just as well,' he said, helping himself to a coffee, his hand edging towards the sports section of Kate's paper. 'Seeing how she's always been partial to a post-hangover fry-up.'

'And you weren't?' Olivia snapped.

God she was moody these days.

'Who was it introduced me to Big Al's greasy spoon? Remember the night after the May Ball, Daniel?'

He didn't remember that particular night but so many had ended in a similar vein. The usual gang staggering down Magdalen Street in Norwich, the girls carrying their heels, packs of Marlborough tucked into their cleavages and the guys' dicky bows stuffed in pockets, leading the way determined on a full English in the hope it might make a dent in the inevitable hangovers.

'Olivia, do you always have to drag up the ancient history of your time at university?' Emily's voice was sharp. 'For God's sake, you left years ago! It's so boring,' she snapped.

'Sorry, Emily, it's just that mornings after the nights before always bring back memories of the famous Al's fried bread,' replied Kate, unusually trying to diffuse the situation.

'So that's why you visited Olivia so often.' With his words he gave Emily a conspiratorial wink to include her. She pouted for a moment and then her face softened with a grateful smile. He must remember that it had to be difficult for her, all this shared history stuff. She was bound to feel a bit left out.

'Why else?' Kate answered with a smile.

'Thanks.' Olivia took mock offence. 'Nothing to do with sisterly love then?'

He caught her shooting Kate a sharp glance.

Awkward undercurrents he wasn't party to swirled and he took the line of least resistance and turned to the football pages, propping them up in front of him against the coffee pot.

Out of the corner of his eye he saw Kate check her watch and pull a face. 'I have to head off. I'm going back with the folks. Dad wants to get home for lunch. Goodbye, Emily,' she said. 'Bye Daniel. Nice to see you again.'

He stood to kiss her.

'Good luck with the Old Bodgers cricket match,' said Kate. 'I hear Dad's looking forward to trouncing you!'

Emily's eyes tightened.

Shit, thanks Kate. He'd really hoped to break that one gently. Cricket matches were hell on long distance relationships. Took up far too much of the weekend and Emily wasn't that keen on coming down to watch. Not that he lived that far from the girls' flat in London – only the other side of Maidenhead – but Emily didn't like the idea of coming out and commuting back to work in the morning. She relied on him coming over to her.

'What match?' Her soft voice sounded hurt already. He'd meant to talk to her about it, explain this wasn't your ordinary match, but much more of a social occasion and would be a lot more fun for her.

'It's a bit of an annual event in the village,' explained Olivia. 'A couple of years ago Dad's team was supposed to be playing a fundraising cricket match, but the other side let them down at the last minute. Daniel rounded up a replacement team—'

'A team of young, fit—' interrupted Daniel.

Olivia poked her tongue out at him. 'Yes, and who made the mistake of suggesting to Dad that perhaps you should mix up the teams so that you wouldn't have the unfair advantage of youth on your side?'

He laughed and Emily looked even more confused.

'Red rag to a bull casting aspersions on their age,' he explained.

Emily looked none the wiser.

'That's where the name came from,' said Olivia. 'Dad decided that his Old Bodgers team had wisdom and experience on their side—'

'And got trounced,' added Daniel with satisfaction. 'So, of course, we had to have a rematch the next year ... and the next year.'

'It's a great day. We have a barbecue afterwards and—'

'Cricket,' said Emily, scrunching her face in dismay. 'I don't think so. It's so boring.'

He shrugged her comments off, laughing at her expression.

'Oh, that's all right,' Olivia said. 'You don't actually have to watch the game. You can help me with the teas and there are lots of—'

'Teas? Do you wear a "naice" pinny à la nineteen fifties?' There was no mistaking her disdain. 'Olivia, you need to get a life. There's no way I would be seen dead.'

He watched Olivia's mouth snap shut. Oops, he was pretty sure Emily hadn't meant to be so disparaging about Olivia helping with teas at the club but Emily did begrudge the amount of the weekend his cricket took up. It had become an increasing bone of contention. The fact that Olivia embraced the social life there didn't help.

He was going to have some bridges to build with Emily later.

It was as if fate was determined to keep throwing him and Olivia together. She was at reception when he went to pay his bill.

The blonde receptionist in her tidy uniform with her keen-to-please smile that had a genuine ring of sincerity was talking to her. 'A taxi to Reading station, you said. And the London train?'

'You are bloody joking.' The words came out before he could stop them, but for crying out loud she was doing his head in.

He felt her stiffen beside him and to his surprise she looked a bit hurt.

'Christ, Olivia. Are you going back to London?'

She nodded, looking disconcerted and so she bloody should. Why was she playing games? So the boyfriend hadn't turned up and her lift had fallen through. Why the hell couldn't she just say so and ask to go back with him and Emily? Their destination was the same.

'What my car not good enough for you?' Then it struck him that maybe she wasn't going home.

'No, I just didn't want to play gooseberry,' she said, lifting her chin.

'So you are going back to the flat?' God he sounded accusing, he had to remember he wasn't supposed to know and it wasn't as if he was her keeper.

'Where else would I be going?' she asked all innocence, and for a moment he almost believed her.

'Well, why the hell didn't you ask for a lift back then?'

She blushed. It confirmed everything and with a flash of awareness, he realised he'd been hoping that Emily might have got things wrong and there was no married lover tucked away somewhere.

'Oh, for God's sake,' he rolled his eyes in mock disgust and turned to the receptionist. 'Don't worry, she doesn't need a taxi. She can have a lift with me.'

Memories of a hundred and one other journeys slipped into his head and without thinking he turned back to Olivia and quipped, 'You can go in the front with the window open.'

'Oy.' She slapped at his arm and grinned at him. 'I'm not that bad any more.'

He raised an eyebrow and shook his head at the receptionist. 'World's worst traveller, this one. Don't suppose you've got any spare sick bags in the back there?'

''Fraid not.' She smiled warmly at him, clearly approving. 'Have a nice trip home.'

A queue was building behind them and they moved into the wide lobby area.

'Right, I'll go see how Emily's getting on. I'll see you back here in ten minutes.'

'Are you sure this is OK? I mean, I don't want to cramp yours and Emily's style. I was trying to give the two of you some space.'

Staring at her earnest face, he gripped the car keys in the palm of his hand, feeling the metal bite. When had she turned into such a good liar?

'Don't worry about it,' he snapped and turned on his heel.

Although I really didn't want to travel home with Daniel and Emily, it was the most logical thing to do. Perhaps I could doze off in the back without feeling sick. I knew it was a hopeless wish.

'But, Daniel ...' said Emily, her voice quavering with the unfairness of it as we left the hotel reception. She wasn't happy that he'd relegated her to the back seat.

'If Olivia goes in the back seat we'll have to stop every few minutes because she'll feel like throwing up. Believe me, we have history.'

I winced. Did he have to say that? Emily was twitchy enough about our long-standing friendship without being reminded of it at every turn.

'We'll be lucky to make it back without at least one stop as it is.'

I felt like the troublesome family dog.

The tree-shaded car park was almost deserted when we got to Daniel's Audi, most of the wedding guests having already departed.

I climbed into the passenger seat, feeling guilty.

'Got your two pences?' asked Daniel in a clipped voice, as he slid into the driver's seat.

'No ... good idea.'

He beat me to it, producing two shiny copper coins from his wallet before I could open my bag. 'Here you go. Don't spend it all at once.' He handed them over, with the semblance of a smile and started the engine.

I watched as he put the car into gear, his tanned, capable forearm scant inches from my knee and then held onto my breath a second too long as he put his arm across the back of my seat to reverse out of the car park.

I closed my eyes momentarily.

It wasn't fair. With his tousled blond hair, twinkling blue eyes and that endearing slightly chipped front tooth which showed when he smiled, why did he have to be so damned irresistible?

The first time I met him I'd gone all gooey.

There'd been a card on the Student Union noticeboard: Available – lift share to Maidenhead area. Half petrol costs. It didn't say people with chronic carsickness need not apply.

When he pulled up in his tiny Mini he had to ask twice if I was Olivia. My tongue had glued itself to the roof of my mouth. Wearing loose, faded jeans and a Diesel T-shirt, he'd unfolded his six-foot frame from the car and given my hand a firm shake. At that point I'd have said yes if he'd asked if I was Edna from Edinburgh.

Him being the perfect gentleman was an added bonus. He stopped three times on that first journey to let me heave up my breakfast.

You'd think I wouldn't see him for dust after that but

no, he kept offering me lifts, cementing a strong friendship. Let's face it, you cover an awful lot of ground in a three hour car journey and you can't help but love a guy who brings you a new travel sickness remedy to try each time. We went through wristbands, Joy-Rides, ginger biscuits – which I later discovered are for morning sickness – and mint tea before discovering that, for me, clutching copper coins works best. In my defence, I'm OK on short hops, when I'm driving or in the dark, but any journey as a passenger longer than an hour and my stomach starts to misbehave.

'Any ideas, Olivia?' asked Emily, once we were speeding along the M4.

'Uh – sorry, I was miles away.' I was concentrating on Windsor Castle on the horizon, another motion sickness essential.

'Come on. Please help me,' she wheedled. 'Fiona wants a proposal for tomorrow's meeting. I should have done it last week. It's not fair. She's always on my back.'

Fiona McIntyre, Emily's boss and high-flying head of beauty public relations at Organic PR, didn't suffer fools gladly or otherwise.

'How am I supposed to think of a new way to launch lipstick?' Emily asked, wrinkling her china doll nose as if perplexed that the task had fallen to her.

I bit back the obvious, 'Because it's your job.' Emily always got very stressed when she had to present her work to Fiona. Instead I said, 'Well, what's different about it? Can't you just say it does what it says on the tube?'

Daniel didn't join in. He seemed to be concentrating on his driving.

Emily gave an exasperated huff and shifted in her seat. 'You've spent too much time working on construction accounts.'

She didn't consider what I did to be proper PR. My job at Organic was very tedious compared to hers. She worked on glamorous beauty accounts and thanks to all the freebies she brought home, our bathroom could give Boots a good run for its money. Attending sparkly launches of new make-up and skincare products in the sorts of places where you'd rub shoulders with A-list celebrities sipping their mohitos was all in a day's work for her.

Not me. I spent my days trudging around thirty foot trenches wearing wellies three sizes too big. No comparison really. I can't think of a single perk of doing the PR for a major road-building company – unless you're partial to the odd yellow hard hat.

'The Marketing Director at Beautiful Babes Luscious Lips wants it to be an aspirational brand. The celebrity's favourite. This lipstick's going to be the summer's hottest new product. Beautiful Babes isn't selling to a bunch of guys with their bums hanging out of their jeans.'

'Ooh, I don't know. Think of it as a unique strategy. Transvestite builders. You're targeting a whole new market.' I caught Daniel's eye and he gave me a tiny smile. I heaved an internal sigh of relief. His mood seemed to be lightening. I had no idea what had made him so cross earlier.

There was no reply from behind me. I turned round. Emily's blue eyes had narrowed and her lips were twisted into a sneer.

'This is serious, Olivia. I'm dreading going in tomorrow. If you aren't going to help me, then just say so.'

Well, I didn't want to look bad in front of Daniel, did I?

'Sorry. Just stream of conscious to get me warmed up. What about ... celebrity kissing? Yes ... get celebrities to wear the lipstick ... then they put their lip prints on ... shirt collars and ... you auction the shirts off for charity.'

I grinned at her, my brain taking off as suddenly a

whole raft of ideas popped into my head. I carried on with enthusiasm as I could see the shirts clearly in my mind. 'You could do a launch … lots of models in short, white shirts. The tabloids would love it. There you go. One idea for free.'

'Thanks, Olivia, but with respect,' she said, not being respectful at all, 'the celebrity auction thing has been done to death.'

I felt like a balloon that someone had just stuck a pin in. I was only trying to help.

'Shame,' said Daniel joining in. 'Sounds fun. I wouldn't mind going along.'

My hero. I shot him a grateful smile.

'Daniel!' said Emily.

Looking outside, I took a deep breath. My stomach was starting to misbehave. At my age I should have grown out of this.

'You all right?' Daniel asked, opening my window a fraction.

I breathed in the cooler air gratefully. 'I will be,' I replied between gritted teeth. His hand covered mine with a comforting squeeze so fleeting I could almost have imagined it, except my heartbeat took off at a gallop.

Just as we joined the A4 another idea for Emily came to me. Surely she'd like this one – although she didn't deserve any more suggestions.

'What about commissioning a designer dress covered in giant lipstick kisses – each kiss in one of the new season's colours – and then invite a celebrity to wear the dress to a top-notch event like a film premiere or something?'

'Yeugh! That is sooo clichéd. Just as well you work on the boring accounts.'

Why did I bother? Miserable cow.

Chapter Three

'You haven't confirmed with Barney yet!'

Drat and I'd been so clever at avoiding Kate's calls all week.

'Admit it. You've been avoiding me. Don't forget you promised Auntie Bren.'

'I did no such thing!' I said. 'Well, it wasn't exactly a promise.' I wasn't going to give into Kate too easily. 'Look, I will go on this speed-date—'

'But?'

'It's just—'

'What, for God's sake? What can go wrong?'

I could make a complete fool of myself. Dry up with stage fright. The list of potential humiliation ran into pages. In fact in my mind it was positively encyclopaedic.

'Nothing, I guess. Just nerves. The thought of having to try and impress—'

'Olivia! You put your make-up on, wear something gorgeous and be yourself. That's all you need to do.'

Easy for her to say that. The whole idea filled me with dread.

'OK. OK.'

'If you don't call Barney, I will.'

With an obvious sigh of resignation, I said, 'I'll call now.'

'Go on then. Don't forget, I have spies.'

She didn't need them. Auntie Bren's purple-shadowed eyes would haunt me forever if I didn't go on one of Barney's dates.

Now was probably the right time to phone him, while I was feeling grumpy and out of sorts. Slowly I picked at the buttons on my mobile.

'Barney Middleton,' a voice snapped in my ear.

'Hi, Barney. It's Olivia.' I resisted the urge to say, 'Your grubby, disreputable younger cousin here.'

He's had that effect on me ever since I was sixteen when Kate told him about the massive crush I had on him. God that sounds as if I go in for crushes on a regular basis. I don't. I've had two in my life, Daniel and Barney. One of which was deserved, the other was NOT.

As an arrogant eighteen-year-old, already good-looking and self-assured, Barney found my crush very entertaining. He and his mates never missed a chance to embarrass me. Did me a favour though – I went right off him.

'Hold on a sec.' In the background I heard him say, 'Get me another one in, Charles, would you? Same again ... No, only one of my cousins ... No, the other one.'

I could hear muted laughter.

'Wondered when you'd call,' he drawled. 'Good job Kate's on the ball. Said you'd phone eventually. You're in luck. I've saved you a place.'

I pulled a face. Like it was really that popular.

'See you on Friday. I usually insist on payment up front but because it's you, you can pay on the night but make sure you turn up.'

It was as if he was doing me some massive favour out of the kindness of his heart. Not possible. He didn't have one.

'Friday!' My voice came out as an embarrassing squeak. That was way too soon.

'Yes, Friday, Olivia. Think you can manage that? Bloody lucky I can squeeze you in. Normally there's a waiting list.'

'Thank you so much, Barney.' It was hard but I managed through great will power, not to add, 'However can I repay you!' What I did say was, 'Don't suppose you might be able to tell me where and when?'

'Eight o'clock. Café Lulu. Don't be late.'

Oooh! My fingers clenched involuntarily into tight fists. There's something about Barney that just brings me out in hives.

He broke off again and over the hubbub in the background, I heard him say, 'Make it a bottle then ... get a decent one, Charles, none of that house muck ... here stick my card behind the bar ... Still there, Olivia? Make sure you turn up.'

'I'll be there.'

No point asking where Café Lulu was. Obviously it was so hip any idiot would know. Thank God for the Internet.

Before I knew it Friday had crept up on me and the little gold top I was planning to wear was hanging up on the wardrobe door, ready for the big date. It kept talking to me every time I walked past.

'I'm far too gorgeous and grown up for you ... and even with that bra everyone will know you're a titless wonder.'

My original plans had changed at lunchtime when Emily had flounced over to my desk and perched on the edge, fiddling with the paperclips and rearranging my pens for a minute.

'You OK?' I asked, knowing full well that she wasn't.

'No, I am sodding well not. Daniel has cancelled on me tonight.'

'Really?' That didn't sound like him.

'He's going out with his dad and stepmum for a family dinner instead.'

'Oh, bit rude if he'd already made arrangements with you.'

'Yes, bastard. Now I'm stuck in on my own on a Friday night.'

Poor Emily, her idea of hell, having to entertain herself.

'You could always come with me,' I joked, never for a moment thinking she would.

Her eyes glittered dangerously and her mouth firmed into a line. I'd never noticed how thin her lips were before.

'Do you know what ... I think I will.'

Oh shit, now what had I done? The determined lift of her jaw suggested she was deadly serious.

'Are you sure ... I mean ... I had to book ... there might not be any places.'

'Don't be dense, Olivia. There are always places at these things. What are you wearing?'

In the end I had no choice but to agree to take her with me, and she insisted on accompanying me in my lunch hour on my mission to buy the perfect bra.

Of course she talked me into the most complicated thing known to man, but it promised serious cleavage no matter how under-endowed you were and was marginally preferable to the one that inflated with – no joke – a little pump. That shopping trip was quite an eye-opener. Chicken fillets, super-boost, balconies – who knew that bra designers needed degrees in mechanical engineering these days.

'When are you going to get ready, Olivia?' asked Emily, hopping up and down outside my bedroom door. Already made-up, she looked gorgeous as always – no wonder Daniel was going out with her – and was halfway through straightening her white-blonde hair. Natural, of course, she had Scandinavian ancestors. If mine had been of a Nordic persuasion you could bet they'd have been great, hairy Vikings, not flaxen-haired princesses.

'Sorry, on the phone to Mum.'

Emily shrugged. 'We need to leave in an hour and a half. Thought you wanted a bath.'

No chance of delaying tactics with her around. She was itching to get going. Obviously she had all her questions worked out. Me, I was still dithering over my opening lines.

Was there any way of getting out of this evening? Perhaps I could do myself an injury with those bra straps. An evening in A & E had appeal. I've watched *Casualty* and *Holby City*. Hospitals are teeming with handsome specimens striding the wards in pristine white coats – although I've often wondered why in their profession they never seem to come into contact with any bodily fluids, like blood or vomit.

Maybe a quick trip to Guy's was a viable alternative to speed-dating, although knowing my luck, Emily would pick up Doctor Hunk while he was untangling the straps from around my windpipe. How could he fail to be impressed by her fortitude in the face of her flatmate's total incompetence?

Turning on the taps in the sunlit bathroom, I perched on the edge of my beloved, recently installed, double-ended bath. Paying the mortgage didn't leave much left over for home improvements but the bath had been a priority.

What the hell was I going to ask? Three minutes per date. Do you come here often? Hardly bowling-over material.

'Can I just grab my deodorant?' asked Emily, sailing in.

'Mmm. What questions are you going to ask? I'm stuck.'

'Ask who?' She looked blank.

'The dates, tonight.'

'You think too much. I thought I'd leave it up them. They're the ones who've got to impress me.'

Sometimes I had to admire her attitude. Then again, with the amount of cleavage she was showing, none of her dates would be able to string a sentence together. Even with the new bra, I wouldn't have that advantage.

Despite racking my brains for three whole days, no clever questions had come to mind. My grey cells were threatening to go into meltdown. In desperation earlier I'd even Googled 'Good questions + speed-date'. No help at all. The advice fell into two camps; 'Avoid talking about films' or 'Ask your date about their favourite film.' There was, however, universal agreement that you shouldn't 'Ask if they want babies?' As if!

Perhaps questions would just pop into my head as I met each date. I tried to imagine what they might be like.

Lying back in the warm bath, two successful candidates popped into my head, leaving me with the delicious dilemma of which to keep. One was a famous architect, who wore Paul Smith suits and wined and dined me in all the best places in London.

Unfortunately my imagination had a practical streak, which insisted anyone that successful – he'd just designed the equivalent of the Gherkin in New York – would also be horribly busy at work and bound to be unreliable.

Alternatively there was the airline pilot who was proving irresistible. Much more laid-back with a wicked sense of humour, he wore nice crisp shirts that exposed just a smattering of blond hairs. His faded jeans encased long lean legs and he had lovely broad shoulders with just a hint of well-defined muscles – he was quite a sexy package. Although I could do without the little chip in his tooth my imagination had unhelpfully provided. What's more, he was desperate for me to go with him to Fiji.

As I was lying back in the warm water, daydreaming, listening to the gentle, pfft pfft of foam bubbles, the pilot just edged into the lead – chipped tooth and all – and was in the process of producing first-class air tickets, when Emily interrupted with a loud rap on the unpainted bathroom door.

'Are you planning on the lobster look, Olivia?' she yelled through the frosted glass.

Bugger. Time to get a move on.

'Got your questions sorted?'

'Nooo!' I wailed, scrambling out of the bath, grabbing my watch. I abandoned thoughts of Fiji. I needed questions.

I could still only think of, 'Do you come here often?' Then, it occurred to me that it could be a great question if used with irony. The ideal, 'Are you on the same wavelength as me?' test.

It would have to do.

Sod's law. The train came on time and arrived at Waterloo several minutes early. There was even a tube waiting on the platform. Hopping on, Emily grabbed the nearest seat, while I walked down the carriage to snag the last seat next to a middle-aged man with a ponytail listening to an iPod. The volume was so loud that I could hear the tinny synthesiser of some horrible '80's arty thing. Laurie somebody. 'I'm not home right now... but if you wanna leave a message ... O Superman.'

I smiled to myself. Superman. That was it. I had the perfect question.

Fifteen minutes later we arrived outside Café Lulu. Through the huge plate glass windows, the décor and furniture shouted 'massively trendy'. My stomach was doing an impression of a washing machine on maximum spin.

At the door we were given a covert up-and-down by an Amazonian blonde drenched in an overpowering perfume, who obviously had strict instructions to weed out any riff-raff.

'You are?' she barked in an East European accent. Even I had to crick my neck to look up at her. She looked capable of slinging out undesirables by the scruff of their necks. Perhaps she'd been a female wrestler in a former life. I'd managed to text Barney that afternoon to tell him, rather than ask him, to expect one extra.

We must have passed the test because we were waved over to a set of brightly lit stairs leading up to the private members' lounge. It was packed. Impressive. Maybe Barney had had to squeeze us in after all.

He was standing at the entrance and barely gave me a

glance, far too busy snapping out orders to another blonde sporting a chest of magnificent proportions. With clipboard in hand and wearing one of those headsets with a microphone, she looked as if she knew what she was doing. She smiled at us. Not a single wrinkle or dimple spoilt her foundation. It was only when she asked our names that Barney twigged it was me.

'Blimey, Olivia,' he gasped, his eyes zeroing in on my cleavage. 'Have you had a boob job?'

Laced in like a Victorian lady, I was rather proud of the results. Good job I hadn't gone for the inflatable version. I wouldn't have put it past him to stick a needle in.

'Murdered any hamsters lately?' I didn't say it, although it was on the tip of my tongue. Another childhood incident. Instead I managed to muster up a snide 'This all looks very professional.' The unspoken, 'For an amateur,' was implied by my surly tone.

Emily gave me an irritated look. 'Children, children,' she interceded with a flirtatious smile. She would. Barney was just her type.

'You're on table seven, Olivia, and you,' Barney gave Emily an approving smile, 'are table twelve. Would you like me to show you to your tables?'

'No, it's fine. Just point the way to the bar,' I said, anxious to put as much distance as possible between us. 'You're obviously rushed off your feet.'

Botox Barbie's smile slipped for a second, her face sour as she muttered under her breath, 'Hardly.'

My glass of wine was window dressing as my stomach was still on its final spin. It might be a long evening. Emily and I positioned ourselves so it looked as if we were talking to one another, when in fact we were scanning the room over each other's shoulders.

The room was almost circular, the circumference ringed by

alcoves containing tables lit by angular desk lamps. The line, 'Ve hav vays of making you talk', ran through my head.

'Seen anyone interesting?' asked Emily, tossing her long blonde hair back over her shoulder for the fifth time.

'I'm trying not to make it seem too obvious.' I gave my wine another tentative sip. 'If I catch anyone's eye they might think I'm desperate.'

'Olivia, people go speed-dating all the time. They're probably all veterans.'

And that was supposed to make me feel better?

Dotted around the room were the odd twosome, like us, pretending not to be eyeing everyone else up. A few brave solitary souls, clearly mad or desperate, were busy examining the huge curved pieces of artwork that hugged the walls.

One man stood out. Nothing mad or desperate about him. If anything he seemed to preen under the curious glances, self-assured and haughty as he gazed airily around the room as if looking for inspiration before reapplying himself to his *Times* crossword.

It went quiet as Barney strode into the centre of the room to explain the rules of engagement. I thought it was all pretty obvious but Barney had to make a meal of it. At last, just as I was thinking about sidling out of the room, he finished with, 'Ladies and gentlemen – good luck.'

'Who does he think he is, head of MI6 sending us off on a mission?' I whispered, my stomach lurching in panic. Emily tossed her hair again and gave an excited little skip.

I almost expected a bell to ring to start us off, but with an imperious, 'To your tables,' Barney clapped his hands and we all jumped like well-trained sheep.

'Show time,' sang Emily and sailed off to her table, her hips swinging.

Searching out table seven, I arrived before my date.

Slipping into the chocolate brown leather banquette in my allocated alcove, I stuffed my bag at my feet with shaking hands and then hopped back on to my feet.

What was speed-date etiquette? Should I stand and wait, or sit back down?

Before I could decide one way or another a tall figure loomed over my hunchbacked position. Crossword Man. He held out a slim tanned hand before coiling himself onto his chair.

Up close he was gorgeous. Even my one-man libido sat up and took notice. Smooth coffee skin, sleek black hair, perfect teeth and dark brown eyes with amber flecks, but there was something distant and aloof about him.

'Anthony,' he announced in a deep voice adding, 'and you are?' His mouth curved with a slight hint of disdain, as if there was a nasty smell under his nose.

'Hi, Anthony.' My heart thudded uncomfortably. Why had I let myself in for this? 'I'm Olivia.'

Settling himself onto his seat, he seemed at ease, almost as if he was conducting an interview. I wished I felt that confident or could even pretend to be.

'Do you come here often?' he asked, inclining his head and nodding as if he was a professor in a tutorial. It threw me.

'Bugger, that was my question.'

There was a startled flicker in his eyes. Oops, shouldn't have sworn so early in the date.

'Of course, I meant it purely in an ironic sense.' I couldn't miss the patronising edge to his tone.

'Y-yes ... of course,' I stuttered, feeling wrong-footed already

'You know. I meant to imply the opposite of what—'

Great, not only was I foul-mouthed, but stupid too.

'Yes, I do know what irony is.' Perhaps I should have brought my degree certificate along.

He leaned back and paused for a moment, as if putting a great deal of thought into his next words. With great ceremony his fingers came together in a delicate point under his chin. 'Tell me. What was the last film you saw?'

The grave expression on his face should have told me this was a potential deal breaker, but my mouth had disconnected itself from my brain and the words, '*Pretty Woman*', popped out.

Whoops. Should have gone for something more worthy. What the hell was the name of that film all the critics had liked? The one I fidgeted all the way through.

'What was the last film you saw?' I asked in desperation.

'*Idle Airs in Blue*. Don't suppose you've seen it?' His tone suggested that I'd probably never heard of it either.

'That was it,' I said with relief. See not a total philistine. 'Just couldn't remember the name.'

Scepticism was written in capitals all over his face.

Arrogant sod. Time to pull out the big guns. Show him that I did have a brain. 'Great film. The cinematography was incredible, those sunrise shots with the main protagonist were breathtaking, and the acting was superb but there were a few flaws in the plot, didn't you think?'

He blinked, his eyelids dipping so slowly he reminded me of a languorous lizard. I didn't give him a chance to speak. 'The lead character was totally unbelievable and unsympathetic. As if she'd go back to teaching. A very anti-climactic ending. Do you know? I think the writer and director ran out of steam. Just thought, "We've done our bit, let's wrap this up sharpish." '

'My brother wrote the screenplay.'

If there's a God, he hates me.

'Wow.' I ignored his icy stare. 'Bet your mum's really proud.' Please don't let her be dead, blind or have abandoned him at birth.

'Yes, she is. We all went to the premiere together.'

There was an expectant pause.

'Did you meet many of the cast?'

Back on safe ground, I listened hoping my look of rapt attention was convincing. I didn't need to say much, just interject with the odd, 'Really? How lovely,' and 'Gosh, how fantastic.'

Who knew that three minutes could last such a long time?

Apparently the director's second assistant's boyfriend (or was it the second assistant's runner's boyfriend) was now one of Anthony's best friends and could get him cheap tickets for *Phantom of the Opera*. At that point I couldn't summon up a single nice comment. I've never liked Phantom, too much wailing and moaning. Give me *Joseph and the Amazing Technicolor Dreamcoat* any day.

The penguin, one of a variety of kitsch novelty timers that Barney had thoughtfully supplied to each table, finally buzzed into life so violently that it was in danger of vibrating its way off the table. Around the room half a dozen lemons, chickens and assorted peppers began to jump about.

Clutching the quivering penguin with gratitude, I almost fell over the table leg in my haste to get away. I'd known I'd be rubbish at this. Stopping to rub the lump already appearing, I was caught by Barney who hissed in my ear. 'Girls stay put.'

As Anthony disappeared, I heavily circled around the 'no' box on my little scorecard. Not that I needed to, judging from the curl of distaste on his full lips, he wouldn't be ticking my box. One down, another nine to go.

Date number two loomed over me. Hoping he hadn't seen my vehement reaction to his predecessor's tick box, I bobbed up to say hello, shoving the scorecard under my bum.

'Hi,' I muttered from my Quasimodo position, half-standing and half-sitting. He immediately grasped the table and pulled it, giving me room to straighten up.

'Thank you.' My thighs relaxed in relief. 'I'm Olivia.'

'Ned. Do you want to sit down now?' He waved his hand at the banquette and I promptly sat, like a plummeting pigeon. Off to another great start then.

There was a pause, which lengthened and was just fighting shy of awkward when I opened my mouth at the same time as him.

'Do—'

'Do—'

I let him carry on. 'Do you come here often?' He looked round at the décor with a barely concealed shudder.

My lips twitched but I felt on safer ground with this guy. With watchful brown eyes and a grave but gentle smile lurking around his mouth, he gave off an unassuming air.

'I assume you're being ironic.' I grinned at him.

'Of course. How about getting down to the nitty-gritty?' His eyes kept politely shying away from my fake cleavage and looking at the abstract picture behind my head. 'Do you have some pre-prepared questions à la *Blind Date* or shall we just go with the flow?'

'I thought of some earlier, but ...' Now I wasn't so sure. Having made such a spectacular idiot of myself with Anthony, I was loath to make it a double.

'Go on. Let's try one out for size.' He leant his arms on the table moving closer. I checked them out. Slender forearms with dark hair – but not gorilla – and a chunky, trendy watch.

'OK then. Rugby or football?'

'Definitely football,' he said, his face lighting up. 'Been an Arsenal supporter man and boy. Didn't go to the kind of school where they played rugby.'

Not a public school boy then, not that he dressed like one; his crumpled corduroy jacket was more trendy sociology teacher than ex-Etonian.

'Tea or coffee?'

You'd have thought from the childish 'yeugh' face he pulled, I'd said cod liver oil or Babycham.

'Neither. I don't like hot drinks. Can't stand all this cappuccino nonsense.' He shook his head. 'Give me pubs over coffee bars any day. Next one?'

'OK, which super power would you chose – invisibility or flight?'

He looked at me with stunned admiration, planting both elbows on the table, cupping his chin as a frown of concentration wrinkled his forehead.

'Corker of a question!'

I preened. Ben, my lovely, vague brother has a nice line in these surreal musings. I'd pinched it from him, prompted by the song I'd heard on the tube.

'Phew. Difficult.'

I had to give him credit – he was giving the question plenty of consideration.

'If I say invisibility ... and I'm tempted ... you might think I was a bit of a perv. But there'd be so many benefits.' His face lit up as if a particularly naughty thought had crossed his mind. 'Would you still be able to see my clothes or would I have to strip off to be, you know ...?'

I hadn't given it that much thought. My eyes strayed to the smooth line of his olive-green Timberland T-shirt – no bulging pecs, but no man boobs either. My gaze slipped further down. No podgy overhang clutching the top of his jeans which a lot of blokes get as they near thirty.

He caught my eyes straying downwards. I blushed. Oh God, did he think I was checking out his tackle. He'd think I was right old slapper.

'No,' I squeaked. 'Invisibility cloak, I think, like in Harry Potter.'

His face crinkled in amusement. Nice brown eyes. Warm.

'Now that would be cool.' His eyes shone with the

possibilities. 'I think I'm going to have to nick your fantastic question. Do you think it will work on any of this lot?'

We peered round the corner of the banquette, scanning the uniform selection of streaked blondes with dead straight falls of hair in skinny jeans and ballerina pumps.

'Mm, perhaps not. How good are you on shoes and handbags?'

His eyes widened in instant horror. I couldn't help it, I laughed out loud at his panic.

'Christ, I wouldn't have a bloody clue.' He ducked his head under the table. Popping up again he said, 'I don't suppose those came from Clarks did they?'

'No, they bloody didn't.' I figured it was safe to swear with him. Cheeky bugger, there was well over £100 worth of leather on each of my feet. 'You say that to anyone here and they'll lynch you. With shoes, stick to Jimmy Choo or Manolo. Handbags, Gucci or Prada or you could try Mulberry.'

'Whoa. That's way too complicated. Who's Jimmy Choo? Couldn't I ask if they wear Nike or Puma?'

'No, this is important stuff.'

'So what should I ask?'

Just as I began the penguin buzzed into life again. 'Too late.' I grinned. 'Now you'll never know the perfect girl question.'

He got to his feet and I was gratified to see he looked regretful.

'Ah well, it's all over when the penguin sings. Maybe see you later.' His eyes met mine and he grinned.

Should I circle a yes around number eight? He had potential. I wondered what Emily would make of him. She'd probably run screaming. She liked a certain level of sophistication in a man.

* * *

Making up my mind, I shoved the card out of sight as the next candidate appeared, hopping anxiously up and down in front of me. Boyishly good-looking but on the small side, he clutched his card to his chest. I could see his Adam's apple bobbing furiously. I smiled, hoping to put him at his ease. Now I'd got the first two dates over with, I felt much more relaxed. In fact I was quite curious now to see what the evening would bring. The new guy didn't say anything just stood rigidly in front of me, arms stiff down at his sides and his legs slightly apart, as if rooted to the spot.

'Hi, I'm Olivia.' I leant forward and put out my hand with another encouraging smile.

'Peter.' He straightened and pushed out his chest. I bit back a smile wondering if he had a slight Napoleon complex, he was a good few inches shorter than me.

'Hi, Peter.'

He nodded and sat down, fussing to pull his chair neatly into the table, looking down underneath it as if to check the legs were square.

'I have three questions,' he announced formally, his eyes meeting mine with a candid stare.

'I started like that but ... I've given up on those already. I find it easier to try a bit of an ice-breaker.' Still elated by my previous success with Ned, I launched in. 'This is a good one ... I promise.'

A flash of disapproval so brief I might have been mistaken crossed Peter's face and for a moment I wondered if I'd been a bit presumptuous. 'If you had to pick a superpower ... what would it be? Flight or invisibility?' I grinned at him in what I hoped was an engaging fashion, my eyes drawn to the hopelessly dated, knitted tank top he wore.

'Flight or invisibility?' he echoed deadpan, as if he'd never heard of either.

'Yes.'

He stared at me, blue eyes behind thick lenses dissecting every feature of my face.

'You know, like Superman or ... the Invisible Man.'

'They're not real.' He looked pained for a second and I felt a bit guilty. I guessed some people were taking this very seriously.

'You're supposed to ask proper questions. To find out if we're compatible.' He pulled a leaflet out of his pocket and I recognised some of Barney's marketing blurb. 'You're supposed to find out what I like. What I'm looking for in a woman.'

I was tempted to remind him that it was a two-way deal, but I decided to let it go. It didn't seem worth the effort.

'So what do you look for in a woman?' I asked, almost wincing as I said the words out loud.

'Good manners. Smartly dressed. Ladylike.' His mouth narrowed. 'I don't really like girls that wear trousers all the time. It's not very feminine.'

That counted me out then. 'And I don't like too much make-up.'

Unable to resist, I sighed. 'Me too. I hate it when men wear too much make-up.'

Something blazed briefly in his eyes but it didn't stop me asking, 'So what do you bring to the party?'

'I'm loyal, steadfast and one hundred per cent reliable. I don't mess people around or let them down.'

Admirable enough qualities, but not enough to make me ignore the rampant male chauvinism. I opted for discretion as the better part of valour and killed the remainder of the time with a string of questions about him.

Chapter Four

In the cab on the way home, Emily was positively fizzing. She perched on the edge of her seat, one leg crossed, jiggling up and down with excitement.

'Well, who'd have thought? That was an interesting night. I'm so glad you suggested we go.'

I didn't have the energy to remind her that she'd invited herself.

'Barney definitely knows all the right people.'

'Mmm,' I replied, feeling a bit woozy. Despite my best intentions I'd succumbed to an extra glass of wine or two. I felt a bit sick as the taxi swayed around corners.

'What fun, though. Such a mix of people. Olivia – are you still with us?'

'Sorry, my brain's a bit scrambled.' And my stomach. 'Wish I'd taken notes – some of them blurred into another towards the end.'

Ned turned out to be as good as it got. There were enough sparks there to fire up a very small Bunsen burner. Two others had been a bit on the hopeless side. Both probably still lived with their mother and were the kind I needed to steer clear of – the ones you go out with because you don't want to hurt their feelings and three weeks later you're inventing dead relatives and funerals in the Outer Hebrides to avoid another date.

At least with this speed-dating malarkey it was much easier to be hard-hearted. You could say no at the outset without hurting anyone's feelings.

My fabulous question had met with mixed results but sorted the men from the gentlemen. Not one of them, not even Ned, came up with the right answer, which was, of course, flight as long as you don't have to wear the tights. I've always had a bit of a thing for Clark Kent.

Emily was still fidgeting. She'd clearly enjoyed herself.

'I can remember them all. There was one complete weirdo, asking me whether I could fly? Complete beer monster. Too boy next door for me.' She wrinkled her nose.

That would have been Ned then.

'That tall guy was nice, good-looking and very smart. Likes Japanese food and knows this lovely restaurant in Soho. His brother's just written a screenplay. Offered to take me to a private screening.' She smiled for a moment. I might have known she'd find Anthony attractive.

Then her face dissolved into a disgruntled scowl. 'Oh my God. Did you get that short chap? Did you see that tank top? His granny must have knitted it. So much for exclusivity. How on earth did he get in past the pneumatic blonde bouncers?'

She did rattle on sometimes. My brain was addled. I was ready for bed.

'Who?'

'You must remember.'

I forced myself to concentrate. Tank top? And then it came to me. 'You mean the one in blue chinos, a bit of a Tom Cruise lookalike.'

'He was short enough, I suppose.'

'Don't be mean, Emily, he did have a touch of Cruise about him. He was quite good-looking in a Clark Kent kind of way. If he took those glasses off and did something with his hair he'd look a lot better.'

'You and your CK fixation.' She tutted. 'He was all right, I guess but you'd have thought he'd lash out and buy a new pair of glasses. You know, try and make a good impression. Did you see the state of them? That silver duct tape holding the lenses in. Talk about style disaster.' She shuddered.

'So you didn't tick his box then?' I asked, expecting her to say, of course not. She shifted in her seat, picking at her thumbnail.

'Speaking theoretically,' she began.

A get-out clause if ever I heard one.

'If ... I was in the market ... which, of course, I'm not ... because I'm going out with Daniel ... but if I wasn't ... there were a couple of guys, you know ... I might have been interested in. That screenplay guy was quite promising. Do you know he completes the *Times* crossword every day?'

'Yes he did mention it.' Three times.

'And he loves sushi.' She sighed. 'Clever, sophisticated and gorgeous.'

Surely she must have realised the only person he was ever going to be interested in was himself.

'Knows some really impressive people. Great contacts. I might meet him for a drink or something. You know ... purely platonic ... because ... you know, I am seeing Daniel. Just networking, you know? Did you see the guy in the Hugo Boss suit and that tie? He was at Eton. Something big in property now. A developer, I think. Offices in Kensington.'

'Emily, he's an estate agent.'

'Are you sure?' Her forehead crumpled.

I nodded. 'Definitely. He's a mate of Barney's. I've met him before. Once tried to sell me a broom cupboard in Wimbledon.'

Her face fell in disappointment. 'Nice suit though. How about you? Going to see anyone again?'

'Not sure. There was one guy ...' I trailed off. Ned had been quite nice and it had only been three minutes. Could there be more there if I gave him a chance?

'Which one?'

'Guy called Ned, he was all right.'

'Why not give it a whirl? What have you got to lose? It's

time you had a bit of fun. Get you out of the flat. I know you had a disaster with that Mike bloke at uni, but when was the last time you went out with anyone for longer than a month? You really need to start trusting again. You'll never find the one mooching around at home with Daniel and me all the time.'

As the cab pulled up outside the flat, Emily's face fell. 'Shit,' she said, looking up at her bedroom window.

'What?' I asked alarmed.

'My light's on. Daniel's here. I wish you hadn't given him that key.'

'I'm sorry but that was before you were going out. Came in handy for someone else to have a key if I locked myself out. I thought you said he was meeting his folks for dinner.'

She shrugged. 'Yeah, at the Oxo Tower. He said there was a chance he'd come by afterwards if it wasn't too late.'

She'd changed her tune, she hadn't mentioned that earlier.

'I'm surprised he didn't invite you to meet them?' And that she wouldn't jump at the chance for a posh dinner. 'They're very laid-back. Lovely, especially Miriam, his stepmum. She's quite a character.'

Emily shrugged. 'He did.' She gave an impish smile. 'I'm not a meeting-the-parents kind of gal.'

Maybe she was right. Let's face it, she had more luck with men than me.

'So,' I said, fumbling with the handle of the door while shoving a ten pound note at the cab driver.

'I don't want him to know where we've been. He's been a bit off …' She stepped down onto the pavement.

Off what? Off hand. Off as in going off her? I was dying to ask, but there was no way she'd admit a man was losing interest.

'Where have we been?' she said, pulling on my arm to slow my progress to the front door. 'Think.'

'We've been out. For a drink.'

'Yes, but where?'

'Café Lulu, perhaps?'

'We can't tell him that!' she hissed in an outraged whisper.

'Why not? It's the truth. Just don't mention the speed-date bit.'

'What if he knows that they have speed-dating there?'

'Emily, even if he did, why would he think that we'd been?'

She shrugged, pushing past me as I opened the door.

'Don't mind me,' I muttered, watching her disappear up the stairs as I hung up my coat.

'Daniel!' Emily's excited squeal carried down the stairs. She should have been on the stage.

Just my luck, Daniel was sitting on the sofa, looking completely at home.

'Hi, Olivia. Been somewhere nice?'

'Hi—' I got no further.

Emily busily taking off her coat and dumping it on a nearby chair, interrupted. 'We've been to this fabulous bar tonight. Café Lulu, just off Charlotte Street. Really nice, wasn't it, Olivia? Absolutely packed. Loads of people. Met Olivia's cousin there. Barney. Of course you know him? He was with some friends. If I'd known you'd be here by now, you could have joined us. Why didn't you phone?' Emily stopped for breath.

Daniel looked bemused by the rapid information download. 'I did. A couple of times, but it went straight to voicemail.'

I glanced at Emily remembering her switching off her mobile, saying she didn't want Daniel ringing mid-date.

'So how was Barney?' asked Daniel looking at me. 'Hasn't he set up some speed-dating business? That's what Kate told me at Lucy and Piers's wedding.'

Emily's mouth opened and shut, her eyes widening with a quick-say-something look.

'Loathsome as ever.'

'Are you ever going to let sleeping hamsters lie?' he teased.

'Nope.'

'Surprised you met up with him. What happened to your hate-hate relationship?'

'Strong as ever,' I said, shooting a now-look-what-you've-done glare at Emily. 'Sadly, we bumped into him. Tea anyone?'

'I'd love one, Olivia,' said Emily.

Daniel frowned at her. 'Thought it kept you awake.'

Blithely she completely ignored him and muttered, 'Must take these shoes off,' before disappearing to her room.

Hoping to escape I headed for the kitchen, only to find Daniel on my heels.

'You know, Olivia, perhaps you should try one of Barney's speed-dates.' The gentleness in his voice made me wish things were different. 'Get a man of your own.'

A furious blush raced along my cheekbones, I could feel it.

'No good waiting around, hoping things will change.'

My stomach lurched, that horrible dip-in-the-road-feeling. How embarrassing. I kept my head down. If I looked at him, I might burst into tears. God, how mortifying. He knew how I felt about him. And so typical of him, giving me a gentle warning off.

Suddenly his arm was around me and he was giving me an awkward hug.

'Olivia, I care about you.' His fingers brushed the top of my arm and I started at the soft tingle they left. 'I don't want to see you hurt.'

I swallowed the lump forming in the back of my throat, breathing in the faint tang of citrus. God, he was lovely even when he was telling me he wasn't interested. Don't cry. Think happy thoughts. Smile. Pretend.

I managed a faint smile but tears were threatening to take

over. 'Think I'll forget the tea,' I said in a strained voice, and fled to my bedroom.

He frowned as he followed Emily back into her room. There were undercurrents present this evening that he couldn't keep up with.

'Sorry about that,' whispered Emily. 'We were out with you know who.' She shut the bedroom door.

'I guessed as much from the odd atmosphere when the two of you came in. I don't get it though, she doesn't seem happy.' He wasn't going to ask what the guy was like. Nothing to do with him and why should he care?

'It's difficult,' said Emily, turning away fiddling with the hem of her dress. 'You staying tonight? Thought you were playing cricket tomorrow.' He detected the sharpness of her tone.

Cricket was still a sore point. He didn't want to give it up – he'd played for the club since he was twelve. After a week at work he enjoyed getting out on the pitch, but he could appreciate it was a bit of a drag for Emily. They didn't usually finish until seven or eight. Even the compromise of playing every other weekend didn't seem to have placated her.

'Yeah.' He grinned and slid his arms around her, getting a noseful of a perfume so strong it almost made his eyes water. 'But I don't have to leave until eleven tomorrow.'

She pouted, her eyes sad and doleful. 'It's hardly worth you staying; you might as well go home now. You'd probably rather anyway.'

He immediately felt guilty and doused the temptation to call her bluff. He didn't want to upset her. Something he seemed quite good at. Despite her outward confidence and bouncy attractiveness, he'd found quite quickly that she was desperately insecure, needing constant reassurance and although her fragility made him want to look after her, sometimes it could be wearing.

He shifted the pile of clothes on the chair, transferring them to the bed and pulled her down onto his lap. 'Emily, I'm here now. I can stay tonight.'

Chapter Five

At the end of the speed-date we were supposed to pop our scorecards into a special post box at the bottom of the stairs on our way out. Amazingly, despite mine still being screwed up in my coat pocket, I received an email from Ned on Sunday evening. All my foreboding about Barney's business ethics was borne out. Either that or he'd recruited a psychic speed-dater.

Apparently Ned had got his hands on a second-hand invisibility cloak and wondered if I fancied testing it with a shoe-lifting expedition to liberate a pair of Jimmy Chews. (His spelling.) I was intrigued and after Friday night's kitchen tête-à-tête, drastic measures were needed to show Daniel I wasn't pining after him.

Emily was sprawled the length of the sofa half-heartedly watching *Antiques Roadshow* and flicking through *Heat* magazine.

'What are you smiling about?' she asked lazily, stretching and yawning, already in her pyjamas.

Sunday nights were sacrosanct in the flat – ironing, followed by hair washing in readiness for the onslaught of a week at work. All of which was always rounded off with rubbish Sunday telly and a nice bottle of cold Pinot Grigio or whatever was cheapest in Tesco that week.

'Barney and his underhand tactics. Have you heard from anyone?'

'What underhand tactics?'

'I ... didn't actually hand my scorecard in.' I pulled a rueful face. 'Chickened out. At the last minute. Didn't put it in the slot.'

'Olivia. You are hopeless!' Emily tutted.

'Didn't make much difference. Barney's still passed my details on. I've got an email. Have you had any?'

'What?' Her left eyelid flickered before she said quickly, 'No, of course not. What do you think it's worth?' She pointed to the screen and a very ugly painting. 'They're getting all excited. Bet it's less than two hundred pounds. Wonder how they know? Do you think they make it up sometimes?'

The minx. Her sudden absorption in *Antiques Roadshow* didn't fool me.

I hadn't seen or spoken properly to Kate since the speed-date and when she phoned on Monday morning with her glib claim that she was in London that afternoon and could meet me after work for a drink, she didn't fool me. She wanted gory details, I knew her too well. She and Barney were close so he was bound to have filled her in. In fact, she may have even put him up to giving Ned my email address.

I was still wondering, as I walked to the hip bar she'd chosen, whether I should go out with Ned. His email had made me laugh. I'd have to come up with an equally witty reply. I tried out various lines in my head. They were all way too corny.

As soon as I got to Asia de Cuba I spotted Kate perched on a high bar stool around one of those impossibly trendy stainless steel pillars that double as a table or a leaning post. She already had a bottle of wine at the ready with two glasses.

The cross-examination began before I'd even taken my first sip.

'How did Emily get on?' asked Kate. 'Has she had any emails?'

Since when the interest in my flatmate? What about me?

'No ... well, not that she's admitting.'

'I bet she has.' My sister smirked, pausing dramatically and taking a large glug of wine before announcing, 'She ticked three boxes.'

'Three?' I echoed. I stared at her open-mouthed for a second, my glass halting before my lips. 'And how do you know that?'

She grinned and preened a little.

I shook my head and tutted. 'Typical Barney. No concept of client confidentiality.' I paused before asking idly, swirling the wine in my hand. 'So do you know whose boxes she ticked?'

'Not so worried about client confidentiality now?' crowed Kate.

I pulled a face at her, wrinkling my nose and wriggling uncomfortably. The bar stools were designed for someone with more flesh on their backside than me. 'Just spit it out, you old harpy.'

'Some chap called Anthony. One of Barney's mates, Charlie, and I can't remember the name of the other one.'

Three!

'Blimey. Poor Daniel,' I said in disgust.

'Olivia, what planet have you been on for the last few months? Surely you can see what she's like. I don't know what Daniel sees in her. He's way too good for her.' Her eyes narrowed. 'I always thought—'

I interrupted her. There was no way I wanted her going down that road. 'Emily's not that bad.'

'Olivia. Yes she is. She's one of those girls who are always on the lookout for their next victim. She'd be out on-the-pull the night before her wedding, just in case. Has she ever not had a boyfriend?'

Kate was being unnecessarily harsh. Although on reflection, in the time I'd been sharing with Emily, she'd always had someone in tow, some overlapping occasionally.

'No,' I said trying to be fair. 'But that's because of her mother's disastrous marriages. She's very insecure.'

'Huh, she hides it well.' Kate's face said it all.

'You don't know her that well. Her mum's had two husbands walk out!'

Kate sniffed with a marked lack of sympathy. 'What was it Oscar Wilde said? "To lose one, may be regarded as a misfortune, to lose two seems like carelessness."'

'Kate, you are so heartless.' I pretended to be shocked. She grinned at me. Was it my imagination or was she spikier than usual these days?

'Sorry,' she said unrepentantly. 'Tell me about your speed-date. Barney says you made quite an impression on one of the guys.'

'Did he now? That would be the Barney that blatantly ignored the fact that I didn't hand in my card.'

Kate grinned.

I had wondered if she hadn't put him up to it. Now I knew she bloody had.

'Barney must mean Ned, the guy with ESP, who worked out my email address all by himself,' I observed dryly. 'He was quite nice. I'm thinking of meeting him for a shop-lifting session.'

'Pardon?' She raised her eyebrows and, giggling, I told her about the email which then led on to a lengthy digression about what shoes we'd steal. Kate was firmly in the Christian Louboutin camp and had seen a pair of the red-soled beauties in Selfridges for a snip at £750. My hankering was for a pair of Jimmy Choos, drop dead gorgeous black courts which even in the outlet village were still £300. We agreed stealing them was our only option because, as Kate pointed out, how many people can really justify spending the cost of a small holiday on a pair of shoes, no matter how lovely?

It wasn't until we'd downed a whole bottle of white

wine and a couple of caesar salads that Kate steered the conversation back to Ned.

'So, Olivia, are you going to meet this guy?'

I shrugged. 'I might meet him for a drink ... but that's all. So don't get excited and start telling Mum or anyone.'

She looked at me over the rim of her glass. 'You should go for it. It's well past time you started seeing people properly again.'

'Why?' I held her gaze.

'To prove you're over Mike.'

'I am,' I said indignantly.

Mike! Give me a break. I hadn't thought about him in years even though he had done the dirty thoroughly. She was dipping her toes in the wrong ocean. Mike, love of my life in my university days, had been well and truly eclipsed by someone else.

'Olivia!' she said crossly.

I pointedly avoided meeting her eyes. If she said another word I would start humming. Childish, I know, but I hated talking about Mike. Not because it still hurt, but because it was totally embarrassing. How could I have been so stupid?

In exasperation she slammed her glass down, the dregs of her drink splashing over my hand that was busily shredding a beer mat.

'For God's sake. You're so stubborn. Don't pretend. It still bothers you.'

'I have to go,' I said coolly, gathering up my mobile phone and purse, shoving them into my handbag. 'Early start tomorrow. A meeting in Derby. I need to leave early. I'll call.' After Daniel's words the other night I was still feeling a bit raw. I couldn't handle a heart-to-heart session with Kate just now.

'That is so typical. Just bury your head in the sand. You need to talk about it. You're in denial,' she snapped.

'Denial, schmial ... you're not a bloody psychologist. There's nothing to talk about. You, Mum and Auntie Bren are the ones with the hang-up. Having a boyfriend who drives a Porsche and gets a massive bonus every year, is not a marker of success,' I said, having a little dig at Kate. 'It doesn't mean you've made it.'

With that I pulled on my jacket, swung my legs off the stool and left to her parting shot that I was a stubborn pain in the proverbial.

As I stomped down Long Acre heading for Leicester Square tube I felt pissed off. Thinking about Mike always left me feeling churned up. He'd made such a fool of me.

No one was going to do that to me again and, by the same token, I couldn't do it to anyone else. Trust. Honesty. They made up my moral compass, but Mike had sent everything West.

Striding down the platform I glared at every man whose eye I happened to catch. When the train pulled in, I threw myself into a seat and brooded on the past.

In my second year at University I'd been swept off my feet, quite literally, by the Brad Pitt of the campus. Mike was the kind of guy that everyone went 'phwoar' about, even though none of us had ever spoken to him. He could have had serious halitosis or a major speech impediment for all we knew.

The memories flooded back as the train pulled out of Leicester Square, plunging into the tunnel and picking up speed. I could still remember my first encounter with him, another thing I could blame on Kate. Her and her bloody Agent Provocateur knickers.

'Don't forget these,' she'd said, grinning as she shoved the tiniest pair of leopard-print silk knickers through the driver's window of Daniel's car when he came to pick me up to go back to Norwich.

Daniel roared with laughter. 'I'm seeing a whole different side to you.'

'As if I'd wear them,' I'd retorted, blushing bright pink. 'Bloody Christmas present. I was hoping to accidentally leave them behind. Can you see me down the launderette with them?'

He wasn't laughing when his girlfriend discovered them under the passenger seat a week later, igniting all her jealousy of our cosy chats on the M11. Determined on ritualistic humiliation, she decided to hand them back in the crowded campus coffee bar.

Luckily for me, Daniel whispered a few words in the ear of one of his rugby teammates. It was one hell of a surprise when two steps over the threshold of the coffee bar, I was scooped up by a man of demigod status. Hauling me along, he drew us away from the curious stares in the coffee bar, across the courtyard and down a walkway to a doorway hidden from view. At which point he pressed a scrap of something into my hand. Looking down I spotted the infamous pants. It was my very own Cinderella moment!

Looking around the carriage I caught the eye of a teenage girl opposite, who gave me a funny look. Had I been talking to myself while remembering all this? Even now the memories gave me goosebumps.

'Dan asked me to give you these,' Mike had muttered apologetically as I nodded up at him, my heart bumping. Even now I couldn't be sure whether my breathlessness had been the result of the surprise of the ambush or the proximity of a very manly chest in a crisp, white T-shirt, centimetres from my nose? I remember gazing up into his dark brown eyes, and the magic of that first kiss, when his head dipped and I couldn't help myself. I didn't put up an iota of resistance. Well, you don't when the campus heart-throb is suddenly giving your lips his exclusive attention. It wasn't the sort of thing I normally did and certainly not stone cold sober, in public and before 11.00 a.m.

I caught the eye of the girl in the carriage again as I winced. She must have thought I was a nutter. If only the rest of the memories were as nice. At first I got the fairy tale ending when Mike and I became a couple. And it was so easy, no niggles, no jealousies and no hidden agendas. I should have known it was too good to be true.

Ironically at the same time, Daniel split up with his girlfriend, thus starting a pattern where he and I were never single at the same time until the evening he and Emily had got together. I'd been so hopeful that our relationship might finally change that night.

In flagrante delicto always sounds vaguely amusing; a situation comedy moment, with people hopping about with one leg in their trousers. In reality it's anything but funny. It's about as bloody unfunny as things get.

Even now gazing at my reflection in the tube window, I could still feel the dismay at the sight of those lovely muscled buttocks rhythmically heaving, all graphic and porn film ... with someone else.

I pulled a face at myself. Stupid cow. Any feisty film heroine worth her expensive lingerie would have charged in, slapped his arse smartly, yelling, 'You bastard'. Not me, I crept away unnoticed. Numb. In shock.

Embarrassed I looked around the carriage. The girl was openly sniggering. Bloody typical. Even now, eight years later, I was making myself look stupid over Mike. I'd had other boyfriends but I'd always made sure I kept things light and superficial. No chance of getting hurt that way. Unfortunately light and superficial had worn thin of late. I wanted more. Through the window I could see the words Embankment. I needed to keep my wits about me. I hadn't realised we were nearly at Waterloo.

I remembered Mike's face when he realised I knew.

'Busy weekend?' I'd asked coolly, when he'd finally turned up at my door.

'No, not really,' he'd said smiling, charming as ever. 'I had to get an essay done. Sorry babes, meant to call you but spent the whole weekend holed up in my room, burning the midnight oil to get it finished.'

'Really, and here I was thinking you'd spent the whole weekend shagging some strange redhead,' I snapped viciously

Shock registered in his face as his eyes widened. The big, fat, lying, slimy git.

'Mike, you didn't lock your door,' I'd told him with quiet despair.

It turned out that the girl with red hair, Tracey, had planned her visit as a surprise. She'd certainly accomplished that goal. She was the girl from his home town, the one he'd been seeing since they were both sixteen. Fed up with Mike's constant excuses of a huge workload, she'd arrived unannounced. Mm, that would be the workload that involved three hours of lectures a week, fifty-three down the pub and the rest shagging me.

Scowling, I pulled myself out of my seat as we drew into Waterloo. It wasn't that I harboured any feelings for the bastard. It was the deceit. Would I have ever known if I hadn't caught him? Never once had it occurred to me that there might be a Tracey waiting for him at home at the end of every term. I was, inadvertently, the other woman. Me! That was the ultimate irony. Fidelity ranked number one on my list of relationship prerequisites and another reason that made anything with Daniel impossible. He was Emily's now.

I weaved my way along the platform heading up to the mainline station feeling depressed and cross with myself. Time to change things. I would go out for that drink with

Ned. I ought to give him a chance, after all, three minutes was hardly any time at all and look at Piers and Lucy now.

When I left the flat at six the next morning, I felt decidedly groggy. I hadn't slept well. I'd had one of those bizarre dreams that feels as if it's lasted all night. My subconscious had run riot and conjured up one unlikely scenario after another, taking place in an airport, a junior school and a garden shed respectively. Throughout I'd been married to Mike, phoning Daniel with whom I was having an affair that Mike knew all about and had Anthony – crossword man from the speed-date – camped out in the garden shed waiting for me to run off with him to go and live on a canal boat moored beside a flour mill. I blamed Kate for stirring things up.

When she texted me at Junction 29 on the M1, I'd just refuelled the car and myself. The Starbucks coffee had worked its magic and I almost felt human. The text finished the job nicely.

'Sorry, sorry, sorry. Lots o love K x'

Kate and I didn't do touchy feely very often, but I shouldn't have snapped at her. Now that she was living in Australia, I missed her desperately. In only another two weeks she'd be flying back again. I could never stay miffed with her for long and at the moment it was even harder. Besides she could always bully me into forgiving her.

Coming off the motorway just outside Derby, I got horribly lost which made me late for my meeting, but I texted Kate back anyway before I went in.

'Forgiven, forgiven, forgiven. Love O x'

With the message sent, I switched off my phone. It had been beaten into me by one boss that it was totally unprofessional to have a mobile ring during a client meeting.

The meeting with three burly site managers who smelt of mud and sweat went on and on. I wasn't offered anything to eat apart from some manky Nice biscuits. Tasty when you're eight but disappointing when you need lunch.

On the journey home I was also regretting not stopping to go to the loo, but there had only been a men's Portaloo on the building site and at that point I wasn't that desperate. By four o'clock my misery was compounded by the traffic lady on Radio 5. I was ready to kill her. Did she really have to be so perky about a major hold up on the M1? I didn't need to be told there was a ten-mile tailback. Any fool could see the red brake lights stretching out as far as the eye could see.

Should I send her a rude text message? Less chirpiness, please. Some of us are stuck in said traffic with a bladder the size of a basketball. Then I remembered my phone was still switched off.

Rummaging in my bag, with half an eye on the stationary traffic, I pulled it out and switched it on. It lay silent and still for a second before vibrating into life with great indignation. Three texts and six messages later, the phone shuddered to a halt.

Message one was mild. 'Olivia, it's me. I've had an email,' wailed Emily. 'Can you call me, please?'

Message two a little more agitated. 'Olivia, call as soon as you get this.'

Message three was a curt. 'Call me now.'

By the sixth message she'd reached full frontal expletives. 'For God's sake, where are you? What's the point of having a fucking phone if you don't fucking switch it on?'

What the hell was going on? I was about to phone her back when I caught sight of the driver behind. He shook his head so slightly that I might have imagined it, except he was driving a dirty great police car. I dropped the phone back on the passenger seat, my fingers twitching longingly but there was nothing I could do.

My battery died an hour later. Two minutes after that, on went the blue light and Mr Policeman shot off. Typical.

By the time I'd crawled off the M1 and through the London rush hour traffic, I was exhausted. A showdown with Emily was the last thing I needed. Grabbing my briefcase and rubbing the knots in my shoulder, I hurried towards the flat, nearly tripping over Charlie.

As usual he was lurking outside the front of the junk shop below the flat. It was a funny little place, crammed full of second-hand furniture and the sort of things that might have been antiques had they not been just a bit too tatty, chipped or broken. Although my flat was directly above the shop, the space below far exceeded the square footage of my lounge, kitchen, bathroom and two bedrooms. It spread out along the street from room to room, none of which could be differentiated by any particular theme or style of products. On my occasional forays in there, I'd never seen a single other customer.

Charlie was probably waiting to follow his owner to the home they shared further down the road. He was a friendly little thing, pure black apart from two white paws, always purring a welcome whenever I came home.

I stopped to stroke him, as he wound his way round and round my legs, his tail tickling the back of my knee. I could have done with cheering up, and if it weren't for Emily I would have smuggled him in for a cuddle, but she said she was allergic to cats.

Although we were on the first floor above the shop, our front door was at street level, which meant you stepped into a long hallway that then led to a flight of stairs. Unfortunately the stairs rose straight into the lounge. There was no way of sneaking in without being seen.

Brazening it out was the only way. 'Hi, Em, are you home?' I yelled. With any luck she might not be in.

'Didn't you get my message?' she said, appearing at the top of the steps, hands on hips in warrior stance.

'Which one?' I asked sarcastically, taking the stairs slowly. 'I couldn't phone you. The motorway was hell and I had a policeman up my bum nearly all the way back. Then my battery ran out.' I might as well have been talking to myself.

'God, what am I going to do?' she wailed.

Reaching the top, I put my hand on her shoulder. 'Whoa, slow down, Emily. What's happened?'

Her mouth crumpled and she looked as if she was about to burst into tears. 'Disaster. Damn speed-date business. I only bloody ticked the wrong frigging box. That saddo ... you know, the one with the glasses, has emailed me.'

I sighed, slipping off my jacket, the tension easing out of my shoulders. No one had died then.

'Which one?' I cast my mind back.

'The one with the knackered glasses.'

A few had worn glasses. I still couldn't think which one. The guy with the red hair? The insurance one? And then I remembered.

'You mean the glasses with the tape?' I said, his image suddenly clicking into view as I perched on the edge of the armchair looking up at Emily. The metal frames had been held together with silver insulating tape.

'Yes, him,' she said vehemently, striding over to the magazine-laden coffee table. 'He emailed me this morning. I can't believe I ticked the wrong box. He's weird!'

'He seemed harmless enough. Have you replied to him?'

'Duh, no!' She slapped her forehead to make her point. 'Look at this.' Tipping a magazine off the table she pulled out a crumpled piece of paper and thrust it at me.

-----Original Message-----
From: Peter Cooper [mailto:PeterC23@bbtl.com]
To: 'Emily'
Subject: Dinner

Dear Emily

I knew when your email address was passed on to me that you must have felt that special connection between us. I was surprised at first. I have to admit your hair is not quite what I envisioned in my perfect mate. I normally prefer girls with shorter styles, but as you appear to have character enough to recognise my worth, I can overlook something that can, after all, be changed.

Let's meet for dinner. Email me back with your preferred dates this week and a suggested venue. If it's appropriate I will book a table for two. I look forward to hearing from you.

Peter

'Blimey, he's sure of himself.' I handed the sheet of paper back to her. 'Are you positive it was the little Tom Cruise lookalike? He was a bit wimpy. This guy sounds full on.' Although the male chauvinism rang true.

'Olivia, you're not listening to me. I didn't tick his box. He's labouring under a delusion. Cheek, he doesn't like my hair.' She tossed her head. 'I didn't like anything about him. I was only humouring him.'

'Really?' I asked, wandering past her down to the kitchen. I needed a drink. Remembering Peter now, I was surprised. Knowing Emily and how rude she could be, how could he have possibly thought she might be interested? Had the kitten voice misled him?

'What on earth did you talk to him about that night?' I

called from the kitchen back to the lounge. 'Something must have struck a chord.'

Emily's feet padded down the hall. 'Knitting,' she said, spitting the word out with disgust as she came into the room.

'Right,' I said, before asking with a puzzled frown, 'Why?'

She rolled her eyes as if it was obvious. 'His home knitted tank top was so vile, I couldn't think of a single thing to say ... then I had a brainwave. Last month's *Marie Claire* had an article about knitting being back in vogue.'

'Do you want a glass?' I interrupted, waving a bottle of wine at her.

'Do you need to ask?' She carried on, 'I just regurgitated everything the article said about Fair Isle patterns. He lapped it up. I was taking the piss. Surely he didn't believe me. I told him he was dead trendy and retro.'

'You didn't?' I exclaimed, turning to face her.

'For God's sake, Olivia, he was awful. He was never hand-picked by your cousin. As if any of us would look twice at him.'

'Emily,' I remonstrated, pulling the cork out with a satisfying plop.

She was right but at least I'd tried to give him the benefit of the doubt. Those three minutes were hard work. When my penguin buzzed, all I knew was that he worked with computers.

'What?'

'Nothing.' She wouldn't have felt a grain of remorse.

'So what shall I do?'

I was dying to say, 'Tell him he's got you all wrong' but I decided against it. 'He sounds intense but harmless. You should be flattered you made such an impression.'

'Hardly, his comments about my hair weren't great. Talk about weeeirrd.'

'Emily, it's just an email.' I shrugged. 'It's not as if we signed a contract. Just ignore it, although it seems a bit rude. Why not send him a nice chatty reply? Nice to meet him but you don't feel ready for a relationship at the moment.'

Emily looked blank. Gentle let-downs weren't her style.

'It's very irritating,' she said grumpily. 'I wanted to meet the film guy again. I hope there hasn't been a mix-up.'

I glanced at her sharply. She knew my feelings on fidelity.

'Not as a date,' she blustered. 'He has great contacts. You know for work. By the way, your mum phoned. You need to phone her back before eight o'clock.'

'I'd better call her now then,' I said looking at my watch, grabbing my wine glass and scurrying up the hall.

'Have you spoken to your sister recently?' Mum was a great one for caller ID. It did away with any of that boring old 'being polite' preamble.

I tucked my glass of wine conveniently between my knees.

'Hi, Mum,' I said sarcastically. 'I'm fine. How are you?'

'Sorry, dear. I was waiting for you to call. When did you last speak to Kate?'

'I saw her last night. Why?'

There was a pause before Mum spoke. 'Did she seem all right to you?'

'Fine. Possibly even more bossy than usual.'

'I'm not sure she's quite herself at the moment.' Mum sounded distracted, as if she was thinking of something else. 'I did try to talk to her, but she bit my head off. Can you give her a call? Make sure she's OK.'

'Sure, Mum. It could be that she's just missing Greg.'

'I don't think so, darling. I don't think it's all that serious. She never mentions him and I've never heard her call him.'

Mum had no idea about Facebook, MSN or Twitter and was no doubt oblivious to Kate using any or all of them to contact Greg. No point trying to even explain, she had enough trouble with texting.

'Now, Olivia, darling, I need to talk to you about ...'

The rest of the conversation was taken up by who was doing what at the Old Bodgers' match. It was agreed that I would do teas – as I did every year – which involved making copious amounts of sandwiches and buttering a scone mountain while Mum would be in charge of the evening barbecue. Apparently Dad was getting very excited about the forthcoming match and thanks to some sneaky recruiting had found some brilliant Aussie bowler. He was already counting his wickets.

Chapter Six

The reception at Organic PR is manned by Piranha One and Piranha Two. I don't bother learning their names any more as they are replaced by updated identikit models every couple of months. Whatever that job ad promises, it must be a pack of lies because they never last long. The necessary qualifications must include a rigid expression – or they're paid in Botox treatments – a distant superior manner and the ability to wither plants at ten paces with one icy look.

Yet all of them have this unnerving ability to morph into a human being the minute they spot an important client or a board director. Forget asking them to order a courier – which I believe is part of a receptionist's duties. From the twitch of their immaculate lips – so much Botox they don't curl any more – you'd think that you'd asked them whether their Prada handbags came from Next.

As Emily and I crossed the hall to the lifts, carrying hot drinks we'd picked up from Starbucks next door, Piranha One lifted her head and said in clear cutting tones, 'Emily! Could you explain to your boyfriend that we are not here to pass on personal messages to staff? And remind him that our email is working perfectly.'

'Pardon?'

'I think you heard,' and with that she turned back to her wordsearch hidden below the desk.

'She is so bloody rude,' Emily seethed. 'How much longer has she got?'

'Another six weeks of that one. Time's nearly up for Piranha Two. What was she on about? I thought Daniel always phoned your mobile?'

'Haven't a clue. Probably got me muddled up with Emily Parr in Accounts.'

I'd just sat down at my desk, prised the lid off my hot chocolate and fired up my computer when a grumpy-faced Emily appeared in front of me.

'Olivia, I've had another bloody email.' Scowling she stomped back to her desk.

I followed. Peering over her shoulder I read ...

-----Original Message-----
From: Peter Cooper [mailto:PeterC23@bbtl.com]
To: 'Emily'
Subject: Tardiness

Dear Emily

I emailed you yesterday and I haven't heard back from you. I was worried you never got my email. Your receptionist tells me, however, that this is unlikely and that your system is very reliable. (She's rather abrupt for one in her position.)

However I wasn't confident she knew what she was doing so I popped in to ensure that she had checked properly. A proper little madam but that's so many women for you. Knowing you as I do, I'm sure there's a good explanation as to why you haven't answered my first email. That stupid female on the front desk was covering up her own incompetence ...

Oo er and yikes.

'He popped in!' My voice went up. 'No wonder the Piranhas were ruder than normal.'

'Bloody cheek. How dare he?' exploded Emily. 'Who does he think he is? Checking up on me? He can piss off.'

'Emily, calm down. There's obviously been a mix-up. Poor

chap. Thought Santa had done a personal delivery when he heard you'd ticked his box.'

'I didn't tick his sodding box! I've a good mind to ring your cousin. Get him to explain the cock-up to this Peter.' She was pacing furiously up and down in front of my desk, oblivious to the curious looks she was getting.

'As far as he's concerned you did tick the box,' I said gently.

'Well, I didn't,' she roared at me. 'I'm going to email him. How the hell did he find out where I worked?'

Er hello, a quick Google on the web and Facebook and he could have found Emily and where she worked in seconds. Peter didn't need to be Einstein to work out her email address.

'Emily, just let him down gently,' I pleaded. 'Imagine how he feels.' In this mood there was no knowing what response she would fire off.

'I was hardly going to email, "Piss off you loony and don't darken my inbox again", was I?'

Actually, I wouldn't put it past her. She wasn't renowned for her subtlety. 'Just do the standard-nice-girl fob-off, "you're-far-too-good-for-me-and-I-just-want-to-be-fair-to-you."'

She looked at me quizzically.

I heaved a big sigh. 'Do you want me to do it?' It was the only way to stop her upsetting him or so I thought.

'Would you? You're so much better at that sort of thing.'

I rolled my eyes. She was the one that wrote press releases about magical lipsticks staying put for forty-eight hours, when everyone knew they'd never pass the 'one swig of a Bacardi Breezer' test.

We went over to her desk and plonking myself in her chair, I started typing.

'Should it be, "Hi Peter" or "Dear Peter"?'

'Try "Oy Weirdo". Works for me.'

'Ever considered a career in the diplomatic corps?' My sarcasm was wasted.

Emily looked blank. 'I couldn't give a toss. We just need to get rid of him.'

I blinked at the casual 'we' but let it go. It was easier for me to get on and compose a gentle but firm rejection email explaining that 'I' wasn't ready for a relationship just at the moment.

Emily tutted and tossed her head throughout. Every time I asked her opinion she pursed her mouth. Half an hour later, after much negotiation, I had an email that we were satisfied with. Emily pressed the magic 'send' button.

'Happy now?' she asked.

God, she could be a pain. If we weren't sharing a flat, I would have stuffed the keyboard down her throat. Instead I went back to my cold hot chocolate and a curt voicemail message. My usually mild-mannered boss, Max, was pissed off. Where was I? Thanks to Emily I was five minutes late for a client meeting.

By lunchtime I'd eaten my home-made sarnie. In fact it had gone before eleven. I needed something else; something nutritious and filling like a pack of Marks & Spencer's Percy Pigs.

I set out down Oxford Street with good intentions, but the minute I got to Marks my stomach took charge, making outrageous demands and before I knew it my basket had mysteriously been filled with essentials like feta stuffed olives, pastrami bagel chips, and chocolate-covered peanuts.

If I hadn't been so absorbed in my Percy Pigs I might have been paying more attention as I shouldered my way through the damp crowds, dodging umbrella spokes on the way back to the office. Someone rushing by shoved me sharply and glancing up I caught a fleeting impression of glasses mended with electrical tape. Whipping my head around, I tried to get a second look but whoever it was had vanished in the flow of people undulating around me. Bloody Emily and her emails. Now I had Peter on the brain ... and a wet neck, as I barged into an umbrella knocking a torrent of water down my collar.

I planned to sneak into the office hiding the telltale bag under my coat to avoid the universal chorus of 'I wish you'd said that you were going'. I needn't have worried – my entrance went completely unnoticed. An excited crowd was gathered around Emily's desk. Had some major coup in the beauty world happened while I was out?

'What's all the excitement?' I asked, as Helene, a junior on Emily's team, bustled by importantly.

'Miranda Baker has just said she'd do it,' she gushed. 'It's a real coup.'

The mind boggled. Just what was it that Miranda had agreed to do? The ex-star of one of those teen soaps, she was one of those irritating minor celebrities who popped up everywhere and pretty much did everything.

'Do what?' I asked.

'Miranda has agreed to wear our dress at the premiere of the new James Bond film,' burbled Helene. 'We're so chuffed. It's amazing.'

I glanced quickly at her. What dress? What premiere?

I hadn't heard anything about this before. I glanced over at Emily's blonde head, pennies dropping at speed.

'For the Luscious Lips launch by any chance?' I asked.

'That's right. It was Emily's idea. Isn't it amazing? We're having an amazing dress made especially for Miranda.' Helene's eyes shone with enthusiasm.

I couldn't resist saying, 'That's amazing.'

She didn't bat an eyelid, instead she leaned forward

confidingly and said, 'Do you know ... the dress is going to be white with big lip prints all of over it.'

'Let me guess,' I said. 'Each one will be in the new season's colours.'

'Yes!' squealed Helene, squeezing her hands together.

'Amazing,' I said cuttingly this time.

'Emily is so clever.' Helene was almost skipping with excitement.

Wasn't she just? Although it wasn't that long ago, on a car journey along the M4 no less, that Emily had thought the very same idea clichéd. I looked over at her, surrounded by an adoring crowd. She looked up and caught my eye.

Some people might have had the grace to look sheepish. Not Emily. She just looked at me defiantly. Shocked, more by the insolence of her expression than anything else, I turned away and went back to my desk.

I realised that it wasn't that much of a surprise, Emily presenting the idea as hers. She did tend to cut corners, and if she could get away with something she would. I remember her once walking out of Topshop with a dress accidentally tucked under her arm, which she didn't realise she'd done until we were half way down Oxford Street. Funny that, and I might have believed it was an oversight if she hadn't spent ages cooing over the dress, pouting when I reminded her she still had her half of the electricity bill to pay. Funny too, I said, that the security tag hadn't gone off, to which she'd responded that there'd been men working on the electrics at the door.

No, honesty and Emily didn't sit that well together.

Ignoring everyone else I busied myself at my desk, pressing the send and receive button on my email several times, hoping somewhere out there in the ether there was a message that needed an urgent response or something to keep me very busy for the afternoon. Nothing appeared in my inbox.

* * *

Emily found me as I emerged from a cubicle in the ladies later that afternoon. She was leaning against one of the sinks. I nodded, letting her do all the talking.

She threw her hands above her head dramatically.

'All right, Olivia, it's a fair cop,' she said defensively, the old chestnuts glibly tripping off her tongue. 'Blow the whistle, if you want, but you do know that there's no such thing as a new idea.'

I said nothing.

Looking into my face, she said in a low urgent voice, 'Look, I know it was your idea but I honestly didn't think it was a goer.'

Huh, a likely tale.

'When I got to the meeting with Fiona, it just came out.'

'Really?' My tone was dry.

'Yes and she liked it. Really liked it. I couldn't believe it, she never likes my ideas.'

I washed my hands very thoroughly with soap, not looking at her. 'That's because it wasn't your idea.'

'Technically, yes.' Emily was now trying to catch my eye in the mirror. 'But at that point I could hardly say it was yours. Have you any idea what it's like working for her? You're lucky. Max lets you get away with anything.'

If she was expecting me to sympathise as usual, she'd misjudged things. This time I was seriously pissed off. I narrowed my eyes and turned to face her.

'Fine, Emily,' I said, firmly making eye contact for the first time. 'But why didn't you tell me? I'm hardly going to march over to Fiona and say, "Actually it was my idea".' Did she really think so little of me? 'Blimey, it's not as if you haven't had ample opportunity. We do live together. From the sound of things you've been negotiating with Miranda for a few days.'

With that said, I flounced out of the loo, stomping back to

my desk. After all the help I'd given her that morning with Peter's email! Well, she could bloody well sort her own mad emails out from now on.

Unfortunately that's just what she did.

I was so fed up with Emily that I phoned Kate for a moan, but she wasn't particularly sympathetic, in fact she was bloody miserable which reminded me of Mum's conversation the previous evening.

'What are you doing tonight?' I asked.

'Meeting up with Caroline for a drink, except she's just phoned. Typical, I'm already on the train to London and she's held up. I'm going to have hours to kill. What are you doing?'

'I've got an idea. Give me five minutes and I'll call you back.' I knew just the thing. Isabelle on the floor above was always offering me complimentary visits to one of her client's places.

'You have such a brilliant job,' Kate said, letting out a long heart-felt sigh as she tucked her towel tighter around her chest, and wiped her hair off her face.

'Mmm.' It was all I could do to answer her. Lying full-length in the delicious heat, the warmth was penetrating my muscles unfurling the knots of tension in them. I hadn't realised how much Emily had wound me up.

'I could get used to this.' Kate's voice sounded wistful

That sounded like a good cue to me. I sat up. Too quickly! I felt light-headed for a second in the hot air.

'You missing Greg?' I asked sympathetically.

'What?' asked Kate, looking confused for a moment.

'Gorgeous Greg, the surf-stud?' I teased. 'He of the six-pack.'

'Six? You mean eight. Everything's more macho in Australia, Sheila.'

Clearly that wasn't the problem, so what was it? Was Mum imagining things? There was only one other thing I thought it might be.

'Poor old Bill. I bet he's only got a six-pack,' I said.

'Where did that come from?' she asked rather sharply, looking at me. 'What about Bill?'

Bingo. As I suspected.

'It's not every day you get picked to play rugby for England. He's been in every newspaper this week,' I answered. 'I just wondered if you might have had a change of heart.' I used my towel to dab at the water dripping down my neck.

'As if that impresses me,' she snapped, looking up for a second and sticking her nose in the air.

I looked at her and opened my mouth in astonishment. 'Gosh, it impresses the hell out of me. He's done so well to be selected and how great would it be to say you're going out with an England rugby player?'

'There was never any chance of that,' she said more gently, shaking her head, clumps of hair plastering her damp cheeks. A small part of me relished her looking dishevelled.

She sighed. 'Much as Bill hoped, nothing was ever going to happen.'

'Why not?' I asked, turning my palms up to the ceiling. 'What was wrong with him?' I never did get it. Bill reminded me of Hugh Grant in his bumbling, gentle way. The same floppy hair and bemused expression although that's where the similarity ended. At six foot five he was much taller and twice the width. Bill didn't play in the back row for nothing. For some strange reason he adored Kate and never bothered to hide it, to her total embarrassment.

'He was my boss for one thing,' she said, tapping the wooden slat beside her with her fingernail. 'And you know he's not my type.'

'You mean he doesn't work in the City and wear pinstripes,' I said cynically.

Her fingernail was still tapping. 'Don't knock it. It might not matter to you but it does to me.'

True. We were totally the wrong way round. I had the job with the smart clothes and restaurant lifestyle and while I enjoyed it, it wasn't essential to my happiness in the same way it seemed to be to Kate.

When she'd stuck at Gainsboro's Plumbing Supplies for more than the usual three months, Mum thought perhaps she'd found her niche. Aside from Bill's devotion, Kate acquired a fan club among the plumbers thanks to her designer's eye and constant suggestions for tiles, fittings and sanitaryware.

'I want someone who's going places. Not some family-run business where the pinnacle of success is a contract supplying gold-plated taps to footballers in Chelsea Harbour.' Her finger tapped in time with her staccato sentences. 'Someone with ambition. Style. Money.' Tap, tap. 'Someone who doesn't buy the same pair of trousers ... in three different colours ... from the same shop because' tap '... they're comfy.' Her voice rose as she finished.

'Not Bill, then.' I said sadly. Shame, he was lovely. Each to their own and all that. I'd be seeing him again in a couple of weeks time. Daniel had recruited him to play cricket in the forthcoming Old Bodgers match. Hang on! I remembered now.

'I forgot to ask you,' I said, shifting to lie on my stomach. 'Did Bill get in touch when he was in Oz a month or so ago? He asked me for your number?'

'Yes ... er ... no.'

I raised my eyebrows and twisted my head round to look up at her on the top shelf of the sauna. 'Which?'

'He did get in touch ...' she faltered, and lay down abruptly.

'And?' I pushed, intrigued. I couldn't see her face any more. Was she deliberately avoiding looking at me?

'We ... there wasn't time to see him.'

I couldn't help pressing to find out more. She'd always taken Bill's adoration for granted. 'Of course, rugby players are gods out there. Bet there were women falling all over him.'

'He was training very hard most of the time,' snapped Kate, sitting up again and slipping off the bench. 'That's why.' She reached for the door. 'I'm going for a shower.'

There was a brief blast of cooler air before the door was slammed. Did Kate have an attack of sour grapes? Surely not, she said she didn't want Bill but that didn't mean she didn't want anyone else to have him, did it?

Poor Kate. I loved her to bits but despite all her front I wasn't sure she really knew what she wanted. The whole Australia thing still seemed out of character. She wasn't exactly raving about living there.

'That feels so much better,' I said, rolling my head and stretching my neck as we stepped out onto the street. 'I can't believe I've never taken Isabelle up on the offer before.'

'Great idea. Thanks for taking me.' Kate paused on the pavement. 'Sorry I've been so grouchy. I ... just feel ...' Her voice trailed off. 'Must be change of climate or ... something.'

Did I imagine the momentary look of alarm that skittered in her eyes? 'Don't worry. Sure you don't want a quick drink before you meet Caro?'

'No, there are a few bits I need ... want to get in ... Boots.' She screwed up her face thoughtfully.

Didn't she have enough lotions and potions? Her toilet bags in the bathroom at the wedding had looked close to bursting.

'Are you going to get everything in your suitcase?' I asked sceptically.

'What?'

'Hello, earth to Kate.'

She gave me a tight smile. ''Course I will. Mum can sit on the case for me.'

'I'd better make a move,' I said, not wanting to but she clearly wasn't going to tell me what was on her mind. 'I have to face Emily some time.'

'Olivia, stand your ground.' Kate took hold of both of my shoulders and shook them gently. 'Don't you dare go apologising to that little madam. She's the one in the wrong.'

'You're right but you know me. Anything for a quiet life.'

Kate tutted loudly. 'What am I going to do with you?'

I grinned at her and giving her a last hug, set off down the street.

When she went back to Australia I'd miss her desperately.

It was a relief to find that Emily wasn't in when I got home. Taking full advantage of her absence, I ran a deep bath, draining the hot water tank and helped myself to a generous measure of her Chanel No 5 bath gel.

There's nothing quite like the guilty pleasure of ill-gotten bubbles. Served her right. It wasn't as bad as pinching other peoples' ideas and taking all the credit, though. I shook my head, the ends of my ponytail dipping into the water.

Well, good luck to her. Thank God I wasn't the one that had to make it all happen. Imagine having to deal with Miranda, a dress designer, the film people and everything else involved.

If only I'd known.

It wasn't until the next day at work that I discovered what Emily had done. I was on my way to make a well-deserved cup of tea when she waylaid me in the kitchen.

Now what? I was still being cool with her. Glancing up, I

could see her freckles standing out in stark relief against her pale skin. Her lips devoid of lipstick looked bloodless as she gnawed them anxiously.

'Are you all right?'

Tears welled up in her eyes. She shook her head but still didn't say a word.

'What's wrong?'

'Come see this.' She inclined her head. Clutching my tea mug, I followed her back to her desk.

'There,' she said.

Running across her computer screen in large red capital letters was the word BITCH. It was on a continuous loop and as soon as the B disappeared on the right hand side of the screen, the word began to reappear on the left hand side.

I looked at her sharply. 'When did this happen?'

'Just now. I went out for lunch. When I got back it was here.'

Tentatively I leaned over to move the mouse and as I did the words disappeared immediately, leaving an innocent word document.

'It's just the screen saver,' I said, slightly relieved. As far as I knew – not much admittedly – an easy fix.

'I think it might be Peter,' said Emily in a low voice.

'Why?'

She paused avoiding my eye, fiddling with the seam of her pale blue miniskirt. 'He sent me another email yesterday.' Her fingers plucked at the linen fabric.

'Another one?' I asked. 'He's a glutton for punishment.' I looked closely at her.

She was still picking at her skirt, her eyes down.

'What did you do?' I asked. I had a really bad feeling about this.

She flushed slightly before blurting it out. 'Well ... he wasn't nice this time. Had a go at me about leading him on. Said I was just like all the rest.'

'And ...'

'I was having a terrible day,' she said defensively. 'His bloody email was the last thing I needed and you weren't speaking to me.'

So it was all my fault now.

'I sent him one back, except ...'

'What did you say?'

She went very quiet, opening her mouth once before thinking better of it. 'I told him to piss off and leave me alone.'

'Subtle,' I said sarcastically.

'What was I supposed to do, Miss Goody Two Shoes? He wasn't very nice and I was having a very stressful day. Miranda is being quite difficult. You have no idea how hard it is working with celebrities.'

'Spare me, please.' I leant down to study the screen. 'So you think this is from him?'

Her eyes scanned the room and she lowered her voice. 'Well, who else is it going to be?'

'I don't know. Who else have you upset recently?' I tried to be funny but it didn't go down terribly well. She glared at me.

'Sorry, Emily.'

'What am I going to do? How did it get here? Do you think it's some kind of virus?'

I only had one answer to all her questions. 'I haven't a clue. Check your emails,' I said, seizing on something practical to do.

Sure enough, there in her inbox was Peter's name. His response to Emily's 'get-a-life-you-sad-loser' email was a rambling, nonsensical rant about the faithlessness of double-dealing women and their evil wiles. His personal philosophy seemed to be based on a mix of misogyny, Greek mythology and homespun chauvinism. Unfortunately no handy confession, 'By the way, I've messed with your computer.'

'He's not a happy bunny boiler, is he?' I observed.

'That's not even mildly funny.'

'Oh! I don't know.'

'Do you think he hacked into the system to do this?'

My approach to modern technology was strictly need-to-know. I had no idea but I did remember at the speed-date Peter had said something about working with computers.

'I think you'd better give Dom in IT a call. He'll know.'

'You do it. Dom likes you.'

Only because I always asked for his help nicely, instead of screaming at him down the phone as most people did when their computer threw a wobbly.

I made the call. Dom, our office IT boffin, spoke in another language most of the time about mainframes, motherboards and Ethernets. Once I spilt a whole glass of Ribena over my keyboard and he gave me a new one without reproach, after he'd stopped laughing.

'Dom, it's Olivia.'

'Don't tell me. Let me guess? If it's Coca-Cola you don't stand a chance—'

'Dom, it's urgent. Please could you pop up to Emily's desk? No ... it can't ... can you come and look now?'

He agreed to come straight up from his little cramped cubbyhole down in the gloomy basement. His choice – apparently he liked it down there. There were days when I was tempted to join him.

When he arrived, the first thing he did was that irritating 'I don't like the look of this' head shaking, flicking his long wispy hair over his stooped shoulders.

'Nasty.' He was a man of few words. We looked expectantly at him. He looked back at us. It was one of those moments when you want to crank someone up. Insert a clockwork key in his back and give it a couple of sharp twists.

'So,' I asked eventually, 'has someone hacked into Emily's computer to do this?'

'Nah.'

'So ...' I prompted.

'Inside job.'

God it was like pulling teeth. 'What does that mean, Dom?'

'It weren't a hacker. Someone did this here.'

'What here at my desk?' asked Emily horrified, taking a hasty step back from the computer as if it might bite her at any second.

'Yeah,' said Dom.

'What, they just used my computer?'

'Yeah, that's what I said.'

'How?' I asked.

He looked at me. 'Durr, like this.' He took the mouse and with a few quick clicks the screen saver was changed back to the default one. 'Came prepared though. Must've had a disk wiv 'em.' He leaned back in Emily's chair. 'You 'ad a bit of a row wiv someone?'

Emily and I exchanged glances. I called over to Cara who sat at the desk next to Emily's. 'Has anyone been near here while Emily was out at lunch?'

Cara's sleepy brown eyes looked puzzled. 'No,' she said, hesitating for a second. 'Only the plant man.'

'Plant man?'

'You know, the people that come in and water the plants, polish the leaves. One of them came in – didn't say much. The other girl's much friendlier.'

'What did he look like?' I asked sharply.

Cara looked more bewildered than usual. 'Um, he had a hat on and a watering can.'

'What sort of hat?' I asked, trying not to let my impatience show. Cara was the sort that needed careful handling otherwise she'd get nervous.

'Baseball, I think it was green ... or it might have been red.' Cara pulled an apologetic face. 'Sorry, should I have said something to him? I thought he was quite helpful. When he knocked Emily's bag on the floor he put everything back.'

She turned to Emily and shrugged. 'I knew you had your purse with you so I wasn't worried he was going to nick anything.'

Emily looked anxiously at her bag.

'Do you think he's ... you know?' she asked me, reaching out and touching the conker-brown leather.

'What?'

'You know, tampered with it or something?'

'What booby-trapped your bag?' I asked, although given the computer stunt it wasn't beyond the realms of possibility. He could have left something in there.

We looked at her pride-and-joy bag. It appeared innocuous. Was there anything nasty lurking inside, like a dead mouse or a mouldy sandwich? Had he emptied his watering can in there or tossed in a couple of handfuls of compost?

Emily poked nervously at it. 'If he's put something in my Fendi bag, I'll kill him. This bag cost me a fortune.'

Didn't we know it? It was a limited edition – one of only fifty in the country.

Gingerly she started removing everything, which took some time – she had half of Selfridges' make-up hall in there. Finally she reached the bottom.

'That's all right then. I was worried he might have ruined it.'

That was so like her, whereas I would have been worried about him taking something. Had she checked everything was there?

'Emily, is anything mi—'

She patted her bag as if it were her favourite pet. 'As long as my bag's OK. You know it's a limited edition. There are only—'

'Emily, we have to tell someone,' I interrupted urgently.

'Tell them what? We went on a speed-date and picked up a lunatic who's emailed me twice and sabotaged my computer. It's hardly Jack the Ripper.'

'Yes, but what if he's done something else?'

'Like what?' Emily was renewing her acquaintance with her lipstick collection. Opening each one and putting a smear of colour on her hand.

I wanted to shake her.

'I don't know, bugged your phone, set up something that sends copies of all your emails to him. I've no idea about all that.'

'Lets 'ave a look.'

I swung round guiltily. I'd completely forgotten Dom was still there.

He grinned cheerfully at us. 'Speed-date eh, girls? You shoulda said. I could fix you up with a coupla mates o' mine.'

I smiled weakly at him, while Emily looked down her nose with complete disdain. Quickly to stop her saying anything – we needed Dom's help – I said, 'That's very kind of you.'

'Jus' lemme know next time,' he said, swinging back to the keyboard.

We stood in silence behind his hunched back, watching as his fingers tapped away, a blur of motion, while he muttered under his breath. He was a lot chattier to the computer.

After a while he leaned back, put his hands behind his head and swivelled the chair to face us, smiling grimly. 'It's clean. Only changed the screen saver. No time to do nuffink else. Wot 'ave you bin doin' to upset 'im?'

Emily rolled her eyes. 'You might say I was doing a friend a favour.'

As Dom heaved himself out of the chair and slouched off shaking his head, she turned to me again. 'All's well that ends well, then.'

'You think?' I asked, looking at the restored screen.

'He's made his point, although we can't prove it was him.'

'Suppose not.'

'I shall just ignore it,' said Emily disdainfully. 'I'm not rising to his pathetic little tricks. If he thinks I'm a bitch – that's his problem, not mine. He's burnt his boat now. Hardly going to bother me again, is he?'

I was still worried. Very worried. Coming in here to make his point was pretty risky. Would that be the end of it?

In the meantime there was no harm in letting Barney know. I was quite looking forward to that. It might wipe the smirk off his face for at least ten seconds.

Chapter Seven

Barney thought I was making a fuss about nothing.

'Seriously, Olivia. What do you want me to do? Peter's totally harmless.'

'What? You know him?'

There was a brief pause and I tapped my mobile phone impatiently.

'Not know him, know him.'

I might have guessed. Bloody Barney and his bullshit marketing crap.

'He's not exactly my type, darling.' Barney's voice was filled with scorn. 'He came recommended though.'

'I thought you said you vetted everyone.' I enjoyed a moment of smugness, I've never managed to get one over on Barney.

'Olivia,' his exasperation showed. 'We're not sodding MI5. Besides define vetting. We check up on people.'

'And what does that entail?' I said, determined not to let Barney have the last word.

'They have to bring their driving licence and proof of current address with them.'

'And that's it?'

'What more do you want?' he spat down the phone.

He had a point. A driving licence was pretty official.

'Well, is there anything you can do? He's freaking Emily out and I've got to live with her.'

'I'll make a few enquiries.'

And that would be the end of that, I thought with a sneer.

'I'm sure ... *if* it was him, it was an isolated incident but don't hesitate to call me if anything else happens.'

What! Had hell just frozen over? Before I could summon up the capacity to speak again, Barney had gone.

In contrast Kate thought it was all highly amusing.

'Serves her right,' she sniggered down the phone later that afternoon.

'It's not funny,' I said, the handset tucked in the crook of my ear as I carried on typing an email. 'I think it's a bit scary. Emily's just pissed off.'

'Probably because the wrong guy emailed. Let's face it, Olivia, she ticked three different boxes – there are still two other guys out there she's not moaning about at the moment.'

True, Emily hadn't said a word about any other contact she'd had. I glanced up at her on the other side of the office. She was chatting away to Cara, perched on her desk as they both poured over a page of *Hello!*.

'So how's the packing?' I asked, changing the subject. 'Did you get everything you wanted in Boots?'

There was a pause and a sigh as if she was about to say something and changed her mind. 'A nightmare.' Her voice wobbled. 'Mum has gone out and bought grocery supplies – half of Asda. I'm never going to get it all in. You'd think I was emigrating for good. I'm only going back to Oz for another six months.'

'Can't you extend your visa?'

'What the hell for?' she snapped.

'Sorry, I thought you loved it there.'

'It's all fine. Greg is great. Australia's great. Everything's just great.'

'Sure?'

There was a pause and a deep breath. I thought she was going to launch into some confessional but her voice was back to its usually perky tone. 'It's all fine. My biggest worry is getting through customs. I can see it now, surrounded by hysterical sniffer dogs driven wild by Mum's Marmite stockpile.'

I giggled. 'I'm sure they're used to it. All Poms travel with the stuff.'

'Not ten jars of it.'

'You'll get it all in. If not, you could leave me a couple of pairs of shoes.'

'Not bloody likely. I'd rather ditch the Marmite.'

Things on the Luscious Lips launch were starting to get hectic. Emily was still in the office at six-thirty, which was unheard of, and her shoulders were so tense her neck had almost disappeared.

Across the room her face was turning redder and redder as she carried on a conversation on the phone. I got a 'God-give-me-patience' eye roll before she slammed down the phone and hurled a pen at the wall opposite.

Shrugging on my coat – a flak jacket might have been safer – I wandered over.

'You OK?' I asked briskly, as she tossed papers into her file tray.

'What does it look like? You have no idea. You wouldn't believe the hoops we're jumping through to please "darling" Miranda.'

Served her right. Although it was still nothing compared to my afternoon. An hour long phone call placating my client, a doppelganger for Jabba the Hutt, when a planning application didn't go his way. His company had just seen several million go down the Swanee.

She looked appealingly at me. If she was looking for sympathy, she'd come to the wrong place.

'I suppose you could say it serves me right,' her voice softened. 'I'm sorry, Olivia. I should have told you that we were using the dress idea.'

Normally I would have said something conciliatory like, 'Don't worry about it.' But an ear bashing from Jabba had left a full-blown disco beat pounding in my head. All I wanted was to get home.

'I'm leaving,' I said wearily. 'Now.' Just talking to her was taking too much effort.

'I've said I'm sorry,' she said in a lost little voice. 'Please don't be mad at me.'

It was just like being back in the playground.

'Emily, at this moment I couldn't care. I just want to go home. Swallow half a dozen Anadin and wallow in a bath. Coming?'

Casting a look of loathing at the piles of papers spread across her desk, she scooped them all up and dumped them in her pending tray. Then, leaning down, she gathered up a selection of files from the floor and shoved them in, too. I watched horrified, hands twitching. Talk about disorganised – no wonder she was stressed.

'I shouldn't but ... I can speak to Miranda's agent in the morning. You wouldn't believe the stuff Miranda wants. Do you know—'

'I'm going, now.'

'All right. All right.' Suddenly she looked at her watch. 'Shit, I forgot. Daniel's coming. He phoned earlier. He's got a meeting first thing so he's staying over tonight.' She pulled a face. 'I could do without it. I'm not cooking.'

Cooking? Emily! That would be the day. She liked being taken to restaurants and was very old-fashioned when it came to splitting the bill.

'He'll have to make do with a takeaway. I've got a bit of a headache. Not that I need to worry on that score.' She snorted. 'I can't remember the last time we had sex.'

And she thought she had problems. I wasn't sure my body still knew what sex was.

* * *

I tuned her out as we left the building. Every other word was Miranda.

Tottenham Court Road was heavy going, thick with bus queues and dawdling tourists blocking the crowded pavements. I wound ruthlessly in and around the throng of people and Emily had to jog to keep up with me, which was deliberate. If she was concentrating on breathing she'd have to stop talking.

I was halted mid-stride by a sudden, sharp tug on my jacket as Emily grabbed my arm and pointed to the other side of the busy road.

'What?' I snapped. All I wanted to do was get home.

Her mouth was moving but the words were incoherent. The wall of red double-decker buses made it difficult to see what she was pointing to.

'Did you see him?' she exclaimed.

'Who?' I asked impatiently. It was impossible to pick out anyone with so many pedestrians waltzing between the bumpers of the stationary traffic.

Emily was always spotting famous people. Last month it had been Elton John in Starbucks, wearing a fluorescent jacket and hobnail boots. She wouldn't believe it wasn't him until he left the coffee shop, put on his hard hat and walked onto the building site next door.

Just outside the entrance to a tube station was a bad place to stop, especially in rush hour. A few choice words were hissed at us as people jostled past.

Emily frowned, rubbing her forehead. 'He's gone now.'

'Who?' I asked exasperated, starting down the steps, rubbing my hip, which had been jabbed by a briefcase.

'Perhaps I'm imagining things. I thought it was him. Peter the emailer.'

'You sure?' I looked round, examining the people coming down the stairs behind us.

'No, it was just a glimpse. Broken glasses mended with tape.'

Goosebumps rose along the hairline around the back of my neck.

I nudged Emily downwards, anxious to keep moving. 'We're in the way. Mind that pushchair. Here.'

Shoving my bag into her hand, I went to the rescue of a tired looking woman who was trying to manoeuvre a buggy down the steps. I felt for her, she had a toddler to deal with and I had Emily!

Once down on the platform, having said goodbye to my grateful new friend, Emily and I stood six deep waiting for our train.

'I think I just imagined it.' Emily laughed nervously. 'I've got him on the brain.' But we both took an unconscious step back from the platform edge, eyeing up other commuters.

'Mm,' I responded reassuringly.

When the train arrived the flow of bodies inched into the carriage. The doors slid closed just as one last chap squeezed between the doors. His hand reached up to clutch his glasses. Through the heads crammed in the space between I could just see the silver tape holding the frame together. From the look on Emily's face she'd seen it too. I tried to get a better look but the mass of people and newspapers got in the way.

'What do we do?' she whispered, her teeth gnawing her lip. 'Is it him?'

'I can't see properly. Can you? Don't catch his eye.'

'You're taller, you look.'

Taking a deep breath, I sneaked a glance over my shoulder. A gap appeared in the crowd. The hand obscuring his face had moved. My shoulders relaxed as the tension whistled simultaneously out with my breath. I stepped aside so that Emily had a clear view. The man by the door, huddled into an old trench coat like a cold war spy, had wispy grey hair in a comb over and was well into his sixties.

Relief made us giddy and silly. Our sniggers grew to wholesale giggles and by the time we got to our last stop, they'd turned into peals of laughter. The rest of the carriage thought we were idiots and as the passengers thinned, George Smiley glared at us over his horn rims.

'Can you believe it?' snorted Emily as we doubled over on the street again. 'Talk about neurotic nellies. Totally harmless and we're nearly wetting ourselves. Bet half of London tapes their glasses together.'

'It's certainly made me forget my headache.'

'And me, Miranda. We deserve a glass of something. Let's stop at the offy and I'll get a bottle.'

For once, Emily and I were united in rare accord. Sometimes she could be very generous. Not just with wine, frequently she tried to press her clothes on to me, even though most of her tops would go round me three times and her trousers only reached mid-shin. No such problems with her accessories though and she owned a fabulous selection.

Luxuriating in the hot water, which I'd just topped up for a third time, I was tempted to ignore the polite knock at the door.

While I'd been in the bathroom I'd heard Daniel arrive.

Was it him at the door? Emily was more likely to have hollered through the glass.

'Hi, Olivia.' I closed my eyes.

As if everything else wasn't perfect enough. Why did he have to have a lovely deep voice, too?

'We're getting an Indian takeaway. Do you want something?'

'Yes, please. Can I have a chicken dhansak?'

Behind the closed door Daniel chuckled. Did he have to do that? Even that was attractive.

'Creature of habit.'

'Sometimes I have prawn pathia,' I yelled back. Sticking to the same thing was much easier. It saved having menu envy.

'Anything else, modom?' he teased.

'No thank you, Jeeves. That will do nicely.'

'No wonder you're so skinny, woman.'

'Slender,' I admonished, thinking it was a good job he didn't have X-ray vision. Throughout my life I'd grown up to the refrain, 'Aren't you lucky? You're so thin.'

No, I'm not. Being thin has its downsides. My knees are dead ringers for large knots of wood on a twig and I look like a boy from behind. Glumly I looked down. As for my boobs; they'd been described as a pair of nasty mosquito bites. Of course, whenever I moaned about them, Emily would pat her 36 double Ds complacently.

'Grub up in about twenty minutes,' he said.

I heard a muffled confab with Emily before the front door slammed shut. I stretched lazily in the water and gave myself a stern talking to. You have to pull yourself together. Think of him as an ordinary bloke. Ordinary. Well, not ordinary. Think brick walls. Not about that chip in his tooth when he smiles or ... the time we once kissed.

I closed my eyes and in a rare moment of weakness let the memory come burrowing out of the hole from where it was normally firmly tucked.

We'd both had a bit to drink. Well, I'd had quite a lot. Still reeling from Mike's betrayal, I'd spent that particular evening proving for his benefit what a great time I was having without him. Daniel decided, for the welfare of both my liver and dignity, to intercede and insisted on taking me home.

I repaid his kindness by weeping all over him the minute he settled me on my sofa. With his arm round me, hugging me, the scent of him filling my nose, I gave into the attraction that had always simmered just below the surface since the day I'd met him and leaned forward to trail a series of kisses along his jaw line to his lips.

The only saving grace of this cringe-worthy memory was that it wasn't entirely one sided. Gentleman that he was, he didn't push me away in disgust, but let me kiss him. I remember moving my lips over his, the tingle of the first touch and then that joyous burst of sensation when his lips moved beneath mine.

I squeezed my eyes closed and slid further down into the bath water, recalling the feel of his hand sliding into my hair to pull me close and the kiss that went on and on with a headiness as if neither of us could get enough of the other.

As the memory smouldered, I felt my cheeks heat up. There'd been longing and pent up passion in those kisses which led to a breathless embrace where I found the long lean length of Daniel's body fitted perfectly against mine.

The crash of the front door announcing the return of my housemates made us spring apart. The horrified look in his eyes made me feel slightly sick. There was no time to say anything as the others burst into the room.

The next day I pretended I had absolutely no recollection of the previous night.

Sloshing water everywhere I sat up quickly and hauled myself out of the bath, trying to ignore the dull ache around my heart. I was an idiot. How on earth did I think rehashing old memories was going to help?

Food was a great distraction and it was fine while we were eating. Shared moans of appreciation filled the flat, as the lids were peeled off the foil trays to reveal the turmeric infused sauces, the fragrant blend of spices and my all-time favourite smell, the distinctive aroma of basmati rice.

It was only after I'd tidied up – no surprise there then – removing the foil trays littering the coffee table and taking the plates through to the kitchen, that I started to feel uncomfortable. Emily had found an old episode of *Friends* to watch and had moved to sit on the sofa next to Daniel who was wrestling with a Sudoku in the *Times*.

Suddenly Emily squealed in delight. 'Look, Daniel. It's Sebastian.'

Daniel raised his eyebrows. 'Haven't you seen this ad before?'

On screen Sebastian, Daniel's younger, prettier brother, was wafting around a horribly contemporary flat, all white and dark wood, spraying air freshener to mask the scent of gorgeous girlfriend number one's perfume before the arrival of stunning girlfriend number two.

'Definitely art imitating real life.' Daniel grinned good-naturedly.

Sebastian's exploits with women were legendary, but he was so charming and handsome all his girlfriends forgave him.

In a way, he and Emily would have been better suited. With a modelling and acting career, he had the celebrity lifestyle that she aspired to.

As I was watching TV I became conscious that Daniel kept looking at me. Had I got curry on my chin? Every now and then I would look up to find him staring at me, as if trying to solve some puzzle. I couldn't help feeling it had nothing to do with the Sudoku.

With *Friends* over, Emily switched channels to some comedy drama on ITV. Speaking personally, the trials of some thirty-plus woman and her on-off relationship with a married man left me cold. My heartstrings resolutely refused to be tugged when her car broke down on a dark night in the pouring rain. Cue the shot of lover boy in a warm, cosy Indian restaurant with his wife, ignoring his ringing mobile.

'What a bastard,' chimed Emily.

'Dumb bastard more like,' said Daniel cuttingly. 'Messing up two lives. The girlfriend needs to wise up. She'd be better off on her own.' He turned and looked at me with a challenging look on his face. 'Nothing ever comes out of going out with a married man.' Then he said more gently, 'No matter how much you hope it will.'

Surely after Mike he knew my views on that sort of thing? Embarrassed, I just shrugged and kept my gaze glued to the screen until the credits rolled.

Jumping up without looking at Daniel I announced I was heading to bed.

'By the way you've got something on your chin,' muttered Emily glancing up. 'No other side,' she directed, as I brought my hand to my face. My fingers touched a slightly sticky patch. No wonder Daniel had been looking at me. He could have told me. Feeling foolish I sloped off to bed leaving the two of them like an old married couple; side by side but not touching, he engrossed in his paper and her watching television. It wasn't my idea of a romantic evening.

Snuggling into bed, not even bothering to take my make-up off, I tried to ignore the feeling of dissatisfaction. Turning over I plumped up my pillow and after a long while I drifted into a lovely dream; lying on a warm beach, bathed in sunlight, wearing the perfect tan-enhancing bikini with a cleavage to die for – when some bastard picked me up by my ankle, and dropped me into a dark icy pool with a loud crash.

Sputtering to the surface, I realised that the cold wasn't a dream. It took me a moment to come to. What had happened? A jagged draft of freezing night air swept over me from the window, which couldn't be right. It was closed. I sat up and winced, my ankle hurt. It more than hurt, it throbbed but as I moved to examine it in the half-light, the wind caught the curtains, which billowed up revealing a large hole in the window. Through the broken glass, in the quiet of the night, I heard the crunch of gravel underfoot. I went completely still. Someone was outside.

Heart thudding I listened, not daring to move or put the light on.

Suddenly my bedroom door was thrown open and Daniel burst in.

He shoved the door open, his heart pounding. 'Olivia! I heard a crash. Are you OK? What's happened?'

It took a minute for his eyes to adjust to the change in light but then he saw Olivia raise a shaky hand and point to the window.

Crossing to the shattered glass, he looked out of what was left of the window.

'Careful,' she said, 'there's glass everywhere.' Despite her calm words, her voice had a distinct wobble to it as if trying to be brave. 'Can you see anyone?'

Peering into the lamp lit street, he craned his head right and left. Nothing moved in the shadows below.

'They've scarpered. Probably messing about after a session at the pub. Are you OK?' he asked again automatically. Then he turned and looked at her properly.

She looked awful. The colour had bleached from her face and the harsh beam of the un-shaded bulb in the hall threw her features into relief making her look haggard and haunted.

Splinters of glass were strewn across the bed and her arm sparkled where a sprinkling of tiny shards punctured the skin. It was only when he snapped on the overhead light, that he saw the blood. Bright, vivid, scarlet, red, pouring down her arm. Fear lanced through him as he followed the glistening river to its source – a large triangular slice of glass embedded in her forearm.

Shit, that had to hurt like hell but she didn't seem aware of it, not yet anyway. She started to haul herself to the edge of the bed still not saying anything. That worried him the most. She seemed almost catatonic.

'Wait,' he said, conscious that the blood needed to be stopped but putting a pad on the wound was going to be impossible. Shit, his first aid training ended at being a boy scout a million years ago.

She stared down at the wound as if mesmerised by it and then a sudden grimace shot across her face. He guessed the pain had finally kicked in over the shock and surprise, but he felt relieved that she'd reacted and lost that numb look.

Blood welled up around the angry looking wound with mini rivers of ruby red spilling down her arm, pooling and leeching into the pure white duvet. The stark contrast made him want to shudder but he couldn't let her know that.

Her eyes went blank as if she was about to black out.

'Olivia,' he said, making his voice deliberately calm as he didn't like the look of the wound or the amount of blood she was losing. 'Don't move.' He lifted the bad arm as carefully as he could. There were tiny specks of glass everywhere. Pursing his lips, he blew gently over the surface of her skin to try and loosen them. It didn't work. He needed something else, something soft.

'Have you got a make-up brush?' he asked, unable to keep the concern out of his voice. 'Like they use on archaeology digs?'

She stared at him as if he'd gone mad but still didn't say anything.

'I don't want to risk pushing some of these tiny splinters in further.' He lifted her chin and looked into her eyes with a calm smile trying to get through to her. Was she in shock? To his relief she finally responded.

'No. Um. Yes, I mean. There.' She nodded to the dressing table.

With great care, conscious he had no idea whether this was

the right thing to do or not, he dusted away the fragments, smearing the minuscule blood spots into little red tears.

Under his fingers he felt her jump slightly and her pulse raced under his thumb. With a rallying smile, he tried to reassure her but she still looked dazed, so he touched her face as if to check she could still respond. Her head tilted exhaling warm breath that brushed his hand. Awareness punched into his stomach, tightening his groin as he looked at her full, plump lips. He'd been this close before, kissed her before. And she didn't remember a damn thing about it. That thought hurt like a physical pain making him want to kiss her more than anything else in the world.

Her shoulders shuddered, loosening a thin strap that fell down her arm, pulling her camisole top low. The rise and fall of her chest drew his attention. He wanted to stroke and soothe the skin, ease her breathing, scoop her up and hold her, take away the frozen look in her eyes.

With his girlfriend just next door. Shame slammed into him. What the hell was he thinking? Besides, Olivia didn't want him, she was in love with someone else.

Abruptly, he put down the brush and holding on to her arm, he lifted the bedcovers away from her legs, dislodging the brick lying on the stained duvet.

'So that's what did all the damage.' He scowled. What if it had hit her head? 'Let's get you out of here.'

He helped her off the bed doing his best to keep his touch impersonal, needing to put some distance between them. She groaned in pain as she put her foot down. A big blue egg was already appearing on her ankle.

'Shit,' she said, as it gave way.

He caught her weight and without thinking put his arm around her, his earlier resolution vanishing. His fingers brushed her ribs through the thin fabric and he lifted them as if burnt.

He heard her sharp intake of breath.

'Sorry, did I hurt you?' he asked.

'Mmm,' she muttered.

As he helped her to hobble through to the lounge, conscious of her warm skin and his fingers skimming underneath her left breast, Emily finally emerged, hovering in the doorway.

'What happened? What was that noise?' She clutched her throat like some 1940's movie star posing in her nightgown. For a brief, puzzling moment it was like looking at a woman he'd never seen before.

'Someone's chucked a brick through the window,' he said, steering Olivia towards the sofa.

He saw the two girls catch each other's eye. Neither of them said a word. The hairs on the back of his neck stood up. He stiffened. Funny they weren't asking more questions, as if they knew more than they were admitting.

'Emily, get a towel,' he snapped, as Olivia sank into the cushioned seat. Emily dithered for a moment. 'Now,' he shouted.

She looked hurt but he didn't care. He'd had enough of whatever game the two of them were playing. 'And a bowl of warm water and cotton wool or tissues,' he yelled after her departing back, as Olivia slumped against him.

Her teeth began to chatter and his anger dissolved. Capable, sensible Olivia looked done in, vulnerable and scared, her eyes meeting his and holding his gaze as if her life depended on it. Tonight he needed to focus on getting her to hospital. Tomorrow he'd be asking some questions.

Totally inappropriate curls of lust snaked in my stomach. How was it possible that with blood spurting everywhere and a three-inch piece of glass lodged in my arm, my libido suddenly decided to come to life?

Keeping my eyes riveted to the shiny point sticking out of my skin, I gritted my teeth. I couldn't let him see how my body was responding. Luckily physical signs of shock started to set in, disguising my reactions. My teeth began to chatter and I couldn't stop the tremors shaking my muscles.

There was already a trail of crimson drops on the floor. My eyes were drawn to a wide smear across Daniel's bare chest. Without thinking I touched the warm skin. The fine dusting of hair across his chest felt surprisingly soft and I didn't want to move. For a second he went still, before putting his hand over mine.

'Are you OK?' he asked, his face softening.

I nodded, a huge lump in my throat.

'Come on, let's get you sorted. You need ice on that ankle. Then, I'm afraid it's a definite casualty job.'

The blood trickle had slowed and was starting to congeal in an ugly puddle around the embedded glass.

'I daren't touch that.' A gentle finger skirted around the wound as he spoke.

Despite the soreness of my arm, a small fizz of electricity followed his tender tracing. My heart did that funny miss-a-beat thing. Not now, I firmly told myself, staring fixedly down at the glass point. Talk about bad timing.

I sank into a chair. Thank God, Daniel had had the presence of mind to pull on some jeans. My pulse had speeded up even more at the sight of the smooth muscled abdomen right in front of my nose. It was rattling along like a runaway train. I couldn't help my gaze following the direction of the dark arrow of coarser hair tapering down into the faded denim. If I didn't get a grip I was going to have full-scale palpitations.

Emily reappeared, slopping water from a bowl as she hurried over. Her gaze narrowed as it came to rest on Daniel kneeling in front of me.

A timely reminder. Daniel was hers.

He glanced up at her. 'We need something for Olivia's ankle – ice, frozen peas?'

Ankle? Forget that. My whole body needed cooling down.

'Peas. Right,' she said, shooting off again. Folding the towel he slipped it under my arm to soak up the worst of the blood. Gently he dabbed away, as I winced with every stroke. When he'd finished, he moved closer, crouching between my legs. Our eyes were level as he gave me a reassuring smile and his warm hand closed over mine, squeezing it comfortingly.

'I'll take you to A & E.'

I kept my eyes firmly on his, terrified I was going to give myself away. God, if I so much as looked at his mouth, he'd know.

'What time is it?' I asked, forcing myself to think of the mundane. Outside it was dark and I could just hear muffled early morning sounds; a car accelerating a street away, the distant rattle of a train.

'Quarter to two,' said Daniel, his eyes flicking to the clock behind my head. 'Hopefully casualty will be quiet. The drunks will have been cleared out. Let me get dressed.'

I settled into the chair, gritting my teeth as the pain began to bite in earnest. Wages of sin. Served me right for thinking unseemly thoughts. What was worse? The stinging in my arm, the steady pounding of my bruised ankle or my mind doing a slow motion replay of when Daniel touched my hand on his chest?

As I closed my eyes, resting my head wearily against the sofa, I was conscious of agitated whispering in Emily's bedroom. I winced. She hadn't seemed very sympathetic to my injuries. Any second now I expected her to say, 'She fancies you'. Instead I heard her hissing, 'You can't leave me here on my own. What if they come back?'

'What? To inspect the damage?' replied Daniel, his words ringing with scorn.

Then he lowered his voice and I didn't quite catch what he said next. It sounded like, 'Probably his wife'. What was he talking about? That TV programme must have fired his imagination.

Raising his voice again, he carried on, 'If you're worried, why not ring the police? You'll have to anyway for insurance. That window will have to be replaced.'

'Fine,' said Emily petulantly. 'Don't worry about me. You'd better get precious Olivia to hospital.'

As Daniel's car pulled into the hospital car park I began to shake again and then I started to cry. Not gentle sniffs and delicate tears – no, they were great, strangled gulps and guttural sobs accompanied by a runny nose. Very unattractive, but I couldn't help it.

'Hey, come on, Olivia,' said Daniel, as he pulled deftly into a parking slot. 'It's all right.'

'S-s-sorry,' I gasped. 'I c-c-can't …'

He leaned over, pulling my head onto his chest. Gradually my tears subsided. I gave my nose an elephant-blow into the pristine white hanky he'd pressed into my hands. With one eye I tried to assess the damage to his sweater. There was bound to be a snail trail of snot and yesterday's mascara down it, but there were extenuating circumstances. I made the most of the situation and snuggled in to his broad chest. I could feel his heart beating, strong and steady under the soft lambswool.

As I grew calmer, he shifted, cupping my chin in his hands to wipe away the tears with his thumbs. Instantly my heart took up a salsa rhythm. Adrenaline rush, I told myself. Just shock. I can handle a 300 bpm heart rate. Deep breaths. That would help.

Unfortunately I over did the breathing and started to hyperventilate. At which point Daniel started stroking my back, his arms around me, as if soothing a highly strung racehorse. The last thing I needed.

It was a relief when he finally opened his car door and said, 'Come on, sweetheart. Let's go and get you sorted out.' From the back seat he pulled out a blanket, which he tucked gently around me.

Sweetheart? Could my heart stand any more havoc? Had he really just called me that?

Calm down, he's just being kind because you're injured. If I wasn't careful I was about to make a terrible fool of myself.

We passed a few diehard smokers just outside and as we stepped through the automatic doors of A & E, the harsh institutional strip lighting stung my tear-stained, swollen eyes. Although it was the middle of the night, there was still a sense of efficient purpose about the place. Soft soled shoes squeaked on the shiny vinyl floors as medical staff strode by.

Daniel escorted me to a grey plastic seat, arranging my blanket around my shoulders before going to speak to a middle-aged lady sitting ramrod straight behind the bare reception desk. No pictures or flowers just dismal public health warnings about smoking and heart disease. Their low voiced conversation washed over me as I closed my eyes drowsily, happy to let him take charge. He managed to get so far, remembering my date of birth and postcode but had to come back and rouse me for my GP's details.

Eventually, all paperwork completed, Daniel returned and sat down beside me. It seemed completely natural when his hand took mine. He squeezed my fingers.

'You OK?'

I nodded, not daring to move, conscious of his warm fingers wrapped around mine.

'They're going to get a nurse to take a look at you, but they don't want you to eat or drink anything until you've been seen.'

'That's OK. I don't want anything.'

'How are you feeling?'

'Tired. A bit spaced out.'

'Here put your head on my shoulder.' He put his arm around me. I snuggled in. Just as I drifted off I thought I felt the graze of lips on my hair as he shifted position or was that wishful thinking?

My first thought when I woke was that my bunny slippers looked decidedly out of place in A & E. However my bloodstained arm fitted right in with the beaten up survivors of a brawl who were sat opposite. Both had black eyes, split lips and long ladders in their tights. Propping each other up, they were swaying slightly. One kept nodding off, her head slipping down the other's shoulder, at which point she would start awake before her head began to droop again.

I checked the clock. We'd been there for over two hours. Lifting my head, I checked I hadn't dribbled down Daniel's sweater. No, all clear. No damp patches. He unhooked his arm, stretching and wriggling it.

'Sorry, I didn't mean to go to sleep.'

'You're fine. How are you feeling?'

'Better. I'm not going to be—'

Our attention was diverted by a short dumpy nurse in a crumpled and stained blue uniform. 'Shannon Cripps,' she called briskly.

One of the two drunken girls twitched, recognising her name and lurched unsteadily to her feet. The nurse went over to offer her an arm.

'Wot you looking at?' hissed the girl belligerently, spittle flying from her mouth, spraying the nurse who grimaced slightly.

'It's my job to look at you. I'm a nurse,' she said ultra-politely. Her teeth must have been so firmly gritted she could have ground peppercorns with them.

'Fuck off. You ain't lookin' at me,' slurred the girl.

Her friend, a blonde with three-inch black roots, muttered. 'Thas right, Shan. You tell 'er, Shan. You wan' me to 'it 'er?'

The nurse discreetly flicked her eyes up to the ceiling. You could see her summoning up every last reserve of patience.

'Do you want treatment or not?' she asked in a very reasonable tone.

'Go on then. Bin waitin' bleedin' long enough.' Shannon moved with exaggerated care.

It crossed my mind that surgery without an anaesthetic was too good for Shannon. The nurse caught my eye. I gave her a sympathetic smile. She smiled back saying, 'You're next.'

The blonde girl who had roused herself long enough for this exchange, dozed off again and, without Shannon's shoulder, slid to the floor, her plump thighs splayed in front of her like a pair of outsize sausages.

I looked at Daniel. He grinned. 'Ah, the fairer sex.'

'God,' I sighed. 'It's only midweek. Can you imagine what it's like in here on a Friday and Saturday?'

He shuddered. 'I dread to think. Feeling OK?'

'A bit sick. More the thought of what they're going to do to me in there. How will they get that glass out?'

'Don't worry. They'll numb it first ... with a very big needle. One jab in your bum. You won't feel a thing.'

I wrinkled my nose at him. 'Daniel,' I protested. 'You're supposed to be reassuring me. Anyway ... I don't mind needles.'

'You haven't seen this one.' He grinned.

At last I was called. Just as I went to follow the nurse, Daniel caught my good arm. 'Do you want me to phone anyone for you?'

'Thanks. It's OK. I'll call my folks tomorrow. There's no point worrying them tonight. They can't do anything.'

'Sure there's no one else you want me to ring?' he said, his face looking fierce for a brief second.

'No,' I said wearily. Who else was I going to phone at that time of day?

He gave my hand a brief squeeze and with a regretful smile said, 'That's sad.' At least I think that's what he said. It made no sense to me.

My doctor looked weary; his skin tone matched the institutional grey walls.

'What have we got then? Another stabbing?' he asked unsympathetically, looking at my bloody arm.

I glared at him and his grubby white coat. You never saw that on *Casualty*.

'No,' I said angrily. 'Someone threw a brick through my window and I've got glass in my arm.' I enunciated every word carefully to make sure he knew I wasn't a mate of Shannon's.

'Ah.' He looked chastened. 'Let's have a look then.'

The next hour was something I'd rather not dwell upon. Despite a hefty injection of something – in my arm, not bum – I felt every move that doctor made and it wasn't pleasant.

Chapter Eight

Five-thirty and London was sluggishly waking up. Following the milk float down the street, he pulled to a halt in the nearest parking spot and turned to watch Olivia dozing next to him. She didn't wake when he switched off the ignition. The painkillers must have kicked in.

Studying her face in the early morning light, he traced the outline of her chin, the high cheekbones and long fair lashes resting on her skin. He'd known her for so long, he took her attractiveness for granted but now looking at her uninterrupted, he realised how gorgeous she was. That bastard, whoever he was, had better appreciate her. It should have been him there last night, holding her, wiping away her tears, distracting her from the pain. Did Olivia realise that she'd settled for second place and that it would always be like this? A wave of sadness gripped him and he wanted to scoop Olivia up into his arms and hold her, tell her that he would look after her. Like he had last night.

She stirred, her face screwing up with pain and muttering. He gave a self-derisory half-laugh at his stupidity. Strong, capable Olivia, she always knew what she was doing. Who was he kidding? She didn't need rescuing.

He gave her a prod, perhaps harder than necessary and she jolted awake. Yes, he was a jerk, an out of sorts jerk. Lack of sleep probably. It had been one hell of a long night. Glancing at his watch, he figured he could grab an hour and half's kip before having to get up. Being his own boss might mean he could pick and choose his hours, but it also meant that too many people were relying on him. Since taking over the organic nursery from his dad, business had gone from strength to strength and they were now supplying a couple of supermarket chains with salad produce. A slew of meetings today meant he had to go in. He could have delegated but at this short notice it was hardly fair.

'Come on, sleepy head. Let's get you inside.'

With dopey eyes and drooping eyelids, she looked at him, confusion clouding her expression. Sleepy, adorable and totally trusting. God, he was a sucker.

He got out of the car and stomped round to the passenger door. Olivia all but fell out. Sighing to himself, he scooped her up into his arms and carried her down the street to the front door. Her hair tickled his nose as her head snuggled into him. It smelled of apples and sunshine. Just shampoo, he told himself.

'Mmm ... D'nel ... thaaa ...' she slurred, her breath warm on his neck. She felt limp and soft and he tightened his grip, worried she might slip right through his arms. Holding her as he reached the door, he realised neither of them had a key. Tough, he'd have to wake Emily to come down and let them in. At least she'd had some sleep.

There was nowhere to put Olivia but on the sofa, bundled up in an old sleeping bag that Emily managed to sulkily produce.

He gritted his teeth as he stood in the doorway of Olivia's bedroom looking at the blood-soaked bedding. Shit, what a mess. Some, but not all, of the dark red stain had faded to brown. Exasperated he rolled up his shirtsleeves. Why should he have expected Emily to sort it out?

He strode to the kitchen and grabbed a couple of black bin bags.

'What are you doing?' asked Emily in a plaintive voice. 'It's nearly six in the morning. Come to bed. I've got to go to work soon. I need some more sleep.'

'We can't leave Olivia's bedroom like that.'

Emily shrugged, her hands fluttering as if that might make the mess magically disappear. 'I don't see why not. It's not going to make much difference now.'

He closed his eyes and counted to ten. It would have made a difference if someone had at least stripped the bed a couple of hours ago instead of letting the blood seep into the mattress. He stomped back to the bedroom.

He stuffed the sheets straight into the black bags. No point trying to save them or the double duvet. Hopefully Olivia wasn't too attached to them. If it were him he'd want new. These were stained with nasty memories and you couldn't be sure you'd get all the glass shards out. The glass in that window must have been quite old.

He could order her a new duvet today and it could be delivered tomorrow. The mattress he'd sponge as best he could and then she could always turn it over and she had spare bed sheets.

He hoisted the black bags over his shoulder and took them down the fire escape steps and through the shared yard at the back of the junk shop, to the wheelie bins arranged in a neat row like sentries on guard. He didn't hang around, the enclosed yard was full of dark corners and shadows.

Olivia had fallen asleep again, scrunched up on the sofa, her head at an odd angle. He went over and shifted the cushion under her head. She didn't stir but she looked a bit more comfortable now.

Half past six. No point in trying to go to sleep and he didn't want to disturb Emily again ... no, not strictly true, he wanted to avoid her, avoid saying something that would upset her. His hands clenched, tension rocking up his arms into his shoulders. Tiredness had scoured out his eyes and they felt gritty and sore.

Making a cup of tea, he sat in the kitchen staring out of the window. How had life suddenly got so complicated? He rubbed at the stubble on his chin, things felt different but he couldn't quite figure out what it was that had changed.

'Olivia? Do you know where my house keys are? I can't find them.'

These were the first words Emily addressed to me the following morning as I lay on the sofa, bundled up in a sleeping bag. Had she forgotten I'd been at the hospital half the night? Of course I hadn't seen her bloody keys. She was always losing them.

'When did you last have them?' I asked patiently. Irritatingly, she stared at the ceiling as if mentally retracing her steps.

'Can't remember. You used your key last night after work. The night before that I was home after you – so you let me in. I thought they were in my handbag.'

'Tried your coat pocket? Changed handbags?'

'No, they were definitely in my bag. My new one.'

She wouldn't have changed that then, not her limited edition special.

'You'll have to let me in later. I can't be bothered to look for them now. It's not as if you'll be going anywhere?' She nodded towards the swathe of bandages around my arm. 'How did you get on? Daniel said the cut wasn't too bad after all.'

Thanks for the sympathy.

'Actually, it wasn't the best evening of my life. They've Steri-Stripped it. Luckily I didn't need any stitches. I was—'

'It wasn't much fun here, either.' She glanced over her shoulder down the hall to the bathroom where Daniel was taking a shower. 'I was terrified. I think Peter threw that brick. Who else could it have been? It must have been him on Tottenham Court Road yesterday. Do you think he followed us home?'

'No,' I said, rubbing my eyes. 'You've been watching too many films.'

That sort of thing didn't happen in real life.

Now in broad daylight, fear had receded and my imagination was back under control. As if anyone was going to chuck something through a window just because someone wouldn't go out with them! That was *Coronation Street* not Earlsfield Road. That brick was just a random act of vandalism.

'What if it was Peter?' asked Emily, her words running into each other she spoke so quickly.

'It can't have been,' I said, shaking my head with a confidence I didn't feel.

'Even so, he's still odd. You should tell your cousin that one of his hand-picked candidates is a bit dodgy. Did you get hold of him?'

'Yes, he said he'd vetted him.' I crossed my fingers under the sleeping bag, not wanting to go into the detail of my conversation with my cousin. 'But I'll speak to him again.' Although what was I going to say? Again, I had no proof that Peter was behind the incident.

'See you later,' trilled Emily, as she sailed through the lounge. 'Come on, Daniel. Have you seen the time?'

Her tone had changed considerably since our earlier conversation about Peter.

Daniel came into the lounge. 'Feeling better?' he asked, with a diffident, almost shy smile, looking quickly at his watch before pulling a pristine white cuff back over his wrist, the crisp cotton emphasising his slight tan and the blond hairs on his arm. My stomach lurched with longing.

'Thanks, Daniel. For looking after me. You must be shattered.'

'Yes,' he said, making no move to leave and suddenly finding his shoes of great interest.

'I ... em, really appreciate you taking me to casualty and waiting and ... you know everything ...' God, I sounded a complete idiot. My tongue was well and truly tied in knots. 'I don't know what I'd ... have done, if em ... you hadn't been, you know... here.'

'Phoned an ambulance?'

Did I detect a trace of amusement?

'You might have picked up a paramedic,' he quipped, although from his tone I don't think he was trying to be funny.

I decided to follow his lead. 'What covered in blood and wearing my best bunny slippers? I don't think so.'

His face creased into a broad smile. I felt a small, golden glow inside, as if the sun had come out.

'You have no idea what those bunnies do to a man,' he mocked.

A little voice inside me was dying to say, 'No tell me'.

'Right then ...' I said awkwardly.

'Yes ... I, um, need to get going.'

In my head The Three Degrees had burst into song with a rousing rendition of 'When will I see you again?'

I got up, took a tentative step forward and laid my hand on his arm, about to kiss him on the cheek. Just to say thanks, of course.

'Daniel. Hurry up.' Emily's voice was shrill, as she appeared at his side, threading her arm through his and marching him off to the front door.

There was a lot of faffing about downstairs with Emily snapping that she needed an umbrella. With an almighty slam that made the letter box rattle, the door closed on her strident tones.

I let out a sigh and waited for my heart to slow again.

Looking round the empty flat, I decided there was no point in being a wounded soldier and not making the most of it. Selecting a large bar of Dairy Milk from my secret stash and with a mug of tea, I switched on Radio 1, slipped back inside my sleeping bag and settled down.

The night's disturbed sleep caught up with me and succumbing to the soft-edged focus of the painkiller, I dozed off.

I woke to the sound of a key in the lock and started. Was that Emily coming home already? Had I been asleep for the whole day? It didn't feel like it.

No, the clock on the wall said it was only quarter past ten. Puzzled and still half asleep, I called out. 'Emily?'

No answer. Dopily I swung my feet, still in the sleeping bag, onto the floor. She'd found her keys, then. I called her name again. What was she doing home at this time?

Not coming back to play Florence Nightingale that was for sure.

She still hadn't answered. I waited and listened. A faint click. The front door closing. My heart lurched.

'Emily.' I yelled it louder this time – as if sounding confident and a touch belligerent might scare off whoever it was, if it wasn't Emily.

Still no sound. Making as much noise as I could, I shuffled across the lounge to the top step, bent and looked down. From there I could see the bottom of the stairs but not the front door at the end of the passage.

'Hello,' I called, feeling daft. As if a burglar was going to answer me!

Disentangling myself from the sleeping bag, I crept down the top six steps protectively holding my injured arm and paused. From here I could see the glass front door. There was no one there. I hesitated. It wouldn't do any harm to put the chain on.

As soon as I reached the bottom step I scooted to the front door. Like a child running and jumping into bed, frightened of a monster lurking underneath. I was about to shove the chain in place, when I spotted the black bundle leaning against the glass on the other side of the door. I opened the door carefully. Charlie, the junk shop cat, was curled up in a ball, meowing piteously.

'Hey, puss,' I murmured softly, worried by his obvious distress. Gently stretching out my hand, I tried to stroke him but to my surprise he hissed, jumped up and ran off up the street limping. Strange, he was normally so friendly.

I slid back the chain on the door and turned to go back upstairs. That was when I stepped into a cold damp patch.

Looking down, my foot seemed small in the centre of the large sodden footprint outlined on the carpet. Far larger than Emily's delicate size fours.

Emily's keys! My mind raced, making terrifying connections. Had her keys been missing since the day of Peter's visit to the office? I tried to remember the scene. Emily had taken everything out of her bag that day. Had Peter taken them?

Heart racing, I fled back up the stairs, grabbed the phone and bolted myself into the bathroom.

Fingers shaking I tried to call Emily's work number, stabbing and missing the buttons on the phone. My heart was pounding double time and my injured arm was throbbing.

'Emily! It's me. Olivia. He's been here ... he's got your keys,' I burst out. 'He's—'

'Olivia, slow down—'

'He's been here ... he must have your keys. He got in.'

'Who's been there?' asked Emily impatiently. 'What are you on about? I've got my keys. '

'You've got your keys?' I repeated stupidly.

'Yes, they were at work all the time. At reception. I must have dropped them here.'

'Thank God.' I sighed with relief, my heart immediately

slowing but still thudding furiously. 'Sorry, Em, I really thought ... I thought ... Doesn't matter. I must have been dreaming. Lack of sleep.'

'I bet the painkillers have confused you as well. It was a bit of an eventful night. No one can believe it here.'

Emily would have embellished the tale, no doubt exaggerating the copious quantities of blood I'd shed.

Putting down the phone and unbolting the bathroom door, I gave myself a stern talking too. You're tired. Overwrought. It was a bad night. Lots of painkillers. Your imagination is racing.

That wet patch could have been made by Emily or Daniel leaving this morning. It was raining. There were hundreds of reasons why they might have stepped outside and then stepped back in. The carpet was cheap nylon; it probably would have retained the wet for ages.

When I got off the phone from Mum, who'd given me oodles of sympathy, and offered to drop everything and come and take charge, I felt a bit better. Tempting as it was, I knew she needed the time in her studio. With some big exhibitions in major galleries under her belt, her reputation in the ceramics world had grown and she was working on a special piece which she hoped would 'blow the pants off' the owner of a famous ceramics gallery in North London.

The arrival of a very garrulous glazier from The Glass Brokers – 'The people who take the pane out of shattered glazing'– later that afternoon did a lot to reassure me. Phil was a big fan of antisocial behaviour because it kept him in business. My little broken window was, 'Nuffink'. He got ten of these every week, more when the weather was warm. Apparently the real money was in the commercial stuff.

'Triple time, between nine and midnight – after that blank cheque book, mate. Blank cheque book.'

Grumpily I reflected, as I made him a mug of tea, one

person's tragedy was another's silver lining – Phil's was made of £50 banknotes.

After he'd gone I rattled around the flat growing steadily more irritable. I'd had enough of smug daytime presenters, I didn't have the energy to tackle any job in the flat and I was too tetchy to read. My arm was itching and the pinprick scabs looked unsightly. I was fed up. Fed up and bolshy.

I knew what was wrong and it had nothing to do with my arm. Determined to take my mind off things, or rather one person, I logged on to my laptop. No joy there either. No new emails apart from the ones from complete strangers offering me Biggadik penis enlargement patches.

A good time to tidy up my inbox. Get rid of all those emails going back six months. My eyes were drawn to the name Ned Hillard. I re-read his email. It was funny. Was he the answer to all my problems? Perhaps he could take my mind off Daniel?

Kate put paid to any more dithering when she called.

'Olivia. It's me. I just heard what happened. Are you OK?' Her voice oozed concern and sympathy down the phone line.

'I'm fine. Bit of an exciting night, though.'

'Well, that's a first,' she mocked.

'Ha, ha.'

'Bloody yobs. It's the same everywhere. Even here. Last weekend someone in the village had his car covered in paint. Some lads found a can on their way home. Bet your window was broken by some lagered-up louts. In that state they don't give a toss if they damage something.'

'Well, that something was me,' I said crossly. 'And I mind a lot!'

'How are you feeling?'

'Crap.'

Kate didn't deal well with other people's problems. Her own life ran so smoothly that she hadn't had the practice. I wasn't surprised when she changed the subject.

'So have you arranged to see Ned yet?'

What! Was she psychic or something?

'No, not yet.' Why do I have to be so honest? It was the last thing I should have said, to Kate of all people.

'You're joking. He'll think you're not interested.'

'I don't know that I am.'

'Of course you are. He sounds a laugh. If he can't afford Jimmy Chews, he might get you a pair of gumboots. Geddit?' She sniggered.

I rolled my eyes even though she couldn't see.

'You are so unfunny.' I giggled in spite of myself. 'Anyway I'm not sure ...' my voice trailed off. The painkillers were wearing off and my arm was throbbing. Where was my magic bottle of pills?

'Know what your problem is?'

I just had to find those tablets. The pain was suddenly excruciating. Kate was still twittering in my ear.

'OK,' I snapped. 'I'll go on a date with Ned.' Anything to get her off the line. There was a surprised silence, followed by a laugh of triumph.

The minute I said it I knew I shouldn't.

'I hear you're going on a date, darling.' That was my mother's opening gambit on Saturday morning when she phoned under the pretext of asking how I was. It hadn't taken long for the family grapevine to rev itself up.

'Very sensible of you,' she said happily. I could virtually see her hopping from foot to foot in the kitchen at home. 'You need something to take your mind off the accident.'

If only she knew. It wasn't the accident I needed to get off my mind. It was the accident waiting to happen. I had to get Daniel out of my head. She warbled on enthusiastically for another five minutes before suddenly remembering that Dad was in the car waiting to take her to Waitrose.

Perhaps I could get away with just making up the date.

I slumped back on the sofa and dreamed up details of the perfect imaginary date – nice wine bar, long boozy lunch followed by a walk around Covent Garden, stopping along the way to watch the street entertainers.

But no such luck. Kate rolled up in person at lunchtime to check up on me. I struggled down the stairs to let her in as Emily had abandoned me in favour of a shopping expedition to Westfield.

'God, you look awful' she said, marching past me into the flat, with a bag of Marks & Spencer goodies. Funnily enough, I thought the same about her. Her hair, as always, was perfect but there were dark shadows under her eyes. Either her favourite Estée Lauder Spotlight had run out or there was something she wasn't telling me.

I'd only got an inch of water into the kettle before she asked, 'So where are you going with Ned?'

No 'How are you feeling? How's your arm?' Trust her to go straight for the jugular. I should have answered her immediately to distract her but I left it that fraction too long. My silence told her everything she needed to know.

'Typical. You haven't fixed anything up yet, have you?'

'Don't nag. I was going to do it today.'

By the time the teabags were being dunked, she had my laptop fired up ready to go. If composing an email with Emily was tortuous, it was nothing compared with trying to write one with my sister peering over my shoulder.

'Let me know, how it goes won't you?' Kate said as she rose to leave.

'Yes, Bossy. Sure you don't want to come and supervise the date properly? In fact, why don't you cancel your flight home altogether ...'

'I'd love to,' she said, suddenly serious. 'I'm not ...' She stopped and sighed.

'Kate?'

'I'm fine. Fine.'

'You don't seem it. What's wrong?'

'Nothing. Australia's a long way away. I miss everyone.'

'Yes, but you've got loads of friends, and the super surf-stud.'

She hesitated. 'It's just not the same. Even though they speak the same language – they don't.'

'You've lost me.'

'*The Clangers* – you remember *The Clangers*?' Her hand grasped the top of my good arm.

'Little pink knitted fellas and the Soup dragon.'

'Precisely.' Her glossy hair slithered forward as she nodded. 'You know exactly what I'm talking about.'

'Yeeees. Because we watched them together.'

'No! People just know, in this country. They're almost a national institution.'

'You've still lost me.'

'Imagine having to explain to someone you don't know what a Clanger is, when everyone else does.' Her voice was rising. 'How stupid do you feel when everyone laughs at you because you don't know some stupid kids TV show?' She bit back a sob. 'It's like that all the time. TV programmes, famous people, politicians. Even everyday stuff. I get asked to pass the Gladwrap.' She raised her palms upward in despair. 'Clingfilm. Do you know what they call Sellotape in Australia? Bloody Durex. How am I supposed to know that?'

There were tears running down Kate's face.

'Kate,' I said soothingly, giving her a big hug, feeling panicky. She was my big sister, always in charge. She hardly ever cried.

'I hate it there,' she snuffled into my shoulder. 'It's so far from home. The news is about places I've never heard of. I can't just pick up the phone and call home because the time difference will be all wrong.'

'Kate,' I said sadly. 'Why didn't you say before?'

'What could I say?' She shook her head. 'Everyone wants to go to bloody Australia, don't they? But to me it's just so alien. No one's on the same wavelength. I don't even have girlfriends. All the women think I'm stuck up and posh.'

So did a lot of people here but it wasn't a good time to tell her that. There was a lot to be said for British reserve.

'You don't have to go back,' I said tentatively. Big mistake.

Pulling away, she looked at me astonished. 'Of course I do,' she snapped.

'No, you don't,' I said soothingly.

'I,' she said with great emphasis, 'do.'

Kate would never admit to failure of any type. I'd had no idea that she was so unhappy.

'Forget I said anything.' The words rattled out of her mouth quickly. 'I'm just having an off day. I've got a bit of an upset tummy at the moment. For God's sake don't say anything to Mum. I'm fine really.'

'Kate—'

'Forget it. Just a wobble. I'd better go. Heaps of stuff to do. See you next week.' She pulled on her coat, her shoulders straightening and her chin going up. I could almost see her physically pulling herself together.

'Let me know how you get on with Ned. I want all the details.' She waggled her eyebrows, some of her natural perkiness reasserting itself.

A classic change-the-subject tactic if ever I heard one.

'Think you'll be all right? When was the last time—?'

'Don't go there.' I was not going to discuss that with her. Some things are best kept private.

'Hopefully that's going to change,' she lowered her voice with a deliberately naughty grin, her tears forgotten. 'It *is* just like riding a bicycle, you don't—'

'Kate, bugger off,' I said exasperated, any second she'd start handing me a pile of condoms.

'You know you're going to miss me,' she said archly.

'Really?' I asked dryly.

Giving me one of her trademark dazzling grins – how did she bounce back so quickly? – she patted me gently on my cheek. 'Don't worry you can always text me.'

Talk about mood swings. Rolling my eyes, I gave her one last hug, watching as her high heels tapped across the pavement to Mum's car. She settled into the driver's seat, checking her make-up in the mirror before giving me a cheery wave and roaring off down the street.

I watched the car disappear. Kate's outburst was just not like her. I couldn't help but be worried.

The final edit of my reply to Ned's email went like this:

To: N.Hillard@yahoo.com
From: ORMiddleton@hotmail.com
Subject: Second Hand Invisibility Cloaks

Hi Ned

While rescuing a child from a burning building I narrowly escaped death when an explosion sent glass flying everywhere. Although a main artery was almost severed, I survived to tell the tale. Sadly my injuries preclude a shoplifting expedition, which is just as well as I've heard those second-hand invisibility cloaks aren't much cop. However a medicinal drink is required. I think copious quantities of wine might help. Know any good watering holes? I'll be the one wearing the bandage.

All the best

Olivia

... which was how I came to be zigzagging my way through Covent Garden, trying to avoid idle tourists ambling through the midday sunshine. Ned had suggested meeting at a pub he knew.

The outside of the pub told me everything I needed to know before I even got in the door. My heart sank, even more so when I stepped inside. It was one of those 'below average places', grubby with too many spillages on the carpet, where men outnumbered women five to one and the wine came out of a box above the bar. A long way from my imaginary wine bar.

'Thought you were joking about the bandage,' said Ned, picking my drink up for me but only after he realised I couldn't manage. Wearing a beige cord jacket and baggy jeans he looked slightly rumpled, as if he hadn't been up for long.

'Better than a rolled up *Times* and a pink carnation,' I said, attempting to be perky. It came out a bit flat. When the painkillers were at full throttle I could forget about my arm. The gaps between paracetamol and ibruprofen weren't much fun though as the wound was still raw. It preferred inactivity and plenty of rest. Traipsing across London was not part of the prescription.

'What happened? You weren't really leaping into burning buildings and rescuing children, were you? Don't tell me you're ...' he looked furtively around the pub dropping his voice to a whisper, 'Supergirl?'

I gave him a dim smile; the best I could manage. 'No, I'm not.' I wrinkled my nose. 'Some kid was practising his shot putting technique. If they make vandalism an Olympic sport, he'll be on the British team. His brick shattered my window and I got glass in my arm.'

'Nasty,' said Ned. 'I thought you said you lived in Earlsfield. Isn't it civilised round there?'

'Normally, yes.' I hesitated very slightly.

Ned picked up on it. He tilted his head to one side. 'Wild partying upset the neighbours?'

'No, our parties are very staid.'

'Shame, I like a good party. So what happened?' He raised his eyebrows prompting me to go on.

'I'm not sure. It's probably just coincidence.' I took a sip of wine, weighing up whether I should confide in him.

Ned leaned back comfortably in his chair. 'You don't sound convinced.' He looked searchingly at me over the top of his pint before taking a deep swallow.

I met his eyes. They were darker than I'd remembered and the brow of his hair slightly further back. Hopefully he would laugh laddishly at my silly fears and tell me I was being a girl.

'Remember the speed-date? Sorry, 'course you do.'

He grinned. 'I've drunk out on it quite a few nights. Most of my mates fancy being invisible. You should hear some of the conversations we've had ...' he trailed off, smirking. 'Then again. Possibly not.'

'I can imagine,' I said dryly. 'Do you remember any of the other guys at the speed-date?'

'Not really, I was looking at you lot.'

I raised an eyebrow and he grinned unrepentantly.

'The ladies.' He looked thoughtful. 'I did notice there were quite a few prats in suits. Arsington-Smythe types.'

'What?'

'You know. Smug gits who like to chuck their money about but do bugger all to earn it.'

Barney's City friends weren't my cup of tea but Ned's chippy attitude made me cringe.

'This guy wasn't in a suit. He was ordinary. Small, dark, a little bit like Tom Cruise, although without the glow-in-the-dark teeth.'

'Really? He looked like that and he was on a speed-date?'

'I said a little – we're talking fractions.' I held up a thumb and finger. 'He took a shine to my friend Emily. Emailed her a couple of times but she wasn't interested.'

'I thought the deal was that you only got paired up if you both ticked boxes.'

Not if you're related to Barney, I thought, taking great interest in a chip on the base of my glass.

'Administrative error,' I said tightly. 'Emily kept getting emails from this guy. Then he turned nasty.' I explained about the day of the screen saver and the coincidental timing of the brick through my window.

'Sorry.' Ned frowned and shook his head. 'I don't buy that coincidence stuff. It doesn't sound right to me. Let's face it. He's a nutter.'

'Nooo,' I said, pulling a face. This wasn't the response I wanted. He was supposed to be on the side of reason and scepticism. Allay my fears, not make them worse. I stared at him, the wine in my stomach rolling uncomfortably.

'Yeah! No matter how pissed off you are – a normal bloke does not blag his way into an office. Let alone start leaving messages on computers. That's psycho territory. You need to tell someone.'

'Do you think so?' I asked in a small voice.

'See that,' he pointed to the bandages on my arm. 'Don't take any more chances. I'd punch the bastard just for the screen saver. If he chucked that brick, you want to make frigging sure he's not going to do anything else.'

'But what if wasn't him?'

He gave an exasperated tut and rolled his eyes. 'And what if it was him? He knows where you live.'

Fear iced down my spine, the hairs on my arm rising. Ned's cold, clear male logic made my stomach contract.

'Do you think I should go to the police?' I asked.

'Yes. You want another drink?'

Obviously we'd covered that topic, it was time to move on.

Halfway into my second glass of wine I asked him what had made him go on a speed-date.

He looked sheepish. 'It was sort of ... a challenge. We were down the Nag's Head. Me and my mates, Graham and Midge.'

I got the impression he spent a lot of time there.

'We were moaning that none of us had had a sh ... girlfriend for ages. My mate, Gram, decided we needed to do something about it. We each had to choose a different method.'

'Choose?'

He smiled weakly. 'We wrote on beer mats different ways of finding a bird – I mean girlfriend – then had to pick one out of the hat. Gram got online-dating. I got speed-dating and Midge had to go to a bar to try to pull someone.'

'Right – and who's winning?' I asked, and immediately wished I hadn't. 'Sorry, that's a bit of a leading question, ignore that.'

He looked at me and shrugged his shoulders. 'I'm the only one who's managed to get a date so far. Why d'you go? You seem well ... quite good-looking ...' He blushed toying with his empty pint glass, 'and pretty normal.'

'What and you're not normal?' I asked laughing, trying to keep things light, pleased at the 'good-looking' bit. He was still fiddling with the empty glass so I asked, 'Would you like another drink?'

He looked at his watch and almost squirmed in his seat. 'Erm, wouldn't mind but not here. Thing is. There's a match on. Big one. Starts soon and the screen here's broken. Do you fancy going somewhere else?'

I paused for a second, football was not my thing.

'To be honest, I might head off. My arm's not feeling too good; I'm between painkillers at the moment.'

His jacket was on before I drained my glass. I caught him checking his watch again.

'Big match is it?'

He rubbed at a bald patch on his cords, a faint flush colouring his cheeks.

'Tottenham v Arsenal – local derby and grudge match. We hate the Spurs.' He might as well have been talking Swahili. I had no idea what he was on about. I good-naturedly rolled my eyes at him as he surreptitiously tried and failed to look at the time again.

'Sorry.' He grinned mischievously and led the way to the door, oblivious to my struggles to get my jacket on.

'Well, it was nice seeing you,' he said, as we stood outside the pub, me still trying to wriggle my arm into place. His foot was tapping.

'And you,' I responded politely, as he did another quick time check. I gave an Oscar winning 'boys-will-be-boys' laugh. 'You'd better go. You don't want to miss kick-off.'

'I'll be in touch.' He half-raised his hand, put it down, raised it again, thought better and lunged in quickly. I felt a brush of stubble on my cheek and then he was gone with the words, 'I'll email ... Maybe we could go for a drink on Friday ... See you,' floating over his shoulder as he scurried off.

Friday, I thought ruefully was probably Nag's Head night with Gram and Midge.

Chapter Nine

'Do these belong to you?' rasped a voice from behind a pair of bright blue, daisy-festooned wellies.

They were mine and were being held up by the big, big boss, David. The MD. Surely I hadn't been summoned to his office on the top floor to discuss my taste in footwear?

'Yes,' I answered guardedly. What was he doing with them? They normally lived in the back of the company pool car. I'd bought them several months ago because there's nothing worse than getting to a muddy construction site and having to borrow warm, sweaty boots.

David smiled his crooked gangster smile, his bright blue eyes piercing. As usual he was perfectly attired in a charcoal-grey suit with a tiny pinstripe running through the beautifully cut fabric. It was worth every penny, hiding his barrel-chested, dumpy shape to perfection.

'No wonder those bastards at Collingwood Construction love you so much. A dolly bird turning up in girly wellies must brighten the lads' day up no end.' He guffawed with laughter. 'They're gonna have to do without you for a coupla weeks though. That lazy sod Max will have to get off his arse for a change.'

He shot me a shrewd look. 'Didn't think I'd noticed who did all the work on that account, did you?'

Poor Max, my immediate boss, a brilliant thinker but rubbish doer.

I didn't answer, not that David expected me to.

Why had I been summoned? David wasn't great on welfare; he didn't do touchy feely stuff, so it was nothing to do with the bandage on my arm. I would bet my entire annual salary that dealings with HR brought him out in hives.

It was only when a very red-eyed Fiona knocked at the door of David's palatial office that all became clear. She was head of the beauty team and Emily's boss. As always she was dressed in a tight-fitting designer suit, the skirt skimming her knee to make the most of her ten-denier clad legs. Only her puffy lids spoilt the look.

'You're taking over Fiona's team. She's got a domestic crisis.' In David speak this had to be a death in the family at the very least.

Without thinking I blurted out, 'The beauty side! I don't know anything about beauty stuff.'

'What's to know?' dismissed David blithely, receiving a weary glare from Fiona. The poor girl looked completely done in.

'Bright girl like you can manage that bunch of airheads. As of now you're hanging up your wellies for a couple of weeks. You're acting Account Director. Fiona'll brief you. And if you wondering about your flower power boots, I've had to pinch the pool car – you won't need it for a while. Some arsehole ran into the Porsche.'

With that he tossed the boots at my feet leaving me with Fiona.

'Arrogant so and so,' she said with feeling. 'Unfortunately he's right. I can't trust them to get on with anything. Luckily, there's nothing major on. Apart from the Luscious Lips launch.'

She sat down heavily in David's chair, smoothing the tight skirt down her thighs. 'I realise Emily's your friend, but unfortunately you're going to have to find a way to manage her.' Fiona shook her head, her lips curling. 'Her attention to detail is truly appalling. We're launching this season's new colours …'

I interrupted her holding up my hand. 'I know all about it. Miranda has been the sole topic of conversation for the last week.'

'Then you know the background.' She looked at me. 'How Emily came up with the idea, I don't know. She actually managed to come up with a winner. But I need you to keep on top of things. Miranda's agent is a complete shark. I don't want to come back to hear that the entire budget has been blown on room service in Miranda's bloody hotel suite or on an entourage of thousands.'

So far, a stylist and a make-up artist had been sanctioned but Fiona had vetoed the nutritionist, Reiki practitioner and personal Pilates instructor.

'I've heard the problems,' I murmured.

'The main thing you have to worry about is Miranda's partner.'

This was news to me. 'Who?'

'Rowan Majors, recently ex-boy-band hero and supposedly heading northward up the charts. Except it's not happening.'

'So?' There was no point even trying to hide my ignorance. Fiona needed to know that I was out of my depth.

Fiona gave me another scornful look. 'If,' she paused with a heavy sigh, 'his solo career doesn't deliver a number one hit in the next week, he's toast ... and we're stuffed.'

Apparently Miranda's ten page contract stipulated we had to find an escort if she needed one. There was even a sub-clause specifying required inside-leg measurements. Fiona wasn't joking!

The contract, legal and binding, was astonishing. According to the densely written paperwork she fished out of her file, the escort couldn't have blonder hair than her (unless there were obvious roots) and his shoulders had to be broad enough to show off Miranda's miniscule size six frame. Last but not least, Miranda had to have final approval.

'God, I hope Rowan stays the course!'

Fiona gave a 'God-give-me-strength' groan. 'He won't. It's my worst nightmare. Or rather, it's yours now,' she said sounding bitter. 'Look I need to go. My mother is desperate.' She looked at her watch grimacing. 'I'll come down with you to break the news to the team.'

'I'm so sorry about your mother …' I said tentatively, wondering what was wrong with her.

'Thanks.' She smiled weakly at me. 'It's not totally unexpected but Mummy's really cut up. She can't believe the surgeon won't operate again. And on top of Daddy, it's too much.'

'Oh, no. Is it cancer?' I asked sympathetically.

Fiona looked at me sharply. 'No, liposuction. She's devastated. She swore she'd never go to Weight Watchers again.'

What could I say to that? If I'd been a cartoon my eyes would have done that bugging out thing where they bounce up and down on springs. All I could do was manage a strangled, 'Don't worry about a thing. I'm sure we'll cope.'

'Of course, Daddy's is a little more serious with his prostate trouble. Mummy doesn't drive so she needs me while he's in hospital having his op.'

Then to my surprise, she stood, smoothed her perfect skirt again and came towards me. Squeezing my good arm with an earnest expression on her face she said, 'You know, Olivia, I couldn't leave my team with anyone else in charge. You're the only other person here who knows what they're doing.'

With that she wheeled out leaving me staring after her in amazement. Blimey! Compliments from Fiona and David? What a day it was turning out to be. Perhaps I should be off sick more often. Now all I had to do was break the news to Emily. Deep joy.

My visit to the top floor had been the subject of much conjecture, so when I came into the office all eyes swivelled my way. I cringed looking at all the curious faces.

Max might just break down and cry and as for the beauty team's reaction, I didn't even want to go there. It was going to be bad enough trying to do the job. Miranda's demands sounded outrageous. She was one high-maintenance chick.

Old Jabba the Hutt had never demanded any more than a hanky to wipe his sweaty brow before a photo shoot. In fact, I'd maligned him. Today, I'd returned to find that he'd sent two dozen scented pink roses and a beautiful card wishing me well.

Predictably, Emily was livid. She couldn't believe it wasn't her stepping into Fiona's shoes. The fact that it was me was a double whammy. Even I could see it was a very public slur.

It was going to be a difficult couple of weeks. Changing desks with one arm was my first challenge. Not one of the beauty team offered to help. Cara was about to but when she jumped up she got a quelling look from Emily and quickly sat down again.

Max roused himself from his perennial laziness to carry over my laptop. Being helpful didn't come naturally to him; he just wanted to moan about how unfair it all was.

'How am I going to manage? Who's going to write the Winton Bypass release? What about the Broughton public enquiry?' he griped, wiping his perpetually smeared glasses.

'Max,' I said with exasperation, handing him a pile of neatly labelled files. 'I'm right here. It's not as if I've been relocated to the Leeds office.'

'God forbid.' He really did look horrified at that. 'But still ...'

'You know all about the bloody Broughton enquiry – and you can read. Everything's in the file.' And even you should be able to write a press release by now, I thought.

'Yes, but Olivia, I've got so much to do for the Management Team Report.'

'Max,' I said raising my voice. 'I write that report for you every month, all you need to do is update it – it's not even my job to do it.' Then lowering my voice I hissed, 'Most of the stuff is confidential, I'm not supposed to know that Ian Riley is on his third warning or that David is considering restructuring again.'

'Yes, but you're so trustworthy.' A wheedling tone crept into his voice. 'I can always rely on you.'

'Well, you can't any more. Not until Fiona gets back.'

'I get the message,' he tutted. 'The power's gone to your head already. Just remember pride before a fall. Don't you worry, Uncle Max will hold the fort for you.'

I rolled my eyes. You'd think I was crossing a crocodile-infested river rather than the short expanse of grey carpet to the other side of the office. Mind you, looking at the grim faces of Emily, Cara, Camilla and Helene, it might be as dangerous.

You could almost see the dark cloud hovering above them, for once united in disapproval. I hadn't dared look at Emily when it was explained that I was taking over for the next few weeks. If looks could kill, Fiona would have spontaneously combusted.

Sensibly, she made a speedy getaway before any of the team could utter a word. Sweeping everything on the top of her desk into her capacious handbag, she thrust a purple folder at me with a hasty, 'You'll need this' and scuttled out of the office.

Dazed, I sank into her chair and opened the folder to find ten pages of colour-coded notes. They made scary reading. Big Sister had been watching them. Helene always took five minutes extra at lunchtime, Camilla was not to be trusted with the petty cash, Cara was too generous with the samples and as for Emily; two pages were devoted to her.

My heart sank. It didn't sound like the happiest of working environments. I cast a regretful glance at Max. His feet were propped up on the desk, surrounded by piles of paper as he chatted distractedly into the phone, the handset tucked into his shoulder while he polished his glasses. He wouldn't know what day of the week it was, let alone whether I'd taken a lunch hour.

Reluctantly I put down the purple folder, wondering whether I should take Emily to one side for a private chat. From the scowl on her face and her hunched position at the computer, co-operation was going to be in short supply.

My first meeting with the team later that morning went relatively well, compared to a train wreck. The 'I'm on your side; I don't want to tread on your toes' speech which I'd rehearsed in the ladies, went down like contraception at the Vatican. The coven, as I'd renamed them, weren't having any of it.

Only Cara showed signs of breaking ranks, which wasn't wholly surprising. She had an Arsenal screen saver on her computer and team stickers all around her desk. Not a typical PR girly. She wanted advice on handling a difficult journalist. This particular beauty assistant who worked for one of the most important magazines was insisting she receive a second sample of a new age-defying moisturiser. At £250 a throw, this miracle cream was like gold dust and samples had been strictly rationed. I suggested a call was put into the Beauty Editor to ask if she minded the assistant getting her sample. Cara grinned gratefully.

The other three were stony faced. It wasn't hard to picture them revving up their broomsticks as they left the meeting room.

'What's this?' I asked sharply.

Emily feigned innocence. 'It's a purchase order.'

'I know that. What's it for?' It was now my job to sign off the triplicate form, which had to be filled out for every piece of expenditure.

'For the Luscious Lips launch.'

It was for £200 and made out to an Otto Omar.

'I realise that but what exactly is it for?'

She looked down at her hand defiantly admiring her polished nails. If she wound me up any more I'd take the nail clippers to them.

'He's the Reiki man for Miranda,' she muttered.

I looked at her in exasperation. 'Emily, Fiona specifically said, "No Reiki". No massage, faith healers or whatever else Miranda's after. I've been through the contract. She can have a make-up artist and a stylist – that's it. There's no budget for anything else.'

'Miranda went on and on about it ...' she trailed off weakly.

'Miranda can go on and on about it. She knows full well what she can and can't have. Talk about trying it on! Don't forget we're also paying her a wheelbarrow full of gold bullion.' God only knew what Luscious Lips put in their lipstick to make it so profitable. 'Ring Otto and tell him his services aren't required.'

Emily stared at me reproachfully. 'I can't do that,' she said horrified. 'I've only just booked him.'

'Well, you'll just have to unbook him, won't you?' This was scary, I was turning into Fiona.

'What now?' she queried, still looking all wide-eyed.

I took a deep breath. Don't shout at her. Instead I calmly said, 'Yes please,' and went back to my keyboard.

Muttering to myself, I typed, 'I will not kill Emily. I will not kill Emily' and forced my shoulder blades back into place. God, I'd only been doing Fiona's job for two days and the stress was killing me.

Emily walked off sullenly. Only after she'd got herself a coffee, phoned Daniel and tidied out her handbag, did I hear her saying on the phone, 'I'm really, really sorry, Otto. Not my fault. It's my boss. She won't let me book you.'

I couldn't care less what she said to Otto, I kept my eye line below the computer monitor. It was the call to Daniel that bugged me. 'Hi, Dan,' she'd tinkled. Dan! I'd never called him that in all the years I'd known him. And did she have to phone him and text him so often? Until I'd sat this side of the room, I'd had no idea they were so devoted.

Recently they'd been out a lot; with a trip to see *Phantom of the Opera*; sushi dinners and frequent visits to posh cocktail bars. In fact, I hadn't seen him since the night at the hospital. His sudden devotion to Emily was impressive, he loathed musicals and his idea of good food was Italian. Emily would have been better suited to someone like that awful guy at the speed-date, Crossword Man.

In comparison, my social life was looking blank. I'd heard nothing more from Ned and Friday was looming.

Ned emailed me the very next day and while I wasn't sure that the vital spark was there, he did have a way with emails. In my book, anyone that calls me Supergirl deserves a second chance.

To: ORMiddleton@hotmail.com
From: N.Hillard@yahoo.com
Subject: Supergirl

Hi Ollie

(Euew! Only my brother got away with calling me Ollie.)

Date great, footie crap – we won but rubbish match. I should have stuck with you. Sorry it probably wasn't the best day to suggest getting together but didn't want to wait any longer. I was afraid I'd miss the boat – there's probably a queue (although I hope not).

How about I show you a really good time, mud

wrestling in Morden, trainspotting in Tooting or birdwatching in Enfield?
You can choose.

Ned

We ended up in the Nags Head, which defied my expectation by being one of those lovely North London Victorian pubs with original tiles and an ornate wooden bar, polished to a rich chestnut. I was expecting a spit and sawdust job with lots of smelly old men super-glued to the stools at the bar.

Ned was obviously watching out for me because the minute I walked into the pub, he jumped up and escorted me straight to the bar. This had more to do with self-preservation than innate good manners. Over his shoulder two very blokish blokes were straining to get a good look.

Despite it being eight in the evening, he still had that rumpled just-got-up-look which was quite cute. His hair kept flopping over his eyes, which he brushed away in a quick impatient movement with the back of his hand.

'Gram and Midge I presume,' I said, nodding towards the pair who immediately beamed and waved.

'Yeah,' said Ned, smiling sheepishly at their antics. 'Sorry about them. Bit keen to meet you.'

That was a good sign. I'd obviously got a good write up, so far. I studied him as he ordered the drinks, exchanging banter with the barman. The jury was still out on whether I fancied him.

'We always meet here on a Friday. What you having?'

Armed with a large glass of wine, I took a deep breath as we went over to sit with them.

Ned made the introductions. There was an awkward silence as Midge's eyes zeroed in on my chest, before moving swiftly up to my face. Gram had a bit more subtlety, he checked my face first.

'Sowhaddyado?' asked Midge, taking a swallow from a pint glass dwarfed by his hand.

I looked blank.

'Work,' prompted Gram. 'Don't mind him, he's a teacher. He's spent too much time with the kids.'

A teacher? He looked more like a builder.

'Ah,' I smiled gratefully at Gram, whose boyish face wrinkled at Midge. His patchy adolescent stubble, still bald in places, was at odds with the prematurely grey tuft of hair sticking up on his head.

'Repeat after me. The rain in Spain—'

'Piss off,' responded Midge calmly, flicking a beer mat at him.

I glanced at Ned. With his elbow perched on the table he was watching the pair of them with an indulgent smile. He gave me a wink.

'Teacher eh? Gosh that must be tough in London,' I said. 'Real front-line stuff.' Compared with that, I really didn't want to have to explain my job.

'You get used to it,' Midge said, with a grin, 'although my first day was a bit of a shock.'

'Really? Was it rough?' He looked as if he could handle a couple of scrapping sixteen year olds. Ned and Gram were sniggering.

'Yeah, I had to tie thirty pairs of laces, open fourteen Dairylea Triangles and one kid weed on me. It's murder teaching reception.'

'Little ones?' I'd assumed he'd teach older ones. 'Do you like kids, then?'

'Only on toast.' He roared with laughter.

It was an old joke. Ned, the leader of the pack, shot him a look. The three of them had obviously known each other for a very long time. They had a habit of finishing each other's sentences and had too many in-jokes. When Ned disappeared to the loo, giving the other two a definite 'behave' look, they both leaned over the table and gave me the thumbs up. Midge looked over at Gram winked and said, 'A babe'. I blushed.

There was a silence, as if without Ned the two had lost the necessary prompt to make small talk. This was broken eventually by Gram politely asking, 'So what do you do?' just as Ned came back.

'She's one of those glamorous PR types,' he said, sinking back onto his stool, moving it as he did so that his leg now touched mine.

'I hate to disappoint but I work on the building side,' I replied. If I mentioned the film premiere it would match all their preconceived ideas. I was conscious of the hard thigh next to mine. Slightly thrown by it, I said the first thing that came into my head. 'My main client is Collingwood Construction.'

All three heads dipped dramatically towards me.

'Really?' said Gram, his mouth dropping open.

'Whoa,' enthused Midge.

'Nice,' said Ned, his leg definitely pressing against mine.

I looked back at them, looking from face to face and raising my shoulders. 'What?'

'You don't know?' said Midge incredulously.

'Don't know what?'

'Collingwood Construction sponsors a box at Arsenal,' explained Ned gently.

I tutted. 'Yeah, the Chairman's always inviting me to go to a match. Says I can take a friend.' Looking up I suddenly felt like a very meaty bone under the gaze of three starving dogs.

'And you've never been?' Midge's voice went up several octaves. Gram's eyes were wide.

'Dear, dear,' said Ned, shaking his head and patting my leg with his hand. 'D'you know people would kill for that?'

'I don't think so, you've never seen Jabba. There's no way you'd want to be in a box with him.'

'The Collingwood box is one of the biggest and the best in the premiership,' said Gram in a strained voice, fanning himself with a beer mat and looking round furtively at the rest of the pub.

'Oh,' I said in a very small voice.

'Next time he offers, say yes.' said Midge urgently. 'I'll come. I'd dress in drag just to see a match.'

'Really. Can't you just buy tickets to see a game?'

Gram put his head in his hands while Midge sighed heavily and glared at me.

Ned explained. 'These days you need to be a season ticket holder to get to a decent game. A season ticket costs a couple of grand at the new Emirates stadium. There's no chance.'

'Duh.' I felt unusually stupid. 'Maybe next time I could see if I could wangle an extra ticket or two.'

When I looked up at them, the starving dogs were back and all three of them were nodding their heads earnestly. From the looks on their faces, it wouldn't have surprised me if either Gram or Midge had nudged Ned in the ribs and said, 'Struck gold there, mate.'

As evenings went it was OK. Without being patronising, they were very sweet but as my lack of knowledge about football so clearly illustrated, I could have come from Mars the amount we had in common.

They weren't really quite sure what to do with me, which made it impossible to relax. In the end after pint number three, I decided to put them out of their misery, even though I was starting to enjoy the proprietary warmth of Ned's hand on my knee.

'It was great meeting you both,' I said, as Ned escorted me to the door, which opened with a loud squeak.

Outside the temperature had dropped and I gathered my

jacket together. 'Right then, I'd better be off,' I said brightly, waiting for him to offer to walk me down the street to the tube.

'They really liked you. Perhaps we could do something next week?'

'Um, yeah.' This was it. I knew the first kiss was coming. Nerves took charge. As usual I talked. 'You never know I might get offered some football tickets.'

'That would be brilliant,' he said quickly. He took a step forward and put a hand on my shoulder, pulling me towards him. Uh oh, kiss time.

Lips first. Not to bad. Not too prolonged. Phew, no tongues. And sadly no sparks. Not a one.

I stepped back out of reach and muttered, 'Night then,' and scurried off without looking back.

I heard the pub door squeak again. Ned must have gone straight back inside.

Just my luck. I arrived back at the same time as Emily. I was hoping to avoid her. We'd had a row that morning, when she'd accused me of borrowing and losing her favourite cashmere scarf.

To be fair, Emily was always lending me things. We were in and out of each other's rooms borrowing things frequently. The scarf was one I borrowed a lot, the deep red looked fabulous with my favourite jacket.

I honestly thought I'd left it draped over the newel post at the top of the stairs two days ago, but it wasn't there now and she was adamant she hadn't moved it. I had a nagging sense of guilt. What if I was wrong and had left it somewhere else? So that night, as I trudged up the stairs behind her, I decided to do what I always did – make the first move and apologise.

If Kate had heard she would have bristled and turned an

apoplectic red. She was always telling me how I should be more assertive but I couldn't bear the atmosphere any longer. Since my temporary promotion had been announced, I'd had four days of the silent treatment at work and at home. It was too much. I wanted things back on an even keel, even if it did mean me doing some crawling. That earlier glass of wine bolstered my courage.

Pushing open the closed door of Emily's bedroom with my elbow, a glass of wine in each hand, I poked my head in before she had a chance to answer.

'Emily, I need to talk to you. I know you're pissed off with me and I completely understand. The job should have been yours.'

The sincerity of my tone won Emily over immediately. I was telling her exactly what she wanted to hear. I handed her a glass and sat down on her bed next to her.

The pursed mouth of righteous indignation which had been part of her permanent expression for the last few days, relaxed and the temperature went up by five degrees.

I knew truce negotiations were well under way when she took her first sip of wine.

'It was just such a shock, you getting Fiona's job. I still don't know why it wasn't me. You don't know anything about the products or the industry – it's a mystery,' said Emily, justifying why she'd been such a cow.

It wasn't a mystery to me. Having worked with the four of them for a week, I now knew exactly why I'd been brought in. Desperate to bring a little harmony back into my life though, I flannelled a bit. Lied like crazy would be more accurate.

'It was nothing to do with your abilities. David wanted to shake things up. It was probably financial. The company couldn't justify having two of us working on the construction side – it was either me or Max joining your team.'

'Max?' she said in a strangled voice. 'That would have been even worse than you.' Ignoring the implied criticism, I laughed and to my relief she joined in.

'Come on. Let's go and sit in the lounge. I'll fill you in on my evening in the Nag's Head.'

Emily pulled a face. 'Nag's Head. Yuk. Was it as bad as it sounds?'

I laughed. 'Not bad. Entertaining.'

Later I apologised to her about the scarf, even though I wasn't convinced it was me that had lost it. As she wasn't the tidiest of people, I was hoping she might say she'd found it. But she hadn't.

'Where's it got to, then?' she asked puzzled. 'I do remember seeing it on the post the other day. You didn't wear it again?'

'No. Look, if it doesn't turn up, let me buy you another one.'

'You can't. It was a one off. That's why it cost so much.'

Great. Make me feel worse.

'Don't worry,' she added. 'It's not like you to lose things. It will turn up.'

After that, there was a distinct improvement in relations, which was just as well because things were hotting up with Miranda and I needed all hands on decks.

Chapter Ten

To my surprise I was getting the hang of things on the beauty team and even starting to enjoy it. At first the incompetence of some of the girls on the magazines amazed me.

'Hi, it's Trudy, on *Babe* mag. I need another sample of the Sunset Pink lipstick.'

'But I've already sent you two.'

'Yah, but I left one at the shoot and well the other ... yah, the photographer stood on it. Be a poppet and send another ... two. You know. Just in case.'

There must be a black hole in Soho full of make-up and skincare products.

By the end of the first week, I was an old hand and didn't bother asking what had happened. I just gaily shoved more products into horrifically expensive padded envelopes to bike round to them. Our budget for sending out make-up and moisturiser was twice the national debt of a small dictatorship.

As I learnt the ropes I was relieved to find diplomatic relations were holding up, although Emily was no help at all. It wasn't deliberate, she was just incompetent – spectacularly so. None of the things that she was supposed to do ever got done.

Luckily Cara had warmed up and was quite helpful. I suspected that her cheerful attitude today had something to do with Arsenal winning their latest match. Her mood did tend to depend on their results.

Most of the time she was quite cheery so I guessed they were quite good. Her supporting them might come in handy, as I could get the inside track on this football business. Which reminded me. I'd promised Ned I'd speak to Jabba about tickets to the box and a game.

* * *

Everything was going well until two days before the premiere. Miraculously Miranda and Rowan's relationship had lasted longer than their dual celebrity average had suggested – but then he'd gone and blown it, which I only discovered when Emily had burst into the flat the previous night clutching the *Evening Standard*. 'I don't believe it. Look what's happened. Miranda's going to go ballistic.' She looked positively gleeful about it.

Apparently while celebrating his number one, Rowan had got roaring drunk and seduced a nearly sixteen–year-old schoolgirl who then sold her story to the *Sun*. Judging from her grainy portrait, the girl could have passed for a twenty-year-old hooker quite easily. Miranda promptly dumped him and was now milking Rowan's betrayal for all she was worth. Telling her heartbroken tale to the *Mirror* took precedence over coming to try the dress on. The headline read, 'Chart Break for Miranda.'

While the publicity was great it did leave a slight problem. With less than forty-eight hours to the premiere, it was now down to me to conjure up a man, and quickly. Short of nipping down to the nearest fire station, I was running out of ideas. Fiona had taken her handy little black book with her. After all, it wouldn't do for me to be too successful.

Then I had a brainwave. Sebastian. Daniel's brother. He would be perfect.

I hadn't seen or spoken to Daniel since that awkward moment the morning after my accident and I'd been trying hard not to think of him. Every time I did, my brain tied itself up in knots trying to figure out whether I might have given myself away that night. Did he have any inkling how I felt about him?

I chickened out and got Emily to phone him. By the end of the day everything was sorted and we had an escort for

Miranda. Sebastian would be meeting us at the hotel the following evening.

One more problem down. All I needed to do now was get Miranda to the sodding dress fitting.

By the time we left the office that evening it was late and I felt as if I was coming apart at the seams, but thankfully nearly everything was in place. I'd even managed to sort out tickets for Ned and me to go to a football match as a guest of Collingwood Construction next week. He was thrilled to bits. I still wasn't sure.

In the meantime, the premiere was front of mind. This time tomorrow I'd be there, as long as I remembered to pick up my dress from the dry-cleaners and go to the doctor's surgery. I was hoping the nurse would down grade my bandage to a smaller dressing otherwise I'd be having a severe wardrobe crisis.

In the course of arranging the evening, Emily had managed to wangle official invites to the premiere in a 'swanning-down-the-red-carpet' capacity for us. The gilt-edged invitation was taking pride of place on the mantelpiece in the flat.

'Remind me, Olivia, to dig out my strapless bra tonight,' said Emily, as we stepped into the lift on the way home. 'I don't want to get to the hotel tomorrow and not have the right underwear.'

Judicious juggling with the Luscious Lips budget and some hardball negotiation with the hotel had ensured that Emily and I had a room to get ready in. With kick-off at seven there would be no time to go home to change. It was the least the hotel could do. Miranda's suite was costing £1500.

Later that evening while I was going through my notes for the hundredth time, I came across the stylist's list of accessories, including a frightening-sounding flesh-toned, super-booster bra. That reminded me.

'Emily. Bra,' I yelled to her. At my shout she wandered into the room looking puzzled.

'Olivia, have you borrowed anything?'

Not the scarf again, please.

'Like what?'

'Underwear,' she said hesitantly.

I stared at her, she looked serious. I snorted. 'You are joking.'

'No,' she said in a small voice. 'I can't find a couple of things. Knickers. My Janet Reger bustier.'

She was definitely joking. Even with a pair of grapefruit, umpteen rolled up socks and an entire box of Kleenex, my meagre bust wouldn't have come near to filling that thing.

'Really?' I asked disbelievingly. She must have misplaced them or put them somewhere else. 'You haven't left them anywhere?'

She glared at me. 'Well, let me think, I've been sleeping my way across London with gay abandon – silly me they could be anywhere between here and Watford Gap. I'm not some floozy you know.'

'I wasn't implying anything. It's just ... you do lose things,' I said apologetically. A polite euphemism for 'You never put anything away'. I was the housework fairy. 'Have you left them at ...?' I couldn't bring myself to say Daniel's name just in case a big arrow lit up above my head and a voice boomed, 'She fancies him'.

'No,' she said crossly. 'I haven't been there for weeks. They're not there. Are you sure you haven't seen them?'

'What?' I didn't mean to say that out loud. So she hadn't been to Daniel's for weeks and he hadn't been here overnight since the accident. The thought that perhaps they weren't sleeping together was enormously cheering.

'Doesn't matter,' she snapped.

From her room I could hear bad tempered thumping as

she resumed her search. Then I heard an angry, 'Bloody hell.' She came storming out clutching a framed picture.

'Do you know anything about this?' She tossed it onto the sofa cushion beside me. The glass was broken. It was her favourite; one of those cloudy portrait shots of her coyly peeping up at the camera. The studio photo shoot and makeover had been a birthday present from her mother. My idea of hell but Emily had loved it. It was a stunning picture, although I thought it was a bit artificial and over-glossed. Shame, really because she was very pretty.

'What do you mean?'

'Er, it's broken.'

A twinge of injustice stirred my mettle. I drew myself up. 'And what's that got to do with me?'

'Sorry, Olivia,' she said more calmly, realising that perhaps this time she'd over stepped the mark. 'You're right. It's just because ... well ... you're the only other person who lives here.'

'I didn't break it.'

'It must have been the invisible man, then,' she said sulkily.

My mind immediately homed in on the memory of that wet footprint. She frowned at my expression, wagging her finger belligerently.

'Don't start that nonsense again,' she said firmly. 'I've not heard from Peter since the last email. Your cousin probably sorted him out. Honestly, Olivia, you are completely neurotic.'

'So would you be if you ended up with a dozen stitches in your arm,' I retorted dramatically. Since my chat with Ned about Peter, I harboured some worries.

'Perhaps it just fell,' I said, ignoring the scaredy cat voice at the back of my head saying 'What about your necklace? The one that was on the floor instead of your jewellery stand'.

The sensible voice in my head reminded me that with the launch tomorrow, I didn't know my arse from my elbow at the moment. I'd probably just knocked it off the stand in my hurry to get to work this morning.

I needed to slow down. After this bloody launch was over I could relax. The Old Bodgers' cricket match was coming up. Bliss. I hadn't seen Mum and Dad for ages. A weekend at home was something to look forward to.

That's not all you're looking forward to whispered a treacherous little voice in my head.

Rubbish. I wouldn't see much of Daniel. As captain of the opposition he'd be out on the pitch and I'd be in the kitchen making sandwiches. It was highly unlikely I'd see him for more than a few minutes.

'So, how's it going with Miss Babelicious?'

Daniel threw his brother a dry resigned look, used to Sebastian's humour.

'Don't call her that. Her name's Emily.' He checked his watch. They'd be on time if they left now. With the trains into London up the spout and knowing that Emily was relying on Sebastian turning up tonight, he'd volunteered to be chauffeur. Now he wondered if he was going to regret it.

He hadn't seen Emily, or Olivia for that matter, since the night of the glass injury. Work had been full on, true, but the whole episode had left him feeling discontent, so he'd deliberately immersed himself in work to give himself some thinking time.

'Why not?' Sebastian grinned, sliding his jacket on and giving himself a satisfied once over in the mirror. 'She's a babe ... although why she's going out with an ugly mutt like you I'll never know.' He shot an amused look Daniel's way. 'Not your usual type.'

He stiffened. 'I don't have a type. Are you ready?' He

jangled the car keys in exasperation to try and speed his brother up.

Sebastian finally took the hint, and headed towards the front door, smoothing down the lapels on his James Bond DJ. ''Course you do. And blonde and fluffy is not your usual type.'

'Rich coming from you,' Daniel observed sarcastically, following Sebastian out of the door, feeling uncomfortable with his comments but not really sure why.

'Aw, but bro, I'm as shallow as a puddle – remember?'

They crossed to the car and Daniel gave his brother a reproving look. Apparently double firsts in Maths just didn't cut it with 'the chicks'. He sometimes wondered if maybe his brother wasn't hanging around with the wrong chicks. But Sebastian was honest and, despite his hefty IQ, he *was* shallow as a puddle in drought and lived life short and sharp, fast and loose. He took after their mother – with the attention span of a toddler in a supermarket.

Except Sebastian never lied to any of the girls he saw or two-timed them. It was something both of them hated. Their mother lived in Kent now, with her new husband, Martin, and two new children.

He and Sebastian had seen at first hand the destructive force betrayal wrought when Martin's wife, a haggard blonde, had turned up on the doorstep of their family home, insisting Dad make his wife behave and leave her husband alone.

Daniel could still remember the shock etched into his father's face reminiscent of Munch's painting, the moment of horror penetrating as he realised that his wife had been having an affair.

The rip in the fabric of the family had been sudden and violent, like a tablecloth wrested from a fully laden table sending crockery and food crashing to the floor without warning or preparation. The resulting devastation too widely spread for anyone to know where to start picking up the shattered pieces.

Olivia really had no idea what she was getting into.

They'd only been driving for five minutes following the signs for the M4 London, before Sebastian spoke again, as if he'd been considering the subject for a while.

'I always thought Olivia was more your type. How is she and that demon sister of hers?'

Daniel swallowed the groan, his fingers gripping the steering wheel as he wished his brother would drop the whole subject. Shallow and a gossip. 'Kate's living in Australia now, though she's home at the moment.'

Sebastian eyed him with amusement. 'Nice curve ball. I always thought you and Olivia—'

'Oh, for God's sake, we're friends! Always have been. Always will be!' he snapped.

Sebastian grinned unconcerned. 'So spill.'

'What?'

'Something's eating you.'

Daniel decided he might as well give it up. He had the whole drive into London with this. 'I'm just a bit pissed off with her at the moment, if you have to know.'

'Ooooh, do tell.'

'Turn down the camp, you idiot – keep it for your luvvies, not me.'

Sebastian just grinned and raised an eyebrow. A trick that irked Daniel but only because he used it himself to the same effect and recognised in it the genetic ability they shared with their father.

'She's seeing a married man,' his words came spitting out with a terseness he'd meant to keep hidden. 'And no, I don't approve, however Victorian that makes me sound.'

Silence greeted his words. Daniel turned to see Sebastian's sceptical, disbelieving face.

'OK, not very pc, but sorry bro but what's it got to do with you? She's a big girl now.' He paused before flashing Daniel a wicked, childish grin, 'Unless you're in luurve with her?'

Daniel slapped the steering wheel. 'I know she's a big girl ... I know she can do what the hell she likes ... it just pisses me off. Thought I knew her better. Thought she would be the last person to ... you know.' He scowled. 'She knew what it was like for us.'

Sebastian groaned. 'Please tell me you didn't.'

'Didn't what?' snapped Daniel, wondering why Seb always had to be so damn obtuse.

'You didn't go bleating to her about runaway Ma, did you? Blimey, I'm surprised she's ever been friends with you. No wonder you never got to first base with her.'

Daniel stamped his foot on the accelerator and swerved into the fast lane, his jaw tight with concentration. Sometimes his brother didn't deserve a response. He took everything back. The little shit was shallower than a puddle in the Sahara.

Fifteen minutes passed before Sebastian piped up again. Daniel had tuned out his presence focusing on the drive time show on Radio 5.

'So, what's the deal tonight? Who's the boss? Emily or Olivia?'

Daniel's mouth turned down. Good question. Whenever he had spoken to Emily this week he'd had an earful of her woes. He sympathised to an extent, he could understand that Emily felt disappointed that she hadn't got the promotion and felt she'd been a victim of office politics, but, he sighed out loud, after a while you just had to get on with it.

'Whatever you do, don't make a big deal of it. Emily's still a bit sore that Olivia got promoted instead of her. Officially Olivia is the boss ... and God knows she's good at the organisation stuff, I saw the brief she sent over for you, talk about detailed. Just don't let either of them down or I'll never hear the end of it. Emily's desperate to make a good impression with this Miranda woman.'

'Shouldn't be a problem. Miranda's hot ... high maintenance, but I can handle that.'

'So's Olivia these days.'

'Really?'

'Yeah, sounds like the promotion ... has gone to her head a bit.' Daniel shrugged. 'Been giving Emily a really hard time at work. Undermining her, giving orders. And then at home, she's been a bit of a cow, borrowing Emily's stuff without asking.'

Sebastian shrugged. 'And again ... it's not your problem. You've got too much of a damsel in distress complex. Want to rescue them all. You want to look after Emily. Rescue Olivia from herself. You need to ease back, mate.'

Daniel glared at him, knowing he was probably right.

Sebastian gave him a rueful smile. 'But ... I know you. Why don't you just talk to Olivia? Say something to her. Com-muuun-iiicate. Talk to her.' He held up his hands in speech marks. 'Tell her you think she's bang out of order.'

'I want to. Feel I ought to, except I'm not supposed to know.' Even as he said it, Daniel felt like kicking himself. He sounded pathetic.

With a curl of his lips, Sebastian said, 'Tough shit. You do know. You either say something or stop whingeing.'

'Put up or shut up,' said Daniel with a wry smile.

'That's about the size of it.'

'You know for a total idiot you occasionally talk sense.'

He would talk to Olivia. The first chance he got. Have a chat with her. Hell, he had nothing to lose.

'Emily. Stop it,' I said, giggling.

'Can't help it. It's so exciting. Everyone thinks we're famous. Shall I wind down the window and wave?'

'Don't you dare,' I said. Even though I was trying to be blasé about driving through the West End in a chauffeur driven car, Emily's mood was infectious. We were like a pair of overexcited five-year-olds on our way to our first party. Frank, our driver, politely ignored the giggles that erupted every time we caught sight of someone trying to peer in the tinted windows.

I was tempted to tuck into one of the bottles of Cristal champagne in the limo's drinks cabinet. I certainly deserved it but I didn't dare. It didn't bear thinking about if a single drop got spilt on Miranda's outfit.

Between us lay the £10,000 Caroline Crammond dress like an elaborate wedding cake.

Fashion philistine that I was, even I had to admit that the finished design was quite simply stunning. Made from blindingly white silk it was covered in six large, coloured lip prints, all of which were the same size, apart from one over the bottom which was twice as big. The strapless style was floor length and created to wrap around Miranda's perfectly proportioned figure like an elegant glove.

It was unbelievable the amount of angst that had gone into all that simplicity. Should the silk be white, champagne or cream? How many lip prints should be hand-painted onto the fabric? Where should they go? Was the large one over the bum too suggestive or too vulgar? And as for the time it had taken to agree the colours! Should we go for muted shades? Should they all be bright? Coral Kiss, Minx Red, Candy Capers or Peach Pudding – the discussions were endless.

Colourful was definitely the way to describe the dress fittings, whether it was blue for Caroline's language or red for Miranda's temper, I'm not sure. Those sessions were better than *EastEnders*. From the moment Caroline whipped her tape measure around Miranda's waist and uttered the words, 'My, you're deceptively thin', war was declared.

Miranda was absolutely tiny; she made me feel like Gulliver which wasn't helped by Caroline's constant needle-like jibes. 'You'll need to breathe in more to be a size 6.' They constantly tried to outdo each other, name dropping all the celebrities they allegedly knew. Their little black books must have been encyclopaedic

The gilt-buttoned doorman snapped to attention the minute the Mercedes pulled up outside The Grayville. He was at the door fractionally before the car slid to a halt. Emily, completely forgetting herself, gave him her hand regally and, to his credit, he didn't bat an eyelid as he pulled her from the car. It was left to Frank and I to manoeuvre the dress out of the back seat without marring its pristine surface.

Shuffling carefully into reception, Frank at one end of the dress and me at the other, we looked as though we were carrying a body. Emily was at the desk, key card already in hand, a man in a white Nehru jacket and impassive face waiting with her bag.

With its pale wood floors, brilliant white walls and sheer voile drapes, the hotel lobby looked more like an art gallery. Instead of upholstered armchairs and sofas, there were small white leather cubes dotted about in between elongated swirls of aqua-blue glass mounted on marble plinths. The whole effect although chic, was cold and stark.

'There you are, Olivia. We're in room 201,' said Emily coolly, in front of the ice maiden reception staff, two almost identical blondes of exactly the same height, with neat, stylish chignons. They looked as if they'd been hand-picked to ensure that they matched the décor. However when they assured me with ice cool *froideur* that they would ensure the dress was delivered to Miranda's suite, I had every faith in their efficiency.

'Miranda's here. She's already in the suite,' Emily whispered in an excited undertone.

I checked the time. There was a twinge of pain as I twisted my arm to look at the tiny face of my dress watch. Phew, that was a good start. We were due to meet Miranda in her suite along with the stylist, make-up artist and hairdresser at half past five.

Miranda's agent, who at the last minute had turned into a human being, had advised us in weary tones to ignore any temper tantrums and stand for no nonsense.

Emily, bouncing up and down beside me as we made our way to the lift, was asking for the fiftieth time that day, 'Do you think the make-up lady will do my eyes for me?' I was ready to throttle her.

Pulling this evening together over the last two weeks, I'd realised that incompetent didn't begin to describe Emily. At home, in the flat, it didn't matter so much. Forgetting to buy milk and toilet rolls was hardly life threatening.

Unfortunately, being scatty at work was a definite hindrance. I'd given up expecting anything useful from her tonight. As we got in the lift and I slotted in the key card to take us up to the penthouse floor, I decided it would be more useful if I got rid of her for a while.

'Why don't you go and find our room? Start getting ready while I go on up to the suite and see Miranda.'

Uncertainty flitted across Emily's face. I could see she was torn. Should she make the most of the time to get ready? After all, it wasn't everyday she got the chance to mingle with celebrities. Or should she maximise the potential of furthering a friendship with Miranda? They'd become quite chummy on the phone.

'Mind you,' I said with a sigh, chewing my lip and looking at my watch. 'It's going to be tight. Once I've seen to Miranda there won't be that much time to change and tart myself up.'

Emily was out of that lift so fast I could see Road Runner style trails of dust following her. She was probably picturing herself in *Hello!* with the type of photo caption that read, 'Emily Mortimer chatting with George Clooney at last month's A-list premiere'.

Once she was gone, I breathed a small sigh of relief, relishing the quiet of the lift as it slid up to the top floor. The doors opened. This was no man's land – only the rich and famous came this high. Up here the carpet was plush, the deep pile almost drowning my shoes as the heels sank in soundlessly. It was like a layer of snow absorbing any sound. I almost expected a large omnipresent voice to boom, 'And what are you doing here, young lady?'

How stupid. I was a professional career girl, doing my job. I could carry off being on Millionaire's Row. Squaring my shoulders, I raised my chin a centimetre and walked with a long confident stride. On the outside, in my best work suit, I looked the part.

Despite the length of the corridor there were very few doors. The rooms must have been enormous.

I stopped and tapped firmly on one of them, without needing to check the name on the brass plate beside the door.

From inside the room I could hear Miranda, her trademark breathy voice replaced by a fishwife's bark.

Bugger. It was too much to hope that this evening would be plain sailing. I drew myself up – I wasn't going to be intimidated by Miranda. My extra inches serve me well in situations like this. The door was thrown open by the diminutive starlet.

'Oh, it's you,' she snapped, turning her back and walking away without even inviting me in. She was still in full flow haranguing the poor stylist, Nikki. My arrival did nothing to interrupt her.

Astounded, I stared around the room, which was full

of boxes overflowing with every accessory imaginable. Handbags and shoes spilt from one, while jewelled hairslides, satin gloves, watches and even things that looked suspiciously like nipple tassels were piled in others. With that lot I could have opened a bijou boutique on Kensington High Street.

Nikki, the stylist, had come highly recommended, so I wasn't too worried about her ability to hold her own with Miranda. When I'd booked her she sounded eminently sensible and experienced. The other option, suggested by Emily, had been a girl by the name of Flissy Fotherington-Flyde – instinct told me not to pursue that one.

Miranda was holding a pair of the sheerest tights I'd ever seen. They were so amazing they could have been made of fairy wings. However, from the wrinkled moue marring her lips, you'd have thought they were cheesy socks.

'I never wear tights,' she enunciated with great distaste. 'I have to have stockings.' Behind her back Nikki was looking mulish and I wasn't surprised, those tights cost more than I earn in a day.

'They are silk,' urged Nikki, valiantly ignoring Miranda's rudeness.

'I don't care. I am not wearing tights. Find me some stockings.'

'I'm sure we can sort something out,' I said smoothly, taking control and looking at Nikki.

She turned away and I could just hear a muttered, 'Yeah, right.'

'Well, you'll have to,' snapped Miranda pettishly.

'Don't worry. We'll get some,' I said, deliberately dropping my voice lower into what I hoped was a reassuring tone. There was no way that this evening was going to unravel over a pair of damn tights.

'Not some,' drawled Miranda. 'They have to be five denier.' The stylist winced.

I didn't even know you could get five denier stockings. Judging from the look on Nikki's face, dodo feathers would have been easier to find.

'I'm not leaving this room until I have stockings. Do I make myself clear?'

I almost laughed out loud. That last part was definitely a line from one of her scripts. Trying hard not to laugh, I kept up my professional facade by locking my back teeth.

'Apart from that, is everything all right?' I asked in my best smooth tone. It was a bloody stupid thing to ask.

The list was endless and to cap it all her horoscope for the day was an 'utter disaster'. Thank God for that brief stint in a nursery when I was a student. I'd dealt with worse. A room full of four-year olds on e-numbers took some beating. At least Miranda's whinges weren't chemically enhanced. Her body, she'd told me, was a temple to healthy living – that or she'd been told cocaine has calories in it.

During this Nikki had disappeared through to the other room, probably to kick something. Looking round to make sure she was out of earshot, Miranda pulled me over to her side and whispered urgently.

'Look, I really can't wear tights. I get horrendous thrush but I couldn't say that in front of her. Just imagine if it got into the papers. I can trust you.'

I looked down into her earnest blue eyes. For a brief second I felt a connection. Underneath it all she wasn't so different from me, there was a human being in there. I patted her tiny hand. She was so little that I felt like her elephant grandmother.

'Don't worry, I'll go myself as soon as we've got everything sorted – just in case there's anything else you need.' To take her mind off her nether regions, I added. 'You're going to look absolutely gorgeous in that dress, it really is beautiful.'

'Thanks, Olivia.'

I did a double take. It was the first time she'd ever called me by my name. She gave me a smile, the warmth of which disappeared as Nikki reappeared.

Sounding more business-like, Miranda turned to Nikki. 'Right, so what have we got to go with my dress?'

She embraced the magic box of shoes with enthusiasm. Although I'm not surprised, it contained some of the most expensive shoes I'd ever seen. Unfortunately they were all size three.

With a mixture of cajolery, flattery and some downright exaggeration, Nikki persuaded Miranda away from the royal blue Manolo Blahnik shoes. 'Yes, Miranda. They are divine but that style is renowned for creating varicose veins. These, however, are perfect. See how slim your ankles look.'

'Wow, they do. Now I like that necklace.'

'Great taste Miranda but ...'

I sneaked a quick look at Nikki's face. She was perfectly serious which was astonishing considering how hideous the necklace was.

'... Kylie Minogue wore this exact one last night for the closing number of her concert,' said Nikki, holding up an elegant Tiffany choker which was much more tasteful.

'Really?' Miranda's eyes were round as she almost snatched the necklace from Nikki's hand. 'It's amazing.'

It certainly was. The concert took place in Sydney. DHL must be using teleporters these days.

With the arrival of the make-up artist Miranda seemed to relax, her edge softening, as the two of them disappeared into the palatial bedroom next door.

The minute the door closed Nikki threw herself onto the sofa with an exaggerated sigh. 'Why do I do this job?'

'The money's good?' I joked. It wasn't bad, I'd signed off the purchase order for this evening.

'Do you know those tights are like blinking gold dust? Huh, stockings – she's just being a cow,' she moaned.

'Never mind,' I said soothingly. I wasn't going to give Miranda's secrets away, instead I said, 'We'll get her some stockings.'

'Five denier! I don't think so. Selfridges is the only place near here that might have them.' She looked at her watch. 'There's no way I've got time to go there, get Miranda into her dress and do the finishing touches.'

'I'll go. Don't worry. She'll be fine,' I said confidently.

Nikki looked dubious. 'She won't pull out, will she? That's happened to me before.' She named a well-known soap matriarch whose reputation was cast iron salt of the earth. 'Old bat was made up and halfway through the hotel's brandy when she announced that she wouldn't wear the outfit the sponsors of the show had chosen.'

'God, what did you do?' I said, wondering what the hell I'd do if Miranda did that to me. Physical violence would probably be the answer.

'Nothing I could do. She'd made up her mind. Did it out of spite – the producers were in the process of writing her out.'

'I think we'll be all right. It is the Bond premiere and if all else fails; I've got Gerry Finberg up my sleeve.'

'What? Is he going to be there tonight?' Nikki looked impressed.

Mr Finberg, a British film director, was going great guns in Hollywood with three mega-grossing blockbusters under his belt. The likes of Miranda would kill to meet him. I looked down at my feet for a second and then up. 'Hypothetically. He might be.' I gave Nikki a conspiratorial grin. She laughed.

'Nice one.'

We agreed that I would go in search of stockings, as fine as I could find. There was just over an hour and a half before we had to leave the hotel. Slipping out of the room, I raced silently down the corridor back to the lift.

Chapter Eleven

I dived out of the hotel entrance to grab the first available cab.

Talk about tizz. I'd never have time to wash my hair, dry it and get made up. It was no good, I was going to have jump the taxi queue. Naughtily I barged in front of an elderly American couple explaining that I was in a terrible hurry. It was an emergency after all.

'And which hospital will that be, love? Chelsea and Westminster, Queen Charlotte's or St Pinocchio's?' asked the cabby, winking at me through the open window.

Obviously the 'sister-in-labour' fib only worked with gullible tourists.

'Sorry.' I grinned unapologetically. 'It really is an emergency. If I don't get back within the next fifteen minutes bearing the finest pair of stockings known to man, my life won't be worth living and I'll have to go to the ball looking like the fairy godmother abandoned me.' I gave him an expurgated version of the tale.

The minute he heard Miranda's name, he put his foot down. I wasn't sure if it was a Pavlovian response to her name or a desire to help.

'Now, there's a madam. We've had 'er in the back. Tried to tell us we were overcharging. Said we were going the long way round. Refused to pay the full fare. Can you believe it? Bet she earns a fortune 'an all. Don't you worry, love, we'll get you sorted.' I was slightly confused by the 'we'. Were cabs and drivers twosomes?

He swung round in a violent U-turn and I clung onto the strap in the back as the cab sped along. May be the 'we' referred to him and his alter ego, Stirling Moss. In seconds we'd gone from nought to hair-raising and were speeding down rat runs to Selfridges.

Running into the store, I weaved in and out of busy shoppers like a mad Artful Dodger. When I reached the haberdashery department, I accosted a bemused shop assistant, one of those supercilious ones who are groomed to within an inch of their lives.

'Help, I need some stockings – five denier. They're for Miranda Baker for the James Bond film premiere tonight. She's getting ready in her suite now. I've got to be back in ten minutes and if I don't get it right, she says she won't turn up.'

'Don't worry, love. Got just the thing.'

She marched off purposefully and I followed her up to the next floor, down one aisle and another into the lingerie section. The prices I glimpsed on the tags made me wince. How could so little cost so much?

'What you want are hold-ups.'

'Honest?' I looked unsure. 'I used to wear those when I was sixteen, and even on my stick-insect legs they left bright red marks and cut off the circulation.'

'The Lycra's very forgiving nowadays. These are the ones you need.' She leaned closer and quietly said, 'We keep this make specially. No one's ever heard of them – just tell her they were imported for Madonna. Works every time.'

'You've done this before then?' I asked her, grinning.

She winked at me. 'This is our best-selling line, love. Just tell her to keep schtum, as Madonna doesn't know the order's arrived yet.'

Thrusting a twenty pound note at the cabbie who had waited for me, with a 'keep the change', I hurtled out of the cab, crossing the foyer at sprint speed. Just as I was about to get into the lift, my mobile rang. Smiling apologetically at a very gorgeous man in a beautifully cut suit, I stepped back out of the lift to take the call.

It was Kate.

'This had better be good. I've just missed sharing a lift with Mr Drop-Dead-Delicious to answer this.'

'More fool you then. I thought you were meeting up with James Bond tonight,' said Kate crisply.

'In my dreams. I'm working. I doubt I'll get very near him.'

'Work?' she sniffed. 'You call that work. Huh. I don't think so. You try working with white-van-man. I really earned every penny. You bloody get paid for swanning about.'

'You're kidding—'

'Dressing up and going to a mega-star party – break out in a sweat, do you? Real work is when the phone never stops ringing, the paperwork is piling up and you're ten deep in plumbers wanting U-bends and copper piping.'

'They all loved you. It can't have been so bad, you certainly lasted longer there tha—'

'Lasted? Thanks a bunch.'

Oops, I had touched a raw nerve. I pressed the lift button and looked at my watch anxiously. Time was running out, only fifty minutes for me to get ready.

'I didn't mean that. You know Bill raved about how good you were. Said you had all those plumbers eating out of your hand and they were getting tons more work because you were designing the bathrooms for them.'

'But it's hardly a job to shout about is it?' There was an unexpected trace of self-pity in her voice. 'Selling a bath waste to a plumber who once worked in a house owned by the Prime Minister doesn't quite compare with going to a James Bond premiere.'

'Honestly, Kate, it isn't glamorous at all. Miranda is a pain to deal with, you don't—'

But Kate didn't want to know. 'Any chance you could

smuggle me in? I came up for lunch today, so I thought I'd hang around and see if I spot you coming down the old red carpet. What time does it all start? Couldn't you slip me in the back entrance?'

'No. Fort Knox has nothing on this.' The lift was back but the plaintive note in her voice made me loathe to hurry her off.

'Sure?' she pleaded.

'Sure.'

'Worth a try. So what time will you be there? At least I can take a pic of my "glam" sister.'

'Officially the premiere starts at eight p.m., but we have to be on the red carpet at seven ten precisely.'

'Precisely, eh?' mimicked Kate. 'Look out for me. Give me a wave. In fact, come over and say hello. Everyone will think you're famous and I can tell them all I'm your more successful sister.'

I laughed. 'Go on then.'

'What are you wearing?'

Oh bugger, I didn't want to tell her.

'Your ... pale blue silk shift dress.'

'Great! My clothes are having a better time than I am. At least you aren't wearing my Armani. That really would have been rubbing it in.'

'Sorry, Kate,' I said wincing. 'You did leave them with me. The blue is the only one that hides the dressing on my arm.' Again I looked at my watch. I was running out of time to get changed.

'You'll look gorgeous in that,' she conceded. 'More your colour than mine. Have a great time. I'll be watching.'

Feeling relieved that she'd finally hung up, I tucked my phone back into my bag. Nice that I'd have one fan in the crowd. Damn, I looked at my watch yet again. Forty-five minutes. I still had to get myself dolled-up. Of course now there was no sign of a lift. Worried about time, I decided to take the stairs and according to the light above my head, the lift was still on floor six. The best thing would be to go straight to my room and hand over the stockings to Emily to take to Miranda.

For a horrible moment I thought it was Daniel coming towards me as I rounded the corner of the corridor to my room.

'Sebastian,' I greeted him.

'Livvy, love,' drawled Sebastian, swooping in to give me a kiss and a big hug. 'Long time no see.'

'Sorry,' I said stepping back. 'I'm a bit ... hot.' Understatement of the century but there was no way I was going to add 'sweaty' to this vision in a black tuxedo, who at that moment could have out-Bonded Bond himself.

He gave me a mischievous knowing grin. He looked so like Daniel, but that was where the resemblance ended.

'Think you need a nice, cool shower.' Those eyebrows danced again, the inference clear. 'What's got you all hot and bothered?' His voice dropped a tone. Flirting came as naturally to him as breathing.

'Last minute aerobics class,' I said acidly. 'I've just run up the stairs.'

He tutted and shook his head. 'I can think of much better exercise.' He gave me a naughty wink.

'Sebastian, you don't get any better.' I laughed at him. 'You'd best behave with Miranda! Have you met her yet? She'll eat you for breakfast.'

With great exaggeration, Sebastian widened his eyes. 'You think so?'

'Probably not.' I sighed. Had this been such a good idea?

'I'm just on my way up to the suite to meet her.'

'OK. You go on up and be good!'

He playfully tugged at one of my curls. 'Don't worry. Duty calls. I promise to behave. Anyway, Daniel's already given me strict instructions not to let you down.'

'Did he?' I was startled for a second and then realised Sebastian probably meant 'you' as in the general universe rather than me specifically.

'Yup. Big brother is watching me.' He mimicked Daniel's voice. 'Don't screw about tonight. Olivia's worked her socks off for this. Which reminds me.' He sauntered over to the lift and pressed the button. 'First rule of the professional. Punctuality. Must be off.'

The bloody doors opened immediately, he stepped inside and they slid closed on him blowing extravagant kisses.

Shaking my head, smiling, I set off down the corridor. There was something infectious about Sebastian. He'd have Miranda tamed within minutes.

'Cutting it fine, aren't you?' said Emily, as I proudly presented the tissue package to her, the distinctive yellow Selfridges bag stuffed out of sight in my coat pocket.

'Just tell Miranda that these were on special order for Madonna and we managed to swipe one pair before she collects them tomorrow,' I panted.

Emily looked impressed. 'Wow, Olivia.'

I wasn't going to tell her the whole truth, not when Daniel was standing behind her looking impressed by my efficiency.

'Some of us have been working!' I snapped as I took in her beautifully applied make-up, artfully piled-up hair and shiny nails, forgetting that I'd sent her to get ready.

'Finding it tough being the boss?' asked Daniel appearing from behind Emily, one eyebrow raised in amusement.

My heart lifted and sank at the same time. What was he doing here? Didn't I have enough to contend with?

Chapter Twelve

Is it possible to register dismay and delight on your face at the same time? My cheeks must have looked as if they were practising for rigor mortis. Daniel was the last person I expected or, in my frazzled state, wanted to see. There he was standing beside Emily, next to who I looked like a bag lady.

'Daniel,' I said in a strangled voice. 'I didn't expect to see you here?'

'Chief chauffeur,' he said, with a teasing raise of his brows. 'There was a problem with the trains so I drove Sebastian up. Otherwise you'd be without his services this evening. Thought I could nip out for a quick burger and catch some football on Sky somewhere while he was working and then take him home.'

My heart did that annoying little lift, which my head slapped down quickly as Emily laid a proprietary hand on his arm.

'Hope you won't be bored, as we'll all be at the premiere,' she said, flirtatious as ever and then turning to me said officiously, 'I've sent Sebastian up to see Miranda and introduce himself.'

'Don't you think you should have gone up with him?' I asked, a little bit miffed. It was all very well for her to be entertaining Daniel in our hotel room, but she seemed to have forgotten that she was here to work and that I might want to get ready.

'I'm on the way, bossy,' said Emily, smiling at Daniel and adding, 'She does fuss so.'

I gritted my teeth. The cow. She was making me look like some power-hungry bitch. I was fuming but didn't want to lose it in front of Daniel. He really would think I was an old harpy.

Trying to sound sweet and reasonable, when I all wanted to do was scream at her, I managed, 'Give her the blessed stockings and just generally make sure she's happy.'

I was going to have to leave it at that. Tonight was a big deal for the company, the Luscious Lips account was worth a lot of money and we couldn't afford for anything to go wrong. Sadly, I really didn't trust Emily.

'Make sure she's on target for our departure time. No last minute panics or tantrums. We must leave at quarter to seven to allow for the traffic and be ready at the carpet point no later than seven ten.'

'Yeah, yeah. I know, if we miss our slot blah, blah, blah.'

I wasn't being anal. Didn't she realise these premieres were run with precision timing? The schedule was everything. Air traffic control had nothing on this. Arrival slots were allocated according to celebrity ranking – if you missed yours you could kiss goodbye to the red carpet. You'd have to circle around the block for an hour before being allowed to arrive at the tradesman's entrance alongside the set designer's mother.

I glared at her. 'Some of us need to get ready,' I snarled, grabbing my make-up bag and pushing past Daniel into the bathroom, slamming the door behind me.

Inside I glared at myself in the mirror. My hair was doing a Medusa impression and after my mad dash across town I was looking very hot and bothered. I wanted to bash my head against the door. Bugger, bugger, bugger. Just once it would have been nice for me to look glamorous. There wasn't even time to take a bath, so I stripped off and took a quick shower. The minute I stepped out I realised I'd left my underwear in the room.

It never occurred to me that anyone would still be in there. Thank God I'd wrapped myself in a bath towel.

I let out a surprised shriek. Talk about heaven and hell. Daniel looked up. Lounging on the bed reading the paper, he'd made himself completely at home, discarded tie flung on the chair, shirt open at the neck and suit jacket hanging on the back of the door.

'Want me to scrub your ...' His grin dimmed as he registered my half-dressed state.

'What are you still doing here?' I snapped.

'My we're a bit snitty this evening. Not what it's cracked up to be, being the boss? Or are you expecting someone else?' he asked, the smile gone. What was it with him and his someone elses?

'I just wasn't expecting anyone to be here. And don't call me "the boss". I'm just doing my job.'

'Not letting it go to your head?' he asked, one eyebrow quirking. It wasn't said in a joking tone, so I knew a little bird had been whispering in his ear.

'No,' I retorted just a bit too defensively. 'Surely you know me well enough. Do you really think that running around after celebrities, sorting out designer dresses is my thing? There are days when I long for my wellies and hard hat. I even miss Jabba.'

'Who?'

'It's a long story,' I said, shaking my head.

'I'm not going anywhere for a while,' he looked sympathetic for a second.

'Aren't you?' I said with dismay.

'It's all right, I'll turn my back if you want. I told you I'm Sebastian's chaperone. Emily said you'd got the room for the evening and that I could wait here until you leave and then I'll snag a lift and go watch with the crowds.'

Did she now? Great – so now I had to get ready in a bathroom the size of a rabbit hutch and hide in there until I could take my Carmen rollers out. Not a look I wanted to parade in front of Daniel, although at the moment his eyes did seem quite fascinated by my legs.

I sidled past him, clutching the towel and rifled one handed in my overnight bag. A sensible person would have stopped and opened it properly instead of trying to retrieve everything through the half-fastened zip.

But I wasn't thinking straight. Of course I managed to knock the bag on the floor, which meant struggling to hang on to my towel, as I bent down demurely so as not to flash my bottom at Daniel. Sneaking a peep at him, I caught him trying to hide his amusement.

'Want a hand?' he asked, raising his eyebrows.

I was going to have to admit defeat otherwise my towel would be joining my belongings on the floor.

'Thank you,' I muttered, avoiding his eye.

'How is your arm?' He nodded at the white dressing on the arm I had clenched to my side, holding the towel in place.

'OK,' I said stiffly. 'Just a bit awkward, now and then.'

'I can see that?' He nodded gravely, his lips twitching. 'Let's see, what are you after?'

I blushed scarlet. He was enjoying this.

'Knickers and bra,' I said red-faced, trying to keep my cool. This was Daniel. We were old friends, I could handle this.

He slid off the bed, right beside me. We were thigh to thigh. He bent down, righting the bag and opening it up properly. If I'd done that in the first place I wouldn't be in this predicament. From the bag he withdrew my bra and went back for a second rummage to produce a matching satin thong.

'Nice,' he said, handing them to me. The gesture immediately reminded me of those leopard print pants. 'Reminds me of the old days ... I'd forgotten this side of you, Olivia.'

'Thank you,' I said firmly, feeling my cheeks fire up as I snatched them from him and dived back in the bathroom. From the other side of the door, I heard a suppressed snort.

'I'm glad you think it's funny,' I yelled, peering round the door glaring at him. 'Why don't you bugger off so that I can get ready in peace?'

'Sorry, Olivia,' he said, his eyes twinkling. 'I was just teasing you. We're mates, remember. You go ahead. Pretend I'm not here. I'll just read my paper until you're ready. And then … I …' His face went serious as if he were about to say something.

He could forget it. Mates eh? Huh! I slammed the door. Pretend he's not there – in a room that size when he's just been fondling my underwear. I'd almost dissolved into a puddle of lust as those warm fingers had brushed my bare shoulders when he leant down to get to my bag. He hadn't as much as twitched. Obviously totally unmoved.

Couldn't he see my pulse about to jump out of my neck? I could have died when he smoothed out my satin bra, stroking the tiny blue bow, before he handed it to me. Please don't let him have seen the double AA label. If Emily's size was anything to go by, he was definitely a boob man.

I pulled a face at my reflection as I unscrewed the top of my foundation and winced as my elbow bashed the towel rail. Dropping the lid, I then bashed my head on the sink while bending down to pick it up. This bathroom really was too small. Bugger. I'd left my dress in the room. It just wasn't my day.

Something flipped. Bloody Daniel. Hogging the room and reading his paper. Completely oblivious to me. Good old Olivia, she doesn't mind. Why didn't he just go away instead of sitting there in comfort while I had to get ready in a room the size of a bloody broom cupboard?

Catching sight of myself in the mirror – flawless make-up, hair cascading in artfully dishevelled curls and in my best underwear, an inner imp urged me on. Mates eh? Not anymore? Forget it. I was sick of him and Emily meeting up with mutual friends and not inviting me. Mates didn't behave like that. He couldn't have it both ways.

Sucking in my tummy, I strolled out of the bathroom as if I didn't have a care in the world. I smiled sweetly at Daniel as I crossed to the wardrobe wearing nothing but scraps of pale blue satin and lace. Turning sideways onto him, I picked up my dress, held it up for a second and out of the corner of my eye took a quick look.

Gotcha! Daniel's face was a picture. He did a discreet but unmistakable double take.

Nonchalantly, I slid the pale blue dress off its hanger and stepped into it. In the mirror I could see Daniel watching as I shimmied into the fitted sheath. I think something in my body had short-circuited, my hormones were simmering.

'Daniel, as you're still hanging around, would you mind doing my zip? It's a bit tricky with my arm at the moment.' I turned my back to him, inviting him to do me up.

He gave a strangled, 'Yes' and came over. His fingers brushed my back as he drew the sides of the dress together to draw up the fastener before slipping under my hair to push it out of the way. As his palm grazed my neck, my insides shimmered with tiny electrical charges, a thousand volts fizzing down my spine. Maybe this wasn't such a good idea after all.

But that little imp had taken hold. No sooner had he let go of my hair, I stepped away to slip my feet into very high-heeled shoes and turned, cocking my head up at him. 'How do I look?' I asked, giving him a knowing smile.

Seeing him swallow nervously was worth every bit of frustration sizzling through my veins. That would teach him. Unfortunately I'd learnt a lesson too. You got burnt playing with fire.

We both jumped when the phone rang. Thank God for divine intervention because I didn't have a clue what to say next.

* * *

For over a week the gilt-edged card had sat on the mantelpiece in the flat. Card. Singular, with the words, 'Admits One', typed in the right hand corner. Gilt-edged card where 'Admits One' means exactly that.

The man mountain at the entrance to the red carpet was immovable; I would have done well to learn from his impassive resistance.

If not once, but three million times, I'd asked Emily to double check with the organisers that we didn't need an additional ticket.

'No, no,' she'd blithely assured me as if I was some neurotic windbag. Anxious not to turn into Fiona, I'd foolishly believed her. Now standing here, with only a fifty-fifty chance of going to the ball, corralled in the waiting area with a couple of lesser known actresses from *Hollyoaks*, I wished with all my heart that I could summon up some of that single-minded self-preservation which Kate and Fiona wore like a second skin.

Did I pull rank when both of us were denied entry? I should have done but as Emily's face crumpled, the fantasy of being in *Hello!* going up in a puff of smoke, I uttered the fateful words, 'You go, Emily.'

She didn't even say 'Are you sure?' Admittedly, she did gasp a tearful, 'Thanks so much, Olivia. I won't forget this.'

As if I had a choice. I had to let her go. Everyone knew she was the magazine addict and a walking-talking mine of celebrity gossip. Not only would she have been devastated, but what kind of jumped-up cow would I have looked if I'd insisted on going?

It looked like I was going to be joining all the star-spotters and well-wishers filling Leicester Square, hoping for a glimpse of 007. Which reminded me, somewhere beyond the crash barriers forming a wide corridor leading up to the front of the cinema, Kate was looking out for me.

I glanced around. At regular intervals, black-clad security personnel manned the metal railings, like trees lining the avenue of a stately home. Each wore sunglasses like a badge of office along with CIA earpieces.

When there's a premiere on the news, it all looks so calm and serene, smiling, white-toothed stars sauntering along, waving and nodding. The reality was chaos, which the cameras don't show, with entourages of bodyguards and minders edgily keeping their charges moving, their dark eyes constantly roving. They reminded me of sharks circling, beadily watching their prey.

'You're going to have to move. No ticket, no entry,' said one of the organisers, earnestly clutching a clipboard, the walkie-talkie at her hip issuing staccato gunfire voices, muffled and unintelligible.

'Just making sure my client got off OK,' I said, bristling at her officiousness.

'Sorry, thought you were a ...' She thought better of finishing the sentence.

I glanced back up towards the cinema. Sebastian and Miranda were still in view, their red carpet moment captured by a thousand flash bulbs. They made a stunning couple, his bow tie matching the big red kiss on her bottom perfectly. Miranda was happily signing autographs to the lucky few, smiling adoringly at Sebastian and he was playing his part to perfection, rakish and handsome, smiling in return at her.

You could almost believe they were a pair. I should have been relieved – mission accomplished. The press had got their pictures; we'd primed them about the dress. Job done. The rest of the evening was celebrity-sitting. I winced. I prayed to God Emily wouldn't muck it up.

Wistfully, I took one last look down the red carpet. I could see the film another day. It was my own fault, all that cynicism about celebrities coming home to roost – hey, so what if I didn't meet Daniel Craig? He was probably dead boring in the flesh.

Cinderella is my favourite fairy tale, the ultimate romance. Of course, she has to scrub a few hearths on the way but it turns out all right in the end. Watching Emily sashay down the red carpet while I went back to the car drop off point, hoping Frank the Mercedes driver might still be there, was a real hearth moment. The problem was, I didn't believe in fairy godmothers. I pulled a face, watching her disappear without a backward glance. Luckily Frank was still jammed into the traffic and at my frantic waving, opened the door for me, ignoring an officious chap who was jumping up and down, waving a clipboard at us, screaming, 'This is a no waiting area, we're backing up, you need to move now.'

'Come on, Cinders. I'll take you back to your hotel.' Frank ushered me into the car, shutting the door crisply, before stepping back deliberately squashing Mr Clipboard's toes.

The journey back was quieter than the one there; the rustle of Miranda's dress was missing, along with the electric current of palpable excitement that had run around the car. I sniffed forlornly, gazing round at the leather seats. A cloud of perfume still lingered, the heady overpowering notes of Miranda's Samsara and underneath the gentler lemon fragrance of Daniel's aftershave. He'd snagged a lift with us, in search of some sports bar just off Leicester Square. The car was a luxury really, as it was only a five-minute walk. Nobody had minded the squeeze, as legs and feet were tangled like computer cables on the floor. Miranda had even said, 'Isn't this cosy?' as she surreptitiously rubbed her leg up and down Daniel's.

'Yes,' gushed Emily, oblivious to what she was up to.

'Would you like a bit more room?' asked Daniel, shuffling closer to me, away from Miranda. The heat of his thigh against the thin silk of my dress made me even more conscious of him.

Nobody had noticed that we were doing our utmost not to look at each other. My bravado had done a runner after my little floor show. The timely phone call had been Emily saying that Miranda was all set to go.

Now in the empty car, the waves of giddy anticipation long gone, I felt bereft. What was I going to do now? I had a whole evening to myself. My feet tapped irritably as we trailed along, through the clogged roads. It would have been quicker on foot, and inside the car I felt as if I was trapped in slow motion.

When Frank deposited me back at the front of The Grayville, I slunk out, keeping my head down. Less than half an hour ago we'd departed in a triumphant procession of colour and verve. As I got out, Frank slipped me a bottle of Cristal – perhaps I would down the whole lot.

'Fancy dinner? There'll be a meal in the kitchens for the drivers. Always good grub here. You can join us.' It was kind of him but both of us knew that I would be lousy company.

I was suffering a post-euphoric hangover. The evening's miasma of emotion, the excitement of seeing everything come together, the pleasure of getting ready for the party, not to mention the stimulation of something else – had eddied into a black cloud of depression. Stealing through the foyer to the lifts, I prayed that no one who'd seen the three-ringed circus depart would still be around.

As I balefully eyed the key slot for the magic penthouse floor, a delightful thought came to me, as my fingers closed over the key card in my bag. I smiled wickedly to myself. The imp was back. This morning Miranda had asked for a car back to Surrey tonight. I'd been livid. I'd hired the most expensive bloody changing room in London – The Grayville was not the sort of place that let you have suites by the hour.

Who could object? The suite had been paid for and I knew just the person who would get a kick out of it.

She answered my call immediately.

'Hi Olivia, where are you? I've seen Emily ... and you'll never believe this, I've just had the strangest conversation with someone.'

'Long story. I'm back at the hotel—'

'When Emily came past, this guy next to me, nudged me and said, "That's my girlfriend." I wouldn't mind but he was quite good-looking, so it wasn't as if he needed to make that sort of stuff up.'

'Probably just some idiot thought she was a celebrity. There are all sorts of weirdos out there. Now ...' I explained the situation to her.

'Be there in ten,' was Kate's delighted response.

Feeling like a naughty schoolgirl I danced down the corridor in anticipation. I was going to enjoy every square inch of that sumptuous suite. I left a note for Emily in her room telling her that I'd see her for breakfast.

Oblivious to the noise of the crowded bar, Daniel picked at the label of the beer bottle. He'd blown the perfect opportunity to speak to Olivia. In fact he had no idea what had just gone on in that hotel room. He'd blown more than speaking to her.

Punching the hard wooden surface in front of him felt like a strong option. What an idiot. It was as if he'd had an out of body experience. He'd vowed to stay out of her way since the night at the hospital and now all he could think about was her smooth skin and the slender body in the flimsiest of silk and satin. The curve of hip bone. The delicate indentation of belly button. Long lean legs. Her slim boyish shape was the antithesis of Emily's voluptuous curves, but all of sudden ten times sexier.

What the hell had just happened back there? He'd missed playful Olivia, the banter that had once been the hallmark of their friendship. How long had it been since he'd seen that wicked, shy smile? It had all come back with one socking great blow bringing pure lust, which had wiped his mind of his plans to talk to her.

He'd been inches from jumping her bones. Forgetting why he was there. He frowned at the damage he'd done to the beer label. This was crazy. Why was sitting down to talk to her proving so damn impossible? That had been the sole reason he'd been hanging around in the hotel room earlier ... and look how well that ended.

The screen above the bar was showing the news, a clip of the premiere. Suddenly aware of the image, he sat up and watched the pictures, abandoning the final shreds of the label. There was Emily waltzing down the red carpet, he'd already seen Seb and Miranda. Where was Olivia? Scanning the picture he looked for a glimpse of her blue dress. Maybe she was out of shot.

He lifted the bottle to his mouth to take an angry swig. He couldn't get her out of his head or the words that he should have said to her back in the hotel room. He knew exactly how he should have played it. Tell her he was worried because he knew what men were like. Given her a male perspective. Made her realise that men took the line of least resistance. Most of them were lazy bastards when it came to relationships, having their cake and eating ...

It was one of those Homer Simpson, slap your own forehead 'doh' moments. His hand froze midway to his mouth as the realisation dawned on him.

Shit, was that really what he'd been doing with Emily? He took a long pull of the beer. This last couple of months. The mouthful of beer soured as he swallowed. It wasn't as if he'd made any promises or talked commitment. But then they'd never really talked much at all about anything that mattered.

He swung his legs off the bar stool and stood up. They'd socialised a lot, meals out, pub visits, shared a bed ... had some, he winced at his own admission, half-hearted sex ... he wasn't that consumed with lust to make a deal of it. It had been too bloody easy – Emily had been easily pleased. Demanding in that she wanted money spent on her, meals, days out ... so easy to do but without much substance behind it.

He finished his warm beer in one last swallow and gave the TV another glance. There was Miranda in the famous dress – he vividly recalled the throwaway words Olivia had made in the car that day when she'd suggested the whole idea to Emily. His brother and Miranda made a handsome couple, chatting and laughing up at each other as if they'd known each other for longer than half an hour.

It looked real. Instant attraction, the right chemistry or a well-honed performance by two professionals?

He had to admit the whole thing had been pulled off brilliantly. Em had bitched like crazy for the last few days about what a slave driver Olivia was, but it had paid off. For all her faults, Olivia was good at what she did.

His phone beeped with a text message. Sebastian. A wry smile crossed his face as he read the text. Stirring it up again. So, there'd been a cock up and Olivia was on her way back to the hotel. Interesting.

Throwing a tenner down, he left the bar. Outside he considered taking a cab and then decided it was excessive. If she'd gone back to the hotel, she'd still be there and besides he wanted to think about what he was going to say to her. With Olivia it was probably best just to get straight to the point.

But what was his point?

'I'm jealous as hell.' His stomach pitched.

Is that what he should say to Olivia? He suddenly realised even if it was the truth, he couldn't say it to her. But it was the truth. He was jealous of this unknown man. Because he and Olivia were friends?

And where did that leave Emily? How could he be jealous of one of her friends, if he was going out with her friend? And that led to the inevitable question, what was he going to do about Emily? She was innocent in all this. Olivia was taking her unhappiness out on her, which wasn't fair or deserved. Poor kid couldn't do a thing right at the moment. He felt a twinge of guilt.

Someone had to tell Olivia she was making a fool of herself. Someone who knew her. Someone who had her best interests at heart.

Entering the suite this time, I closed the door with a firm click, leaning giddily against it. I was queen of the castle. Could one room possibly be worth this amount of money for one night?

It even smelt different up here. Miranda's Samsara was the most recent in a palimpsest of subtle smells, new carpets and leather furniture mixed with Windolene and furniture polish overlaid with liquorice and cigars.

Nikki's boxes had gone. All that was left was the discarded packaging from the stockings and a Hansel and Gretel trail of polystyrene beads. A used glass with 'Minx Red' lipstick smears around the rim was the only other evidence of occupation.

The full-length windows, unfettered by blinds or voile, looked out over the rooftops of London. Nearby I could see the globe atop the London Coliseum and just beyond it the top of Nelson's hat in Trafalgar Square.

I drooled in earnest the minute I pushed open the bathroom door. The rest of the suite was palatial and luxurious in a magazine double-page-spread sort of way. The pillows were plumper than plump, the décor was straight from *Homes & Interiors*, the bed was emperor-sized rather than king and the carpet virtually velvet – it was all stylishly gorgeous. But the bathroom was instant orgasm, the culmination of every one of my Cleopatra fantasies. I clapped my hands to my face in sheer delight, my smile leaking out from beneath my fingers, unable to suppress the squeaks of joy. This was bathroom heaven and you're talking to an aficionado; subdued lighting, black slate, a double-ended bath, a Philippe Starck sink and full-sized expensive toiletries, none of this miniature rubbish. I wouldn't have been surprised if asses' milk poured from the high-spouted tap.

Fresh orchid petals were strewn around the edge of the bath, vivid fuchsia against stark white and black. Bouncy, fluffy towels were piled inches thick on a long wide shelf, from which hung a monogrammed cotton waffle bathrobe. Completing the utter decadence was a flip down plasma TV screen.

I'd definitely be using that bathroom but first I needed an ice bucket and two champagne flutes. Kate and I were going to enjoy this bottle of Cristal.

'I could get used to this,' said Kate, lying full-length on one of the chocolate-brown leather sofas, her head propped up with one arm, clutching a full glass.

'It is rather lovely.' I gazed around looking appreciatively at the gorgeous glass coffee table between us, just one of the many artefacts decorating the room. It was a squat hippo, his small ears, eyes and broad snout rising above a sheet of glass as if it was surfacing in water. Like everything else in the room, it was beautiful.

'I never thought I'd be grateful to Miranda for anything. Here, drink up. I'm a glass ahead.'

To my surprise Kate's glass was still virtually full and then she put it down on the polished table.

'No more, thanks.'

I stared at her flat stomach, her hand hovering protectively above it. Suddenly everything clicked into place. Mood swings. Tiredness. Tummy trouble and Boots. I knew immediately.

'Yes,' she said bitterly. 'I'm pregnant.'

'Really?' My eyes widened. Kate never made mistakes. The first time she applied liquid eyeliner she ended up with perfect Cleopatra doe eyes, unlike me. I looked like a tart who'd been crying for a week. Still gaping at her, I asked what I thought was the obvious question. 'Have you told Greg?'

It was her turn to look startled.

'You know, the father?' My sarcasm was wasted.

Kate's lips twisted. 'He's not the father.'

There was a gaping silence. I couldn't think of a single thing to say. I was astounded. How could she know with such certainty?

'How do you know?' I asked puzzled.

She looked pityingly at me. I was obviously missing something.

'Because,' she paused. 'There is no Greg.'

'What? No Greg. I don't understand.'

'There never was.'

I still looked blank.

'I made him up,' she snapped.

Why? Kate! Of all people. She was the last person who needed to invent boyfriends. Since the age of fifteen she'd been bringing the opposite sex to their knees.

'So,' I asked casually, as casually as I could when I was practically bouncing with agog-ness. 'Who is the father?'

There was a long silence. Kate looked away and picked at

a speck of fluff on her trousers. She swallowed a few times but she still didn't say anything. I waited. Now she turned her attention to the button on the cuff of her jacket.

Then in a very small voice she said, 'Bill,' before bursting into tears.

What! No way. I shook my head, I must have misheard her. Unable to think of a single thing to say, I stared for a moment. How? More to the point, when? And what was she going to do about it? There were so many questions I wanted to ask, I didn't know where to start. Instead, I put my glass down, moved over to sit next to her and held her tight as she rocked back and forth sobbing silently.

'Why didn't you say anything before?' I said, when her sobs finally slowed, smoothing her hair back from her face.

Wiping the tears with the back of her hand, she pulled a face and put her head on my shoulder. 'I thought if I didn't say anything to anyone it would make it less real. Stupid, huh?'

I stared at her waiting for her to go on but not wanting to rush her.

'I suppose you want to know what happened?' Her ribcage lifted and fell with the heavy sigh.

'Only if you want to tell me,' I lied.

It turned out that, despite her earlier denial, she had seen Bill when in he was in Australia. Being a rugby player in Australia was next best to royalty, so he'd been put up in one of the best hotels.

'It was so amazing. The Swarovski crystal fountain in the lobby was incredible and you should have seen the room Bill had. Complimentary everything. Veuve Clicquot champagne, Godiva chocolates, you name it.'

'Wow.'

'I was only going to stop for a quick drink. Say hello, but then he invited me for dinner. And it was so lovely to see him.

I'd forgotten how easy he was to be with. And so English. And the restaurant had a Michelin star.'

It sounded as if she was so homesick and lonely she'd have met him for a Big Mac if he'd asked.

'I went up to his room for a nightcap and … It just felt so good to be held for a change. Someone looking after me. Someone thinking I'm wonderful instead of taking the piss out of my accent and the things I say.' She put her head in her hands, starting to cry again.

I took her hand, squeezing it.

'I didn't want to go back to my place. He was home … and when he kissed me. It felt so right. So I stayed.'

My heart lurched in sympathy. I stroked the back of her hand. 'So what now? How pregnant are you?'

Kate gave me a wry smile. 'Totally.'

We both giggled hysterically.

'Sorry, I …'

'I've done four tests and every time that blue line appears.'

'So, when? I mean how long?'

'Nine weeks.'

Neither of us said anything. I wasn't sure what to ask next. The obvious question was, 'What are you going to do?' but I wasn't sure I wanted the answer.

'Are you going to tell him?' I asked quietly

Kate sniffed, put her head up and stroked her neck thoughtfully. 'There's no point.'

'Kate, whatever you decide to do, you know I'll support you, but don't you think you ought to tell him?'

'What for?'

'He's the father.'

'Olivia, it's the size of a coffee bean, if that. I'm going to have an abortion. In Australia. I've done some research. They do them up to twenty weeks. Anyway Bill won't want to know now.'

I stared at her. Surely, she didn't mean that. 'He might.'

'No, I don't want him to know.'

'But you don't have to go back. Stay here. You can't face this on your own.'

'I have to go back. If I don't Mum and Dad will want to know why.'

'But you can tell them. Come on, they're pretty liberal, hardly the "never–darken–our–door" sort. You know they'd be supportive.'

Her breath exhaled noisily. 'Yeah, and they won't want to know who the father is? Mum will never stop badgering me. The worst thing is they know Bill. They really like him. Knowing my luck they'll tell him or insist I do. He's playing in your bloody Bodgers match next week.'

Shit, I'd forgotten he'd be there. How was I going to face him knowing this?

'But—'

'Olivia. I've made my mind up. I have to ... have an abortion and I don't want him to know.'

'But why not? He's a decent guy. He ought to know.'

'Because ...' she started to cry again

'Because,' I prompted.

'I made a mistake.' She paused, looking at her hands. 'All that time when I worked for him ... I really didn't fancy him. You saw what he was like ... never dressed properly. He ran a bloody plumbers-merchant, for God's sake. That's why I went to Australia. To get away. When I saw him out there, he was just Bill. All those times I'd turned him down. Been rude to him. Ignored him. And he was still prepared to look me up, take me out and look after me. I realised that night ... I'd really missed him.'

'So what's the problem?' It sounded as if she really did feel something for him.

'I panicked.'

'You,' I said.

'Yes. My whole life is a mess. I ended up working with tradesmen who swear like troopers, with a boss who's self-made and would do anything for me. What happened to working in the City and being swept off my feet by a sophisticated banker or lawyer in a Hugo Boss suit? Bill thinks the height of fashion is a pair of Johnnie Boden cords! I thought by going to Australia I'd get away from all that. Make a fresh start.'

'But, Kate, you were good at that job. I thought you enjoyed it.'

'I did. It just wasn't where I thought I'd end up and now it's too late. Bill probably hates me.'

'Why? He spent so long chasing you and then he saw you in Australia.'

'Take it from me. He hates me and even if he doesn't, I don't stand a chance with him now. I've really messed up.'

It turned out that the morning after they'd slept together, Bill thought that they'd got something going but Kate had had too much time in the night to think and in her usual blunt way had quickly disabused him of that idea.

'But you could explain—'

'Olivia. The timing couldn't be worse.'

I stared at her. I was obviously missing something. Her eyes filled with tears again.

'He's just been picked to play rugby for England, hasn't he? All of a sudden he's a big hero. Doing some modelling. A celebrity. So how's it going to look if I roll up and say actually I've changed my mind, I would like to see you and by the way, I'm having your baby?'

I could see her point but I still didn't think going back to Australia was the best plan.

'Couldn't you stay here and have an abortion? Cancel your flight. Don't go back.' A tear began to roll down my cheek.

Kate tightened her mouth and straightened up. 'Olivia, I have to.' She turned and looked at me. 'If I stay any longer someone might realise. Mum's already suspicious. Besides I've got a good job over there. Nice flat. I just need more time to get used to ... you know the culture. But I want you to do something for me.'

'Anything.'

'Don't come to the airport to say goodbye.' She managed a sad smile and with a wet tissue dabbed my tears away. 'I know what you're like. You'll get upset. Give the game away to Mum and Dad.'

'But I won't see you after tonight.' I sniffed. 'You fly the day after tomorrow.'

'Yes, but now I've told you, it's a bit of relief. It's been so—'

The knock at the door startled us both.

'Who?' she asked.

I shrugged my shoulders. I had no idea. Could it be room service? 'I'll get rid of them.'

'I need some tissues. I'll ...' She cocked her head towards the bathroom and disappeared inside as I went to open the door.

Daniel stood there, a tentative smile on his face. With so much emotion swirling around me, for a moment I wanted to hurl myself into his arms and let him take care of me the way he had at the hospital.

'I heard you didn't get in to the premiere. Sebastian texted. Wondered if you wanted...' his voice faltered, and I followed his gaze over my shoulder as it fixed on the pair of champagne flutes on the table. His mouth snapped into a firm straight line and his eyes flashed with sudden emotion.

'You've got company.' He shook his head, a sneer twisting his face. 'I should have realised. I hope he's worth it.' He spat the words and looked me up down.

My mouth flapped feebly, the words completely lost. He looked so furious and disgusted with me, my heart raced. I put my hand out and touched his forearm, to make contact and slow him down.

'Daniel?' My voice wobbled.

He shook my hand off as if it was contaminated and then he wheeled around and stormed off, his long strides eating up the distance back to the lift.

Finally I managed to get my vocal chords back under control. 'Daniel,' I cried. 'Stop. I can …' Even to my ears it sounded a terrible cliché.

Chapter Thirteen

It should have been bliss after the premiere to climb down from 95,000 feet but I couldn't stop worrying about Kate, now back in Australia, and Daniel, who might as well have been.

I phoned and texted him several times. Anxiety at the injustice of not being able to find out what had made him so angry made me sleepless and irritable. It wasn't like him to jump to conclusions or to get so mad without giving someone a chance to explain. I felt aggrieved that he hadn't and still wouldn't talk to me and the more he ignored my attempts at communicating, the angrier I got and the more determined that this was it. I'd had it with his constant about turns.

I certainly wasn't going to say anything to Emily, who happily lapped up the success of the event and the resulting press coverage. It made a very pleasant change for her to be so easy-going. I made the most of it.

The best part of my week was the premiere post-mortem with the happy clients from Beautiful Babes Luscious Lips. They were delighted with all the pictures in the *Sun* and *Mirror* of Miranda and the close-ups of the Minx Red kiss on her bottom. They might have been even happier if we'd been able to show them the five minute slot we got on the BBC news, but someone had forgotten to arrange for it to be recorded.

How many ways can you interpret, 'Please ring the press cuttings agency and make sure they monitor all broadcast coverage'. Unfortunately by the time I realised that Emily had failed to even manage this, it was too late to even resort to BBC iPlayer.

'That went well,' exclaimed Emily, as the client disappeared escorted by David. I glanced at her. She was perfectly serious. No sweaty palms for her then when the client asked where the DVD of the news coverage was. Shaking my head, I started to pack up my desk.

'Well, I've had enough for one week. I'm off. Are you sure you don't want to change your mind and come down with me? Nip back to the flat and get some stuff for the weekend. I don't mind waiting.'

What a total hypocrite. At least making the offer for her to come along made me feel better. Not quite so guilty. She was staying at home by herself while I was heading off for a weekend at home, the big cricket match and to face Daniel. After a lot of heart searching, I knew I needed to make more effort stay away from him. Maybe I should go out and join Kate in Australia. This weekend would be the last event I'd go to where I knew he'd be without Emily. Avoiding him was difficult in the flat, if not impossible, but doable. I would just do social chit chat when I had to and then retreat to my room, making sure I stayed out of his way as much as I could.

Unfortunately there was no way I could back out of the weekend. My family would know something was wrong. I never missed this fixture. It would be a dead giveaway if I didn't go at this late stage.

Emily fidgeted in her seat before looking up at me with a pitying expression on her face. 'Thanks, Olivia, but no thanks. I've got better things to do than play cricket widow.'

It never occurred to me at the time that she really did have 'better things to do'. I thought it was just sour grapes.

'I don't see why I should spend my Saturday making sandwiches for a bunch of blokes I don't even know. Some women might enjoy being a throwback to the fifties, humouring their men – not me. Daniel's welcome to play cricket. His choice, but I'm not giving up my weekend to have the pants bored off me. It's all right for you. You know everyone. You're staying with your family. I'd have to stay at Daniel's and I can't stand his stepmum.'

My guilt pangs curled up and died. They'd done well to survive the snide remarks about cricket groupies and teas that had been tossed my way in the last couple of days. Sod her. I didn't care if she was on her own this weekend.

Heaving my holdall over my shoulder, I was about to leave when David appeared in the office. He didn't say anything but with one finger he beckoned to me. Shit, was I going to be in trouble about the missing BBC coverage? Emily exchanged a quick, nervous glance with me and then shrugged her shoulders, as well she might. It wasn't her problem, was it?

As if I hadn't had enough drama for the week, David's summons to his office was just what I didn't need late on a Friday afternoon. I thought I knew what was coming and was fully expecting a bollocking.

The satisfied grin on his face belied his words. 'I've had a few complaints about you.'

'Really. I'm surprised,' I said coolly. He'd dumped me with the job from hell. If there was any complaining to be done it should be coming from me.

'Miss Emily Mortimer is not very happy with your management skills.'

I frowned at him, that wasn't what I was expecting him to say. Bloody cheek. I wasn't too chuffed with her either.

'Isn't she?' I said grimly, thinking of the missing coverage, the single ticket and her general ineptitude. 'Eleanor Braeburn looked pretty pleased – and she's the client. I'd have thought her opinion counted most. She's the piper after all.'

'Smart girl. That's why I made Fiona give you the job. Eleanor is crapping herself with delight. But don't think you're getting a pay rise out of this.'

'What about a car? After all you pinched mine.' The words just popped out of my mouth. I'm not sure who was more surprised, me at thinking so quickly on my feet for once, or David at my outright gall. He's not used to that. Most people are either so busy tugging their forelocks that they miss the wicked glint in his eye (he does have a very warped sense of humour) or so darn scared of him, he treats them with contempt.

He put his head on one side, studying me. 'Think you deserve one, do you?' he asked, his blue eyes dancing with arrogant mischief as he reclined in his chair, his ankle hooked over his knee.

'Yes I do,' I said, tilting my chin to emphasise that I was taller than him. He pushed himself up. 'Go on then. Speak to HR. I suppose I'm going to have to promote you permanently – which means I do have to give you a bloody pay rise.'

He picked up a small plastic box from the windowsill and tossed it at me.

'You'll need these.'

Typical David. Through the clear plastic lid I could see my name, Olivia Middleton, Account Director. In my head I did a goal scorer's wiggle. One to me.

'By the way, what did you do to upset Emily? You've achieved in two weeks what Fiona's been trying to do for three months.'

I frowned at him, puzzled. There was a letter on his desk, which he picked up and with a flourish he began to read.

'It is with regret that I formally tender my resignation. Since the advent of Olivia Middleton in the role of temporary Account Director, I have found my position totally untenable.'

He tutted, looking sternly at me.

What? Cheeky cow. How many times had I saved her bacon?

David continued. 'Since assuming responsibility for the

team, Olivia has made my working life intolerable with her constant, unfounded criticism and the unremitting undermining of my position in front of other team members.'

I stared at David, my face frozen while my mind raced. Two-faced witch. Five minutes ago in the office she'd given no clue that this was how she felt.

Giving an exaggerated sigh, he shook his head with mock disapproval at me. 'Sadly I have no choice in the circumstances but to terminate my employment with Organic PR.'

He laid the letter on his desk and looked at me. 'What do you have to say for yourself?'

'You don't believe all that,' I started indignantly.

'Noo! Think I'm dense!' He slapped his hand on his desk and cackled with laughter. 'God, she's a pain in the arse. You deserve the car for putting up with the silly cow and not coming moaning to me every five minutes. Bloody Fiona's in here every week. She's—'

'Did you give me this job to piss her off?' I interrupted, clenching one hand behind my back as the pennies and pounds began to drop. My stomach was churning and I felt sick and shaky.

He grinned devilishly. 'It did the trick, well done.' Completely ignoring my outraged glare, his expression changed to one of shrewdness. 'You're a smart girl, Olivia. Luscious Lips pay us a quarter of a million every year – I don't piss about when fees are involved. She's off to another agency. Says she's taking her expertise and ideas where they'll be appreciated. Silly bitch.'

Her ideas. That was rich. Ever since I'd known her she'd been desperate for promotion. Now I knew why it had never happened and why it was unlikely to. I bet she'd taken all the credit for the Luscious Lips campaign to impress the new agency.

'She's on a month's notice. I'll leave it up to you whether she pisses off straight away, or stays for the month. Still have to pay the little madam. Make it bloody clear she won't get a reference if she plays silly buggers.'

With that I was dismissed. He was a wily devil, he knew damn well after reading that little litany that my blood was up but he had just given me carte blanche to do as I pleased.

As I left his office, he growled, 'Just don't tell everyone what a pussycat I am.'

As if.

David might have thought I was a sharp cookie, but he was wrong. The contents of Emily's letter had been a complete surprise. Leaving the top floor, I'd taken the back stairs, very slowly, disbelief running through my head. My hand was shaking so much I could barely grasp the handrail. Any delight at the unexpected promotion was well and truly overshadowed by the tone of Emily's letter. Had I really upset her that much?

By the time I got back to my desk, she'd gone. I had a vague recollection of an arrangement to go to Bar 29 next door for post-work drinks. As the office was virtually empty, I guessed most people had decamped there. No doubt Emily was among them. No one hung around long on Friday evenings. Unfolding the A4 paper, I stared at it, my stomach twisting uncomfortably. The words jumbled up on the page as my eyes ran over the offensive words again and again.

We'd had our ups and downs but they'd always been normal flatmate irritants. Like pinching the last teabag and not buying more, generally her, or using all the hot water, usually me. Although it had been difficult recently, I thought that with the stress of the premiere over we were back on an even keel.

I don't bear grudges. With every fallout we'd ever had,

I was always the first to apologise or smooth things over. I couldn't believe that this was what she really thought of me.

Shaking, I pulled out my phone. Sod the cost, I needed to speak to Kate.

Snatching up my holdall with one hand, my mobile in the other, I headed for the stairs. Pressing buttons as I stumbled down, I never gave a thought to what the time might be on the other side of the world.

She answered as I hit the pavement and the Friday night throng on the street. To get out the way, I ducked into a doorway on the opposite side of the road. From my vantage, I had a complete view of the office, stretching up three floors above the busy street. Waiting for Kate to answer, I eyed the top floor bitterly.

'Kate, it's me,' I said, when she finally answered; I'd had to dial twice.

'Olivia, it's the middle of the night. I've still got jet lag,' she muttered in response, her words blurred by sleep.

I bit my lip, looked anxiously at my watch, and realised it must be about four in the morning there.

'No one's died,' I said, inhaling a sob.

'It had better be good, now that I'm awake. Honestly, Olivia, you are hopeless. You're not still trying to get me to talk to Bill are you?'

'No, it's Emily.'

Stumbling over the words, I told her what had happened. I'm surprised she could understand what I was saying.

'Olivia.' She gave a long sigh. 'It's about time you woke up and smelt the sewage, sweetie.'

That wasn't what I wanted her to say. She was supposed to be on my side. Where was the sympathy?

'I've been telling you for ages. Emily is bad news. You wouldn't have it. Why do you have to always see the best of people, even those that don't deserve it?'

Taken aback, I ventured softly. 'But isn't that better than always seeing the bad?'

'No, it's not. You're too nice. You think everyone is like you – they value honesty and want to do the right thing. Not everyone does.' Her voice was getting louder, as she warmed to the theme. 'People like Emily coast on other people's coat-tails. And yours was a very comfortable ride. Nice flat, great friends, and she even pinched Daniel from under your nose. Easy pickings, thanks very much, Olivia.'

'No ...' I tried to stop her. This was not what I wanted to hear.

'I'm sorry, hon, it's about time you realised she's been using you. Not that I think it was personal. She's a parasite. Latches onto the nearest free meal. It wasn't as if she was that attached to Daniel. He was just handy at the time.'

'It doesn't explain why she had to be so horrible in her letter to David.' That really hurt. Especially all the lies.

'She's just saving face. Anyone that hopeless is never going to get on if they stay put but she couldn't admit it, could she? So you got the blame. Bet she genuinely believes all that guff. Ask yourself, what's Emily ever done for you?'

'She cleaned the flat from top to bottom when I hurt my arm. That was really nice of—'

'I'm not saying she's all bad, but overall she's just not that great. And what about Daniel?'

God she was determined to keep bringing him up, just when I was trying very hard not to think about him any more.

'Don't tell me she didn't know that you liked him.' There was a pause as if she was considering her next words carefully. 'I think she stuck the knife in that night at Ben's birthday party. You told me that one minute Daniel and you were getting on like a house on fire, the next she's waltzed off with him.'

Thanks for sisterly sympathy. Now I felt even worse. Especially when I realised I'd hung up and not asked how she was feeling.

Friday night was hell on the tube. So much for my quick exit from work to beat the rush. David's little meeting and the call with Kate had played havoc with my plans. It was now after six. I felt more like going into the pub and downing a pint of vodka than braving the packed underground.

Feeling bloody miserable, I swung the holdall over my shoulder and I headed reluctantly towards Tottenham Court Road tube and as I did managed to catch the shoulder of a man standing just to the left of the doorway, his eyes focused on the doorway of Bar 29. Turning my head, I offered a fleeting, 'Sorry,' and caught his eye. He looked familiar. Where had I seen him before? Not that I really cared. I was far too pissed off with life, the world, Emily and myself to give it another thought.

Every inch of the concourse at Paddington was packed as I squeezed my way through trying to get to the platform. I only just caught the 6.35, which meant standing nearly all the way to Maidenhead. I was too lost in thought to care and too wedged in to worry.

Kate's words were like merry-go-round ponies spinning, going round and round in my head. I'd always dismissed her views as being typically Kate, overly harsh and disparaging. Grudgingly I could see now that she'd been right. Not in everything but she'd certainly seen more than me.

Looking back, a sense of shame filled me as I thought of all the times I'd let Emily get away with things. So she was inept at work; it wasn't her fault she wasn't as organised as I was. When Fiona gave her a hard time, I'd always sympathised. What I should have done was point out why Fiona gave her a hard time. Now I knew why. Emily was always ready to blame everyone else for her failings. Look how she'd pitched my ideas as her own and got away with it. In a lot of ways, I was as much to blame as she was. I'd never made her face her faults. To keep the peace I'd encouraged her instead of trying to tell her diplomatically that she was the cause of many of her own problems.

I was disappointed as much in myself as in Emily. How could I have failed so badly to see her for what she really was?

I was still brooding when we pulled into West Drayton. Achingly close to Daniel's offices. If she could say all those things in her letter to David, what on earth had she been saying to Daniel?

Getting off the train, I was slightly annoyed there was no welcoming party at the barrier. Where was Dad? He was supposed to chauffeur me home in style in his Jag. It was probably just as well. No doubt he would have asked me what was wrong, given me tons of sympathy and made me feel even more self-pitying.

Wandering past the ticket office and out on to the road, I was hailed by a sudden honking from the beaten-up old Mini parked nearby.

'Ollie, over here!'

'Ben,' I said with surprise. My brother didn't normally get out of bed for anything less than a willowy blonde. 'How much did Dad have to bribe you?'

'Hi, Sis.' He grinned before giving me a big bear hug. I wrestled my bag into the back seat.

'Mum was dropping heavy hints about cleaning the barbecue. You were less hassle, except she wants me to stop off and pick up another barbie on the way back.'

I looked at him and raised my eyebrows. 'Erm, Ben. Just

how do you propose getting a barbecue in here?' I indicated the back seat.

He looked blankly at me. 'Bollocks. Knew I'd forgotten something. I was meant to bring Dad's car.'

Honestly I do wonder about him sometimes. He's about as much use as a chocolate fireguard. The epitome of a dumb blonde. Very cute and sometimes very dopey.

During the summer when his eyebrows and hair turn white blond, he looks just like a Thunderbird puppet. This combined with the surf-boy look he's adopted means that wherever he goes, young impressionable teenagers turn their heads and drool. Not that he would know what to do with a surfboard – I dread to think how much damage he could do with one.

At junior school he was always picked to play Gabriel in every nativity play, until an incident with a black marker pen, a moustache and baby Jesus got him drummed out of the celestial troops.

'Are you sure it won't go in?' he asked, looking puzzled.

'It's a Mini not a bloody Tardis,' I pointed out, my mood beginning to lighten. You could never take anything too seriously with Ben around. He's very easy to be with and at that moment, just what I needed.

'With the best intention in the world – unless it's one of those little portable jobbies …'

Ben's faced screwed up comically. 'No! It's huge. It's Daniel's folks one, you know the one we borrowed last year.'

My heart sank. Five minutes and already his name had to crop up. 'Can't you get him to bring it over tomorrow?'

'Good idea, Sis. He can bring it in the Land Rover. Give him a call.' With that he turned the ignition and slammed into first and tossed his mobile into my lap before wheeling off into the road.

Shit. How did I get out of this one? I tutted and picked up

the phone, my pulse racing. If I refused Ben would only make a big deal of it. I needed to pretend everything was normal and that for some reason Daniel didn't hate me and that he was nothing more than an old mate.

I scrolled through the address book. 'Digger, Five O, Fossil, Foxy, Gasper, Gert ... Don't any of your friends have proper names?' I queried. 'And what's this one, Me?'

'So that I can give people my number. Can't remember it.'

I rolled my eyes and carried on scrolling. I still couldn't find Daniel's name anywhere. 'Ben, it's not here.'

'Five O.'

'Why?'

'Book em, Danno. You know that ancient programme. *Hawaii Five-O*.'

I shook my head. Boy logic, I'd never get it.

Finding the right number, I reluctantly pressed call.

'Ben.'

'I—'

Before I could get a word in, Daniel was saying, 'Make sure you stay off the beer tonight we're relying on your bowling.'

'It's me, Olivia,' I said. For a second I thought the line had gone dead. 'Hello. Are you there?'

There was an empty pause. 'Olivia. Hi. Thought you were Ben.' His tone was clipped.

'No,' I said forcing a cheery note into my voice. Once again he sounded pissed off with me. 'Although I could bowl if you want me to.'

I could almost hear the resigned sigh, as if he felt he had no choice but to talk to me. 'Are you any good? We're desperate.'

'Not that desperate.'

'So where's Ben, why are you using his phone?' His voice held an accusing note.

Ben shot me a questioning look. The last thing I wanted was him picking up on any negative vibes. I had to keep things light. 'He's driving. Allegedly. We've already had several near misses and I've only been in the car five minutes.'

Daniel laughed softly and I felt a hollow ache in my stomach at the sound. Shit I missed him.

'So how many times have you thrown up then?'

'Very funny.'

'Sorry, couldn't resist it. Just arrived?' His voice gentled as he asked, 'How's the arm?'

'It's fine.' My voice went husky at the concern in his. Then I glanced at Ben, who watched me with sharp beady eyes. The little sod didn't miss a trick.

I stuck my tongue out at him. 'Ben met me at the station. Except the half-wit came in the Mini. We're supposed to be picking up your barbie. Is there any chance that you can bring it over on the way to the ground tomorrow morning?'

'Tell him he's bloody useless. I'll ask Dad if I can pinch the Land Rover – we'll probably need the trailer as well as Miriam has done her usual. She thinks she's performing the feeding of the five thousand tomorrow.' I could hear the pride in his voice. His stepmum, Miriam, was an amazing cook.

'I'm in her kitchen now. Every time you open a fridge door you're in danger of being buried alive in chicken drumsticks marinating in stuff.'

I giggled. 'Stuff! Daniel. It's ambrosia.'

There was a grunt and I could hear Miriam berating him in the background.

'I'm about to be beaten around the head with a sausage.'

'Well, give her my love. Are her and your dad coming over to watch tomorrow?'

'Yes, so you can tell them yourself. It's their fifth wedding anniversary this weekend. Bloody embarrassing, they're like love's young dream all the time.'

As he said it, I could hear Miriam's outraged shrieks and teasing threats.

'How about your mob? I heard on the grapevine your dad's been trying to recruit some fast bowlers.'

'We'll all be there, but you know I can't spill team tactics.'

'Excuse me! Where's your loyalty? I don't want any of this family solidarity rubbish. All the young ladies of the parish are supposed to be supporting the good-looking, virile team not the geriatric has-beens.'

I giggled. 'I want to get fed and watered tonight. Dad might withhold my wine ration.'

'If I'd known all it took was a bottle of Jacob's Creek I'd have signed you up as team mascot ages ago. Now there's an idea, we could dress you up to distract the opposition.'

'Dress me up as what?' I asked, my voice squeaking slightly. Ben did a double take, swerving dramatically.

'Now there's a thought.'

Did I detect a slight husky timbre to Daniel's voice?

'How about some cheeky shorts? Get those legs out. That'll get a few pulses racing. You never know their pacemakers might explode.'

His mention of my legs made me blush, remembering when he'd last seen them.

Ben snatched the phone from me. 'I heard that. Think I'm going to be sick. If Olivia gets her kit off that really will sabotage the game.'

I couldn't hear Daniel's response properly.

'Yeah. See you tomorrow, mate.'

The warm fuzzy feeling spreading through my chest dissipated the irritation at being cut off in my prime.

Ben glanced at me suspiciously before sliding the phone into his shirt pocket. 'What's happened to Emily?' he asked slyly.

I looked at him questioningly. He's not normally that quick on the uptake.

'What do you mean?' I asked, jutting out my chin defiantly.

'She's definitely not coming?' he asked, as we careered around a sharp corner.

With my feet wedged firmly into the front well, I jammed myself into my seat wishing he'd keep his eyes on the road. We swerved again. The car was doing sixty down the country lane.

'No,' I said shortly, hanging onto the seat and, through sheer will power, my lunch.

'Oo, have you two fallen out?' he said, in that irritating little brother way.

'Not exactly,' I said dryly. I didn't want to go into details with him, it was too raw and he was the last person I'd confide in. If you can rely on someone to say the wrong thing – it's him. I certainly didn't want anything said to Daniel. I could imagine it all too clearly, something along the lines of 'The girlies have fallen out again'.

'Why isn't she coming? Not that Dan seems that bothered. I did wonder if they were still you know ...' He glanced enquiringly over at me.

'If they're not, it's news to me,' I said brusquely.

His face fell.

Typical, Emily was just his type. I couldn't bear it if she caught her claws into my baby brother. Quickly I added, 'As far as I know, Emily's still dead keen. She just hates cricket. What's Daniel said then?'

'Not a dicky bird. He doesn't say much about her. Just call it my intuition.'

Intuition, I shook my head. Bless him. He wouldn't see a lamp post until he'd walked into it.

'He was asking about you and your fella. Oops, sorry.' He rammed the gears into fourth.

Fella. Hello! What fella? Surely not Ned. I would have asked but the last of the hair-raising turns he was negotiating at top speed was playing havoc with my digestion. It was all I could do to hang onto the contents of my stomach. When we screeched into the gravelled drive, pulling up with an emergency stop scant inches from the bumper of Dad's Jaguar, all I could think about was the relief of being back on dry tarmac.

Chapter Fourteen

Tumbling out of the car, I looked fondly up at the house, with its ancient wisteria curling around the front door. Wellies and trainers littered the large porch and I picked my way through them as I hurried into the house pushing open the door, yelling, 'Hello. We're home.'

Heading straight to the kitchen, kicking off my shoes as I went, I padded across the parquet floor past the wide staircase. We'd lived in this house for as long as I could remember and at this time of day I was guaranteed to find my parents in the kitchen.

I paused in the doorway enjoying the familiar sight of Mum sitting at the huge pine table with a glass of wine peering at the *Telegraph* crossword, with Dad reading the sports section, a half pint glass of his favourite bitter in hand.

Mum pushed her glasses onto the top of head. 'Hello, darling. Good trip?'

Enveloped in her arms I breathed in her familiar Rive Gauche scent.

'Hi, Mum.' I relaxed into the hug. She squeezed me tight.

I leaned over and kissed Dad on the top of his bald head.

'Hi, Sweetie,' he said. 'How are you?'

Mum immediately grabbed me a glass, and without asking poured me a generous slug of wine.

'John, have you eaten all those crisps already?' She tutted affectionately. He blinked with surprise at the empty bowl, giving the room a perplexed once over as if to check that some alien hadn't sneaked in and pinched them all. Dad was a crisp monster. Every night, except for the first few weeks in January – his official post-Christmas diet detox – there would be nibbles on the kitchen table which he would absently hoover up, hand on the paper propped against the table, the other making regular forays to a misshapen home-made bowl. Mum kept all of her pottery disasters.

Taking an eager sip of wine, I sank into the padded cushion on my seat at the table. My place was laid, complete with my own napkin ring, an ornate O engraved into the silver. We all had our own napkin rings, each one different, collected over the years by Mum's incessant foraging at flea markets and antique shops. I was lucky to have an O, Kate's was a C. As a child learning to read this had confused her no end, but Mum said it was the closest she could find. Placid Ben never questioned the W on his.

'Ah, bliss. I love Friday nights,' I said, taking another slurp of wine.

'So how's work? Kate said you were so busy on a new account.'

At the sound of Kate's name I immediately felt guilty and prayed I looked innocent as I enthusiastically told Mum about my promotion.

'Well done, darling. A car as well. That's great isn't it, John?' She prodded Dad who was hidden behind his paper.

He peered over the top. 'What, dear?'

Rolling her eyes she turned back to me. 'I'll be glad when this cricket match is over and I get a bit of sense out of him. He's been on the phone all week, pestering poor Daniel. Stop that, John.' She slapped Dad's hand away, which was now stealing nuts from my little bowl. 'You'll never get into your whites if you keep that up.'

'No, dear.'

I laughed. 'Team's all sorted then, Dad?'

'Yes, dear. Your Daniel has been very efficient and organised. '

'Dad, he's not my Daniel. He's just a friend. He's going out with Emily. Remember, my flatmate.'

Mum snorted and I glared at her. What had Kate been saying to her about Emily? Dad hid behind the paper again. I was far too knackered and dispirited to tell Mum the full story about the resignation note tonight, even though I knew I'd get bucket loads of sympathy and maternal indignation.

'So,' piped up Mum. 'Have you spoken to Lucy since the wedding?'

'Yes, briefly. She told me some hilarious stories. Apparently her mother-in-law was being so vile in the lead up to the big day, that Lucy was having second thoughts. Turned out she'd misplaced her HRT pills that week, and she did actually apologise the day before the wedding, so Lucy decided she would turn up after all.'

'Poor woman,' Mum said with feeling. Dad muttered something under his breath. Mum glared at him over her half-moon specs.

'John, go and see if the pizza is done yet,' she barked at Dad before continuing to me. 'I can't complain. I sailed through the menopause – it was those tablets from Harmony.'

Mum had great faith in tablets from the local health food shop and she was always pressing them on me. I wouldn't mind, but most of them were the size of horse pills and the last lot she'd given me had made my wee bright yellow.

'Well, it's a shame they haven't given you any tablets for senility – you haven't switched the oven on,' Dad chortled. He gave her an affectionate squeeze and turned on the oven.

'With all those crisps you've eaten you won't starve. While you're up, bring some more nuts over for Olivia. She must be hungry.'

I didn't like to confess about the small matter of a king-sized Mars bar that I'd happily munched on the train on the way here.

'How did it go with Kate at the airport?' I asked idly, deliberately not letting on I'd spoken to her earlier.

Mum groaned, 'The usual torture. Every alarm clock in the house had to be set as well as your father's mobile phone. We have to leave it in the garden shed every night.'

'Why?' I asked.

'Because we haven't a clue how to switch the alarm off. It beeps every morning at four-thirty. In fact, John, you might as well go and put it out now, otherwise we'll forget later.'

This was typical. My family are complete Luddites.

'Why don't you read the manual or ask Ben?' I asked. Mum looked blankly at me. Neither had occurred to her. 'Hand it over. Let's have a look.'

Reprogramming the phone, I handed it back.

'So did she get upgraded again?'

It was a standing joke. Kate always got up impossibly early before a flight, not because she was worried about missing it but because she was convinced that appearing at the check-in desk immaculately groomed and accessorised would secure her a place in business class.

'Yes she did but you can't tell her it's pure fluke and most likely because she's travelling solo. She insists it's because she looks the part.'

I smiled. The biggest irony was that Kate's much-loved Louis Vuitton luggage probably cost more than a first class return to Australia.

'She said your date went well.'

I looked startled. That was news to me. Kate must have been talking to Barney again. 'She did, did she?'

'Kate says this chap is very nice,' said Mum, full of confidence, quoting the gospel according to my sister. 'Barney thinks he is very smitten.'

'Really? Maybe we're going on another date – I must ask Barney and Kate what they've arranged,' I said sarcastically.

'Oh dear ...' Mum looked worried. 'Is Barney being a bit ...' she trailed off.

Barney was being a lot … but I didn't expect anything else of him. 'It's all right, Mum. I've been out twice with Ned. He's nice enough but I'm not really interested.'

'Twice, that's not … You could give him another chance.'

'I am. We're going to see a football match next week.'

'Football, you!' said Dad, looking up in surprise.

I shrugged. 'Got to try new things. Thought I'd give it a whirl. We're going to the Emirates Stadium to see—'

'You're going to see Arsenal.' Dad's face had the same meaty bone expression as Gram and Midge's.

'So you do you like him then?' chipped in Mum.

'I don't know. The timing's not been great, what with my arm and—'

'Sweetheart,' she cried. 'How is it? Let me have a look.'

Mum was an alternative health and wholefood freak, so we'd grown up on a diet of lentils and pearl barley. Peeling off the dressing, I resigned myself to Mum's experimental prodding.

'Vitamin E oil. That's what you need.' She stood up and crossed the kitchen to the medicine cupboard, which Dad referred to as 'Mrs Quack's Cure-All Medicine Trunk'. I could hear bottles clinking as she rummaged.

'I'm sure I've got some from the time your father stood on the bread knife.' When she disapproved he always became my father.

Poor Dad rolled his eyes.

'I didn't stand on the bread knife.'

'Really, dear. So how did you get stabbed in the heel?'

'My foot slipped on the knife block when I was painting the ceiling.'

Mum tutted. 'Serves you right. You should have used the decorating stool instead of clambering all over my kitchen units.'

'Yes, dear.' Dad sighed winking at me.

There was a triumphant squawk. 'I knew I had some. Come here, Olivia. We'll do it over the sink. It's messy stuff.'

Arguing with her would have been totally pointless. If it came from the health food shop, it was a magic elixir. The minute she took the lid off the small glass bottle, the smell almost overpowered me; a combination of rotting mushrooms and seaweed.

'That smells awful, Mum,' I complained, screwing my face up as she massaged the oil around the wound.

'Do you want a nasty scar? This will help it heal. Trust me, I'm not a doctor.'

'I know that,' I said teasing her, but Mum's attention was elsewhere.

She has bat ears, probably due to years of listening out to make sure Kate, Ben and I all got home safely in our teenage years. 'John, there's someone at the door.'

Bloody hell. It was Bill. Could my life get any more complicated?

'Hello, Mrs M. Hope you don't mind me popping in?' Bill said with a grin, as he ambled in to give Mum a kiss on each cheek. He is the sort of person you can take anywhere and from Mum's point of view, perfect potential son-in-law material.

'Don't be silly. It's always lovely to see you, but I'm afraid you've missed Kate. She's gone back.'

I shot a sharp glance at Bill but his gaze over the top of Mum's head was completely innocent. Too innocent.

'No, no. I ... em ... thought she'd probably gone back. No. I was passing. Yes, just passing. Thought I could, you know, save a phone call.' He turned to Dad. 'What er ... yes ... er what time does the game start tomorrow?'

I turned back to the sink to hide my face. Poor Bill. He was so sweet. Although sweet probably isn't the word most people would use for someone verging on six foot five, with the breadth to match.

'Hello, Olivia,' he said, suddenly acknowledging me. 'Sorry didn't see you there.'

No because you were too busy looking for Kate I thought, smiling at him.

'How are you?' He shifted on the spot, his head narrowly missing Mum's shelf of cookery books over the door. 'Heard you had a spot of bother. Daniel was telling me about vandals in Earlsfield. Not good.'

'I'm fine thanks, Bill. Just a scratch,' I said warmly.

I really didn't understand my sister. When I first met him, like a lot of people, I made the mistake of assuming from his heavy-lidded, sleepy blue eyes that he was slow and plodding. But I knew that wasn't the case at all. Aside from learning that he had a first from Cambridge, I'd seen him in action. He was like a canny fisherman, biding his time before reeling someone in. It had crossed my mind more than once that he was playing the same game with Kate, deliberately cultivating a laid-back approach by ignoring her spiky comments.

'Excuse the smell. Mum's playing doctors and nurses.'

'Really?' Bill's voice brightened with enthusiasm before he remembered where he was.

Dad chuckled as Bill blushed, and then took pity on him. 'Want a beer?'

'Only if I'm not interrupting. My folks are out for the night. I was just on my way for a quick pint and bite at the pub.'

'Say no more. What'll it be, I've got some Old Speckled Hen, Brains SA Gold, Greene King ...'

Dad led him out to the utility room where we had another fridge that was always well stocked. I came from a long line of lushes.

Mum shook her head. 'Poor boy. Shame Kate was never

interested. Just as well she's gone. Give him a chance to forget about her. Debbie Meakin, the new barmaid at the Pea and Hen's been casting eyes at him. And she's not your normal run of barmaid. Speaks as if she's been at Cheltenham Ladies' College.'

I concentrated on cleaning up the oil, which had left nasty slicks around the sink and had already seeped into my T-shirt. Debbie whatever-her-name was couldn't possibly be a match for Kate, but sadly she was here and my sister was over 10,000 miles away. Surely there must be some way of getting Kate to contact Bill?

Bill ended up staying for pizza. Dad's hope of talking match tactics for tomorrow's game was dashed by the re-emergence of Ben who was star-struck and insisted on talking England rugby. The rest of us weren't much better and soon joined in.

'Wow, Bill. Sounds great,' I said enthusiastically. 'Who can you introduce me to?'

Dad is nothing if not generous with the wine, I'd had far too many glasses.

The conversation degenerated even further when Mum and I started to dissect the team one by one assessing availability, looks and arguing about who had the best bum. Mum was very concerned about Bill getting cauliflower ears until Bill kindly explained that players wear protection these days.

Whoops, you didn't! I giggled to myself. And then appalled stopped quickly.

Dad and Mum disappeared at around eleven leaving me, Bill and Ben at the table with another bottle.

When Ben nipped out to the loo, I felt bold enough to say to Bill, 'Have you heard from Kate?'

He looked startled and hopeful at the same time. 'Not recently,' he answered warily.

'She ... she told me you'd seen her in Australia,' I ventured.

'Yeah.' Bill sighed heavily, putting his head in his hands. 'I'm such a muppet. She's not interested. Not flash enough for her.'

I leaned over and put a hand on his forearm. 'Don't be so sure about that.'

'Yeah, right.'

'What if she'd had a change of heart?'

He looked up, hope flaring in his eyes.

I carried on. 'What if she'd made a mistake?'

The sparkle faded and he shook his head. 'No. To be honest I was surprised she even agreed to have dinner with me, let alone what … well … you know. Anyway if she had changed her mind, she's been home for weeks, she'd have called.'

Not if she'd just discovered she was pregnant and his selection for England had just been announced I thought but couldn't bring myself to say anything. With Kate's previous indifference, would the timing have looked suspect?

'Stupid thing is. I bloody love her. I really do. First time I met her, I knew.' Bill sank his head into his hands again.

I felt for him. He and I had more in common than he knew.

'Bill …' I stopped, pausing to wonder whether I was doing the right thing. 'She's not happy out there. Australia's just running away. She'll be back. Don't give up on her.'

'Really?' He looked up.

'Well, I don't know for sure. She's not said anything but …'

Being the middleman is so hard. I wanted to give Bill hope but I didn't want to let Kate down. After all, what if my last conversation with her was just the hormones talking?

I woke up in a shaft of sunlight, the golden beam slanting through the dormer window. A cloudless, blue sky heralded perfect cricketing weather.

Despite all my good intentions a little voice in my head

reminded me that today I'd see Daniel. Last night's banter on the phone had made me believe that I could maintain a friendship with him.

I'd also see Bill again. Had I done the right thing last night, giving him hope? Maybe I should have told him that Kate was pregnant.

My thoughts were disturbed by a horrible screech from outside. Something was being dragged across the patio below. It must be Dad getting organised.

He and Mum were both horrifically early risers but with very different routines. He liked breakfast with the radio in the kitchen while Mum preferred to stagger down to her studio at the bottom of the garden, coffee in hand and not talk to anyone for an hour. This arrangement suited everyone. Dad was far too perky at that time – and Mum was vile before her first cup of coffee.

Drifting downstairs in my favourite, faded pink dressing gown, I spotted Dad in the garden wrestling with trestle tables. After making a mug of tea, I went out to join him.

Perched on the patio wall, I watched as he washed down the tables and brought me up to speed on who was due to play. He was feeling hugely optimistic, although God knows why. His team was verging on the geriatric.

'Experience, love,' he said, when I pointed this out. 'Wisdom over youth.' I gave him a sceptical look.

'And ... a couple of ringers.' He gave me a gleeful grin.

I bit back a smile. His glee might be short-lived. Ben had been hinting last night that Daniel had recruited a few ringers of his own, but I wasn't going to spoil Dad's fantasies.

By mid-morning, the tables, picnic chairs, cool boxes, and several large Tesco carrier bags filled with sandwich making provisions, were loaded into the cars. As a past master of teas, I knew what I was doing. The only thing I had to worry about was doing battle with the prehistoric urn, which had a mind all of its own.

After a week left to its own devices the clubhouse had a unique smell that hit you the minute you stepped inside; slightly damp and musty with an overtone of sweaty socks. Ted, the trusty groundsman, whose shoulders were so stooped they were almost level with his knees, was striding around the field planting the boundary flags with enthusiasm.

I gave him a wave and in response he pointed to the sky and gave me an enthusiastic thumbs-up. The well-trimmed grass looked perfect and a testament to his devotion to the club.

Armed with her bottle of Dettol, Mum insisted on washing down every reachable surface in the kitchen before I could take anything in.

'No food in here before I finish,' she insisted, frantically scrubbing away as I stood in the doorway, my arms lengthening by the second with the weight of the carrier bags.

'Mum, Dad and Ben eat here most weekends. Neither of them has died of food poisoning yet.'

'There's always a first time,' she replied, attacking the Formica surface with renewed relish.

'Morning, Mrs Middleton. Olivia,'

I turned to see Bill looking surprisingly fresh.

'Hi, Bill. No hangover?' I wondered if this morning he might regret his love struck ramblings about Kate.

He grinned sheepishly. 'Bit slow out of the traps this morning. Must get changed. See you later.' He ambled off to the changing rooms.

With three quarters of an hour to go before the match started, final preparations for the game were underway. Half-dressed players were padding about in socks (no wonder the place smelt the way it did) and Ted was giving the square one last roll.

Dumping the bags and leaving Mum to it, I slipped out onto the white fenced veranda which ran across the front of the clubhouse. Today it offered cool shade from the sun, which was getting hotter. Studded boots clattered past me on the wooden boards as the two teams trooped in and out of the pavilion. Bill and my brother were over in the nets practicing with a couple of other players. At every turn I was greeted by familiar faces.

'Olivia! Haven't seen you here for a while? How's life treating you?'

'Home for the weekend, are you?'

'Wotcha. Seen Ben?'

'Where's your Dad, love? The umpire wants a word.'

'Go on, make us a cuppa.'

Some were contemporaries of Dad's, others mates of Ben's and all were accompanied by wives, girlfriends or children armed with blankets and rugs, deckchairs and cool-boxes. The ground was filling rapidly.

'Olivia! Wait up.'

It was Daniel calling from the car park. I waited on the veranda as he strode over.

There was an odd expression on his face.

Daniel could see her standing on the pavilion steps as he got out of his car. She looked relaxed and happy, not like the last time he'd seen her. Talk about guilty face, wrapped in a bathrobe peering round the door of the hotel suite. He smiled grimly to himself. Bet she'd had a near heart attack with an unexpected knock at the door. Although she was probably used to it. Was that what it was like when you had an affair, in constant fear of being found out or spotted where you shouldn't be? Some people, he supposed, got off on that kind of thrill ... although he didn't see Olivia as the type.

And now he was about to give her the really bad news. He

couldn't believe it. No one had heard from Mike for bloody years and then out of the blue one of the other players dropped out and asked Mike to step in for him. The worst thing was going to be breaking it to her.

There was no easy way to do it.

He caught up with her just outside the kitchen.

'Olivia …' He paused loathe to tell her. 'Porn Star Mike—'

'What about him?' Olivia looked blank.

'He's … coming … today. Sorry.'

'Mike?' Her voice pitched up in disbelief.

He nodded.

For a moment her face crumpled in dismay. At least it was better than the tears she'd shed the first time she confided in him what had really happened between them on one of their shared journeys home. Catching your boyfriend in bed with someone else really sucked. He'd done his best to try and cheer her up, coming up with the stupid name Porn Star Mike – it wasn't really that funny but at the time it had made her smile and then it had stuck.

'Sorry,' he said, reaching toward her. 'We were short. James said he knew someone and I never gave it another thought until he sent through his team list last night.'

'Bugger.' She pulled a face. 'Really?'

'Yeah, I'm sorry.'

'Can't be helped,' she said briskly. 'Not your fault. Ancient history.'

Although she pulled a face and shrugged, he could see she'd put a brave face on. 'No doubt everyone will find him charming and I'm far too "nice" to tell.'

With the misery in her expression, he couldn't help but put an arm round her to give her a quick hug. He breathed in the scent of her newly washed hair, which still felt slightly damp as it tumbled across his forearm. To his surprise she leaned in to him and he could feel her heart pounding against his chest.

It brought back the memory of them lying full-length on her sofa lost in kisses and his own pulse kicked.

With a squeeze, he reassured her with the words, 'Don't worry about old Porn Star. You'll be OK.'

The nickname finally elicited a giggle and she looked up at him, the sadness dissolving in her eyes. Encouraged, he smiled down at her and she responded, squaring her shoulders and lifting her chin with a determined nod.

'I'll try not to call him that, but if I have to speak to him, I can't guarantee I'll be civil.'

'Yeah, right.' He clasped her shoulder and gave her another hug.

They both knew that was rubbish. Olivia didn't have it in her to be rude to anyone.

The knowledge jarred in his mind as a trickle of memories slipped into his head and he remembered all the things that Emily had told him that Olivia had said and done. Suddenly they didn't ring true. Not with the Olivia he'd known all these years. Like a cloud lifting, his thoughts clarified. Emily had been prone to exaggeration; it just hadn't occurred to him how far that might stretch. Now it seemed obvious.

He realised Olivia was speaking and he'd zoned out for a second.

'Just don't let on to Dad who he is. I don't want any homicidal bowling.'

Kate was the only one of the family who'd ever met Mike but they all knew what he'd done.

'If he gives you any trouble I'll put itching powder in his box!'

She laughed. 'Thanks, I'll be fine,' she said amused, and then her eyes shifted as if she was trying to avoid looking at him. Weird. Were they back to those odd games again?

An awkward silence hung between them and he stepped back.

'Duty calls. I need to find out who's here. See you later.' Loping off, he headed into the away team's changing room.

I was grateful for Daniel's warning. It meant that when I did see Mike and his girlfriend I was prepared. I knew exactly who she was from her distinct shade of red hair. I'd seen it once before, fanned out on a pillow beneath Mike.

'Olivia! Great to see you. How're you doing? What are you up to now?' he said all in one nervous breath.

'Mike.' I nodded. Be cool. Distant. 'Fine.' I said, deliberately ignoring all his questions and not bothering to show any interest in him. My chilly response didn't faze him as he carried on enthusiastically.

'So, what are you up to now?'

'I work in London,' I said coolly. Although part of me wanted to tell him I was wildly successful, had a wonderful life and drove a bright red Ferrari, another part wanted to show him that I had absolutely no interest in his opinion.

Tracey had looked suspicious at first, shooting glances at us, checking out our body language but my off-hand manner must have reassured her. I could see her relax and in a throwaway glance totally dismiss me.

She'd obviously decided I was no threat at all, which normally I wouldn't have reacted to. After all she hadn't personally done me any harm, but coming after Friday's moment of epiphany about Emily, her dismissal wound me up. How dare she? I'd wipe that smug look off her face. How come everyone else got away with bad behaviour?

I couldn't help myself, I was feeling bitchy and for once I was going to give into those feelings.

Suddenly I wanted to make Mike squirm. He and Emily were two of a kind, they always went for the easy option in life and in both cases I'd let them get away with it. Not any more and that went for Emily too.

I gave Mike a long slow assessing look and smiled straight into his eyes completely ignoring Tracey. 'It's been a long time. You look well. What are you doing these days?'

He blanched uneasily.

As well he might. Tracey immediately straightened up, moving closer to his side to give him an unsubtle nudge in the ribs.

A look of panic crossed his face. 'Tracey, this is Olivia. She was at Norwich with ... at the same time as me.'

I smiled. The wide, soulless smile of a shark going in for the kill. 'I saw you ... once.'

Mike's Adam's apple dipped and I felt a tiny flicker of satisfaction at his discomfort.

'Really,' she said frowning as if trying to remember meeting me, which of course she couldn't. 'I'm sorry, I don't ... Are you sure it was me? I only went to Norwich once.'

'I'm sure. Very sure. Mike remembers. Don't you?'

He flushed bright red. She intercepted the look and frowned.

Not so smug now are you?

'Yes,' he mumbled and before she could ask for any more details he quickly said, 'See much of Daniel these days?'

I was just about to answer when I saw his gaze move to a point behind me.

'Daniel. Hi.'

Swivelling round I saw Daniel, now in whites, just emerging from the changing room, with a clear warning look in his eyes.

'Mike,' he said, extending a hand. 'Glad you could make it. Still handy with a bat?'

'Don't get much chance to play these days,' answered Mike, with a quick look at Tracey. 'The missus doesn't like it.'

'Only because it's such a waste of the weekend,' she snapped back.

'Mmm,' said Daniel ruefully, nodding at Mike and giving her a polite smile. 'My girlfriend feels the same.'

His words were a sudden bleak reminder of Emily. I needed to put some distance between us.

The hugs he'd given me earlier had been too much. That first one had made my heart give a little skip as every nerve ending went on alert. How on earth was I going to cope? Compared to this, getting over Mike hadn't been so difficult. I could hate him for what he'd done, but how was I ever going to forget Daniel? All the touchy-feely, aren't we mates stuff was torture. Perhaps it was better when he was cold and distant.

I mumbled something about needing to start making sandwiches and began to head towards the kitchen. Behind me I heard Daniel tell Mike he needed to go and get changed.

'Olivia,' Daniel called and in quick strides caught up with me. 'Need any help with teas?'

'I didn't need rescuing,' I said grumpily

He grinned at me. 'I know, but Mike did.'

I pulled a face at him. 'I wouldn't have said anything. Just making him sweat a bit.'

'Heartless woman. He was genuinely upset when you cut him off at uni, you know.'

'And he didn't deserve it?' I said my voice quavering indignantly.

'You were pretty ruthless. Severing all ties immediately.'

Daniel's tone might have been gentle but I was pissed off at the implication that I might have handled it badly.

I didn't say a word leaving Daniel to dig a bigger hole.

'It must have been hard on him. The two of you had been so close. You never even gave him the chance to explain.'

'Explain what?' I spluttered in disbelief. 'Do tell me. What is the proper way of telling your girlfriend that you're sleeping with someone else?'

Daniel had the grace to look embarrassed. 'Sorry. Point taken. All I'm saying is that he was hurt too. He made a mistake. We all do that.'

I didn't like Daniel being Mr Reasonable.

Beyond him through the window I could see Dad and the umpire pacing the pitch.

'Oy! Daniel,' yelled Ben from the veranda. 'You're needed for the toss.'

He lowered his voice, something urgent in his eyes as he said, 'Sometimes you get involved in a situation. You know it's wrong but you just keep going.'

My heart thumped as he held my gaze. Mike? Or, hope blazed for a second, him and Emily?

He carried on, 'Can you honestly say, hand on heart, what you're doing is the right—'

'Daniel, where the hell are you? Get your arse out here,' yelled a voice from outside.

'Shit. Gotta go.' He gave an 'I'm-on-my-way' wave to Dad and the umpire out on the pitch, before squeezing my arm affectionately and heading out.

Why did he have to do that? It was only adding to my confusion.

What was going on? Was he going off Emily? No, he couldn't be. Hadn't he just taken her to see Phantom and then out for sushi?

But he doesn't like sushi.

No one likes sushi.

So that proves it. He must love her.

Chapter Fifteen

Dad won the toss and he opted to put his team into bat. I kept myself busy preparing sandwiches, laying out the plates and teacups, chatting to Mum and her cricket widow cronies and doing my best not to let my eyes drift over the other side of the field to Daniel's tall, lean figure.

Tea came and went, a flurry of players piling their plates high, squabbling good-naturedly over the last chocolate fingers and chattering about the game.

When they all trooped back onto the pitch, Dad's face split with a wide grin in anticipation of unleashing his special bowler, the empty pavilion fell silent except for the rattle of teaspoons in saucers as I went around collecting all the cups.

As I was dumping them into the sink, Miriam sailed into the cricket club kitchen with a pile of tea towels and a pair of bright red rubber gloves, ready to do battle with the dishes. What is it with that generation? They have an obsession with drying up. Surely it's more hygienic to leave things to drain or perhaps that's me being lazy?

'Darling, how are you?' she said, soundly kissing me on both cheeks. She called everyone darling. Daniel once told me it's because she has a terrible memory for names. Sebastian, more maliciously, observed it was an upper-class affectation.

However, anything less like a country matron would be hard to imagine. With her short grey hair cut in a spiky, gamine style, she looked more like an errant pixie. Dark blue dungarees covered her short dumpy figure and the overall look was completed by a pair of maroon Doc Martens.

'Much easier on the bunions,' she'd told me once.

I was surprised when she suddenly grabbed my arm and brought it up to her face, to peer at the wound. Although short-sighted, she was still in denial so never wore the prescribed glasses.

'Nasty. Daniel told me. Unpleasant. I hear the company was interesting.'

I looked at her uncomprehending for a moment.

'You mean the South London ladies of the night,' I said realising what she meant.

'Mm. How the other half lives, eh?' Miriam shuddered. Country born and bred, the concept of a casualty department in the city was as alien to her as an episode of *Dr Who*.

'Help? Want some? You all right with that arm? Wash or dry?' Miriam wasn't a great one for social pleasantries.

'Wash, definitely. Thanks for these.' I nodded at the gloves. 'The ones here are always full of holes.'

'Can't bear the bloody things myself.' She snorted like a dissatisfied horse. 'Came free with a job lot of slug pellets or was it worming pills? Amazing thing about skin. Waterproof. You know. Marketing people, worse than estate agents. Inventing things we don't need.'

'Mm,' I murmured, looking at her hands – definitely the perfect advert for rubber gloves. The people at Marigold would have paid good money to show those chapped, wrinkled fingers.

'Gather you put some work Sebastian's way. If you can call prancing about in a monkey suit work. Looked a picture on the news,' she said.

'You saw him. What at the Bond premiere?' I asked. 'What channel?' I was still talking to several TV companies, trying to get hold of some tapes of coverage of the premiere.

'The Beeb, darling,' she said outraged. 'Wouldn't watch anything else. Can't bear the ads and George does love those David Attenborough—'

'So you saw Sebastian on the BBC,' I interrupted, desperate to keep her on track.

'Yes. On the news. Looked a picture he did. Showed Daniel last night.'

I nearly dropped a cup. 'You've got it!' I exclaimed excitedly.

'Yes, dear.' She looked at me strangely. 'George doesn't trust the video recorder. Sets it to come on half an hour early. Sebastian was on at the end of the news. Only reason we saw it.'

'Video recorder? You've still got one?'

'It works, why throw it out?'

'Can I borrow it?' I asked eagerly.

'What the video recorder?'

'No, the tape of Sebastian. I desperately need a copy for work.'

She looked at me as if I were quite mad. 'You're allowed to watch television at work? How odd.' She frowned as if trying to understand the complexities of life in the twenty-first century.

'Pop round tomorrow morning,' she said airily. 'We're out to the Richardson's for lunch. He's a bloody bore but she's a hoot. Daniel can let you in if we're not about. Come on. Let's get this lot done and then we can have a G and T.'

Great, another excuse to see him tomorrow. Just what I didn't need.

Duty done, I headed out with a rug and a book to enjoy the late afternoon sunshine on the boundary. I avoided looking at the players, especially the one at the crease batting. So much for avoiding Daniel after today, but never mind. Once I'd got that tape it really would be the last time I'd see him.

I was happily relaxed, lying on my stomach, head propped on my chin relishing the warm sun on my back when a cool shadow fell blocking out the hot rays, disturbing my pleasant daydreams. Turning to look over my shoulder, my irritation dissolved as I realised it was Daniel. Even better, he was carrying a condensation-covered glass of wine along with a pint of lager.

'Thought you might like one,' he said, offering me the wine before settling down next to me. He studied me intently as I gratefully raised the glass to my cheek, enjoying the coolness against my hot face.

So much for keeping my distance, his tanned face was so close I could see the faint white lines around his eyes that had been missed by the sun. My mouth went dry.

'Thanks.' I looked over at the players on the pitch trying not to look directly at him. 'Are you out? Sorry, I must have dropped off.'

He nodded. Out of the corner of my eye I saw him pulling a face.

'Bad luck,' I said sympathetically.

'My own fault,' said Daniel cheerfully. 'Stupid bloody shot to play and it was a great catch.'

I risked looking at him and found his blue eyes were twinkling. Clearly being within an arm's length of me wasn't bothering him. I tried to ignore the skittering of my pulse, which seemed to have developed a pace of its own today. 'How many did you get?'

'You mean you weren't watching every majestic stroke?' he said with mock outrage.

I giggled. 'No, remember me, chief sandwich-maker. Chained to the kitchen sink most of the day.'

'Between gossiping with the whole village,' he said teasing. 'I saw you. We're out there slaving over the wicket to bring home a triumphant win and the womenfolk can't even be bothered to watch our heroic efforts.'

'How many did you get, Hercules?'

'Fifty-six. Not bad. We might just win. Mind you, your Dad's surpassed himself this year with that Aussie bowler.'

Another shadow appeared. Ben. Trust him. The original

gooseberry. With a brief grunted greeting, Ben dropped down. His mood wasn't great, he'd only scored a few runs before being caught out by a spectacular catch from Dad's oldest teammate. Lounging next to me, he helped himself to a good glug of my wine.

'Oy, get your own,' I snapped. He would have to spoil the mood.

'Oo, what's bitten you,' he teased in typical irritating brother fashion. 'Girls, eh?' He tutted, looking at Daniel.

I glared at him. 'You're just a bloody scrounger. Go get—'

Ben just laughed and jumped up. 'Stroppy mare. She just needs a good shag.'

I very nearly threw my wine at his retreating back. I could wring his bloody neck. Did he have to say that in front of Daniel?

'I'm not stroppy,' I smarted indignantly, watching Ben saunter across the field back to the pavilion.

I might as well have been talking to myself. Daniel had gone very quiet. He seemed distracted as he stretched out on his back, hands tucked behind his head.

Sipping my wine I looked over at the players on the field, conscious of the silence. Daniel sighed. Then he sighed again. Opened his mouth and then closed it.

If he had something on his mind, I wished he'd just spit it out. But he didn't and the silence between us lasted until another wicket fell. It was only as a new batsman strode into the centre of the pitch that Daniel rolled over to face me, propping his head up on one elbow before finally speaking.

'Shame your chap's not here today,' he began tentatively. 'I mean, with Mike turning up. You could have done with a bit of moral support.' He avoided looking at me as he traced small circles on the grass with his left hand. 'I suppose weekends are a bit difficult for him.' He glanced up with a quick, sympathetic smile.

'What? For Mike?' I was confused.

Daniel was absorbed in the grass again. 'No,' he muttered. 'Your ... you know, chap.'

I looked at the top of his head mystified. 'Pardon?' I wrinkled my nose and waited for him to look up.

It must have been catching. Last night Ben had been wittering on about a fella. My family had a lot to answer for. Chinese whispers had turned a couple of dates with Ned into a full-blown boyfriend.

'It's all right, I know all about it,' said Daniel, his steady blue eyes holding mine.

'Bloody Barney,' I said, disconcerted by his gaze. 'Honestly. Two dates and suddenly my family has me married off.' I tossed my head in disgust. 'Two. Neither a huge success. Ned's not really my type, bit too football mad, but will they listen? Will they hell?'

Daniel's eyes narrowed in confusion. 'So it's finished with the other chap?'

What was it with everyone? They all knew more about my love life than I did.

'What are you on about?' I asked, my voice rising slightly.

'Emily did say you wouldn't want to talk about it.' He looked away, his index finger resuming its circles. 'Must be serious. Never thought you'd fall for a married man.'

My mouth opened but I couldn't say anything. 'What?' That wasn't right.

'I've known for ages,' he muttered, still absorbed in the grass.

'You're kidding!'

'Emily told me that night at the party.' Daniel was still mumbling.

Bloody hell. The scheming cow. Suddenly everything fell into place.

'She told you, did she?' I snapped sarcastically, as I felt

the blush heating my cheeks, which I think he took as guilt because he looked awkward and began apologising.

'You can tell me to piss off. It's nothing to do with me.' He gave a shrug. 'You've got your reasons. Emily warned me. Said you don't like talking about it.'

I'll just bet she did, wait until I got hold of her. Stunned, I stared at Daniel who was unable to hide the disapproval etched clearly in the lines around his mouth and the furrow under his fringe.

I finally found my voice, or rather it found me. I exploded, my words tumbling out in a loud explosion of sheer frustration and fury.

'Daniel Caldwell,' I yelled, and lashed out with my hand at his chest pushing him over onto his back and looming over him.

'Do you,' I poked him hard in the ribs with my index finger, 'honestly THINK' a much firmer poke, 'that I, me, would go out with a married man! DO YOU?' I growled at him in low menacing tones.

Lying beneath me, at the mercy of my finger digging into his ribs, he stared up, his face a picture of confusion, surprise, puzzlement and concern.

I leant back into my heels, my chest heaving. We stared at each other, until my breathing slowed.

Daniel was looking horrified at my outburst and sat up.

Now that he was facing me, I felt a dangerous wobble. Please don't let me cry. If I burst into tears now, it would be a seriously bad mistake. I was bloody furious with him. I needed to stay angry.

He opened his mouth but I wasn't about to let him take charge.

'Daniel,' I said icily, meeting his gaze. 'I repeat, do you honestly think that I would go out with a married man? Really? After everything, everything that happened with

Mike. After what you went through with your mother? You think I … would do that … to someone else?'

He inhaled deeply, his eyes narrowing as if about to say something but I cut him off.

'Just how long have I been having this imaginary affair?' I asked dangerously. 'Just so I know,' I added, my lips twisting in an exaggerated sneer just in case he was in any doubt.

His eyes flashed and his mouth curled. 'Since Ben's birthday party,' he snapped, folding his arms.

'That long. God, I hope the sex was worth it. Have I had a good time?' I looked down, studying the golden hairs on his forearms, tanned against the white cricket shirt.

'Stop being bitchy, Olivia. It doesn't suit you. How was I to know Emily was lying? You've not exactly been forthcoming of late, have you?' There was a sarcastic note to his voice. Rising to his knees as his gaze bored into me and his eyebrow quirked in challenge.

'What the hell is that supposed to mean?' My fists were clenched, my voice tight. How dare he be angry with me? I hadn't done anything wrong.

'We used to be friends. Remember? Now you avoid me like the plague.' His voice was cold, the words snapped out, like ice breaking.

'Excuse me? I avoid you? What am I supposed to do? You're going out with my flatmate. I can hardly hang around being green and hairy.'

'As you weren't around much, I assumed you were busy with your married man, which under the circumstances is perfectly reasonable.'

'You …' Who did he think he was, trying to justify himself? 'Reasonable?'

'Yes. Little clues like the stray brick.'

God I wanted to punch him. 'What the hell has that got to do with anything?'

'Don't swear. That doesn't suit you either.'

'And don't change the subject,' I shouted at him, uncaring that I might be overheard. 'How the hell does that … prove … I'm having an affair with a married man?'

'An irate wife,' he suggested snidely.

'Crap,' I said turning my back on him, rising to my feet, ready to walk away.

'I saw your and Emily's faces that night.' Putting his hand on my arm to halt me, he stood up and said, 'Don't deny it, you knew who was behind it. Didn't you?'

He had me there. I turned slowly, his hand slid down, and the fingers gently encircled my wrist.

'I promise you,' I said looking up into his face, slowing my words, 'That was nothing to do with a married man.'

His blue eyes studied me for a moment. 'So there's no married man?'

I shook my head. Frowning he asked, 'So why did Emily say there was?'

I shrugged. 'You tell me. I have no idea.'

We stood in silence both of us lost in thought. What could she gain from telling him that? Suddenly I knew. 'When did she tell you?'

He frowned again. It took him a moment to answer. 'I told you, that night at the party.'

That made sense. Sadness washed over me. 'What exactly did she say?' I pressed.

'God, I can't remember … something like "Poor Olivia, it's a shame she has to come to things on her own all the time. He'll never leave his wife." '

I felt light headed for a second.

'Then, she said, "Please don't let on I told you, she doesn't want anyone to know."' I could picture it all too clearly. Emily earnestly clutching his arm and whispering urgently in his ear as I walked out of the room.

'Wait 'til I get hold of her,' I said, remembering the feeling of bleakness when I'd come back to find her lips locked with his.

Daniel frowned looking right through me. 'Yes,' he said absently, letting go of my wrist. He seemed miles away.

'Oy, Dan,' called one of the team, coming over with a loping run. 'As you're out, can you come and do a spot of scoring?'

With a rueful look, he called, 'Be right with you.' He glanced at me, his mouth looking grim. 'Talk about timing.'

'Hmph,' I muttered crossly.

'I've got to go, Olivia.' With that he turned away and then immediately turned back, an odd expression in his eyes. 'We need to talk.'

Heavy-footed, I walked slowly back to the pavilion oblivious to the sights and sounds around me, my thoughts were back at Ben's party.

Cringing I could remember the flirty banter with Daniel at the start of the evening, when he'd greeted me with the line, 'Wow, you're looking gorgeous tonight.'

Things were going swimmingly with lots of sparkly-eyed conversation until I was dragged away to supervise my brother's birthday cake. A sugar paste triumph in the shape of a bat and ball.

Drifting through the clubhouse into the ladies toilet, I gazed at my flushed face in the mirror. I leaned against the cool glass for a moment. Was that when things had gone awry? Had I stood a chance with Daniel that night?

Going back over that evening in my head, I remembered that awful kick in the stomach sensation I'd got when I returned from sorting the cake out to find Emily wrapped around Daniel, her arms encircling his neck, kissing him deeply. At the time I'd nearly doubled over with the pain of it.

The memory still made me feel sick and embarrassed. Turning on the cold tap in the cramped toilet, I splashed water on my face, glaring at myself in the mirror. God, Daniel must have found it hilarious, that night. Me, throwing myself at him. What an idiot. Of course Emily was going to be his type, a petite, sexy blonde with curves in the right places. I stared at my reflection. Who'd want a lamp post whose ribs were more prominent than her boobs?

So had Emily's lies put the barriers up? And now that he knew the truth, did it make any difference, or was I about to make the same mistake all over again? What if all Daniel wanted to say was, 'You're a really nice girl but …'

Events were determined to thwart us. Daniel's team won the game, so he was in big demand. Not that defeat seemed to have bothered the opposition, both sides were celebrating equally. The clubhouse was packed, the pints were flowing and the bar filled with empties. Clusters of men were grouped around the tables, discussing in great detail every ball. How did they remember? They spoke another language and I could hear strange incomprehensible snippets: 'Defensive drive … just caught the edge … bowled a googly … silly mid-off' as I circulated chatting to wives and girlfriends.

Towards the end of the evening, I went out onto the veranda to cool down and watched as the barbecue embers gave off a final redundant glow.

It was then that a very chummy Mike arrived beside me, breathing beer fumes, obviously taking advantage of Tracey's trip to the bar.

'Olivia. Gotta talk to you. I hafta splain.' With dusk falling, he couldn't see my look of bored resignation. 'Y'know I was goin' out wi' Tracey … then you came along. Shoulda told you after the first night but I couldn't resist you … couldn't stay away. Your fault.'

I might have had a bit more patience with his drunken rambling but he made the mistake of trying to blame me. Great. Nice to know I was irresistible to someone.

'Never gave me chance to splain. You walked away. That wash you,' he moaned.

What a day. My temper which is normally well hidden under layers and layers of ingrained politeness had been simmering all afternoon. I only needed the slightest excuse to light the touchpaper.

'You bastard,' I hissed at him, ready to let rip but Daniel materialised at my elbow. His timing stank.

'Olivia, there you are. I've been looking everywhere for you.' The breath whistled out of me as Daniel firmly took my arm. 'Excuse us,' he said, before adding. 'Mike, you're a dickhead. Thank your lucky stars that she's too nice to go and spill the beans to Tracey.'

Wheeling me away from Mike, we walked a few steps and now the moment was finally here. Sod's law; I was desperate for the loo.

Would he hang around and wait for me or would I lose this window? 'Sorry, I really need to go to ...' I indicated with my head and fled towards the ladies.

When I came out I almost tripped over him, leaning lazily against the wall. Was that a good sign? Was he was determined not to let me slip away? His arms were folded and a lazy amused smile was on his lips.

'Fancy meeting you here,' I said aiming for a flippant tone. 'Looking for someone?'

'Yes.' He flashed me a smile. 'A tall, gorgeous blonde.'

My heart did a little flutter. I missed a breath. It all went quiet.

'Fancy a walk round the boundary?'

'That would be nice,' I responded suddenly lost for words. I winced. Nice. Where's the witty repartee when you need it?

Was this when we were going to have our 'talk', here in the half-light, protecting us from curious eyes?

'Good game,' I said, after the silence of the first few paces.

'Great,' said Daniel enthusiastically. In the cover of the dusk evening, his fingers brushed mine. A warm tingle ran up my arm and I sneaked a glance at him as we walked on in silence.

'Congratulations.'

'Thanks.'

'Gorgeous evening,' I said inanely.

'Mm lovely,' said Daniel.

I could just make out him grinning. 'You're laughing at me,' I accused him. 'I can see your teeth; you look like the big bad wolf.'

'Are you scared?' he asked. For a second I didn't dare answer. Should I keep things light? What would he say if I said yes, absolutely terrified? Terrified that I'd got it all wrong. I chickened out.

'Nah, he gets outwitted by a little girl wearing a red hood. Pretty useless wolf, if you ask me.'

And at that point I was outwitted by the ring of my mobile. Conditioned by work, I had to see who was calling just in case it was urgent.

I shrugged at Daniel. 'Sorry,' I said, and digging it out of the back pocket of my linen trousers I checked the caller ID. Kate? Quickly I checked my watch. Two in the afternoon there – funny time for her to ring. Some sixth sense of foreboding made me answer.

'Hi, Kate. Your timing is rubbish. Is it urgent?' I said, with a quick glance at Daniel. I could see his teeth grin in the dark. I immediately regretted my words.

'I'm bleeding. I ... I ... don't know what to do.' Her teeth were chattering.

'My God.' Immediately I went cold. 'How badly?'

'Really bad.' She started to cry. 'There's loads. Gushing. I'm losing the baby. I don't know what to do.' Now she was sobbing in earnest, which frightened me. That wasn't like her.

'OK, Kate,' I said slowly, trying to sound more grown up than I felt. 'Calm down. Have you phoned for an ambulance?'

'Yes, but it doesn't work,' she cried.

'What doesn't work? Your phone?'

Daniel had moved closer, touching my arm as he mouthed, 'Is she OK?'

I shook my head and listened hard to Kate.

'No, the number. 999. It doesn't work.' I could hear the panic in her voice.

'Slow down, Kate,' I said frowning. 'You didn't misdial?'

'No,' she wailed. 'I tried lots of times. It's not working. Bloody, shitty country. Even 999 doesn't work.'

Maybe it was different there. I put my hand over the mouthpiece and whispered to Daniel. 'Kate needs the Australian emergency services. 999 isn't the right number. Do you know it?'

'What's wrong with her?' he asked, his face creased with concern.

Without thinking I blurted it out. 'She's having a miscarriage. She needs help now.'

His mouth was a perfect surprised 'O' for a moment before he said, 'What about 911? America?' which I immediately relayed to Kate.

'Have you tried 911?'

Her voice lifted. 'I could try that ... wait there ... never thought.'

The line went quiet for a second before I heard a howl of disappointment.

'No joy,' I whispered to Daniel.

'Wait,' he grabbed my arm, 'the Aussie bowler.'

'Good idea, but for God's sake be discreet.'

''Kay,' and with that he sped off back to the pavilion.

'Kate. Hang on, sweetie. We're just going to ask an Australian player at the club.' I started running after Daniel.

She didn't even query the 'we', all I heard was a low moan on the other end of the phone.

'Kate,' I said urgently, slowing my pace so that I could hear properly. 'Kate. Are you still there?'

'It ... hurts,' she moaned again, weeping down the phone.

I felt so helpless. I stopped just outside the veranda waiting for Daniel. There was no point going inside, it would be noisy and full of people. Looking up at the stars in the midnight blue sky, stars she couldn't see, my heart ached for her. She was so alone.

Daniel reappeared in the doorway with Bill behind him.

Shit just what I didn't need.

'000,' he called, coming towards me. Thank God, he'd asked. I'd never have thought of that in a million years.

'Kate,' I said urgently. She was still crying. 'Kate, it's 000. Can you hear me?'

'Yes,' she sniffed. '000, let ...' she broke off with a long groan. '... me try it.'

There was a muffled hiss and bang as she put down the phone and then I could hear her talking, breathless between sobs giving her address to someone.

'They're on their way.' She was calmer but her voice was dull and lifeless. 'I'd better go.'

'Wait, Kate? Do you want me to come over? I can fly out.'

'It's too bloody far. You can't get here in ...' she cried, anguished and started to sob again.

'Please, Kate, there must be ...' We were both crying now. I was aware of Bill and Daniel standing together on the top step of the veranda, looking down at me with concern on their faces. I focussed on Kate.

'There's nothing. You can't do anything.' She was getting angry now.

'I can stay on the line 'til they get there.' Mentally I was flipping through the ramifications of getting the next possible flight. Passport. Airlines. Work.

As I sank down onto the step, Daniel slipped in beside me putting his arm round me, rubbing my shoulder. Bill stood awkwardly to one side, shifting from one foot to the other as I carried on talking to Kate. We talked of everything and nothing until I could hear a siren in the background.

'They're here. Olivia, I don't know what I'd have done ... I'll call ... Don't tell anyone.'

'Of course not,' I lied blithely, glancing behind me. 'Call me as soon as you can. Promise.'

I cut the call and stared wearily at the phone in my hand.

'What's going on Olivia? What's wrong with Kate? Why does she need the emergency services?' Bill was practically jumping up and down.

Shit. What was I going to say?

I didn't get the chance to think of something plausible. Daniel answered the question for me.

'She's having a miscarriage.' The words hung in the silence.

The guilty look on my face said everything as I closed my eyes and wished I was somewhere else.

Bill's face went white and then he grabbed me, hauled me to my feet and said, 'Is that true?'

Daniel intercepted pulling him off me. 'Oy. Leave her alone!'

'It's OK, Daniel,' I said, squeezing his arm gratefully. Turning to Bill, I nodded miserably, barely able to meet his eyes.

'Is it mine?' he asked heatedly.

Daniel's eyes widened and he swivelled sharply to look at Bill.

I couldn't lie so I nodded again.

'Bloody hell,' said Bill, sinking onto the step, rubbing his head distractedly.

'Bloody hell,' echoed Daniel.

'Sorry, Bill. I couldn't ...' I muttered, anxious to get away.

'Shit. Pregnant. Kate. Bloody hell.'

'Look. I have to go. Kate's all on her own. I need to try and get a flight tonight or tomorrow morning.' My mind was racing with the practicalities of getting home to get my passport.

At this point Bill jumped up. 'I'll go. I've got to see her.'

'Bill, you can't ...' but as his words sank in, part of me thought that might be a very good idea. Kate had admitted she'd made a mistake. If he flew to her rescue she could hardly turn him away. She'd forgive me eventually. Wouldn't she?

'Daniel, can you get me to the airport?' asked Bill, decision made.

'I will,' I said firmly.

'You can't,' interrupted Daniel gently. 'Your folks will wonder why you've dashed off. They'll know it's Kate. Presumably she doesn't want them to know. Besides, you're in no fit state to drive.'

True.

'Ring me when you know about your flight?' I said to Bill as I wished him luck. 'Do you want me to tell Kate—'

'No, don't. If she has time to think she might refuse to see me. I'll call with my flight details. Let me know where she is. Don't worry, Olivia, as soon as I get there, I'll be able to look after her.'

'Thanks.' I sniffed as he gave me a big bear hug, my face only reaching his shoulder. He strode off leaving me with Daniel who turned to me and touched my cheek. 'You OK?'

My eyes met his and my heart did a little flip. I nodded shyly.

'Are you around tomorrow?'

I nodded again. 'I, uh, was planning to, uh, come over to get something from Miriam,' I stuttered. 'She's got a videotape I need.'

'Fine, why don't you pick me up on the way up to the house? Toot at the gatehouse. I'll be there. We still need to talk.' Still facing me he took a few paces back and then without warning, took two strides forward, gave me a brief hard kiss on the lips and then turned away and walked off to the car park without looking back once. There was a catch in my throat as I missed a breath, my lungs stuttering in surprise.

I could see Bill waiting by the car, his phone glued once more to his ear. There was nothing sleepy or slow about him tonight. Pacing up and down, he looked alert and ready to take on the world.

As Bill dashed into his house to collect his passport and overnight gear, Daniel drummed his fingers on the steering wheel. Tension lifted his shoulders and he wriggled uncomfortably in the driving seat. The temptation to call Emily was strong but to be honest he wasn't sure the words would be coherent. How could she lie so blatantly to him? He wanted to punch something. Was there any way she could have genuinely made a mistake? His neck clicked as he tipped his head back against the headrest. Who was he kidding? Christ, he was a fucking idiot.

Of course Emily had lied. It seemed so bloody obvious now. Sitting in the dark car he shook his head and let out a half-laugh of disgust. How had he managed to get it so wrong with Olivia? Again.

Would she forgive him? He'd done her one hell of an injustice. How the hell would he feel? Tried and found guilty without an ounce of proof. It seemed obvious now: he'd acted out of hurt pride that night. Not that that deserved to cut any ice with Olivia. She had every right to be furious with him.

He'd been so convinced that Olivia must have been leading him on, instead of talking to her about it, he'd got his own back by responding to Emily's unashamed come-on. What a dickhead. He'd blown it so badly and now when he appreciated just how badly, he realised how he felt about Olivia.

With a heavy sigh he sank lower into his seat, regret pulsing through him. Arse. Arse. Arse.

'Let's move,' said Bill jumping into the car, a small bag on his lap.

'Any idea which terminal?'

'Three.'

Bill's expression was grim and neither of them said anything as Daniel concentrated on navigating through the village roads until they hit the bypass to take them up to the M4.

Once they hit seventy, he saw Bill's grip on his travel bag relax slightly.

'So ... Kate?' he ventured the question. 'When did that ... er, happen? Not that you have to tell me if you don't want to. I had no idea, the two of ... you ...' His voice petered out.

Bill groaned. 'It's always been Kate. Bet you never thought I stood a chance. Let's face it. No one did, least of all me. Stupid thing was, we got on so well. She just wouldn't give it a go.'

'So how did it happen?'

Bill laughed. 'You mean you don't know?'

'Well, I wasn't thinking it was the Immaculate Conception.'

'When I went to Oz on tour. Looked Kate up. Bloody fool that I am. Couldn't stay away from her. Except this time, she actually seemed pleased to see me. We had a great time. Met up for dinner … and,' Bill groaned again, 'things went from there.'

Bill shook his head vehemently before he spoke again.

'Shit, I should have realised it was too good to be true. The next morning she made it quite clear it had been a mistake and I buggered off sharpish.'

Daniel absorbed all this wondering if he should voice his thoughts and then decided to risk it. 'So why the knight to the rescue act now?'

Bill thrust his hand out and hit the dashboard. 'Because I can't believe that night didn't meant anything to her. I won't believe it.' Bill turned his face toward him, misery etching twin furrows on either side of his mouth. 'And what have I got to lose? I love her. Always have done. Besides she's alone out there. She needs someone. I can't stand the thought that she's lying in some hospital ward without anyone.' Bill's voice cracked, making Daniel think of how he'd feel if that were Olivia.

Instinctively he pressed the accelerator. He needed to get Bill on the next available flight.

Chapter Sixteen

Thank goodness I had an excuse to get out of the house the next morning. There was only so much time I could spend in my room. I was terrified of giving something away to Mum or Dad by constantly checking for messages on my mobile.

The last contact I'd had with Bill was a hasty text from Heathrow the previous evening, which was nothing more than '11.10 flight 2 Sydney. Text when u hr frm K.'

I still hadn't heard from her. I'd tried her mobile a couple of times but nothing. Was she in hospital? Was she OK? As well as the worry, I was consumed with guilt. Mum would kill me if she found out. I tried to tell myself it was better this way. No point in worrying her until there was any real news. As if! That was rubbish. As far as she was concerned, worry was part of her job spec.

Slipping my mobile into my pocket I headed downstairs where I found Mum and Dad absorbed in their Sunday papers. Dad was very chipper. He didn't seem too upset by yesterday's defeat.

'There's always next year,' he said, wincing as he turned the pages.

Mum tutted unsympathetically. 'If you will go diving about thinking you're still twenty, no wonder your shoulder hurts. You should let me put some Arnica on that bruise.'

'Yes, dear,' he murmured, winking at me.

Pursing her mouth she shook her head. 'Men,' she huffed. 'What time are you going to Daniel's this morning? Will you be back for lunch?'

'Not sure,' I said, putting down my mug of tea, forcing myself to take another bite of toast as I surreptitiously slipped my phone onto my lap.

'Not to worry. Only soup and sandwiches. What time's your train this afternoon? Are you staying for dinner? I could do it early.'

I hesitated. 'Thought I might go for a four o'clock train. Don't worry I'll eat when I get in.' My eyes slid down to my mobile.

'You've got to eat something. You've barely touched that toast.'

'Too worried about her teeth, I should imagine,' quipped Dad, looking with amusement at the solid home-made wholemeal loaf on the table.

Mum ignored him. 'Take some leftovers with you when you go ... And stop fiddling with that phone. Honestly we all managed perfectly well without them when we were your age.'

'Sorry,' I said, giving up on my toast. 'Look at the time. I'd better go.'

Daniel's parent's house, just outside Henley, was a beautiful Queen Anne mansion, complete with a pair of octagonal lodges at the gate. To my great envy, Daniel lived in the left hand one overlooking the sandstone coloured gravel drive.

If I'd been Emily I'd have spent every weekend here but she hated it – said it was too quiet and parochial.

'Daniel's house is in the middle of nowhere.'

'No it's not,' I protested amused.

'Yes it is. No street lights. Pitch black. Strange noises all night. It's awful.'

'What sort of noises?' I asked, trying to be being sympathetic.

'Horrible ones. I was really scared which Daniel thought was hilarious. Sounded as if someone was being murdered. He just laughed. Said it was the badgers in the coppice. Is that code for something? I had no idea what he was on about.'

'But isn't the lodge lovely? Didn't you like it?'

She'd looked at me with complete disdain. 'If you like that sort of thing. Did you know he pays his dad a huge rent? Mad. He could get somewhere in London for that.'

What Emily didn't know was that Daniel's rent helped to maintain the lovely big house up the way and that he liked to be around. Although his dad was fine now, a few years before he'd suffered a massive heart attack.

Looking at the lodge house as I pulled up and sounded the car horn, I thought Emily was mad. Why didn't she adore this place? The quaintness of the design; the huge key box in the hallway that held the old iron keys to the estate gates and the ancient oak front door.

I gave my hands a quick wipe on my jeans as Daniel appeared at the upstairs window. To my surprise, he signalled that I should park and come in.

I wandered in through the door he'd left open, my heart thumping. Looking around I gave a little sigh of pleasure.

'Be right with you.' Daniel's disembodied voice floated down the stairs as I stood in the hallway looking through at the six-sided lounge.

Here, contemporary style mixed with traditional features. The room was dominated by a beautiful plasterwork fireplace, which contrasted with the warmth of the polished cherry wood flooring. Two overstuffed cream sofas, filled with tapestry cushions faced each other and there was little else apart from a couple of mahogany occasional tables which probably would have had the experts on the *Antiques Roadshow* wetting their knickers.

'Sorry, Olivia.' Daniel's head appeared over the banisters at the top of the stairs. 'I got stuck on a work call. Do you mind waiting? I've just got to whack off an email. Won't be long. Have you heard from Kate, yet?'

'No, but it's the middle of the night there.' I shrugged.

He gave me a cautious smile. 'Don't worry. She'll be in good hands. Why don't you help yourself to a cup of tea?'

'No, I'm fine,' I said, feeling relieved that there was no strain between us.

'Sure?' he sounded disappointed. 'I was hoping you'd make me one. You're so good at it.'

'Cheeky.' I stuck my tongue out at him

For a single guy living on his own, Daniel's kitchen was fabulous, although the big range complete with wok burner was so clean it can't have ever been used.

What a terrible waste. I'd kill for a kitchen like this. I could imagine it full of people, crowded round the refectory-style pine table, the wok burner fired up with a Thai curry on the go and Daniel dispensing drinks while I ...

I shook my head. Don't go there. Deliberately changing the direction of my thoughts I concentrated on trying to work out the time in Australia. When would I hear from Kate?

I came back to earth as Daniel came clattering down the stairs.

'Right. All done,' he said, rubbing his hands together.

I handed him his tea.

'Thanks. You found everything then?'

'Yes,' I said sighing, turning my back on the kitchen and my daydreams. Now that he was here, my palms felt clammy. Was it time for our talk?

I needn't have worried. Our conversation focused on yesterday's mad dash to the airport with Daniel giving me a complete run down.

'Bill was in such a state. He's pumped up on the rugby pitch, of course, but I've never seen him like that off the field. Talk about a bull on the rampage. Poor girl at the check-in desk. I thought he was going to pick her up by the scruff of her neck.'

'Really? Let's hope he's calmed down when he gets there and is a bit gentler with Kate. She's going to kill me for spilling the beans.'

'You think?' Daniel asked. 'Won't she be pleased to see him? I had no idea anything had gone on between them.'

'Neither did I, until that night at The Grayville when you barged in on Kate's confession,' I said pointedly.

Daniel looked confused for a second, put down his mug and leaned against the draining board with his arms folded. 'Come again.'

How nice it was to take the moral high ground and rub it in that he'd completely got the wrong end of the stick that night.

'Kate was halfway through telling me she was pregnant and hiding in the bathroom when you knocked on the door of the suite.'

Daniel's face creased into a frown. 'Ouch. I got that one wrong.'

'Yes you did,' I said sternly. 'Jumping to conclusions. Which seems to have become a bit of a habit.'

I wished he'd stop staring at me.

'Sorry, I thought—'

'I know what you thought ...'

'I just—' He was interrupted by the ring of the phone. 'Bloody hell.' He glanced at his watch ignoring it. 'We need some peace. Let's nip up to Mum and Dad's, get your tape and go to the pub for a couple of hours. We've got a lot of things to clear up.'

That sounded a great idea. I could do with being on neutral territory in case I didn't like what he had to say.

Just as he was hustling me out of the door, I recognised the voice on the answering machine, which had just clicked in. It had to be Emily, didn't it?

'Hi, it's me. Think I might have missed a call from you

last night. Sorry my phone was erm … off. Call me at home. Catch up with you then.'

So he'd called Emily last night had he? I wondered what for. Was he trying to get her version of things?

The ancient video recorder was in what George and Miriam referred to as the family room, although ten generations of my family would have fitted in there.

Miriam had left the tape on top of the television, clearly marked.

'Do you mind if we watch it quickly?' I asked. 'Make sure it's on there.' Now I was here, my stomach was doing cartwheels and I wasn't so sure about going to the pub.

Wow, Miranda's dress looked brilliant on TV. The white silk of the fabric was luminous against the deep red of the carpet while the coloured lip prints stood out in multicoloured contrast. The camera hugged Miranda's tiny figure, zooming in on the 'Minx Red' lip print over her bottom.

As the camera swung away down to the later arrivals, it homed in on Emily, looking lush and gorgeous in her Marilyn Monroe halter neck. Bloody hell, she looked stunning. I didn't dare look at Daniel to see what he thought. Then it panned out over the watching crowd.

'Look, there's Kate … oh my God,' I breathed, realising who she was talking to. I stared at a splash of red around the neck of the man next to her. The hairs on my arm stood rigid to attention as a curl of alarm tightened in my stomach. Leaning forward, I studied the screen, my hand over my mouth, disbelieving.

'Where's the remote?' I asked in a thin high voice, my eyes fixed on the TV.

'What?' asked Daniel.

'Quick. The remote,' I said.

Unearthing the remote from a pile of papers on the

coffee table, Daniel handed it to me. 'Are you all right, Olivia?'

'No.' My heart thudded in my chest as my fingers found the rewind button.

Pausing the picture, I stopped the tape on one frame. There. Behind Emily, talking to Kate in the crowd, was a familiar face, his gaze snapping back towards Emily intent and fixed on her.

Around his neck was a red scarf, knotted casually at the throat. My hands clenched involuntarily. I knew the softness of that scarf – the suppleness of the cashmere. I felt cold, all the way to my bones. The last time Emily or I had seen that scarf it had been hanging on the newel post in the flat.

My teeth nibbled the edge of my fist, biting hard into the flesh. I felt sick, stomach churningly sick. That damp print on the carpet. Oh God, he had been there while I slept.

'My God, it was him in the flat,' I whispered, staring wide-eyed with horror at the screen. 'He's been in our home!'

Daniel's forehead creased. 'What? Who's been in the flat?' he asked harshly.

I hesitated for a moment. How much should I tell him? Emily might have done the dirty on me but I didn't feel comfortable about telling Daniel about her going on a speed-date behind his back. How would he feel?

Daniel's expression became stern and stony faced. 'Olivia, what the hell is going on? You never did explain the brick.' He gave my shoulders an impatient shake. 'What kind of trouble are you in?'

His eyes held mine, glinting angrily. 'That broken window was no accident. No irate wife. So who was it? You know, don't you?'

'I told you the married man doesn't exist,' I said, deliberately stalling for time not wanting to tell him the full story. Now that I'd seen Peter on the tape, I knew we should have taken his emails more seriously.

'What's the story this time, Olivia?' Daniel's voice had gone dangerously quiet.

His face was level with mine but I couldn't look at him.

'You're going to have to tell me,' he said firmly in a soft voice. I met his angry stare and pursed my lips.

Looking at his grim face, I knew this time nothing less than the truth would do. Quickly I told him all about the speed-date, Peter's emails and the missing scarf.

Worrying at the fingernail on my index finger, I watched him with a sinking heart. I wanted to hide. I felt really small. This time he had every right to be angry.

'Why the hell didn't you tell anyone?' he yelled. I'd never seen him like this before. 'He'd thrown the brick through your window! You had to go to hospital!'

'I wasn't sure it was him,' I said in a small voice. 'There was no proof.'

'Bloody hell. How could you be so fucking irresponsible?' he hissed, stalking up and down the room, kicking angrily at the rug curling up under the sofa.

I'd never heard him swear quite like that before, certainly not at me and not at 95,000 decibels.

'For God's sake you're an intelligent woman! What if he'd let himself in when you were there?'

I bit my lip nervously, dying to put my hand over my ears. Now was not the time to confess that Peter had once.

'We have to phone the police. You need to get the locks changed.' He looked at his watch. 'Today,' he barked, as I stood there, the remote control limply hanging from my hand.

That was the final straw, all the time he'd been shouting at me, I'd stayed calm. Now I lost it but not very convincingly. Seeing Peter had really shaken me up

'Don't shout at me?' I yelled back my voice wobbling. 'It was Emily's fault.' My voice broke slightly.

'Leave Emily out of this for the time being,' he snapped, ignoring the tremors in my voice.

'I can't you ... you ... big dickhead. She's Walter Mitty, not me.'

That shut him up for a moment.

He looked at me bitterly. 'What's Emily got to do with this? Why should I believe that? I've never had any reason not to trust her. Now, all this comes out and ... I don't know what to believe. I've always trusted you, too. We've been ... You're ...' He faltered, a sad expression crossing his face, before he went on in a stronger voice to ask, 'Why would Emily lie to me?'

God, she'd done a good job on him.

'You ... you... dickhead,' I said again in sheer frustration.

'Stop calling me that,' he snapped back.

I glared at him mutinously, saying slowly and haughtily. 'I ... don't ... tell ... lies! Omissions, perhaps. I couldn't tell you about the speed-date, not that it was anything to do with you, because Emily came with me. So then I couldn't tell you about Peter. Emily's your girlfriend, go shout at her!' I stopped to take a few breaths.

All the shouting, his and now mine, was exhausting and suddenly all the fight went. 'Look, Daniel, until I saw that tape I had no evidence,' I explained more calmly. 'No proof. I've no idea how he got in or how often.' I stopped uncertainly.

Silence hung in the air, the crackling anger between us dissipating as we both considered the implications of my last sentence. The thought that Peter had been in my room, touching my things made me feel ill. Daniel seeing the look on my face gave a heavy sigh.

'Olivia.' He leant against the mantelpiece, looking at me,

his eyes blazing with emotion. The intense expression in them lit a tiny flicker of hope that burned low in my belly sending butterflies skittering about.

'Have you any idea how much danger you could have been in? God, I feel sick at the thought of you being harmed.'

'Do you?' I asked in a small voice.

He strode over to me, seizing my shoulders. 'It was bad enough the night I found you covered in blood in your room? That night I realised …' his low impassioned words were like a blowtorch finally sparking full flame combustion.

'Yes,' I prompted, watching the expression on his face hungrily.

'How long I've I wanted to do this …' he murmured as he got closer and closer.

I swear my heart stopped. The tick of a clock echoed in the quiet. God his lips were soft. I wanted more. Tingles of excitement blossomed in my stomach as the kiss deepened. Of their own accord my arms went up around his neck as our bodies pressed together.

'Really?' I asked breathlessly a few minutes later, my whole body reeling from the pleasure of that one kiss. The thundering in my ears was receding. I felt as if I'd been flattened by a herd of stampeding cows and left in the quiet aftermath in a cloud of dust.

'Really,' said Daniel emphatically, nodding his head. His blue eyes meeting mine, a gentle smile filling them.

Shyly, I examined his neck, resisting the temptation to trace my fingers down the strong column to the dark blond hair peeping out of the 'V' of his open shirt. I sneaked a look up at him. My heart flipped at the tender expression on his face. I couldn't help myself, I gave him an ecstatic grin.

'You needn't look so pleased about it. I've aged ten years in this last month.'

'Sorry.' I bit back another smile, averting my gaze back to the smooth, slightly tanned skin of his neck. So kissable, I wanted to brush my lips against it.

'So you should be, woman. What are you going to do to make it up to me?'

There was a challenge in his eyes, which combined with that humorous tilt of his eyebrows made me feel invincible.

'I could kiss you to make it better,' I said tilting my head, suddenly feeling full of confidence as I looked boldly at his lower lip in blatant invitation.

In response he brought his hand to my face, skimming my cheekbone with his thumb and my heart went straight into freefall, spiralling down. I took a sharp intake of breath as he bent his head down again.

Hard hats were most definitely required. That second kiss was even more thrilling than the first, setting off every firework going. Catherine wheels were fizzing through my stomach and when his tongue tentatively touched mine I thought I might just go into meltdown.

'And what exactly were you planning to make better?' he asked, much later when we finally came up for air. I was too dazed to remember.

There was a click and a whirr as the video recorder switched off. Bugger. Our timing was lousy. Reluctantly we pulled apart and stood facing each other.

'We have to do something about your stalker,' Daniel said heavily, smoothing a strand of hair off my face.

I reached for his hand. It was impossible to concentrate when he touched my face. It was making me go all gooey inside and we needed to think sensibly.

'I know,' I replied regretfully, wanting to stay cocooned in that first kiss glow of happiness but I couldn't ignore what I'd just seen.

'And,' Daniel went on, 'I need to talk to Emily.' He looked at me, his eyes boring into mine. 'I have to tell her it's over. Today. I know how you feel about two-timing.'

My happy glow dimmed. What would she say? I didn't want to be around when he told her. Although her resignation made things slightly easier. Another thing I hadn't told him about yet.

It would have been so much easier to stay put, stick to our original plan, go the pub and bask in that heady intoxication of knowing your feelings are returned but I couldn't. I sighed. 'It's no good, Daniel. I'm going to have to go back.'

'No ... we're going to have to go back.'

Mum sussed something was up the minute I got home to drop off her Peugeot, but only because she caught Daniel kissing me as I locked her car.

Typical! She had to open the door at that second, her arms clutching the box of bottles and tins for the recycling bucket.

'You're back earlier than I expected.' She looked at us with a smirk.

'Emergency at work, Mum,' I lied, waving the videotape at her. 'Daniel's taking me back. Need to pack.' And with that I fled up the stairs abandoning Daniel. He was a big boy. He could cope.

With holdall in hand and ready to make a speedy exit, I wasn't surprised to see Daniel comfortably ensconced at the kitchen table chatting away to Mum. He was the only person who ever expressed an interest in her pottery. Too polite for his own good.

'Go on, take it, Daniel,' she was saying, pressing one of her misshapen bowls into his hand.

'Sure?' he asked, turning it around in his hands stroking the glaze.

I rolled my eyes. What a mug. Mum caught me.

'It's not as if any of my family appreciates my work,' she said huffily.

'Sorry, Mum. It's lovely. We're in a hurry.'

'Fine. I'll just wrap it up for you, Daniel.' She flounced off to the utility room and I could hear lots of rustling.

'Creep,' I hissed at Daniel.

'What?' He looked amused. 'I like it.'

'You don't. You're just sucking up. You're as bad as Bill. He was here the other night schmoozing the parents. They won't put a good word in for you.'

'Don't you believe it? Anyway you have to check out the mothers, see what you're getting yourself into.'

He'd had a lucky escape with Emily then.

'Aha, here you go.' Mum reappeared with a newspaper parcel. 'Don't drop it. Before you go, do you want some leftovers ...'

Daniel and I spoke simultaneously.

'Great,' he said. Typical man, thinking with his stomach.

'No, we need to ...'

Mum arched an eyebrow.

'OK, then,' I said heavily, giving in.

When we finally left we were loaded up with little tinfoil packets of cold sausages, chicken thighs and three plastic bowls of rice salad, couscous and cold pesto pasta. Mum has a Tupperware mountain with the right sized boxes and tubs for every occasion.

While she'd been preparing this, I'd phoned Emily for the third time since watching the video. Still no answer. I'd tried on the landline in the flat and on her mobile. Where was she? What if she was in the flat and Peter had let himself in? Closing my eyes I tried to shut out the image of him creeping up the stairs, while she, unsuspecting, with the radio on, never heard a thing. Then him holding her from behind, his hand over her mouth, while the phone rang and rang.

The traffic on the M4 was very heavy and slow going. Daniel could see Olivia's foot was pressed against the floor on the passenger side as if that would speed their journey up.

'Olivia,' he said, rubbing her thigh, his hand entwined with hers. He kept his eyes on the road, intent on the cars ahead. 'That's the third heavy sigh in as many seconds. I know you. Spit it out.'

She sighed again and he nudged her thigh again.

'Sorry.'

'And stop staying sorry.'

'So—' She stopped herself. 'What are we going to tell her?'

He risked a quick glance at her to see her tugging at her lip with her teeth.

'It's simple. The truth.' It sounded harsh but it was what Emily deserved. 'I tell her it's over.' It galled him that she'd lied to him ... and that he'd been taken in by her. 'The rest of it, well, that's down to you. You decide what you want me to do. It's obviously going to be awkward for you if I tell her that I'm finishing with her because ... of you. Especially as you work with her as well.'

'That's an understatement. She already hates me.'

Olivia then relayed to him what had been going on at work and the vindictive resignation letter. He really had underestimated Emily.

'Bloody hell. I suppose it's one less thing for us to worry about.'

'Mmm,' said Olivia, and he could tell she was brooding.

'What's wrong?'

'It's just so ironic. So much for all my principles. After Mike I vowed I'd never put up with any deceit or lies ... but I don't know if I can do this. If we tell Emily about us ...' she sighed. 'Life is going to be hell ... and you haven't seen Emily in all her full bitch glory.' She squeezed his hand. 'Do you know what ... it would be so much easier in the short term, if we kept it a secret?' She threw her head back against the headrest. 'And I can't believe I'm saying that.'

'It's completely up to you. You're the one that's got to live with her and work with her.'

'God, it was bad enough when I told her that I'd got the job on the beauty team ... can you imagine what it's going to be like if I tell her I've nicked her boyfriend as well.'

He grinned. 'You haven't nicked me. I just changed my mind about her.'

'It goes against the grain ...'

He nudged her hard. 'Your lip's starting to bleed, stop chewing.'

She wiped a smear of blood from her lip and gazed down at it. 'Shit. It's going to be a lot easier if we take it slowly and not dive in and announce to Emily that ...' she faltered.

'We're together and you're my ... girlfriend,' he said sternly, enjoying the shocked surprise on her face. 'Besides, I don't think she'll be too surprised, actually. I've been deliberately cooling off,' he said, looking over his right shoulder as he pulled out into the fast lane.

'Cooling off,' she said indignantly.

'What? Apart from the premiere, when I saw more of you – a lot more of you – I've barely seen her.'

Colour flared in Olivia's cheeks.

He took his eyes of the road for a second and winked. 'That striptease was nice, very nice. Are you going to do it again for me?'

'Daniel, going to see *Phantom of the Opera*, dinner at Yo! Sushi and cocktails at Mint Leaf hardly qualifies as cooling off,' she challenged.

'What?' His hands gripped the steering wheel and he

risked a longer look at her. 'Musicals and sushi? Do me a favour?'

'Not you? So who has Emily been talking to on the phone? I heard her arranging theatre trips and dinner dates?'

'Not me.'

'No cocktails?'

'Nope,' he replied, his lip curling derisively. 'Definitely not.'

'I don't understand.'

Suddenly she straightened but didn't say anything. He could almost see her brain furiously ticking over.

'So what did happen at Ben's party?' Her words were flat.

'I blew it big time at your brother's party.'

'Tell me about it. I spent all evening chatting you up. Disappear for two minutes. Come back and you've got your tongue down Emily's throat.'

He winced at the disgust in her voice. 'It wasn't like that,' he protested.

She scowled and snorted.

'Emily made the first move.'

'What? And you couldn't fight her off?'

She had a point. 'Sorry, Olivia. I'm a guy, we do guy things. She was coming on to me, seriously flirty and well ... she's easy on the eye and ...'

She rolled her eyes.

Bugger it he might as well be totally honest with her. 'I was pissed off with you.'

'Me?' she squeaked indignantly. 'Why?'

'You'd been leading me up the garden path all night. Like a trained puppy on a lead. So close and yet so far. I thought we were finally going to get it together this time—'

'This time?'

He risked a glance at her. 'You don't remember, you'd had a few too many, but we kissed one night.' He winced. 'I took advantage of you but I'd fancied you for ages and you kissed me back.' She'd done more than kiss but he didn't think it would be gentlemanly to remind her of that.

'Actually I did remember but I was too embarrassed to admit it. I'd thrown myself at you and you were just being nice.'

'Nice!' He took his foot off the accelerator for a second, hastily replacing it as the engine whined in protest. 'Olivia, there was nothing nice about that kiss. If you hadn't been drunk ... well, who knows where it would have ended.'

'Oh,' she said in a small voice that immediately lit a spark of satisfaction low in his belly.

'I've had a lot of time to think about that kiss over the years and then when I think we're going to get it together, I'm suddenly confronted with the news you're having an affair with a married man. I felt a right fool. Suddenly there was Emily, green light flashing, looking at me like I was Brad Pitt, James Dean and James Bond rolled into one. When she started kissing me and you showed up, I ... you know ...'

Now he'd blown it, maybe there was being too honest.

She stared at him, comprehension dawning. 'You were trying to make me jealous.'

He flashed her a grin. 'I had no idea that Emily was—'

'So, how come you carried on seeing her?'

He squirmed in his seat, not really wanting to answer but there'd been so much misinformation between them he wanted to get everything out in the open. God knows over the last couple of years their timing had been out of sync. Looking back, he could see he'd fancied Olivia forever and a day. It really was now or never and he didn't want to screw it up this time. 'OK. We ended up in bed together. I'm not a total bastard.' Surely that would count for something in his favour. 'I had to see her after that and let's face it, you were otherwise engaged. There was nothing to lose.'

She didn't look impressed. 'So you just kept seeing her. What? Because it was convenient?'

You didn't need a degree in body language to determine her mood from the arms firmly crossed over her chest.

'Don't be like that. It was a mistake. Anyway part of it was your fault—'

'How do you figure that?' she spat.

God, this wasn't going well. How did he explain? He thought the boat had sailed so he made do with second best. Telling her it was the practical option wasn't particularly romantic.

'Going out with Emily was a good excuse to keep seeing you and find out how serious it was with this other guy.'

'Really?' She stared thoughtfully out of the window, watching the woman in her hatchback next to them singing away to her music.

All the revelations of the last few hours had made him realise just how often he'd invented reasons to visit the flat. He was impressed by how devious his subconscious had been. He had been a very regular visitor.

Now it all seemed so obvious. OK, one kiss didn't make a lifelong commitment but he couldn't imagine life without Olivia.

They didn't talk for a little while.

'You could move out ...' he suggested, breaking the silence.

'Where to,' she said gloomily. 'It's my bloody flat.'

Even before he said it he wondered if it was a risk, if it was too soon to say it but hell they'd wasted so much time over the last few years. 'To my place.'

She looked at him, her mouth dropping open into a shocked 'o'. Then she dropped her head and muttered, 'I can't.'

'Why not?' Now he'd said it, it was so obviously the right thing to do.

'Because ...' she stopped. 'Besides, it's too soon.'

'Too soon for what? You can't stay with Emily. It's the obvious solution. Anyway I want you there. Safe. With me.'

'Are you sure?' Her voice sounded choked and out of the corner of his eye he caught her blinking furiously, and then in a typical Olivia move, she lightened the moment by saying, 'How do you know I'm not moving in just for that gorgeous kitchen? You know I've got oven envy.'

He smiled. 'Sweetheart, if you know how to drive it, you're welcome to it.'

As they came off the motorway into the heavy London traffic both of them went quiet. The prospect of facing Emily weighed heavily on him and he couldn't imagine how Olivia felt. The lies, that letter and the two of them having to pretend. No, he definitely wasn't looking forward to that bit.

Olivia tried to call Emily again, but her phone still kept switching to voicemail. Where was she was? Why didn't she answer? Maybe she couldn't.

Chapter Seventeen

Turning the key in the lock, I stopped reluctantly in the doorway, not wanting to go in, even though Daniel was right behind me. His hand was clasped over mine on the key in the door.

'I'll go first?' he whispered.

Following him, I bent to pick up my bag, listening intently.

'Hellooo,' I called out, with only a tiny quaver in my voice. Having six foot plus of lean muscle and warm body with me was very reassuring.

'Emily – are you home?' Nothing. Just silence.

Daniel took the steps two at a time. 'Emily, are you in?' he called more forcefully.

Following closely, my heart was bumping uncomfortably at the same time it was expanding with pride. My hero. My very own Clark Kent. He got to the top step, which opened into the lounge. It was cold and unlit; as if no one had been here for a little while.

An empty mug was on the floor beside Friday's *Evening Standard* along with a plate of congealing beans, a pair of boots, and two different shoes. Assorted clothes, jewellery and magazines were scattered around the room while the coffee table was strewn with empty crisp packets, biscuit crumbs and two discarded yoghurt pots.

'Has there been a struggle here?' said Daniel, bending down and picking up one of the shoes.

'No, Daniel. This is standard.'

'Really?' He seemed surprised.

Of course Emily had made sure she'd kept her inner slob hidden whenever he came round.

'I don't think anyone's here,' he said, lowering his voice. 'I'll check the bedrooms.'

He looked into Emily's room, then mine. 'Clear,' he said, with a more confident smile.

'You sound like you're in an American cop drama or something.'

'Just as long as I'm the good-looking one and not the short fat sidekick,' he said swaggering by, heading towards the bathroom. We were on a roll until he hit the kitchen. When I heard a muttered, 'Shit', I rushed in, fearing the worst, expecting to see Emily's bloodied and bruised body spreadeagled across the floor with spatters of red up the walls. Too much watching of CSI.

I collided with Daniel as he was retreating backwards.

'Oomph,' I muttered into the back of his shirt. He turned, standing tall so I couldn't see around him. My imagination carried on picturing a bloody body.

'God, it stinks in here. The bin needs emptying.'

My height decreased by three inches as the tension left my shoulders.

The bin always needed emptying when I wasn't around. Emily didn't do dirty jobs. There was quite a pong; old curry cartons mixed with rotting teabags and something I couldn't quite identify. Feeling pissed off that it was always me that had to do this, I crossed to the bin and quickly tied up the nearly overflowing black bag and dumped it outside the back door on the fire escape. I'd take it down the stairs later.

Closing the door, I crossed the floor, brushing past him deliberately to savour the bodily contact as I flicked on the kettle. He caught my arm and deliberately pulled me towards him.

'God, woman, this is going to be torture.'

I grinned wickedly up at him. Teasingly I reached up, putting my hand to the back of his neck and pulled his head down to mine.

'You're just going to have to grin and bear it,' I breathed

at the corner of his mouth, stealing a quick kiss. He turned and caught my lips, turning it into a kiss of the slow lingering type. My insides quivered and when he finally lifted his head, I was left wanting more. He returned my grin with an equally naughty one of his own.

'And you're going to have to behave.'

'Not fair,' I said ruefully. 'Bromide in the tea, I think.'

'You started it,' he said calmly, leaning back against the cupboards, arms folded looking smug.

I couldn't resist a quick sneaky glance to see if he was as affected as I was. He lifted a brow. Oops not as surreptitious as I'd thought. I blushed bright red as he smirked and my stomach dropped into freefall.

All this touchy feely, shivery, quivery stuff was very well but it was a long while since I'd been to bed with someone. I didn't have to calculate exactly how long – it was months in double digits. The thought of feeling all the hard and soft bits of his naked body up against mine had set my nerve ends tingling.

Daniel had a knowing look on his face. I could have sworn he knew exactly what was going through my head.

'You would be so bad at poker, sweetheart.' He grinned. I pretended to hit him, and of course he grabbed my wrist, pulling me towards him. When we finally broke apart, I insisted he should go and sit in the lounge so that I could concentrate on making him a cup of tea.

'But can you nip out and grab a pint of milk first?' It was pointless looking in the fridge; the last bottle had been finished on Friday morning. There was no way Emily would have bought any since.

While he was out, I made the tea, then quickly unpacked my bag, putting everything away, before giving my bedroom the quick once over. Just in case.

* * *

Opening the Yellow Pages, I sat down on the opposite sofa facing Daniel who having returned with the milk, had plonked it straight down on the table in front of us. I kept my distance because I was keen to avoid the scenario where we sprang apart like scalded cats the minute we heard Emily's key in the door.

'Blimey, it's big business locksmithery. There are loads listed.' I thumbed through. 'Police registered, contracted … that sounds good.' Daniel opened milk and poured it into the tea.

'Get a few quotes. They're bound to charge extra on Sunday.'

'Here's one that says no call out charge. Or what about this, OAP discounts. Do the over-sixties lock themselves out regularly?'

'Yes, if they're anything like my gran. She had keys all over the village – she was always locking herself out.'

Emily turned up just as I was finishing my call with Locks R Us. I was dreading her rushing up to Daniel and hurling herself into his arms, but I needn't have worried. As she rounded the top of the stairs, a guilty look slid across her face.

'Where have you been?' I asked hurriedly. 'Why didn't you answer your phone?'

'Daniel … Olivia. What are you … doing here?' she stuttered, hurriedly pulling her jacket back on.

I knew why. That skimpy top looked like last night's clubbing outfit to me.

'We've been so worried about you? I was imagining all—'

'What are you on about?' she asked defensively. 'I was at … at Caroline's last night.'

Her eyes didn't meet mine, which suited me fine – my own guilt was probably plastered across my face.

'Do you want to tell her, Olivia?' asked Daniel looking stern.

'It's Peter,' I explained. 'He's stalking you.'

'What do you mean?' Emily pulled a face, rolling her eyes at Daniel as if humouring me.

'Here on this tape I got from Miriam, you can see Peter watching you at the premiere.'

Her eyes narrowed. 'Are you absolutely sure it is him?'

'Definitely.'

Emily's eyes darted to Daniel.

'I know all about it,' he said dryly. She coloured and glared at me.

'I hope you explained that it was all down to you,' she snapped, her voice softening as she turned to Daniel. 'I only went on the speed-date to keep her company – biggest mistake I ever made.'

Not, if she was with the man I suspected she'd been with last night. A certain someone she'd met at the speed-date. Someone who had access to tickets to the *Phantom of the Opera*, liked Japanese food and completed *The Times* crossword every day.

'Emily, I'm not interested,' said Daniel wearily. 'There's a much bigger issue. Peter. He looks like he's been here. Taking things. Like your scarf.'

'Don't be ridiculous! You've been listening to little Miss Paranoia.' She rounded on me. 'You lost my red scarf. Do you think I believe that? Honestly.' She rolled her eyes at Daniel, trying to enlist his support.

'Emily,' I said as calmly as I could, my back teeth grating. 'I'd show you. It's quite clear on the video tape.'

'How convenient. Who still uses video tapes these days?'

Daniel shook his head. 'Emily, I promise you I've seen it. This guy was definitely at the premiere, watching you and wearing your red scarf.'

'My God. That's so creepy. How did he know I'd be there?' Emily hugged herself and sank onto the sofa.

'Dunno. But can you remember when the scarf went missing?'

'It was …' She went silent. 'No, it couldn't …'

'What?'

'You remember I lost my keys?' Emily asked Olivia.

'Of course I do. I rang you in a panic when I thought there was someone downstairs.'

Daniel's head shot up. 'You never said anything about that before.'

'Sorry, I didn't …'

Shit, had we just given the game away to Emily. Her face was an icy mask. Her eyes narrowed on Daniel. Trying to distract her, I said, 'Thought you'd left them at work.'

A brief look of embarrassment crossed her face. 'Not exactly,' she hedged. 'They were handed in to reception. Someone found them outside the front door of the office.'

Everything clicked into place. 'Cara said he'd dropped your bag,' I said, butting in. 'He took your keys.'

'My God. What's he up to? Why's he following me?' Emily looked ashen, her breathing shallow. 'I'm scared. What does he want?'

As if asking permission, Daniel glanced my way before going over and sitting down next to her.

'Look, Emily,' he said, taking her hand. 'A locksmith's on his way to change the locks but you need to call the police in. You have to report this.'

'Why can't Olivia? It's her fault – and her cousin's,' said Emily, turning to him and laying her head on his shoulder. 'What am I going to do? Oh, Daniel. I'm so glad you're here.'

He looked up helplessly. I shrugged. An Oscar winning performance.

'You'd have thought,' she glared at me as if I was

personally responsible, 'that checks would have been in place to stop this sort of thing. Why didn't you warn me, Olivia? You'll have to phone the police. Barney's *your* cousin.'

That's right put all the blame on me. I don't suppose it occurred to her that her inflammatory emails had poured oil on a troubled mind.

'You're the target,' said Daniel exasperated. 'The emails came to you and it was your computer he sabotaged. The brick was probably just random.' His voice softened as he said this and Emily gave him a sharp considering look. 'He wouldn't have known whose room it was.'

Suddenly she was mutinous. 'If we change the locks Peter can't do anything else, can he? He'll know we're on to him. That'll stop him.'

'No, Emily. Daniel's right. We have to call the police.'

She dismissed me. 'Olivia, you're over-reacting. I can't think about this, now. I'm going to have a bath.'

'Emily—'

'What difference does it make if we phone later? It can wait.' She deliberately turned her back on me.

'Daniel,' she said, her tone far sweeter. 'You don't mind if I slip off for a soak.' After a pause she asked, 'Are you ... erm, staying?'

'Actually, we need to talk,' he said ominously. My heart skipped, which was wrong of me but she deserved what was coming. I doubted she'd be too bothered, all the signs were that she'd got Daniel's successor lined up. Then again, she never liked to lose face.

Her fleeting look of worry was quickly replaced by a cocky, knowing look. 'Anyone want a glass of wine? I think I'm going to need one.' Before either of us could answer, she wheeled around and tripped off to the kitchen as my phone beeped announcing a text message.

As I read it anxiously, Daniel studied my face.

'Not Kate,' I said despondently looking up, rolling my head back and kneading my left shoulder which was full of knots. 'Why hasn't she got in touch yet?'

'Try not to worry. It's still the middle of the night there.' He stepped towards me and gave my hand a reassuring squeeze.

From the kitchen we heard a bad tempered bang as Emily slammed a cupboard door closed.

I withdrew my hand and pulled a face at Daniel. 'I'm going to hide in my room,' I whispered taking my cue for a diplomatic retreat.

'Can I come too?' he whispered.

'Daniel.' I tried to be stern but I couldn't help smiling at him, he was doing a puppy dog look. 'Are you a man or a mouse?'

'Definitely—'

Suddenly there was a piercing scream. A cry of such terror that it punched straight through to the nervous system. We both reacted in the same way, running panic-stricken to the kitchen.

An overpowering smell hit us, a rotten, stomach turning stench that made me physically recoil.

Emily was standing in front of the open fridge, gripping the edge of the door. Her eyes fixed on something inside.

Daniel took hold of her, peeling her fingers away from the door and deliberately manhandling her so she could no longer see what was so terrifying. Clinging to him, she burst into noisy heaving sobs, her shoulders shaking. I hovered uncertainly, my stomach heaving as the sweet, bitter smell permeated my lungs. It was the worst thing I'd ever smelt in my life.

'Hey, it's all right. It's all right. We're here,' he soothed, awkwardly rubbing her back.

'Cat. Downstairs. Cat,' she moaned.

What was she talking about? I couldn't make out the words. All I could see was her white face, screwed up in terror and her throat swallowing furiously as if she might gag at any second. I was trying not to breathe through my nose. Daniel passed Emily out of the way and towards me so that he could get to the fridge properly. She was soft and pliable, as if all her bones had been removed and it felt as if she might slip through my arms at any second.

Even though he'd steeled himself, Daniel's flinch said it all. His face paled as he closed the door firmly. His mouth turning down at the corners.

'Don't look, Olivia, it's not nice.' Judging from the smell, that was an understatement.

'What is it?' I breathed, my arm around Emily, holding on tight to keep her upright, every muscle bunched with tension. She'd started to cry and her teeth were chattering. She was slipping into shock.

'Dead cat,' he said tersely. 'The junk shop cat. Now's the time to phone the police.'

My stomach was churning with fear. Had Peter deliberately killed poor Charlie? The room felt incredibly cold. Wrapping my arms around myself, I tried to stop shaking. I wanted a cardigan but didn't want to go into my bedroom by myself. Peter must have been in there. I remembered things now, unexplained at the time, my necklace on the floor, Emily's missing underwear. It all made sense now.

We'd retreated from the kitchen and Emily was weeping copiously, all over Daniel. Shit, it was hard to ignore the way her tiny frame fitted so neatly on his knee, her head just tucked under his chin.

All three of us nearly leapt six feet in the air when the locksmith arrived. It was left to me to answer the door.

There was no way Emily was vacating those muscular thighs. Succumbing to my inner bitch, I thought it was a shame she'd stopped screaming. I would have enjoyed giving her a good slap.

A man of few words, Mr Lukic made short work of installing a new lock, even without my constant interruptions.

'Look, love,' he said with a sigh eventually, after I'd badgered him solidly for five minutes with questions about the security of the new locks. 'There are millions of permutations of these keys. No one is going to have a copy.'

'Are you sure?'

He put down his tools, and looked up at me. 'Yes, love.'

'But what about someone picking the lock?' I asked.

His brow furrowed like corrugated cardboard. 'That happens in films. Not real life, love. Burglars. Opportunists they are. Easy access – they'll take that every time.'

It wasn't a burglar I was worried about. I'd read enough psychological thrillers to know that psychopaths started small, torturing and killing pets before graduating to humans. My stomach twisted. Poor Charlie. What had Peter done to him? How could he? Charlie had been such a sweet little thing. He'd probably walked right up to Peter, weaving in and out of his legs, purring away like he always did. God, I was going to have to tell Charlie's owner? My eyes welled up. What was I going to tell him?

'There, love,' Mr Lukic's raspy voice interrupted my thoughts. 'All done.' Catching sight of my tears, he busied himself putting away his tools. 'Safest thing. Always put the chain on when you're in.'

It cost £120 by the time he'd finished, easy money for forty-five and a half minutes work. Nice work if you could get it especially with all those keyless OAPs wandering around in their slippers. Mr Rolling-in-fivers was handing out fresh keys by the time the police finally turned up.

Given that a murder wasn't actually in progress when we'd dialled 999, the police appeared quite quickly – by South London standards. They called it a 'Suspicious Incident' but I think Emily's hysterics in the background had a lot to do with it. Probably took pity on us – her voice can be a bit high-pitched.

To my disappointment there wasn't so much as a flash of a blue light to herald their arrival. They ambled in, in their black uniforms. Starsky and Hutch they were not.

PC Carpenter and WPC Cartwright were local veterans, so the contents of our fridge didn't faze them too much, even though they pronounced that poor Charlie's throat had been cut. At that news Emily keeled over in a suspiciously neat faint, while my stomach tried to turn itself inside out. Daniel's face turned even greyer.

Despite his youthful appearance, I swear it must have taken him three days to grow that stubble, PC Carpenter had probably clocked up more fatal stabbings and drive by shootings than he'd had hot dinners. He was a fairly weedy looking specimen, while gravelly voiced WPC Cartwright had probably had more packets of unfiltered Gauloise than hot dinners. Pushing forty, her hard, lined face told you that she'd seen and done everything, although she admitted a feline corpse in a domestic appliance was a new one.

She dutifully declined a cup of tea and plonked herself down on the sofa to take notes, propping up her notebook on her knee. It was left to me to relate the full tale, which when told sounded fairly fantastic.

'Did you make it clear the emails weren't welcome?' asked Cartwright, her hand pausing, glancing up from her closely written notes at Emily.

'Sort of,' said Emily wincing.

'How?' persisted the police lady.

'I told him to ... stop emailing me.'

Cartwright was nobody's fool. She just looked intently at Emily.

'All right, I told him to piss off and leave me alone and that he was a sad loser. OK?'

Cartwright's pen scribbled away furiously, asking the odd question about the content of the emails. I got the impression that in her vast and unseemly experience, the emails weren't even mildly offensive. As she explained wearily, there were guys out there beating seven bells out of their wives and girlfriends every night – often killing them.

In the background PC Carpenter poked about the flat, making obvious comments like. 'So this is the bathroom.'

I could see why he wasn't a detective.

As I got to the end of the story, PC Cartwright's back got straighter and her frown of concentration more intense. Coming to the end of the story, I explained how Daniel and I had seen Peter on the tape, and realised that he'd been in the flat, even before we'd come home to find the unmentionable in the fridge.

Cartwright looked sharply from me to Daniel, and then from Daniel to Emily. She shook her head slightly. I think she thought he was running a harem.

'We're definitely dealing with a harassment matter. Have you had any further contact with the young man?' she asked.

Emily shook her head.

Cartwright pinched her lips tightly and hesitated before she spoke again. 'This could escalate. I would like you to be aware of that. What we can do, if you would like us to, is warn him about his behaviour under Section Two of the Harassment Act.'

'What does that involve?' asked Emily, gnawing at her lower lip.

'He's officially warned in person by a police officer and

a record is made of this on computer. After that warning, if he persists in his behaviour, we have the power to arrest him and it could go to court. In that case your tape would then be evidence. In the meantime, you best hang on to it,' explained Cartwright, her wrinkled eyes narrowing into something resembling a sympathetic smile.

PC Carpenter returned from his amble around the flat. 'If you could prove that it was him chucked the brick through the window, you might get him for criminal damage. Did you report it at the time?'

'Yes,' I piped up. 'I've got the crime number.'

'What about your neighbours? Any of them see anything?'

'Doubtful. The junk shop downstairs is empty at night, the owner lives several doors down and we've never even see the people on either side.'

'Might be worth popping round and asking them,' observed PC Carpenter.

'What about the scarf?' asked Daniel.

Cartwright patiently explained that it was circumstantial evidence and unless we could prove that Peter had taken it from the flat, the police had no grounds to arrest him and seize the scarf for forensic examination.

Talk about unsatisfactory. Basically we had no proof.

'What about breaking and entering?' asked Daniel, bewildered that the law didn't seem to be able to help.

'I'd like SOCO to come round and see if they can get some fingerprints from the fridge.' She sighed wearily. 'Normally they wouldn't come out for harassment but this ... well ... I think it warrants it. Don't touch the fridge again until they've seen it.'

'Socko?' asked Emily. 'What's that?'

'Scenes of Crime Officers,' I piped up. Cartwright raised her eyebrows at me. I smiled weakly. 'Too many crime thrillers. Not first-hand knowledge.' I almost added, honest.

I always had a compulsion around the police to let them know I was a good upright citizen.

'Carpenter, can you get on to that right away,' said Cartwright, ignoring us both. 'Might be a good idea to get them here as soon as.'

'Will do.'

'So in the meantime, what next?' asked Daniel. 'Two girls living on their own. The locks have been changed, but what if he comes back?'

WPC Cartwright softened slightly at his visible frustration. 'Look, I understand you're worried. We can flag this address so that if you call 999 there's a note on the computer about what's been going on. If anything happens you'll be a priority. In the meantime we'll contact,' she looked at her notebook, 'Barney Snowdon, and see if he can give us this Peter's contact details. If all else fails we've got his email address and we can contact the service provider.'

God only knows what Barney would say when he heard the police would be in touch. That was one call I really didn't want to make.

Chapter Eighteen

What a day! From the start it had been one long rollercoaster from worrying about Kate through to finding Peter's gift, the arrival of the police and more recently the silent whirlwind of the SOCO team.

Hearing Daniel refer to me as 'my girlfriend' earlier in the car had been the high point, but now seeing Emily with her arm firmly anchored through his and the uncomfortable look on his face, I was going through the fastest freefall in history. She was in such a state that when she sobbed, 'Daniel, please stay tonight', what could he do? There was no way he could leave her, let alone break bad news to her.

Half an hour after Cartwright and Carpenter left, the crime scene guys turned up. They weren't the Hollywood heart-throbs you see on TV. Trooping in carrying their kits, apart from a brief introduction neither said a word. They were both tall, thin and moustached, reminiscent of John Cleese, except without the funny walk. Once in the kitchen they produced outsized brushes, big fat round ones with black bristles, which they whirled in circular motions around the fridge reminding me of a car wash, except instead of cleaning they were spreading black ash, which later proved bloody hard to get off.

I loitered in the kitchen for as long as I could until, after a pointed look from one of them, I disappeared just as they got to the interesting bit. It looked as if they were about to lift off a couple of prints. Within ten minutes their job was done and the two of them trooped back out again, telling me they'd got a couple of prints and someone would be in touch. Now it was just me, and Emily and Daniel.

In sheer desperation I got out the ironing board to occupy

myself. Perhaps my domestic goddess impersonation might impress Daniel.

Of course if Nigella had been doing the ironing, she would have made it look all sexy and come hither, with parted lips as she concentrated on a collar, a gentle toss of her hair as she pressed a sleeve and meaningful glances at the camera through the steam.

I on the other hand looked more like an angry troll taking my frustration out on several pairs of jeans. What with thinking of Daniel and worrying that I still hadn't heard from Kate, my concentration was shot and my favourite T-shirt ended up with a scorch mark on the sleeve.

Just as I was wondering whether Kate was all right, the phone finally rang and a strong Australian accent informed me that she was a nurse on Kate's ward.

'Thank God. How is she?' I asked anxiously. On the sofa I could see Daniel straighten and turn towards me.

'I'm afraid she's lost the baby, but she's doing well. We're keeping her in to keep an eye on her because she's lost a fair amount of blood.'

'How long for?'

'Another day or so. It was an incomplete miscarriage, there's still some tissue left in her uterus, we need to—'

'Can she have visitors?' I interrupted. Much as I love my sister, I didn't necessarily want the full details of her internal bits.

'Only one at a time at the moment,' said the nurse, clearly put out that I'd halted her mid medical spiel. 'She's very weak and, of course, upset.'

The nurse then reeled off the visiting times and ward number. I looked at my watch. Bill would be landing at about 11.30 their time. Could he get to the hospital for visiting time that afternoon?

'So how's Kate?' asked Daniel, as I was texting the details to Bill once the nurse rang off.

'In hospital. Doing OKish.' I didn't want to reveal all the details in front of Emily as I was sure that she was the last person Kate would want to know intimate details of her private life.

Emily lifting her head from Daniel's shoulder looked intrigued but before she could ask any questions I announced that I was going to bed.

'Been quite a day.'

'Yes,' said Emily huffily, as if it was entirely my fault.

Daniel looked at me steadily. 'Night, Olivia. Sleep well.'

'Good night,' I said as I slipped into the bathroom. How bizarre? Wishing him a good night. It was the last thing I wanted him to have. Sitting on the loo, I buried my head in my hands in a moment of self-indulgent despair. If ever I wanted someone to lean on, tonight was the night. Just my luck, so close and yet so far. How could I be missing Daniel so badly – it was less than twelve hours since our first kiss?

''Lo,' I answered groggily, when my mobile went some hours later.

'I know it's late but it's me. I've seen Kate.'

'Bill?'

'Yes, I've just left the ward.'

Rousing myself, I switched on my bedside lamp. It was three in the morning. 'God, what did she say when she saw you?' How much trouble was I in?

'Not a lot. She just cried.'

My heart sank. That wasn't Kate at all, she must be in a bad way. 'When can I speak to her?'

'She's asleep now. But I'm coming back at six for visiting time. I'll call you then, so you can speak to her. Don't worry, Olivia, she's OK, physically. Obviously she's very upset.'

'Seriously, Bill. Is she really OK or is she in a state?'

He took a deep breath. 'Olivia, I'm not going to lie. She's

very emotional, understandably. Very tearful and clingy. But I'll look after her. I promise.'

'Thanks, Bill.' I sniffed.

'I'll call later,' and with that he hung up.

There was no way I could get back to sleep after that. Poor Kate. Always so self-sufficient. Thank God Bill had gone straight out.

I felt so much better knowing that she had someone with her. He would look after her. Despite that reassurance, I still couldn't get back to sleep. I tossed one way and then another, plumping my pillows but it was no good. I had to get up.

Some sixth sense stopped me screaming the house down as something grabbed my calf as I crept through the lounge.

'What are you doing?' I whispered, my heart leaping into my mouth, relived to see Daniel.

'Trying to get some sleep on this very lumpy sofa. Didn't mean to scare you.'

'That's all right then, if you didn't meant to,' I said, as he pulled me down next to him, putting an arm round me. 'Thought you'd be with Emily,' I said tentatively.

'What? Sleeping with her?'

'Not in the physical sense. How d'you get out of it?' I asked 'Oo your hands are cold.'

'So would you be without a blanket.' He was still fully dressed but had pinched my winter coat from the rack in the hall. 'Said there was something on TV I wanted to watch. I was going to pretend that I'd fallen asleep here. Don't suppose you fancy warming me up a bit?'

'Yes. There's a spare blanket ...' I teased half-standing.

He pulled me back. 'Don't you know body heat is the most effective in preventing hypothermia,' he murmured in my ear, hot breath teasing my neck as his hands slipped round my waist and up under my top.

'Hypothermia. It's summer,' I replied squirming as his cold

hands smoothed their way up my back. They might have been cool but everything else was warming up nicely.

Despite that, I was finding it very difficult to relax. The spine that Daniel was so confidently stroking was remaining resolutely ramrod.

After a while Daniel shifted, pulling me round to face him.

'Not having second thoughts, are you?' he asked, looking into my face.

'No, just scared Emily might come out.' In response he put an arm around my shoulder and we sat there in the dark with the moon shining in through the window. It was probably at least ten minutes before either of us spoke. Even my brain had slowed to enjoy the quiet closeness. I'd missed this, the easy companionship of being with someone else without having to talk, no gaps to fill, no uncertainties to question.

'Don't drop off, sweetheart, you need to go back.' It was the third time he'd called me that, and yes I was counting. It sent such a shot of sheer joy through me. I muttered sleepily at him, too content to find words.

'Come on, I can feel you drooping, it's been quite a day, all in all.'

I sighed. 'Do I have to? I like it here.' I would have quite happily stayed there forever, hang the consequences.

'Yes, you do. Remember you work and live with Emily,' he said, quoting my words back to me. 'I was planning on hanging around in the morning, I have to speak to her tomorrow. Knock it all on the head.'

'You know, Daniel,' I said hesitantly. 'I'm not sure that she's going to be too upset.'

'Really,' he asked turning his chin, bumping my head. 'Sorry that sounds big headed. Do you think she knows?'

I shifted, looking up at him. 'No, let's just say I have an inkling your replacement's already been lined up.'

A chagrined expression crossed his face. I put my hand up

to stroke his cheek saying flippantly, 'It's OK, I still lo—' I stopped. His hand trapped mine, an eyebrow quirking. There was a silence. I chickened out. 'I think that she might have been elsewhere last night. She didn't exactly seem pleased to see us.'

'Now you mention it, was it my imagination or was she a bit shifty?' he observed.

'Mm, if it wasn't you she was out at Phantom with last week or Yo! Sushi, I've got a good idea who it might have been.'

Now if Daniel had been a girl he would have been straight in there wanting to know all the details, but he seemed to take it as a green light. A slow smile crossed his face, a knowing look in his eyes. All of a sudden he seemed far more interested in trying to spark some life into my erogenous zones. A considerably warmed up hand was making a new foray, slinking up the side of my ribs, dancing on the edge of ticklish and wildly erotic. I couldn't help it, a small moan escaped. He took complete advantage of my half-dressed state, the palm of his hand spreading, his thumb inching over my nipple. A zing darted downwards; my lips met his, move for move and before I knew it I was sinking back, the warmth of his body spread over me, our mouths fused in a delicious kiss.

I woke up cold and alone – virtue intact. Damn it! I'd returned to my empty bed at about five and, despite every nerve end tingling with frustration, had amazingly dropped straight back to sleep.

The morning got off to a good start when I got my first love text. 'Gd mrng sweetheart. Sleep well? Xxxxxxx'

My heart did a funny little flip and I lay back on my pillow, a silly grin on my face, counting the kisses on the message. How sweet was that? He was only the other side of the wall.

From there it all went downhill.

It should have been a relief when Kate finally phoned, but she was listless and weepy. I felt so helpless. All I wanted to do was give her a big hug. Never had I felt so far away.

'Hi, sweetie. How are you?'

'OK,' she said wearily. 'I want to go home but they won't let me.'

'How's Bill?' I asked warily.

'Fine,' she said.

'Oh,' I was flummoxed. Pulling teeth would have been easier. 'Just fine?'

'Yes,' she said her voice breaking.

'Kate, don't. I thought you'd be mad at me for telling him.'

'Too late now,' she said with a sniff, her voice sounding thick as if she had a cold. 'He knows. Anyway there's no baby, so he doesn't need to stick around.'

'Kate. You know that's not true. If you'd seen him the night he flew out.'

'How was he?' she asked pathetically eager.

'In a state.'

'Honest?' she asked quietly.

'Yes,' I said exasperated. This wasn't like Kate. Normally men fell like ninepins at her feet with her stepping over them with careless abandon. When had things changed? Was Bill really that important to her?

'For God's sake, Kate. The poor man dropped everything, hopped straight on a flight and flew twenty-four hours to see you.'

'You think he really cares?'

Duh! I was trying to be gentle with her, she clearly wasn't herself. Good job she was so far away, otherwise I would have given her a good shake. 'Kate! Listen. Of course he bloody does. You can ask Daniel if you don't believe me. Shall I put him on?'

'Daniel?' her voice sounded puzzled. 'He's with you?'

'Erm, yes. Actually I meant he's here in the flat but now you mention it, I could say "with me". We're still working on it.'

'You and Daniel.' She brightened up. 'Yay. About time. You finally dislodged him. I want details but not now. Bill's going to be here soon.'

There was a pause down the line, followed by a small sob. 'What am I going to say to him? It was his too.' She stopped.

'Kate, it's not your fault. He's not going to blame you for having a …' I couldn't bring myself to say the word. As if saying it made it more real. Until now, Kate being pregnant had been almost hypothetical.

'What if it is my fault? I didn't want a baby and now it's gone.' Her voice went up. 'And now,' she was crying in earnest, 'I do.'

My fingers tightened on the phone as I bit my lip at the anguish in her tone.

'I was going to get rid of … my baby … it … I said that. As if my baby was nothing. How could I? Now I've been punished for being so … It was my fault. Maybe I shouldn't have flown back. Air travel can't be good for pregnancy. What if I never have another chance?'

'Kate, stop. It wasn't your fault. These things happen. It's a cliché, I know, but they do happen, much more often than people realise. There's some statistic, one in three—'

'That's marriages ending in divorce. Not babies,' wailed Kate.

My shoulders slumped. This conversation was so hard over the phone. I would have done anything to be sitting with her, on the end of her bed, holding her hand.

Trying to distract her, I changed the subject. 'Do you want me to say anything to the parents?'

'Noooo!' she cried. 'I can't … No … not Mum. Don't tell her yet. Wait 'til I'm out of here.'

Finishing the call, I looked at my watch. I was running late but I just didn't care. Poor Kate. Then again, there was no way I wanted to hang around the flat. After everything that had happened this weekend, work would be a break. Hopefully it would take my mind off everything else.

Last night Daniel had said that he'd wait until I'd left to talk to Emily. No doubt she'd be demob happy and only working minimal hours. Shit. I had to speak to her about that today. It wasn't her day either.

As predicted, Emily had decided she would be late in.

'I'm far too shaken up,' she explained wearily from the bathroom, where she was busy applying her make-up. 'You can explain why.' As if it was entirely my fault.

'OK,' I said, dying to ask where Daniel had got to. There was no sign of him and my coat was neatly hung back on its peg as if last night had never happened.

'What are you doing about the fridge?'

My immediate thought was 'not a lot'.

'Don't think I'm going anywhere near it,' she announced, tossing her head, mascara wand in hand. 'Daniel's had to go out to buy a pint of milk. Yesterday's smelt funny.'

I replied resignedly that I would sort it out. PC Carpenter, it had turned out, was originally a country boy. As a result he'd had a lot of experience with dead animals. His view was that the smell would take a while to get rid of. He had to be joking, there was no way I was cleaning out that fridge. I had every intention of buying a new one today, that's what credit cards were for.

There was something I could do about the fridge in the meantime.

As soon as Daniel came back from the corner shop, I asked him very loudly so that it was all above board in front of Emily, to help me move it out onto the fire escape.

'Come on, then,' he said, discarding his jacket and putting his shoulder against the fridge to heave it towards the door. I paused as Emily appeared in the doorway, although he couldn't see her.

'Come on. No slacking,' he admonished. 'Your mission, should you choose to accept ...' He broke into the *Mission Impossible* tune. I caught Emily's eye. She was stony faced, her mouth curved downwards in a crescent of disapproval as she stood watching our antics.

I couldn't stop myself giggling. Daniel was wearing a tea towel mask and darting around the room, arms flailing as he made random karate chops in the air. With slow motion care, he opened the back door, poking his head in and out several times, before pulling lots of faces to show me that all was clear.

'Why don't you grow up?' tutted Emily, her lips pursed as she directed her narrowed eyes at me, making it clear we were about as funny as a pair of nine year olds on laughing gas.

'Sorry,' I said meekly, trying hard not to snigger as I caught Daniel pasting a look of mock innocence on his face.

'Hmph,' muttered Emily, glaring at me and ignoring Daniel, as she turned to stomp back down the hall. She paused, 'When will you sort out a new one?'

'Don't worry. I'll get one today.'

'Good.'

We giggled quietly, pulling the tea towels off. I cast mine aside ruefully. 'I'd better go. I need to get to work.'

'Haven't you forgotten something?' teased Daniel, with a tilt of his head.

I glanced at the door, the coast was clear. It seemed totally natural to slip into his open arms, my own coming to rest around his waist.

'When am I going to see you again?' he asked. 'After work tonight?'

'Only if you don't mind coming to John Lewis with me to buy a new fridge.'

'Can do.'

Quickly we arranged to meet in front of the store and a moment later, I pulled away. 'I really have to go,' I whispered regretfully.

'I'll see you later. I've got a meeting in the West End later this morning which is going to last nearly all day. I'll take the car and park up in Portman Square, it's right behind the store. Quarter to six outside.'

I bit my lip and nodded.

'Take care, Olivia. I don't like the thought that Peter's still out there.'

'Well, at least he hasn't got keys.'

'Yeah, but ...' He shrugged and took a step forward. 'Just be on your guard,' he muttered, giving me one last kiss before I slipped down to the front door, grabbing my jacket on the way.

The shiny new lock, which glinted at me as I pulled the door too, was an unwelcome reminder of another thing I had to sort out. Barney.

God, he was going to be so pissed off that the police were involved.

I flicked open my mobile as I walked down the street, a spring in my step and a fierce glow in my chest. The postman looked distinctly amused when I gave him a big grin and gave me a knowing wink.

'What – this had better be good,' snapped Barney in my ear, as I finally connected with him.

'It is. Remember the guy that I spoke to you about. Things have escalated – he's broken into our flat and left a dead cat in the fridge.'

There was a gratifyingly stunned silence for a few seconds before he breathed a heartfelt, 'Fuck.'

'Fuck indeed. Emily found it.'

'Emily? Oh God. Is she all right?'

I felt ready to scream. Emily was bloody fine, lapping up the sympathy, while muggins here had to sort everything out.

'Have you told anyone about this?'

'The police came round yesterday. Sorry they needed your details to contact Peter.'

To my surprise, he didn't object. 'Fair enough. They haven't called yet, but I've got Peter's address. I dug it out last time you called. Olivia, I'm really sorry. It never occurred to me that this might happen.' His voice dropped and for one second I almost believed he was sincere. 'Mind you, if I did vet everyone, it would make us so much better than all the rest. Great marketing.'

'As long as no one hears about this,' I snapped.

''Spose so.' There was a pause before he asked, 'You haven't told your mother have you?'

I sent a silent appeal heavenward. As if.

'No, you're off the hook. Mum doesn't know, so you'll still be the blue-eyed nephew.'

'Do you know, Olivia, sometimes you're a shrew. I meant that I could reassure her that I'm checking Peter out.'

Bugger, I hated it when Barney showed his kinder side. I always assumed people like him had no conscience.

Chapter Nineteen

To my surprise the bored tone of the man at the council offices never altered as I recounted my tale when I phoned him from work that morning. For a very reasonable fee he offered to send someone round to collect the fridge.

This still left the question of what to do about Charlie. I couldn't let the council dispose of him as well. I'd knocked on his owner's door after speaking to Barney but to my relief there'd been no answer. Telling them that Charlie's body was in my fridge was going to take some explaining. I was going to have to buy some industrial rubber gloves and a face mask to remove him. It would have been easier to leave his body in a shoebox on the doorstep but I couldn't do that to Mr Gregory.

'Where's Emily?' From the way Cara's eyebrows were creased over her soft brown eyes, she must have overheard some of my bizarre conversation.

'She's going to be late in this morning,' I answered shortly, not wanting to go into details, especially as over her shoulder Helene and Camilla were both listening avidly. It was obvious Emily had already told them she was leaving.

Cara stepped back, giving me a mild look of reproach. Bugger, she didn't deserve that. She'd been my first ally on the beauty team. Easily worth ten of Emily.

'Sorry, Cara. Didn't mean to snap. Been an eventful weekend.'

'I kind of gathered. If there's anything I can do ...' her voice trailed off weakly as she gave me a sympathetic smile and went back to her desk, absently flicking at the Arsenal pennant stuck to her computer.

Arsenal. Football. I suddenly remembered. I was supposed to be taking Ned tonight.

'Actually, Cara, there is something ...' Was it a bit of a cheek to ask her to go to a football match with a complete stranger?

I'd underestimated the power of the Arsenal football team.

Cara's eyes lit up. Ned could have been Quasimodo for all she cared. All that mattered was that she going to 'the Arsenal' as she called it.

'Thank you. Thank you. Thank you, Olivia. Sure you don't want to go?'

'It'll be wasted on me. Plus I need to do something urgent this evening,' I said, turning back to my to-do list, adding Ned's name to the bottom. With a million phone calls to make, a bulging inbox of emails and a feature deadline to meet, my day was going to be hectic. My phone never stopped ringing that morning. David, to tell me that Fiona was due to return, so was popping in for a meeting later today; journalists chasing photos, printers wanting artwork and ... I still had to talk to Ned.

Thank God for work. If I'd had time to think my brain would have melted into a puddle. It had been an eventful few days.

I should have worked diligently through my to-do list, but thanks to considerable procrastination, it was late afternoon before I managed to get hold of Ned and then I bottled it. How could I tell him?

'All set for the big game tonight?' he asked, when I finally got through to him.

''Fraid not. Sorry, Ned, I can't make tonight. It's a bit complicated.'

He didn't say a word, so I ploughed on quickly. 'Don't worry. You can still go, but you'll have to go with a work colleague of mine. She's a big Arsenal fan. In case the client asks, it'll look better if someone from our company is there.'

'OK,' he said slowly. I could tell he was pissed off. Not

that I blamed him but my emotions were like glitter in a snow globe. They were so mixed up I couldn't summon any guilt.

'Look, I'm really sorry,' I explained dropping my voice. 'It's been a hell of a weekend. My sister lost a baby.'

Immediately I could tell he perked up. 'Shit, sorry that's bad news.'

'Yeah, well. She's in hospital.' I didn't add 'in Australia'. Thank God she'd got Bill with her. And Ned didn't need to know about Daniel, just yet. Let him enjoy his Arsenal match. Not that I was big headed enough to think that he was smitten with me but telling him now would only hurt his pride unnecessarily.

Feeling relieved to have avoided any unpleasantness, I arranged that he would come to the office to meet Cara at 6.00 p.m., by which time I would be long gone.

At five-thirty on the dot, I switched off my computer, handed over the tickets to Cara without a grain of guilt and left the office. My mind was on other matters.

Anyone seeing me skipping down Oxford Street might have questioned how much coffee I'd been drinking. Anticipation and excitement had added an extra bounce to my step.

As I spotted Daniel outside the front of John Lewis, my stomach twisted with nerves. I speeded up and he looked up, catching my eye as I got closer. For a moment we looked at each other without saying a word. My mouth went dry as one corner of his mouth quirked.

'Hi,' he said softly. My heart lurched as I smiled shyly back.

'Hi.'

Giving his head an amused shake he stepped forward and slid a hand across my cheek, into my hair and pulled my head towards him for a kiss.

'That's better,' he said afterwards, putting his arm around me and steering me inside. 'How was today?'

'Busy,' I said. 'I didn't get a chance to speak to Emily as she wasn't around much. How did she take it?' I asked, our hands linked, as we sailed upwards on the escalator.

He winced. 'My ego feels as if it's been ripped out, chewed up and spat out again. Be gentle with me.'

'That bad?'

'Hell hath no. The worst boyfriend on the planet.' He sounded reasonably cheerful about this as he pointed to himself. 'Rubbish relationship material.'

She hadn't pulled any punches then.

'I'm a boring old git with an unhealthy obsession with ball ... sports.'

'Have I made a terrible mistake?' I teased.

'I never go to decent restaurants.'

'What never?' I asked, in mock outrage as we stepped off the escalator.

He drooped his head in dejection. 'Nope.'

We wound our way through the electrical department to find the fridges.

'You don't need to worry then,' I said cheerfully, sailing past the televisions, tugging at his hand as he stopped briefly. 'It's your kitchen I'm interested in – we can eat in.'

'It gets worse ...'

Playing along, I sighed heavily and stopped. I turned to face him. 'What there's more?'

'I'm crap in bed.' His eyes twinkled, his lips twitching.

'That's it then. Sorry ...'

'Oy,' he tickled my ribs. 'You're supposed to be on my side.'

I lowered my voice, there were other people around. 'Perhaps you just need practice?'

'Are you volunteering?'

That took the wind out of my sails.

'Well, surely you must have some good points,' I said

bracingly, as I turned and pulled him along towards the household appliances.

He sucked in his breath. 'No,' he said firmly. 'Not one.'

'Sure? No redeeming features at all.' I thought for a moment. 'I might have to reconsider.'

His arm snaked round me and pulled me closer, his warm breath teasing my neck. 'I've been through the verbal wringer. I need first aid and sticking plasters, woman. What are you going to do about it?'

'Depends. Are you young, free and single again?'

'Resoundingly, yes. Emily never wants to set eyes on me again. Mind you, she's not overly fond of you either at the moment. What have you done to upset her so much?'

'What? Apart from breathe?'

'I asked her about your married man but she stuck to her guns. Insisted he existed – even after I said I believed you. At which point she spat your name out, reminding me, I might add, of an indignant llama, and said you wouldn't know the truth if it came and slapped you.'

I laughed. I could so clearly picture Emily's face. 'And what did you say to that?'

'Well,' he hedged slightly.

'Daniel,' a note of warning creeping into my voice.

'I didn't mean to let on about us ... but I might have been a bit ... vocal in support of you.'

'Can I help?' A small man stepped out in front of us, his wrinkled neck reminding me of a tortoise.

I gave Daniel a look, my heart filling with a little burst of pride as he gave me a little wink. 'Er yes, we're looking for a fridge,' I said self-consciously. Shopping for white goods in John Lewis wasn't quite how I'd envisioned spending my first proper date with Daniel but I felt a little definite thrill. Shopping for two made a change.

Our little man was a mine of useful information. He really

knew his fridges, although discussing the merits of automatic defrost when your libido is on fire takes some doing.

Everything went swimmingly until we got to the taking possession of our chosen model part of business. It turned out choosing a fridge was easy. Having it installed before the milk went off was another matter. Delivery took at least a week.

'Dad's got a spare fridge in the garage we use at Christmas,' volunteered Daniel as my face fell. 'Let me give him a call. I could bring it over tomorrow after work.'

Our helpful assistant beamed at this, although looking at my credit card clutched in his hand, it would have been a fight to the death to get it back from him.

Having someone to look after me, after years of self-sufficiency was rather nice. In fact it was blood tinglingly gorgeous. We went for a drink, strolled hand in hand through Covent Garden and stopped for dinner. It should have been perfect but annoyingly thoughts of Peter kept intruding. I did my best to keep them at bay by telling myself that he wouldn't dare do anything else now. Would he?

Although I didn't mention it to Daniel I was conscious that he too kept surreptitiously scanning the crowds as we walked along.

As it started to get dark we headed towards the river and both relaxed as we left the crowds behind. We made extremely slow progress across Waterloo Bridge. Daniel kept pointing out landmarks.

'Look.'

'Where?' I asked, stopping only to find his head dipping towards mine and his lips brushing my mouth.

'The London Eye,' he said grinning as he lifted his head. I soon joined in the game.

'Look, Big Ben.'

It took half an hour's sightseeing to get over the bridge and ten minutes to get up the stairs into Waterloo station.

'Daniel, you don't have to put me on the train,' I said, as we looked up at the departures board, standing arm in arm, cheek to cheek. 'You've still got to go all the way back to the West End to get your car. I'll be fine, honest. There's a train in five minutes.'

He shrugged.

'I'd rather ...' He looked round at the busy concourse before kissing my cheek. His lips worked their way to mine. 'Plus I'm not going to see you 'til tomorrow night.'

I pulled a face and kissed him back, eyes closed, revelling in the warm glow of his words, as I ignored the little voice that wondered what Emily would have to say when he turned up tomorrow with the fridge.

I missed that train and the one after.

When I got home, to my massive relief, Emily didn't emerge from her room although she was clearly awake as I could hear drawers and wardrobe doors rattling as if she was feverishly searching for something.

As I quickly made myself a cup of milk less tea, I resolved to tackle the contents of the fridge. Tomorrow.

When the train arrived the next morning it was packed. As I squeezed my way on, I couldn't help checking every face even though it meant raising my head. My mascara stained eyes must have looked a sight. On the way to the station I'd finally caught up with Charlie's owner.

Handing over the box that had once contained new boots made me feel like a murderer. Mr Gregory answered the door in a royal blue sweatshirt and half-mast jogging bottoms, which revealed skinny grey haired ankles.

'Chew know what time it is?' he growled, throwing the

door open and stepping towards me. Glaring down at me, I felt positively small which doesn't happen often.

'Ssorry, I ...' Without thinking I offered him the boot box.

'You the new postman,' he snapped, looking me up and down as he started to open the box.

'No, no.' I put my hand on the box. 'It's Charlie. Your cat.'

He looked at the box in his hands and then sharply at me.

'Know where Charlie is, d'ya?' His voice softened. ''Ees been missing for a coupla days now.'

I took a deep breath, hoping it might stop me bursting into tears. No such luck. 'I'm ...' A sob escaped as a tear slipped down my cheek. 'So,' I sniffed. 'Really sorry.'

Mr Gregory's bushy eyebrows drew together under a deeply furrowed frown. He grasped my arm firmly and for a horrible moment I thought he might think I was responsible.

'Now, now love.'

I nodded towards the box. 'He's dead. I ... I found him.'

He lifted the lid of the box and his face crumpled, his mouth drooping and his eyes disappeared into crinkled creases as he blinked furiously.

'Charlie lad, Charlie,' he murmured, reaching into the box and stroking the black fur with one bony finger. He looked back at me, nodded, turned away and with his shoulder closed the door leaving me on the doorstep.

Talk about shitty start to the day. Not getting a seat on the train only made things worse. My eyes felt tired and gritty and I had the beginnings of a headache. Bloody Peter. Slipping my phone out of my pocket I tapped in a quick text to Barney. 'Any joy in tracking P down?'

Five minutes later just as the train pulled into Vauxhall, my phone rang.

'Barney?'

'Olivia. Thought I'd let you know. I've spoken to the police and gave them Peter's address.'

'Great. So you spoke to the person who recommended him? What did they say?'

'Not much. But I gave him short shrift for being so casual about it all. He was horrified. Got a feeling he might have words with Peter, even though I told him to leave it to the plods. I've drafted up some new terms and conditions to make sure this doesn't happen again.'

That was unexpected. 'Thanks,' I said, voicing my surprise.

He sighed. 'Olivia, you're family. This guy's been terrorising you and it's indirectly my fault. I'm not all bad you know.'

'No,' I said grudgingly. 'I suppose you have improved a bit since you were eighteen.'

'Don't overdo it, will you.'

'I wouldn't want you to get big headed,' I replied sweetly, and then more sincerely. 'Thanks Barney.'

'Speak to you later.'

Emily made a brief appearance in the office and then left just after lunch to go to the dentist, which I thought was odd as she'd not mentioned it before. Taking advantage of a client meeting finishing early, I decided not to go back to the office. It wasn't like I didn't put the hours in normally.

When I got home, I surprised Emily.

Black bin liners and boxes overflowing with clothes were spilling from the open boot of the cab parked outside the flat. No wonder she'd been avoiding me for the last 24 hours.

The driver was lazily smoking a cigarette leaning against his car door, jabbering unconcernedly on his mobile. A box emerged from the flat, piled with books, CDs, one of my saucepans and a bedside lamp and was dumped into the back of the cab. Emily's bottom backed out, straightened and turned walking right into me.

'Olivia!' Her voice was high-pitched and strangled. I was obviously just that bit too early.

'Going somewhere?' I asked.

She squared up, her jaw thrusting out pugnaciously. 'I'm moving out. Well, you'd hardly expect me to stay ... a stalker in waiting and you mooning all over my boyfriend.' Rehearsed to perfection her bitter words came tumbling out. 'Let's face it. You've been making cow's eyes at him for ever. Idiot ... do you think he's interested in you? Cricket turns him on. Wouldn't surprise me if there weren't some serious homo-erotic leanings there – you know naked men together ... in the showers, that sort of thing.'

She stalked past me up the stairs back towards her room.

My eyes did a 'you've got to be kidding' wide-eyed thing as I followed her. The naked bit I could imagine but that's where our imaginations parted company.

'That's what turns him on on a Saturday night. He was never into sex. We haven't slept together for weeks.'

She grabbed another bag from her bedroom and turned to face me.

What could I say after that little outburst? Although at her last words, I did an internal goal scorers wiggle. Feebly my response was, 'So where are you going?'

Every bit of pity and disdain she could muster was summoned up and delivered in her scathing glance. It was completely wasted on me, bouncing right off into the ether. My mind was busy lighting candles, setting the scene for seduction.

'I'm going to stay with someone. You know him quite well.'

I had a pretty good idea. All the clues suggested Mr Loathsome from the speed-date who liked sushi and knew someone who could get tickets for Phantom, but a little gut instinct kept telling me it didn't stack up. He was a bit too smooth.

I pulled a face and shuddered very deliberately which was a bit theatrical and downright rude but she deserved it.

'You're just jealous,' she said, dismissing my childish gesture, flouncing past me towards the stairs, 'that your cousin likes me more than you.'

Cousin!

'Barney!' I squeaked. She had to be kidding.

She shrugged. 'Why not? We really clicked that night at the speed-date. Who did you think it was?'

I couldn't bring myself to admit how wrong I'd been, instead I opted for the cheap way out. I hadn't planned to do this but she was such a cow she deserved no mercy. I delivered the *coup de grâce* as she was carrying the last box out.

'David told me you'd resigned.'

A sly smile lifted the corners of her mouth. She looked like the cat that has swallowed the golden canary as she preened, waiting to hear the next bit.

'He said ...' I let her preen a bit longer, 'it was up to me ...' I enjoyed the dimming of her self-satisfied smile, '... when you go.' I paraphrased him. 'So you can either piss off tomorrow and we'll pay you up to the end of the week, or you can work the full month, bearing in mind your reference depends on how well you behave.' The power had completely gone to my head, I really wasn't a nice person – but God I enjoyed it.

Her face darkened with rage.

'You can't do that,' her voice cracked. 'I'm on a month's notice.'

'What like the month's notice you're giving me?' I asked, looking pointedly at the box in her arms.

'I was going to give you the rent,' she said haughtily. We both knew that wasn't true. It was hard enough getting her share of the bills at the best of times. 'Anyway, you still have the deposit. In fact you'll owe me, that was a month and a half rent.'

'What after bills?'

She shrugged. 'Let me know what I owe. My new job pays a lot more. I can afford it.' And with that she tossed her head and marched down the stairs.

The decisive slam that accompanied her departure almost shook the foundations, and for a fleeting moment I felt sad that it had come to this but that was quickly overtaken by indignation that she could get away with behaving so badly.

It was amazing how quickly I'd become so reliant on Daniel, my first thought was to ring him but then I remembered he was probably already on his way with the temporary fridge. Until then, I had the flat to myself and I knew exactly what I was going to do. Perhaps I'd just give him a quick call and ramp up the anticipation. Tell him that Emily had gone and we had the place all to ourselves. There was time enough to tell him the shocking revelation about Emily and my cousin.

My throaty message on his voicemail was full of invitation. Whether he would arrive in time to scrub my back in the bath was debatable.

In my next life I might come back as a hippo – there's nothing quite like having a bath to calm you down, especially when you're wallowing in someone else's expensive bubbles that she had left behind.

Breathing in the scent of mimosa and frangipani and watching the steam rising off the water, I wriggled my shoulders in satisfaction deliberately ignoring my mobile ringing in the other room. It finally rang off, the answer service must have kicked in but less than a minute later it started again. Bugger it, I was staying put. Let it ring.

When I finally emerged from the bathroom, and looked at the dratted thing, there were five missed calls. All from Barney.

There was one message from him.

'Call me. On my mobile. ASAP. I need to talk to you.' Against the background sound of traffic, he sounded slightly breathless as if he was walking quickly along a busy street.

I didn't want to call him, guessing he wanted to come clean about Emily. Bet she hadn't told him the half of it. I still felt shocked. Emily and Barney. Never saw that one coming. But what if he was ringing with news on Peter? I had to call, but he didn't answer. Where the hell was he? Now my curiosity was piqued. I left a quick message desperate to know what he had to say.

His call had undone all the good of my bath. Restlessly I wafted round the flat rearranging things to my satisfaction; stacking all of Emily's magazines in a neat pile on the coffee table, moving the sofas so that they didn't both face the TV and putting the ugly spare dining chairs into her empty room.

When the knock at the door came I jumped in eager anticipation, glancing at the clock. Daniel had made very good time. He must have left work early.

Chapter Twenty

Quickly I tousled my hair and kicked off my bunny slippers, changed my mind and slipped them back on again. It was only as I skipped down the last few stairs towards the opaque front door that some sixth sense slowed me down.

Of course, it might not be Daniel. Was it my imagination or was the height of the outline through the rippled glass too small or had the knock been too urgent? In the pit of my stomach there was an uncomfortable sensation, as if something was rubbing the wrong way. Whatever it was it made me put the chain on the door.

I'd never even looked at the little brass chain before. It suddenly seemed very flimsy. Don't be so paranoid, I told myself as I slid the chain into place very quietly so that whoever was on the other side of the door didn't know what I was doing. I could see their outline shifting impatiently.

A gruff voice in an offhand tone said, 'Delivery. Needs signing for.'

Phew. I needed to get a grip.

He had his back to me as I opened the door. All I could see was neatly cropped brown hair and a red scarf tucked above the collar of a dark brown anorak. Below this he was wearing a pair of sand coloured cords, which finished an inch too high above scruffy brown brogues. Hang on. Delivery man? Dressed like that? Those trousers didn't say courier to me.

He slowly turned round, bringing his face right up to the crack in the door, brown eyes glinting at me. The red scarf.

My legs suddenly seemed unable to take my weight and wobbled beneath me.

'Hello.' He grinned. 'Like my last delivery?'

Before I had a chance to slam the door closed, he had thrust his arm though the small opening and grabbed my arm. 'Gotcha,' he rasped and then giggled.

My heart was slamming into my ribs as I tried to pull away but his fingers tightened. Looking down I could see them short and stubby at the end of forearms, thick with gorilla hair. I shuddered. The chain rattled alarmingly as his leg now forced its way through the gap, jamming open the door to its fullest extent. My throat felt tight, as I opened my mouth. No scream came out.

The door. I had to close it. With all my weight, I threw myself at it, hurting my hip as it slammed into the door.

There was an angry grunt from the other side as he let go of my arm. Thank God the chain was holding. Still pushing at the door, hoping that he would pull back and go away, I dodged his arm that was flailing blindly towards my head.

Not fast enough! The next moment he had a handful of my hair. With a sharp violent twist he pulled hard slamming my head into the metal door frame.

For a moment, white lights flashed in my eyes and a wave of sickness grabbed at my stomach.

'Nmph,' I grunted. As the pain radiated in waves down my face I rocked for a second trying to breathe. The hand grasping my hair loosened briefly. Then ... thunk. I felt the cold metal bite into my cheekbone. With sickening anticipation, I felt his fingers pulling tight on my hair. Please, don't let him do it again.

Raising my hands to my head, I dug my fingernails hard into his hand and ignoring the pain of my hair pulled tight away from my scalp, I gave a desperate tug.

I couldn't believe it. The relief as I flew backwards. But as I looked up my relief turned to horror. My God. The chain. The links had burst apart. It dropped uselessly to the floor. Then Peter came falling through the door after me, his arms flapping like a windmill as he tried to stay upright. He tumbled to an ungainly heap, hitting the wall on his way down.

Without waiting to see more, I turned taking the stairs as fast as I could. The kitchen! From there I could get down the fire escape to the yard and get away.

As I reached the kitchen, pausing momentarily to listen to Peter's footsteps thudding up the stairs, I could hear my mobile ringing in the lounge. If only I could get to it.

God, he was still coming. Grabbing the handle, I opened the back door straight onto the fridge that was still waiting for the man from the council. Please let Peter be bigger than me, I prayed, squeezing past, my hips protesting as I barely made it. He was small for a guy but surely his frame was still wider than my skinny one.

Halfway down the stairs, my heart sank as I noticed the large padlock on the back gate. Shit, how was I going to get out? Could I climb over the fence? It was over six foot.

Glancing back through the metal steps I saw that the door to the junk shop was open. Jumping the last four steps, I twisted as I landed and scooted through the door. Above me I could hear the grate of metal and I could see the fridge moving. I didn't wait. Instead I ducked quickly inside.

Hands shaking I pushed the door closed very quietly, searching in the gloomy half-light for a key. Nothing. Groping up and down, my fingers felt the door frame. My eyes were adjusting to the dim light as my fingers gripped cold metal. Relieved, I slipped the bolt into place. That would give me time to get out of the front of the shop onto the street.

Outside I could hear Peter's footsteps ringing on the metal treads.

I moved quickly though the little hallway, darting into the main room of the shop. This was the biggest room, with the till and the entrance. Over to the right was a smaller room that led into two even smaller ones. Trying to get my bearings I moved left quickly, bumping into something at thigh level. Another bloody bruise. Odd shadows merged together in the half-light making unknown shapes.

It was a while since I'd been in here. There could be anything barring my way. Last time I'd popped in, the place had been filled with threadbare old sofas piled high alongside everything from old comics, horse brasses, fireguards and saucepans.

Something caught the sleeve of my blouse, momentarily anchoring me. Damn, I had to free myself. From the cold metal under my fingers, I guessed I was tangled up with a cast iron bed frame. Wrenching my arm violently, I ripped the sleeve of my top, the screech of fabric sounding horribly loud. I stilled for a second. Then there was a crash at the back door.

I needed to get to the entrance and fast. My eyes had adjusted to the light now. Damn! Seeing the door properly I realised there was no way I could reach the deadbolt at the top.

Frantically I pulled at a chair and leapt on the arm. It was no good. Still not high enough.

From the hallway, I could hear the strangled squeak of wood being smashed. My ears roared, it sounded as if the door was being broken down.

There was no way out. No way past him, unless I hid in here and hoped he went into the other two rooms. Then I could sneak out of the back door and back up the stairs to the flat.

Another louder crash. I had to move and quickly.

Instinctively I dropped to the floor, where I could feel the tickle of dust irritating my nose.

There was a sideboard at the other side of the room, if I just squeezed behind it, I would be hidden from view. Scuttling along the floor, I just made it, curled against the wall and the furniture, my head brushing the floor, as I heard a final crack of the outside door finally giving way. Footsteps tapped briskly towards me and then stopped.

The room was completely quiet, except for the intermittent rush of cars outside. The dust had made my nose run but I didn't dare sniff. The trickle was inching down my upper lip. Listening carefully, in between the cars, I could just hear the soft shuffle of a shoe.

'I know you're in here,' said a matter of fact voice. 'You can't go anywhere and if I have to find you, I'll get cross.' There was a short silence. 'AND YOU WON'T LIKE IT WHEN I GET CROSS.'

God, he sounded like a villain in a film, except this was all too horribly real. On the back of my neck, my hairs stood to attention. A river of sweat inched down the 'V' between my breasts. I crouched lower fighting an overwhelming instinct to curl up into a ball and whimper. I wasn't going to give up.

Being so close to the floor, I could hear the crunch of the dust on the concrete floor, which was cold and gritty underneath my cheek.

Crunch. Crunch. As each step got nearer, my muscles turned to jelly. I couldn't move. The steps stopped, an ominous scrunch along with a puff of fine grit grazing my forehead. He was right in front of me. Nothing happened. I waited. My heartbeat was roaring in my ears. Kaleidoscope patterns danced behind my tightly closed lids. Orange and yellow like demons swirling.

There was a slight scratch as if he'd shifted his weight. And then his steps moved away. Still rigid I didn't dare raise my head.

Every now and then his steps would stop and then move off again. My knees were stiff. I'd never be able to move quickly if I stayed put much longer. Did I dare make a run for it? How long had I been here?

I had no idea what time it was but there was no sound. Peter must have moved through to one of the other rooms. Easing up from my cramped position, I tentatively raised my head above the sideboard.

No sign of him. As quietly as I could I stood and forced my knees into action, creeping silently towards the back door.

I could see daylight and there was still no sound from behind me. I took a step into the yard and took a deep intake of breath. Thank God. I'd made it.

'Guess who?' sang a cheerful voice. Jumping, I didn't even get chance to turn around. My heart contracted, my bladder almost emptying as an arm slipped around my neck.

Daniel cranked up the CD, the infectious rock music suiting his mood perfectly. Even the hideous traffic on the A4 couldn't wipe the smile off his face. Olivia's sultry voicemail message showed a new side to her, one that he'd like to get to know better. Although looking at the time, her bath water would be stone cold by now. He'd have to scrub her back another day.

Damn the traffic had come to a complete halt now. If only he'd left work early like he'd intended, instead of getting stuck in a meeting that had dragged on and on. It meant hitting the worst of the rush hour.

When his phone rang he reached eagerly for it, hoping it might be Olivia but to his dismay it was Emily. God, hadn't she said enough to him? Boy, he'd been taken in by the soft Marilyn Monroe voice and winsome smiles. He hadn't told Olivia half of the things she'd spat at him. Disappointment rankled and he couldn't decide which was worse, that he'd been such a dickhead for being so taken in or that she could be such a bitch when she didn't have to be. Hell, she had tons going for her. She didn't need to behave like that.

He shook his head grimly. Women, he'd never get them ...

apart from Olivia. Straight down the line. He knew exactly where he was with her. How could he have ever believed Emily's lies? He had to concede she'd been smart in knowing which buttons to press.

He tossed the phone back on the seat. Within seconds he heard the strident beep of the phone again. She wasn't giving up that easily. Eyeing the standstill traffic he warily answered.

'Daniel, it's Emily. Do you know where Olivia is?' Her words tumbled down the phone in a breathless rush.

'Yes, she's at the flat.'

He heard muffled conversation as if Emily had put her hand over the phone.

'Are you sure?'

His senses went on alert, the hair on the back of his neck rising.

'Yes, she rang me a couple of hours ago, said she was at home. Planning to have a bath.'

Another voice muttered in the background and then Emily spoke again. 'Barney's been doing some digging ... I'll hand you over.'

'Daniel,' Barney's voice, clipped and decisive spoke. 'It's Barney. I'm trying to get hold of Olivia but she's not answering her phone or the one in the flat.'

Daniel's heart faltered and for a second he felt as if he were falling. Her message had told him she was waiting for him. She'd hardly have gone out.

'Where are you?' he snapped, trying to work out how long it would take him to get there.

'On my way to the flat. Emily's got a key.'

Daniel didn't ask why Emily was with Barney. At this moment it didn't matter.

'How far away are you?'

'About ten minutes. Do you think Olivia's home? Any chance she might have gone out?'

Daniel wanted to think she might but in his heart of hearts he knew it was unlikely. He tried to think of all the reasons she might not be answering the phone. Her battery could be flat but then the landline would ring. She had her iPod on full blast and couldn't hear a thing. Maybe she'd slipped in the bath and had hurt herself and couldn't get up ... or was lying unconscious ... and might have drowned.

Or, he didn't want to think it but the idea wouldn't go away, Peter had found a way in. But that wasn't possible. They'd changed the locks.

'I'm about twenty minutes away. Have you phoned the police?'

'No, don't you think that might be a bit—'

'No!' he snapped. 'They've got the address flagged. Call them. Did you track him down? I thought you were going to give details to the police.'

'Turned out the guy I knew who brought Peter along shared a house with him. I went round this afternoon.' Barney paused. 'Not good, I'm afraid. Shares a place with a couple of other guys. They let me in. Said he was odd but thought he was harmless. I saw his room.' An uneasy silence followed the words.

'And ...' Daniel dreaded to think. Peter had killed a cat and put it in a fridge, that wasn't normal behaviour on any level. The guy was a nutjob.

'Weird. Loads of photos of Olivia and Emily. Looks like he's been following them for weeks. Work, home, in the street. And their stuff, clothes, underwear ... really creepy.' He paused. 'It gets worse ... there were knives, a couple of kitchen ones lined up in size order. He'd slashed a lot of the pictures and clothing.'

Bile rose and Daniel's stomach churned. A horn blared behind him. Dazed he looked round to see that the traffic had miraculously freed up and they were moving again.

Numbness spread through him as he tried hard to quash the images of the damage a blade could do to a face, to skin. To Olivia.

Barney spoke again, 'If it's any consolation, it looks as if his main target was Emily.'

Daniel slapped the steering wheel. 'No, it bloody isn't. What the hell were you playing at? Didn't you check on any of the psychos? Your own bloody cousin.' Part of him knew losing his rag like this wouldn't help but he needed to rage at someone. If this traffic didn't start moving, he'd just get out and leave the damn car here. It would be quicker to run.

Up ahead a space in the traffic opened. He let out the breath he'd been holding for too long. 'Don't hang up. I'm on my way.' Tossing the phone, the line still open, onto the passenger seat, he floored the accelerator and raced down the wrong side of the road, darting in front of the queue slowly crossing the traffic lights. By the skin of his teeth he whipped back into the line of traffic to a chorus of angry horn blasts.

'I'll be there in ten,' he yelled, hoping that Barney could still hear. 'Meet me, there.'

Driving like a complete maniac, he managed to piss of virtually every driver south of the river. Overtaking on corners, cutting people up, tailgating ... the adrenaline coursed through him as he weaved through the traffic without a care for the paintwork or bumpers of his or any other car.

'Out of my way, you arse,' he yelled, as a young woman dithered at the roundabout ahead of him. Why was the world filled with crap drivers? Couldn't they see he was in a hurry?

Finally he pulled out into the stream of traffic ignoring the indignant blares of horns in his wake. This was life or death.

Twisting and turning through Wandsworth, he thought he'd never hit the Earlsfield Road.

'Come on, come on,' he muttered, tapping the steering

wheel, his foot hopping up and down on the accelerator revving the engine rudely. 'Now lady, now.'

Narrowly missing two schoolgirls hopping off at their bus stop and trying to cross the road, he swerved round the bus and picked up speed down Garrett Lane. Sod the forty-mile an hour signs. If anything, he hoped the police would spot him. He'd lead them straight there.

Finally he turned into the street and threw the car into a space, uncaring that most of the back end stuck out into the stream of traffic. Grabbing his phone, he cut Barney off and tried Olivia's phone again. It rang and rang eventually cutting to her voice, perky and upbeat inviting him to leave a message.

His voice dried in his mouth. What to say? There were a million things he wanted to tell her but he couldn't get the words past the lump in his throat. How he felt? Where was she? Why wasn't she answering? Punching the off button, he stuffed the phone in his pocket, threw open the car door and slammed it shut behind him. Horns blared as he raced across the road, putting his hand up in apology at the on-coming cars. As he came to a stop outside the flat, he anxiously scanned the first floor windows above the shop. Nothing. No sign of life. No lights.

Then he went cold. The noise of the traffic receded and for a moment everything went black. He struggled to take a breath as his chest tightened at the sight of the scarlet coil of wool nestling into the doorstep like a pool of blood.

Every pulse point pounded as he tried to focus, the horrible facts adding up faster and faster.

'Daniel! Over here.' Barney's voice came from a few houses up the street. 'We just got here.'

Daniel immediately zoned in on Emily and without preamble, said, 'We have to go in.'

'We?' In another situation the horror on her face might have been comical. 'I'm not going in. What if he's there?'

'Exactly,' snapped Daniel. 'He is here. Look.' He pointed to the cashmere scarf.

'My scarf. I've been ...' Her words ground to a halt and she stared up at Daniel, her face paling.

'I thought we'd agreed that neither of you would be alone in the flat until he was caught,' accused Daniel.

Emily opened her mouth as if to come up with an excuse but quickly thought better of it. 'I ... I ... I thought you were being over the top. Besides, he's probably harmless. It's probably nothing to worry about.'

'Nothing to worry about.' Rage pulsed through him. 'Which bit of weird do you not get?' he asked through gritted teeth. 'This guy broke in and left a dead animal with its throat cut as a message. A fair clue he's dangerous, don't you think? I'd say we can be reasonably confident he's here. Olivia's on her own, she said she would be here ... and she's not answering either phone. It's not looking that great to me.' He'd never hit a woman in his life but the urge to slap Emily itched at his palms. Even Barney looked impatient.

'What if he's holding a knife to Olivia's throat?'

For a moment she looked shamefaced.

Barney turned to her. 'Em, you have to go in. See what he's doing? Find out the lie of the land. We can't all just barge in there.'

'You are joking.' Her eyes widened. 'No way.'

Daniel took a step towards her and drew himself up. 'Olivia could be in a lot of trouble in there. We have no idea what he's capable of ... but given his track record to date, I'm not prepared to risk another minute. You have to go in. We'll follow behind quietly, he won't be expecting us.'

'Besides,' Barney looked at Emily briefly and gave her an apologetic smile, 'having seen those photos, it's you he wants.' He took both her hands and held them, looking sincerely into her eyes. 'Don't worry, we'll be right behind you.'

'Actually,' he had had a moment to think. It was no use blindly charging in, they had no idea where Olivia was, where Peter was and whether he had any weapons on him. 'It would be better not to scare him or alert him to the fact we know he's dangerous. Emily should go in as if she were coming home from work as normal.' He paused to make sure Emily got the point. 'You and I, Barney, need to go in quietly as back up, so that we can surprise him. I suggest Emily leaves the latch off and you sneak in after her and I'll try and get in at the back so that we've got two lines of attack, especially as we have no idea where they are in the flat.'

'Or even if they are in there!' snapped Emily bitchily.

His palms twitched. 'Let's stick with worst case scenario.'

He gave her a look of disgust and focused on Barney. 'We'll time it exactly. Emily you need to make as much noise as you can, so that I can come in through the back. I might have to break the window in the kitchen or force the door. Give me five minutes from now and then you go in the front.'

Emily put her hands on her hips but he could see her defiance deflating rapidly. 'Do I have to?'

He glared at her.

'You'll be a hero,' said Barney, hugging her to him, eying Daniel over the top of her head.

Daniel swallowed the metallic taste of fear in his mouth and glanced again at his mobile phone, willing it to reveal that he'd missed a call from Olivia and this was all crazy supposition. The screen remained blank.

Where was Olivia? And why wasn't she answering her phone?

Chapter Twenty-One

Peter had been lying in wait for me. With my windpipe under pressure there was no way I could fight him as he forced me towards the metal staircase to the flat.

As he pushed me at the first step I could smell the strong scent of carbolic soap as the rough hair of his strong forearm rubbed under my chin. I could barely make the steps, my knees were only just working and my thighs shaking.

'Ups-a-daisy,' said Peter, kneeing me sharply in the back of the leg.

'You know the police know all about you. You can't get away with this,' I said, my teeth gritted so that the betraying tremor in my voice didn't escape.

'Can't get away with what?' he answered his voice pleasant and reasonable, remonstrating with me for my deplorable manners. 'That's no way to greet a guest, not very friendly at all.' He tutted and shook his head. 'You should have invited me in. Shall we start again?'

We reached the kitchen and he let go and shoved me in.

'This is the part where you invite me in.'

'I'd rather you left.' I tried to sound firm. It didn't work, my voice came out weak and wobbly.

His lips twisted unpleasantly and I caught a fleeting something in his eyes.

'No can do. It's Emily I'm here to see but I see she's out. So I'll just have to wait. In the meantime, you're in the way.'

What the hell did that mean?

'I can leave,' I said stupidly, never believing for a moment he'd agree.

'I think not. Don't worry you won't be in the way while I wait.'

'But Emily's gone,' I said urgently, wondering whether telling him this was a good idea or not.

'Really?' Peter cocked his head, an amused smile on his face.

'No seriously, she's moved out.'

He laughed politely. 'What since yesterday? I don't think so.'

'But—'

'Enough!' he shouted his face darkening. I jumped at the change in mood. He stepped forward menacingly and grabbed my arm.

'This way,' he snarled and pulled me through to the lounge.

Once in the other room, he picked up a rucksack from the top of the stairs, headed straight over to the dining table and pulled out a chair. He had it all planned.

'Sit,' he said, thrusting a knee into my stomach forcing me to sit down. 'Don't move or I'll kill you.' He was calm again. Digging carefully into the bag, he produced a Stanley knife with a flourish. His dark eyes never left my face.

My stomach dropped with a horrible loop the loop, falling away sensation. The hairs on my forearms rose jumping to attention like iron filings to a magnet and my thighs were doing a jig all by themselves.

With a sly smile he pulled out a roll of silver tape. My stomach calmed for a second. Was that what the blade was for? I'd been so afraid he would use it on me. With every loop of tape, he became more confident and positively chatty.

'I hate to say this, but it's not you I'm interested in.' He sneered at my chest. 'Sorry, you just don't tempt me. Now, Emily, on the other hand. She's all woman.' A scowl crossed his face and his expression hardened. 'Unfortunately, she needs teaching a little lesson but no matter, she will learn.'

Admiring the Formula One track of tape that wound

round my wrists and forearms, securing me to the chair, Peter walked round me poking the tape, before putting one last strip firmly over my mouth. He gave a little skip and sat down on the sofa. Then crossing one leg over his knee, he sat there flicking through one of Emily's magazines as if he were waiting for a doctor's appointment.

The minutes ticked by on the green numerals on the DVD player in the corner. The right side of my face was pulsing with pain, my hip bone ached and my feet were gradually going numb.

Emily was never going to come. Daniel would probably come and go. He'd give up when I didn't answer the door or my mobile. My phone had rung several times in the last forty-five minutes. Every time Peter grinned matily at me. At the second call he mocked, 'Want me to get that for you?' and after the fourth, 'Popular, aren't you?' before carrying on flicking through his magazine.

Daniel was bound to drive off in disgust at being stood up. And what about Barney? Had one of the calls been from him, or maybe Kate, or Bill or Mum?

The straight edge of the tape was cutting into my nose, sharp and uncomfortable, making me sniff. I tried hard not to. The last thing I wanted was for Peter to think I was crying.

Now that my heart had slowed, I felt calmer but painful pins and needles were taking over my feet. To take my mind off them, I studied Peter. What if I needed a wee? Would he let me? No chance. He'd leave me to do it right here and sit in my own puddle.

He didn't know that Emily had gone for good but he was ready for the long haul. Judging by the controlled calm of his approach, he was very good at waiting.

As marauding maniacs went, he looked like a twenty-five watt version instead of the thousand watt Hollywood neon variety. No maniacal gleam in his eye. No inarticulate mutterings or frothing at the mouth. He looked totally nondescript. Harmless even.

As the minutes ticked by Peter got more comfortable. He even went and helped himself to a bottle of red wine and two glasses. Pouring a glass he raised it in a silent toast and with a sly smile took an appreciative gulp.

'You girls do know your wine, a very good year this one,' he said, smirking at me. The fact that he'd got the glasses and wine so quickly showed he knew his way around the flat. Just how many times had he pawed through our things?

My shoulders forced back had passed through the screaming stage and were now numb and tense. Where the tape touched bare skin it pulled at the hairs, a constant reminder of pain every time I moved. Not that I could move very far. I never would have believed how uncomfortable it could be forced to stay in one position for such a long time.

Worst of all was the knowledge that no one was coming. Self-pity crowded in. No one would miss me until work tomorrow, even then they might just wonder why I hadn't phoned in. How long would it take for someone to notice? As a silent tear escaped, I turned my head, so that Peter couldn't see it.

Peter snapped to attention upon hearing the scratch and chink of a key in the front door. And so did I. It was the last sound I was expecting. The only person with one of our new keys was Emily. It couldn't be her, could it?

Peter turned and smiled. 'She's home,' he said with a grin.

For the first time, I could see the shine of saliva on his lips. He was licking them feverishly, his tongue darting out lizard-like and his Adam's apple bobbing in time. Tremors began to rack his slight frame as he rocked forward and back trying to contain his excitement.

He put his fingers over his lips as if to say 'sh' and giggled conspiratorially. I could see the anticipation in the sudden tension in his shoulders.

To my absolute amazement and total confusion, Emily issued a very loud and surprisingly chirpy, 'Hi, Olivia.' She carried on quickly, almost booming the words. 'You'll never guess who I bumped into. I knew you'd be dying to see him, so I invited him round. He's coming in ten minutes.'

What on earth was she on about?

'Yes, Olivia. Barney. Your cousin.'

Peter's face was watchful now. As was mine. I knew who Barney was. What was she trying to tell me? Did she know that Peter was here? Was that why she'd come back?

Peter had stooped to pour a second glass of wine. Then he stood waiting for her to appear over the balustrade, Stanley knife clenched in hand.

She was still shouting, talking absolute nonsense, especially given our last conversation. 'Blimey, Olivia, have you gone deaf. I'm home. God, I had a horrendous journey on the tube. You've no idea how awful it was. I was so pleased to see Barney.'

Finally I heard her pound up the steps. She was making a hell of a racket. Was that also something coming from the direction of the kitchen? And why with all that noise hadn't I heard the front door slam?

At last Emily appeared. Her eyes widened as she let out a stunned gasp when she saw me trussed up. If I hadn't been watching her so carefully, I'd have missed the quick dart of her eyes away down the corridor to the kitchen. My heart rose for a second. Was the cavalry on its way?

Peter smiled as he picked up the second glass of wine and went over to Emily as if this was entirely normal.

'Emily, my darling. Thought you'd never get here.'

'You!' she said theatrically, swallowing nervously.

'Yes. Waiting for you. I knew you'd be here eventually.' He shot me a look of distaste before smiling at her. He looked like a lovesick puppy. 'I've been waiting a long time. Come, sit down. I've got you a glass of wine.'

'Er,' stuttered Emily. 'Look Peter, I ...' Her voice was loud again. She looked wildly at me. I gave my shoulders a fatalistic shrug. There was no point looking at me.

'You haven't been very nice to me, Emily.' He waved the Stanley knife at her. 'Those emails. Not kind. I thought you were different.'

Emily's eyes caught mine again and frowned in thought for a second. There was a perceptible lift to her spine.

'Do you know Peter? You're right. I wasn't very nice, was I? But Olivia had nothing to do with that. Do you think you could undo her?'

Peter gave me a dismissive look. 'No, she's not been very nice to me.'

That was rich but I thought that giving him the evil eye at this point might not help my cause.

'I'm sure if you let her go we could sort everything out.'

She went over to him, stomping over making a lot of noise, staunchly ignoring the knife and took the glass of wine and sat down at the other end of the sofa. She smiled at him.

'Those emails. I was having a really bad week and I took it out on you. I shouldn't have. I'm sorry. Email isn't good.'

It was an amazing performance. Emily was trying hard and from Peter's body language, I thought he might just be buying it. He put the knife down on the table.

The whole time I'd been listening carefully. There had to be some reason for Emily's noisy entrance and subsequent shouting and reference to Barney. So when I saw Barney's head peep around the stairs, my whole body slumped back against the chair. Thank God. How I managed not to beam at his reassuring wink, I'll never know.

So who was in the kitchen? While Emily had been making all that noise downstairs, I'd definitely heard someone in there.

However, as long as Peter had that knife so close at hand, there on the table, no amount of knights in shining armour was going to save us.

'Peter, why don't we start again? We got off on the wrong foot,' said Emily silkily. I had to admit she was bloody good at the femme fatale bit, even with a man who was clearly not sane.

I watched as Peter sidled along the sofa to sit closer to her, leaving the knife just that bit out of reach. Any minute now as he got nearer, he would have to turn his head. My opinion of her rose several notches, when she didn't even flinch but sat there, smiling at him.

The minute he turned his back on me, I lunged forward, ignoring my tingling feet, and launched myself on top of the coffee table, even though I was still attached to the chair.

Thank God! The knife stayed sandwiched between the table and my layers of tape as Peter whirled round, spraying wine everywhere. He stood up and from my position, I saw him lift a foot, inches from my head. My eyes squeezed tight and my teeth locked in anticipation of the kick.

At that moment I heard Barney leap up from the stairs and a roar of rage from the kitchen. Lying prone, still glued to the chair like a small beetle, I opened my eyes to see Daniel appear from the kitchen like an avenging god. His face was thunderous as he grabbed Peter from behind, his arm hooking round his throat in a bruising neck lock.

'Don't you dare touch her again, you bastard,' he ground out angrily, his arm jerking with fury. From this angle I could see Peter's chin ratcheted up notch by notch as Daniel's grip tightened.

Barney was beside me, ripping at the tape securing me to

the chair. I think I passed out because the next thing I heard was the clumping of feet on the stairs. Suddenly the lounge was full of black soled shoes which was pretty much all I could see from my position. Two pairs of feet came to flank Daniel's brogues, relieving him of his burden and rescuing Peter from imminent strangulation.

Then Daniel's denim clad knees dropped in front of me as he elbowed Barney out of the way. 'Olivia! My God.'

I mmm mphed through the tape. Daniel hesitated before picking at the edges. I screwed up my eyes as he ripped it off, tearing a good strip of skin off my cheek. Being able to breathe through my mouth again was such a welcome relief though that I forgave him the brutal exfoliation.

Having been brave for so long, I should have been able to have hung on a bit longer but as the tape was ripped off, my bravado collapsed like a tent in a force nine gale. Tears poured down my face mingling with the snot from my liberated nose.

Totally ignoring the slime trail of salty tears and unmentionables coursing down my face, Daniel scooped me up, chair and all, and laid his cheek against mine as he righted me. His eyes were drawn with horrified fascination to my throbbing cheekbone, which I could feel had swollen to Elephant Man proportions. Vaguely I was aware of helping hands ripping at the tape binding my arms to the wooden chair back.

Released at last, my shoulders were screaming having been pinned back in such an unnatural position for so long and I slumped forward in relief. Daniel grabbed my hands rubbing them between his. I looked up completely defeated, whispered, 'Thank you,' and laid my forehead on his shoulder. 'How did you know?'

'Tell you later,' he muttered into my hair.

Around us I could hear the tinny sound of police radios,

deep voices all talking at once. Daniel and I were in a private oasis, two alone in the midst of all the activity. My fingers, the pins and needles flooding them, wiggled their way to intertwine with his. My eyes were closed and I stayed there shutting everything out, absorbing the strength and warmth of Daniel's presence, his steady breath in my ear, the firm grip of his fingers and the warm flesh under my forehead. I didn't need anything else.

PC Cartwright materialised. 'Can you tell us what happened?' she growled in her smoke laden voice.

I tried to lick my lips and winced, they were so dry despite the excess of saliva that had revoltingly collected in my mouth.

Daniel flicked her a distinct, 'Leave her alone,' look before piping up, 'She needs water.' At a slight nod from Cartwright, another WPC darted away and was back in seconds with a glass.

I sipped gratefully. Across the way, Emily was sitting on the sofa, her head in her hands. Peter was being held forcibly by two constables who wouldn't have seemed out of place on the back row of a rugby pitch. He looked unperturbed gazing choirboy like at the ceiling.

I thought police procedure would take forever but they were amazingly quick and incredibly sympathetic. I heard Peter being read his rights and arrested before he was escorted down the stairs.

'We'll need you to make a full statement,' Cartwright said to me, her face softening to granite. 'But we'll wait for the paramedic to get here.'

'Can't it wait until tomorrow?' asked Daniel, indicating my bruised face.

Cartwright pursed her lips. 'Sorry, we need witness statements from all of you.'

Emily stood. 'Why don't I give you mine now? Olivia needs to ...'

The words go home were left unsaid. I was already at home, after all, but there was no way I wanted to stay.

I smiled weakly at Emily. 'Thanks.'

Cartwright turned to me. 'A uniformed officer will stay with you and accompany you to hospital. I really think you should go.'

She raked my face with an experienced eye. 'That cheek looks a bit of a mess, although believe it or not you got off lightly.'

Got off lightly, who was she kidding? I dreaded to think what someone who hadn't looked like. My face felt as if it was on fire and my head hurt if I so much as blinked. On top of that I felt so limp and defeated. All I wanted was simply to sign on the dotted line and say, 'I hereby hand over my body – somebody please take charge of me'.

The paramedic, a vision in bilious green, arrived looking more like a kindly leprechaun than a hero of the emergency services. His twinkly avuncular manner belied a core of steel and before long I had agreed to go to the hospital with him. By this time, statements had been taken from Emily, Barney and Daniel and they were all free to go.

Before I left Emily came over. 'Clothes and now men. You always did like my cast offs.' She smiled wryly to show that she was joking. Daniel melted away disappearing into my bedroom. 'Sorry, Olivia. I always knew you liked him.' She sighed heavily. 'I should have given him back earlier.' That was as close to an apology as I was ever going to get. 'Take care of yourself. I won't come back here.' She laughed tonelessly.

She directed a quick look at Daniel, who'd emerged from my room with a bag in his hands into which he was stuffing a pair of my jeans. 'Bye then. Are you coming, Barney?' She gave him a flirty smile. Typical, he was so her type.

He grinned back. 'Well done. Bloody brave of you to brave the lion's den. Back to my place?'

'Please, that would be nice.'

She turned to Daniel. 'Bye, Daniel.'

'See you, Emily,' he said calmly, looking totally unconcerned.

'I doubt it,' she replied, airily tossing her hair so that he would remember exactly what he was missing. I watched him from under my lashes, as he eyed her thoughtfully as she and Barney disappeared from view in the wake of WPC Cartwright.

Chapter Twenty-Two

Daniel and I left the flat in the hands of the crime scene guys. The twilit sky was awash with blue flashes; the unsynchronised lights illuminating the faces of curiosity seekers crowding around the scattered police cars.

'This way.' The attractive brunette WPC who had been assigned to accompany me to hospital ushered me into a waiting car. Daniel, sliding into the back with me, perked up momentarily. His first time too. He was leaning over the seat avidly looking at the different gizmos. I managed a wonky smile. He gave my hand a squeeze.

'Which one do you think is the siren?' he said in a loud stage whisper. WPC Jennings gave us both a 'and-no-one's-ever-said-that-one-before' patient smile.

Once again she went through the procedure at the hospital. We'd be met there by a specially trained SOCO who would 'harvest' any evidence – her description – and she would be taking my statement as soon as I felt up to it.

The journey to the hospital, despite the novelty of the transport, went by in a haze, as was my time there. I remember clearly Daniel being a constant, at my side the whole time. Everything else had a dream like feel; the low gentle tones of my police lady as she took copious notes, the crime scene photographer taking hundreds of pictures of me, gently angling my head this way and that to get close ups of every bump and bruise and the low hum of the hospital beyond the cubicle curtains.

The only one bonus to the evening was that I was seen very quickly. The doctor wanted to admit me, but when I questioned her closely about my injuries, she said in patronising tones that if I wanted to, I could go home but she wouldn't advise it. 'You'll need someone with you,' she said acidly, when I said that I really would rather.

'She's coming home with me,' interjected Daniel, giving the doctor a tight smile. He hadn't said much in the last few hours, his face had been grim for much of the time. A little light bulb lit up within me – only a fairy light admittedly, given the way I was feeling. I looked at him gratefully, although he didn't see, he was busy looking at his shoes. I craned my neck to see what was so interesting but couldn't spot anything.

Never in his life had he needed to hold on so tightly to his temper. Escorting Olivia for the second time out of the automatic doors of the hospital, he shook with the control he needed to stop himself giving into the desire to lash out at something. If he started, he wasn't sure he'd be able to stop a descent into a frenzy of violence. Every knuckle on both hands hurt where they'd been clenched so hard as if physically clutching onto his self-control. He found talking difficult, in case he upset Olivia.

Guiding her outside, he saw passers-by glance quickly at her poor face. Wide-eyed, almost punch drunk, no wonder they looked, she looked so fragile and bruised.

He consoled himself with glaring at them, the only outlet for the violence he held in check, he worried if he let it show it would push her over the edge.

He took Olivia's hand into his. It was the only part of her he dared touch. It also kept her at arm's length. The swelling on her face, the streaks of blood on her clothes were a constant reminder of what she'd suffered and he knew if he didn't keep a distance, he would breakdown, hug her too him and never let her go. She needed him to be strong.

Getting her home was the priority. Once they were there and safe, he could let go of the terrible anxiety spiralling through him. Seeing her so vulnerable, at the mercy of Peter had tugged at a frail thread inside. He'd never felt so helpless or useless. Just thinking about it made his breathing shallow. He gritted his teeth and forced himself to concentrate on ushering her towards the taxi rank.

It never occurred to him to ask her where she might want to go, he was taking her home with him and keeping her by his side for the rest of the night. If not the rest of his life.

As the taxi dropped them at his car, still parked haphazardly outside Olivia's flat, he unlocked the door with the remote. Glancing around, he settled Olivia in the passenger seat and then checked there was no one nearby, resisting the urge to lock the doors as he moved around the back of the car to get to the driver's seat.

It was funny how everything suddenly dimmed into insignificance. All the wasted time, Emily's lies, the near misses. As he started the engine, immediately soothed by the revs under his foot, he turned to Olivia. Her eyes were closed and her lips pressed tightly shut. He let out a breath, slipped the car into gear and glanced at the clock. In another hour they'd be home.

Daniel couldn't have driven all the way home in second gear, but I don't remember him ever relinquishing my punishing grasp on his hand. My lap was full of first aid remedies pressed upon me by the sulky doctor, antiseptic salve for my face and industrial sized boxes of paracetamol and ibruprofen. The latter were just starting to work, so the journey was a blur of cat's eyes on the road. There was silence apart from the purr of the car and low music that I was aware of but unable to hear. I felt strangely disconnected. The warm hand in my lap was the only thing linking me to the world. I wanted to speak but couldn't form the words. They were stuck at the back of a tunnel that my brain couldn't dig its way through.

As I stepped out of the car, the shadows and rustles of the country night immediately soothed me. Emily had said she found the country night alien but I felt comforted by the dark. It felt safer here. The urban jungle was far scarier, concealing the feral under a civilised veneer. The only predators out here were the four-legged variety – I could cope with those.

Daniel unlocked the big, solid wooden door, ushering me in. He put my bag down at the foot of the stairs. In the dim light of the hall, he looked the worst I'd ever seen him. Tufts of hair stood ranged across his head, his face grey and eyes shadowed.

He caught me staring at him. 'This way.' He nodded towards the kitchen. It was hard to believe that it was only two days ago that I'd been here, all a flutter, with the promise of things to come. I smiled wanly.

'Daniel, I'm sorry. You must be absolutely bushed,' I said in a low voice. He ran a hand through his hair. No wonder it looked as bad as it did, he'd been doing that all evening.

'It's been quite a night,' he said looking at me.

Now that we were inside there was a physical distance between us. I was shy and he seemed to be avoiding touching me all of a sudden.

Had he changed his mind? Had I been too needy in the last 24 hours? Perhaps all this knight in shining armour stuff had got a bit tedious. It was ironic. When he had seemed unattainable I'd managed to bury my feelings for most of the time. Pretending that they weren't there and getting on with my life. Now, since yesterday morning, I'd been unable to resist examining them like a shiny new penny, polishing them in private. What if that was taken away again? I felt hollow.

'I don't know about you but I'm starving.' he said finally, moving away. I watched him open the fridge, his head disappearing inside like an eager Labrador on the hunt for food. He emerged clutching a white carton. 'Would you like some soup?'

Ugh. My stomach quivered. I wasn't sure if it was rebellion or hunger. Horribly conscious of all the trouble he'd already been through, I ignored my natural reaction and said politely, 'That would be nice, thank you.'

He busied himself, getting out a pan, opening the carton of fresh soup. 'Aubergine and red pepper all right?' he asked blandly. 'Miriam's been to Waitrose again. I get all the things Dad refuses to try. Red pepper gives him indigestion.'

'Sounds lovely.' I tried to sound bright but my voice came out strained.

He looked sharply at me. 'I can find something else if you want.'

'No, that's fine, honestly.' I pulled out one of the chairs and sat down sideways on. I was still huddled in my coat. The painkillers had done their job but I felt washed out. I didn't even have the energy to offer to set the table.

Daniel seemed grimly efficient, crisply moving about the kitchen, concentrating on his tasks. Only when the soup was in a saucepan with the gas ring lit, the soup bowls ready and bread buttered did he stop. Carrying two spoons to the table, he looked at me and slid his eyes away quickly. They came back to rest on the top button of my coat.

'Don't you want to take that off?' he asked.

I shrugged. Disappointment bitter in my throat. Fumbling sausage fingers failed me as I tried to undo it. Those paracetamol were working overtime and affecting all my nerve endings.

'Come here,' he said, a trace of exasperation in his voice.

I stood awkwardly looking down, watching as his fingers deftly undid the buttons. I felt like a five-year-old at school, I expected to see mittens on strings poking out of each sleeve. His hands came up to tug the lapels from my shoulders, they brushed my neck. Three thousand volts registered immediately but even as the brief flash died away, despair flooded in. His eyes had slid away from mine, his hands jumping away. Had I imagined the merest flicker of distaste in them? My shoulders slumped, a tiny rogue sob escaped.

'Hey,' said Daniel softly, his face creasing in concern. This immediately set me off. More sobs broke through, my eyes filling with tears that poured helplessly down my cheeks. God, men hate tears. He must have had enough tonight. Which made me sob harder. Bloody hell. I couldn't look at him.

I felt him push my coat down my arms. Heard the buttons chink against the floor as he tossed it aside. Strong arms enfolded me, pulling me into a hard chest. The next thing I knew I was sitting, tucked onto his lap, close enough to see the soft stubble breaking through on his chin.

'It's OK, you're safe,' he murmured, his eyes looking directly into mine. They looked worried. Leaning closer still, his mouth began tracing up the trail of my tears, wisping past my damp eyelashes and coming to rest on my forehead. 'It's OK.'

Weeping uncontrollably now, I sputtered incoherent apologies. 'I ... I'm ... sssorry.' My gulping breaths interspersed the words.

His hold tightened, pulling me closer. We sat like that for a minute as my heaving sobs calmed. Apart from the hiss of the gas ring and the plops of soup bubbles, there was silence. I could feel the rise and fall of his chest against me. Then very gently his lips moved downwards, until they found mine.

Instant conflagration! The second they touched, something burst. Every pent up emotion – all the fears of the day – were poured into that kiss. Thank God for painkillers! Our mouths were urgent. His lips firmly moulded mine and I kissed him back wholeheartedly. There was no hesitancy or gentle teasing. This was tongues duelling; breath gasping harshly; his hand holding my head firmly. Spontaneous combustion was only seconds away.

The bitter acrid smell of burning soup butted in. As I pulled back slightly, Daniel tightened his hold and carried on kissing me. I twisted my head to mutter against his mouth.

'Soup .... burning.'

'Sod ...' He kissed me again, pulling my head back to slant his mouth back over mine. 'The ...' Those delicious mind numbing lips honed in again before coming up to murmur, 'soup.'

I was starting to melt. The kiss was penetrating erogenous zones I didn't know I had. My body was beginning to do that pliable thing – bones going all supple and all the while a core of heat building.

Any doubts about my desirability and whether he still wanted me had gone up in smoke. Literally.

BEEP, BEEP, BEEP – the ear piercing shriek of the smoke alarm censored the kiss. We drew back, chests heaving, little pants escaping, looking at each other.

'And I was worried about damaging you any more,' he said dryly, his lips brushing against my face as he spoke.

I gave a wan smile and touched his face. 'Just what the doctor ordered – definitely the kiss of life.' My shyness receded. 'Better turn that soup off – we don't want to make it a hat trick with the emergency services by needing a fire engine. I think we've used up our 999 call out ration for today.'

Tipping me to my feet and grasping one hand, he switched off the soup with a deft flick of the wrist, marched up to the alarm and pinged out the battery. Still clutching my hand, he led me through to the lounge. Flipping on a lamp, he pulled me down with him onto the sofa, pulling me close with an arm around my shoulder.

'I've lost my appetite. Now where were we?'

'Mouth to mouth resuscitation, I think,' I said, eyeing his

lips longingly before very slowly and deliberately sliding my gaze to meet his.

'Do that any more and I'm not going to be responsible for my actions. I'm having a difficult job trying to keep my hands off you as it is.'

'I don't want you to. I'm all right,' I said, my hand lifting to stroke his neck and slide up into his hair.

'Sweetheart, you don't look it.' He softened the words, gently circling my bruised cheek. 'After tonight, I might need a bloody pacemaker fitted. My heart damn near stopped when Emily and Barney phoned me. Then when I saw you with blood pouring down your face and tied up in that chair, I wanted to ...' He shook his head, hands tensing, the tendon's standing proud. He didn't need to finish. I had a pretty good idea. I'd seen his face at the time.

'It was a hell of surprise when I heard Emily come in. Suddenly she was being as nice as pie – only an hour before she was trying to tell me you were gay.'

He looked startled. 'What did you say to that?'

'Sorry I didn't get the chance to defend your honour. In the next breath she told me you'd never be interested in me.'

'Well – at least you know the latter's wrong even if you weren't too sure about the former.'

I looked up at him, took a deep breath and said, 'I did then. I've been ... having doubts since we got here. I've caused you so much trouble in the last 24 hours. You seemed a bit ... I thought ...'

God was I being weak and needy? Was he just being nice now – because I've had a traumatic experience? One of my voices sarcastically shouted, 'Yes, of course he's just being nice – with a kiss like that.'

'Olivia, have you any idea how much control I've been exerting? I hate to say this but you're looking pretty banged up. After what you've been through today, you might not want me manhandling you – although …' his Adam's apple dipped as he swallowed, 'I realise now, I got that bit wrong.'

Smiling gently, he traced my collarbone with one finger. 'I really regret not insisting you moved in the other night. I should have done the cave man thing, slung you over my shoulder and brought you back here.'

'I was trying to make life easier with Emily. Although I guess she knows now.'

'Yeah, I kind of gave it away tonight,' mused Daniel, a reminiscent smile on his face.

He brought both hands up to my face, smoothing my undamaged cheek with his thumb, looking intently at me. A little shiver unfurled down my spine in anticipation. 'I should have told you first, but surely you know? You must have realised on Sunday. I don't make a habit of asking women to move in with me. You are the only woman I've ever even considered wanting to have here. You do know that I'm absolutely one hundred per cent crazy about you?'

My heart flipped with happiness and my stomach dropped as if I'd jumped out of a plane.

'In fact, I still owe you for that little performance the night at The Grayling.'

'That?' I gave him a mischievous smile, trying to breathe normally as my heart was still going skitter scatter. It felt as if at any moment it might burst out of my chest. 'You deserved it.'

His eyes glinted playfully. 'Er … run that by me again. How?'

'I was mad at you, treating me like one of the lads.'

'Sweetheart,' he kissed me, 'you are most definitely not,' he punctuated his words with another pert kiss, 'one of the lads.' He ended with a final peck on my lower lip. 'None of them have underwear like that. I tell you I was in a terrible state in the car that night. I'd been doing my best not to think about you since Ben's bloody party because I thought you were in love with someone else and suddenly it hits me like a truck that I have the serious hots for you. I have a rampaging hard on and, you, cool as a cucumber, saunter off telling me to go downstairs to wait for the car.'

I grinned at him, a little shudder of cat-that-licked-the-cream running through me.

'Sorry,' I said not meaning it, which he knew damn well from the twitch of my lips.

'Honestly, I am keeping you under lock and key. Don't even think of going anywhere without me for at least a century. I don't think my heart can take it.'

I placed my hand on his chest, I could feel the steady beat, beat, beat of his heart. 'I think it'll survive ... with lots of love and attention.'

'Promise.'

I nodded slowly, my eyes drinking in the tenderness in his. There was a pause, my own heart slowed, it was my turn.

'Daniel, I'm not going anywhere. I've been tying myself in knots since that night in casualty. It was so bad that I nearly didn't come this weekend ...' I tutted showing my irritation, 'except I couldn't stay away. It was supposed to be my one last ...' My words were swallowed with an enormous yawn.

'You need to go to bed, you must be shattered.'

I looked ruefully at him, another yawn escaping. 'Sorry.' I sighed. 'I've been running on adrenaline for ages. I've just hit empty.'

'Come on,' he said firmly, pulling me to my feet. 'Bed time.'

A lightening tingle shot through me as his fingers slipped between mine. Switching out lights as we went, he led the way up the little staircase, both of us ducking our heads at the top narrow corner. Outside the bedroom door, he let go of my hand and opened it to let me through.

* * *

I'd taken a quick look at my injuries before I'd left the flat but with a stampede of policemen about, I wasn't given time to dally. I nearly died when I saw myself in the bathroom mirror. My cheek had swelled to Quasimodo proportions; my mascara would have rivalled that of a seventeen-year-old Goth; and I had marginally less colour than a corpse. At my horrified squeak, Daniel came to stand behind me, his mouth tightening. I touched my cheek, wincing, it was starting to feel painful again as the tablets were wearing off.

'You could have told me how awful I look,' I said with a pout.

He quirked an eyebrow in response.

'OK, maybe not, but I could have cleaned up.'

'Now you know why I've been trying to summon up some restraint,' he growled into my ear, his arm snaking round my waist. 'Much as I'd like to ravish you, I'm worried about hurting you and don't deny it you've winced through every brush stroke of your teeth, I saw you. It's more pills, an ice pack and bed for you – nothing more ... tonight.'

My hormones gratefully acknowledged that they were all talk this evening and slipped into standby mode. There was always tomorrow. The last thing I remember is Daniel lifting me into bed and sliding in next to me from the same side. He shuffled me into the middle of the bed and nestled me into him.

I made a tentative stroke of his chest, breathing in his smell, exhaling warm breath over his smooth skin. He caught my hand, and turned his head to mutter in my hair.

'Olivia, you need to rest, I'll still be here in the morning, but I can only take so much.'

I snuggled into his warm body, and I fell fast asleep to the beat of his heart pumping away, solid and safe.

An arm was idly tracing the length of my rib brushing along just under my breast. Even as I came to, my nerve endings were already leaping into action. They were at the starting post. The rest of me was trying to catch up. Sleepily I rolled over to face Daniel, who was lying there, head propped up on one hand, watching me indulgently.

'Morning, sleepy head.' He smiled, his hand stilling for a second. 'I didn't wake you, did I?' The wickedness of his grin notched up.

'No,' my voice was husky as it found itself. I felt so much better. I tried an experimental smile and lifted a hand to touch my cheek, the swelling had definitely gone down and the pain was low grade, quite manageable which was just as well.

'How are you feeling?' he asked, scooping his arm around me to pull me nearer. I squirmed savouring the delicious feeling of naked body, deliberately rubbing against him.

'Better,' I murmured. 'Much better.' One of his legs slipped over mine. A tiny gasp escaped me. The hair roughened skin had set light to a thousand little nerves racing up my thigh. His other arm slipped under my shoulder and he pulled me close. His bare chest was warm and solid, my breasts crushed against it, the smattering of hair tickling slightly. My heart bungeed its way down to my toes, lurching with instant desire.

His eyes were dancing with mischief. 'Did you sleep well?'

'Yes, I'm sor—'

He laid a finger on my lips to stop my apology. I gave it a gentle nip, just touching it with the tip of my tongue. His eyes widened for a second, the pupils darkening in surprise. Watching him mischievously, I gently sucked on the top of his finger.

'Sure you're OK?' he whispered, as a warm hand slid up my stomach. Holding his gaze, I nodded, my heart thumping. He touched my cheek very gently, before moving in to plant a long slow kiss. My lips were positively tingling as I sighed into that kiss. My hips inched forward, I couldn't help myself. I was past caring if I was a hussy. It was a sinuous move, nudging up against him, urging him on. Immediately the kiss deepened, my body melted into his, as one hand smoothed my breast teasing the nipple, which immediately jumped to attention. Forget butterflies, my stomach had taken off with all those fluttery feelings.

My skin felt hot where those warm hands were sliding back and forth. An involuntarily moan slipped out. Daniel lifted his head, looked down at me and gave me an arrogant smile. Well two could play at that game. My hand slipped down his back, sliding over his hard hip and down, stroking down the length of him with a feather-light touch. A delicious gasp escaped him and I grinned delightedly at him.

'Minx,' he growled, cupping a hand round my head and moving over me. Heat was sweeping downwards. Passion was building, a slow sure fire being stoked by every writhe and move. Our sighs punctuated the morning and little murmurs of acquiescence danced on the air as the momentum and urgency built.

All shyness, that early tentative exploration was gone now. The experimenting and teasing was over. Our breathing roughened as small moans of demand filled the air, a delicate negotiation of desire taking place as unspoken pleas for this and that danced back and forth.

Finally when I didn't think I could bear it any longer, my hips nudging and meeting his, he looked into my eyes and I gave him a complicit age-old nod. We slid into that moment of intimacy; bodies locked together driving towards a climax.

It was a far cry from Earlsfield, the sunlight pouring through the sash windows, bird song outside and … a gorgeous man in my bed. I stretched, my stomach full of squirmy feelings of happiness. My hand absently brushing against Daniel's thigh.

'Oy, give a man a chance.' He grinned, pulling me on top of him. I stared down into his laughing face, sheer joy lighting me from the inside out. I was glowing and it wasn't just physical.

'Now that you've had your wicked way with me, I need to phone work. I ought to put in an appearance at some stage today.'

'It's a good job your boss is so understanding,' I teased.

He swatted me on the bottom. 'He's a fool but he's madly in love with a very troublesome wench. You know the type.'

I pouted at him, before registering the first part of his sentence. I stilled and raised an eyebrow. 'Is he?'

Daniel rubbed my nose with his, Eskimo style. 'He most certainly is, although he's not sure how the troublesome wench feels.'

I moved kissing his jaw line, working my way towards his ear. 'The troublesome wench is madly in love with him too,' I whispered happily.

Shifting so that we were facing each other, he looked at me, his hand stroking the 'V' between my cleavage and moving to trace under my breast. He smiled gently. 'That's good.'

As we lay there luxuriating in the warm, cosy duvet moment, I looked at Daniel. 'If you had a choice, which super power would you pick, flight or invisibility?'

His eyes narrowed at me, giving the question the due consideration required. He tipped his head to one side, eyes screwed up in concentration and mouth moving as he ruminated.

'Hmm,' he said. I waited watching him closely. He knew this was serious stuff. 'Is there a right answer here?' he asked eventually, a worried crease appearing on his forehead. I nodded very slowly

'Yup.'

'Any clues?' he asked.

'Nope.'

'Right.' A heavy sigh followed. He screwed up his face, looking out of the window. 'Flight ... definitely flight ... as long as I don't have to wear the tights. I always thought those shiny legging things were a bit nineteen eighties disco, not really very superhero.'

Bingo, one hundred and eighty. I flashed him a kilowatt smile.

He looked smug, laying back into the pillows his hands behind his head. 'So what do I get then? What's the prize?'

I think he was quite satisfied with his reward.

Epilogue

I did get to have my lovely Thai dinner party in our wonderful new kitchen. It was a noisy, boozy affair. Which was just as well – no one noticed that the jasmine rice was overdone or that I only had mascara on one eye. Daniel said it was my own fault for doing my make-up in my underwear.

We'd planned to make a formal announcement at the end of dinner, the champagne would have been nicely chilled by then ... but eagle-eyed Kate spotted the rock on my finger just as I was ladling out Nam Pla soup. Her squeal of surprise nearly pierced everyone's eardrums. Yes, Kate was back from Australia. Bill had taken charge very thoroughly and brought her back with him. Trust her to spot the ring straight away, perhaps because she was still so conscious of her own.

Daniel had surprised me by proposing exactly six months to the day I moved in. As we were celebrating our anniversary he asked me whether the superpower of my choice was still flight? With my answer, which of course, was yes, he produced a tiny figure of Superman, complete with his very own necklace, a gold band with a seriously super-sized diamond on it.

Mum was immensely relieved; she'd already chosen and bought her mother of the bride hat the week after I moved in with Daniel. Dad was delighted and immediately embarked on a campaign of blackmail threatening to refuse to hand over the bride in church unless Daniel agreed to join his cricket team.

A lot has happened in those six months. I only went back to the flat once. Daniel and I popped in very briefly, packing my things as quickly as we could. There were too many memories there and I put it up for sale.

The correspondence from the Crown Prosecution Service about court dates and witness appearances seemed endless but in the event the trial was straightforward and I only needed to make a very brief appearance. The barrister defending Peter, who'd insisted on pleading not guilty to aggravated burglary, false imprisonment and ABH. had a tough enough job. He wanted my time in the witness box to be limited, which suited me fine. The photographs of my beaten up face so horrified the jury that Peter was sent to prison for two years.

It would have been nice to say that I'd left all the horrors of that day behind me in my rosy glow of happiness, but in the days before the trial the nightmares were frequent. No matter how many times I put the chain on the door in my dreams, faceless men with many arms shot through the door. Daniel was always there to hold me in the dark, stroking my hair while my heart pounded; the sound almost audible in the quiet night. Even now I still occasionally jerk awake, the sense of being chased filling my thoughts as I come to.

The only proper contact I had with Emily was at the trial. We exchanged emails to sort out the bills and detritus of sharing a flat and the odd friendly one about how fantastic her new job was and how much better it was there than at Organic PR. But gradually these petered out, as did her relationship with Barney. Thank goodness. I wasn't sure I could have stomached seeing her over family Christmas lunches. Apparently she'd latched on to a client who also happened to be a multi-millionaire.

Amazingly my boss, David, was incredibly supportive during the trial. In fact immediately after the hostage situation as Dad tensely refers to it, David insisted on providing me with trauma counselling on the company. My team, Cara, – who, conveniently for me, did get together with Ned – Camilla and Helene, without Emily's malignant influence, became good friends, as well as Daniel's unofficial fan club. All are completely besotted with him. Whenever he visits the office, his ego swells tenfold.

I can hardly complain. I have to agree he is pretty wonderful. Bless them, they're still complete air heads but nice air heads. Fiona was absolutely delighted to find Emily gone. She's a huge fan of mine – especially as my promotion paved the way for her move up to the top floor to board director. Now I organise the posh parties and it's quite good fun. I don't miss my hard hat as much as I thought I would and those girls at the magazines – well, let's just say they grow on you.

About the Author

Bred but not born in Yorkshire, Jules considers herself an honorary Yorkshire woman and, despite living in the Chilterns, still misses proper hills. She's always wanted to be a writer and blames this on her grandmother taking her at a young age to the Brontës' parsonage in Haworth.

After reading English at the University of East Anglia, she found herself in the glamorous and deeply shallow world of PR, which she rather enjoyed, and spent a number of years honing her fiction writing skills on press releases.

Upon completing a creative writing course and finding no local writing group, she set up the Tring Writers' Circle. As a result it was incumbent upon her to set a good example and actually write, which was rather fortunate as with a genuine allergy to cleaning, she finds writing offers the perfect displacement activity. *Talk to Me* is Jules's debut novel.

More from Choc Lit

If you enjoyed Jules's story, you'll enjoy the rest of our selection. Here's a sample:

The Wedding Diary

Margaret James

Where's a Fairy Godmother when you need one?

If you won a fairy-tale wedding in a luxury hotel, you'd be delighted – right? But what if you didn't have anyone to marry? Cat Aston did have a fiancé, but now it looks like her Prince Charming has done a runner.

Adam Lawley was left devastated when his girlfriend turned down his heartfelt proposal. He's made a vow never to fall in love again.

So – when Cat and Adam meet, they shouldn't even consider falling in love. After all, they're both broken hearted. But for some reason they can't stop thinking about each other. Is this their second chance for happiness, or are some things just too good to be true?

Visit www.choc-lit.com for more details including the first two chapters and reviews, or simply scan barcode using your mobile phone QR reader.

A Stitch in Time

Amanda James

A stitch in time saves nine ... or does it?

Sarah Yates is a thirty-something history teacher, divorced, disillusioned and desperate to have more excitement in her life. Making all her dreams come true seems about as likely as climbing Everest in stilettos.

Then one evening the doorbell rings and the handsome and mysterious John Needler brings more excitement than Sarah could ever have imagined. John wants Sarah to go back in time ...

Sarah is whisked from the Sheffield Blitz to the suffragette movement in London to the Old American West, trying to make sure people find their happy endings. The only question is, will she ever be able to find hers?

Visit www.choc-lit.com for more details including the first two chapters and reviews, or simply scan barcode using your mobile phone QR reader.

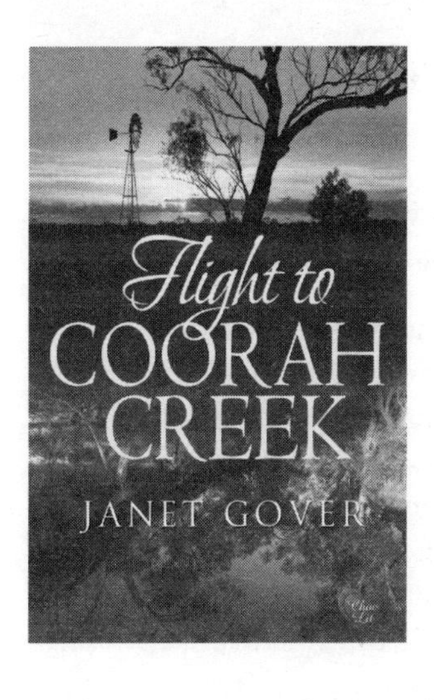

Flight to Coorah Creek

Janet Gover

What happens when you can fly, but you just can't hide?

Only Jessica Pearson knows the truth when the press portray her as the woman who betrayed her lover to escape prosecution. But will her new job flying an outback air ambulance help her sleep at night or atone for a lost life?

Doctor Adam Gilmore touches the lives of his patients, but his own scars mean he can never let a woman touch his heart.

Runaway Ellen Parkes wants to build a safe future for her two children. Without a man – not even one as gentle as Jack North.

In Coorah Creek, a town on the edge of nowhere, you're judged by what you do, not what people say about you. But when the harshest judge is the one you see in the mirror, there's nowhere left to hide.

Is this Love?

Sue Moorcroft

How many ways can one woman love?

When Tamara Rix's sister Lyddie is involved in a hit-and-run accident that leaves her in need of constant care, Tamara resolves to remain in the village she grew up in. Tamara would do anything for her sister, even sacrifice a long-term relationship.

But when Lyddie's teenage sweetheart Jed Cassius returns to Middledip, he brings news that shakes the Rix family to their core. Jed's life is shrouded in mystery, particularly his job, but despite his strange background, Tamara can't help being intrigued by him.

Can Tamara find a balance between her love for Lyddie and growing feelings for Jed, or will she discover that some kinds of love just don't mix?

Visit www.choc-lit.com for more details including the first two chapters and reviews, or simply scan barcode using your mobile phone QR reader.

CLAIM YOUR FREE EBOOK

of

talk to me

You may wish to have a choice of how you read *Talk to Me*. Perhaps you'd like a digital version for when you're out and about, so that you can read it on your ereader, iPad or even a Smartphone. For a limited period, we're including a FREE ebook version along with this paperback.

To claim, simply visit ebooks.choc-lit.com or scan the QR Code.

You'll need to enter the following code:

Q211403

This offer will expire June 2015. Supported ebook formats listed at www.choc-lit.com. Only one copy per paperback/customer is permitted and must be claimed on the purchase of this paperback. This promotional code is not for resale and has no cash value; it will not be replaced if lost or stolen. We withhold the right to withdraw or amend this offer at any time. Further terms listed at www.choc-lit.com.

Introducing Choc Lit

We're an independent publisher creating
a delicious selection of fiction.
Where heroes are like chocolate – irresistible!
Quality stories with a romance at the heart.

Choc Lit novels are selected by genuine readers like yourself. We only publish stories our Choc Lit Tasting Panel want to see in print. Our reviews and awards speak for themselves.

We'd love to hear how you enjoyed *Talk to Me*. Just visit www.choc-lit.com and give your feedback.
Describe Daniel in terms of chocolate
and you could win a Choc Lit novel in our
Flavour of the Month competition.

Available in paperback and as ebooks from most stores.

Visit: www.choc-lit.com for more details.

Keep in touch:
Sign up for our monthly newsletter Choc Lit Spread for all the latest news and offers: www.spread.choc-lit.com.
Follow us on Twitter: @ChocLituk and Facebook: Choc Lit.

Or simply scan barcode using your mobile phone QR reader:

Choc Lit Spread

Twitter

Facebook